# PSYCHO-TROPICS
## Dorian Box

FRICTION
PRESS

# PSYCHO-TROPICS

This is a work of fiction. All names and characters are invented or used fictitiously. Any resemblance to real persons is coincidental. Events are the product of the author's imagination. The cities where the book takes place are real, but most locations within them are fictional.

ISBN 978-0692371350

*For Kody*
*The Heart of the Heart*

**psychotropic** (sī´kō-träp´ik) **adj.** mind-altering - **n.** a psychotropic drug - **ex.** "That crazy @#&% needs a *whole lot* more psychotropics."

# JUNE
# 1995

# 1

IT WASN'T FAIR that Albert Thumpet had to die just because he was the most boring member of the Seminole High School Class of 1975. Killing Thumpet wasn't anything personal. They never even met. Just something he had to do, like eating pancakes on days of the month divisible by three.

He picked Thumpet out of a little book put together by the organizers of the twenty-year reunion. More than three hundred graduates responded to a questionnaire, more graduates than he'd ever known, including Thumpet.

His own high school was a circle of broken-down trailers on the outskirts of Ocala, horse country in North Florida. Thumpet's alma mater was a world away in Hollywood, sandwiched in the Gold Coast slime that began at Fort Lauderdale and oozed all the way to South Miami. He wasn't sure how big his graduating class was, having been kicked out in the tenth grade for setting fire to one of the trailers, but he'd be surprised if it was more than a couple dozen.

Thumpet was the perfect victim. *Poor little Thumpet, sat on a trumpet ... along came a spider ...* He lost his concentration fighting off a tarantula that attempted to seize his brain stem.

Lots of people think they're poisonous, but they're not.

*Thumpet!* Single, no kids, an accountant living far away in Bismarck, North Dakota. If you wanted to become nobody, you couldn't do better than Albert Thumpet. He basked in the discovery for a month, the memory burning so brightly it kept him awake at night.

Getting a copy of the reunion booklet was easy. Just walk into the administration offices and stutter the magic words, *"I'm a gg-gg-raduate."* An hour later he was sitting at a secluded table in the public library confirming Thumpet's lonely life in a moldy yearbook.

No clubs, no sports, nothing. No one was gonna miss the little dweeb.

But waiting in Thumpet's bedroom to kill the accountant when he got home from work, he was having second thoughts. Thumpet's yearbook was open on the nightstand.

Probably wetting his pants to get back to South Florida to relive the life he never had. He started feeling a little sorry for Thumpet, but remembered he didn't have any feelings. Dr. Lazlo told him that.

He leafed through the yearbook wearing latex gloves. The good ones. He bought a value-pack. The only entry was a *Good Luck, Albert* across the picture of a gray-haired biology teacher who surely had croaked. He flipped to the back, to the picture he lucked upon in the library. *The Sweetheart Couple of the Year.*

"Al Thumpet shouldn't have to die for you."

He was tempted to spit on the picture, but didn't want to leave any double-helixes hanging around the crime scene. Besides, a hawker would trivialize the *splendido plandido* he set in motion before leaving Florida. He scowled at the smiling couple then crisply turned pages until he found *her.* He touched her face and slammed the book shut.

If Thumpet knew he was getting killed for such a good cause, maybe he wouldn't mind.

No, people are selfish.

The yearbook and Thumpet's reunion invitation might come in handy later. He shoved them in the backpack and removed the small-caliber junk gun he mailed ahead to a private Bismarck post office box. He didn't plan to use it—the brand's most notable feature was an exploding barrel—but never went anywhere unprepared.

He missed his authentic German Luger, but couldn't risk losing it in the mail. *Quality.* He loved the Luger more than just about anything. If he had a kid, he'd name it Luger. "Here Luger!" If it was a girl, she'd be Lugi, like Carli or Brandi.

He'd toss Mr. Saturday Night Special after he killed Thumpet. It only cost sixty bucks in a parking lot deal at the Sunny Beaches Gun & Knife Show. He slid the pistol in his belt and rummaged for the survival knife. Unfolding the saw-tooth blade, he sat on the bed taking in the orderly surroundings of Albert Thumpet.

Books on a shelf were arranged according to size. Diplomas hung perfectly spaced around a certificate for *1993 Accountant of the Year.* Starched white shirts on matching hangers stood like soldiers in the closet. Shiny shoes in a neat line reminded him of boat slips and made him homesick for Florida.

He appreciated Thumpet's orderliness. If he wasn't going to be dead in five minutes, they could probably be friends. *Good ol' Al.*

Keys jangled in the front door. He leaped up. The bed creaked gratefully. Moving behind the bedroom door, he twirled the knife and rehearsed once more how he would grab Thumpet's hair as he came through the door, yank back his head and cut his throat. Easy peasy.

Thumpet was clattering around in the kitchen. The refrigerator opened and closed, followed by a pop. Probably a beer. That made him feel better about killing Thumpet. He hated alcohol. Bottled evil. Anyone who didn't believe him could ask his mother. They'd have to dig her up first and she still probably wouldn't answer, but they'd get the point.

Thumpet was singing. It sounded like *Rainy Days and Mondays* by the Carpenters with William Shatner on lead vocals.

Too much traveling, too much strange surroundings. *Edgy.* He shifted the knife to the other hand and wiped his sweaty palm on his 100 percent worsted wool catalog-order slacks. Quality.

Hurry up! He leaned against the wall, jostling a string of rosary beads and large cross hanging from a coat hook.

"Jezzzus."

This was not good. The Lord's Cross hanging—*hanging*—right here, not two inches from both of his eyes. Two inches. Two eyes. *Oh-man. O-men.* A pair of twos. He hated twos. He squeezed his eyes shut and prepared for the inevitable chattering of synapses that came in times of stress. His teeth were rattling when, in an epiphany, his panic dissolved.

It was an omen, but not a bad one. A *great* omen of *triangular* symmetry. One, he was the avenging angel. Two, the scums back in Florida were Satan's triplets. Three, Thumpet was the sacrificial lamb.

Point, *triple-point*, point. *Hah!* Bonus points.

Relieved, he stroked the rosary beads. He hoped Thumpet hadn't heard the omen. He didn't think it was possible because it was his omen. But then, they were Thumpet's rosary beads. That could make a difference.

Thumpet interrupted his consideration of the issue, entering the bedroom stuffing a turkey sandwich in his mouth with one hand and carrying a can of soda in the other.

The first thing he noticed was that Thumpet put together a decent-looking sandwich. No wonder he was in the kitchen so long. The second thing was that Thumpet had no hair to grab onto. In his yearbook picture he had enough to stuff a mattress.

No time to be inflexible. Improvising, he grabbed Thumpet's shoulder and rammed the knife into his spine. Thumpet dropped his dinner, managing to turn and see his killer just before slumping to the floor.

"Sorry, Albert."

He might have spent more time being sorry but there was something wrong with the knife. It wouldn't move. He pulled and twisted, but it didn't budge. Wouldn't you know it?

"Albert, I've gotta hand it to you," he said, wiping his brow. "I went over this plan a thousand times. I thought of everything that could go wrong, from you having a mother to you *being* a mother, but the possibility of my knife getting stuck in your spine never occurred to me. There's a lesson to be learned here."

He had to straddle Thumpet's body and yank with both hands. When the blade came loose, he almost stabbed himself in the testicles.

Studying Thumpet, he made a decision. He rolled the accountant on his back and unbuttoned his shirt. What to his wondering eyes should appear but a ribbed undershirt.

"*Hah!* Of course you would have a ribbed undershirt, Al. It's even one of those muscle numbers."

Beneath the undershirt was a white belly, soft and round as a baby's.

He raised the knife and plunged it into Thumpet's stomach. He didn't do it to punish Thumpet for having dense vertebrae, although that did annoy him. Just being careful, having read too many true crime stories about victims left for dead who weren't. One guy apparently took six bullets to the head and just swallowed a couple of aspirin before waltzing into court and sending his shooter to the electric chair. Thumpet had to be one dead graduate.

Satisfied Thumpet had joined the ranks of the living-and-breathingly challenged from the Seminole Class of 1975, he went to clean up. He had hoped to kill Thumpet without getting messy because Orenthal James Simpson had been able to do it, but staring in the bathroom mirror he realized O.J. must be innocent after all.

No matter. He brought an extra set of threads. Always prepared. The Eagle Scout of schizophrenics.

He set the artificial log he bought at a drugstore in Thumpet's fireplace and torched the ends with his prized silver lighter. Built to last, unlike the mother to whom it once belonged. The rubber gloves caught quickly, sizzling and spitting like bacon, which made him hungry. He arranged the clothes on top.

"I'd like to relax by the fire and talk about our relationship, Albert," he said, warming his hands, "but I have a plane to catch."

He showered using the tiny bar of soap he swiped from the airplane. As always, he sang, but heard the words *lonely clown* leave his mouth and stopped cold.

*Rainy Days and Mondays!* No friggin' way. Lonely clowns made him sad, and he never liked the Carpenters. Cranking the hot water as far as it would go, he switched to *Mama Told Me Not to Come*, his favorite song of all time.

His skin was red as an apple when he climbed out.

In fresh duds, he roamed the apartment with a dish towel, dumping drawers and tipping books off of shelves. The cops would think Thumpet came home and surprised a burglar. He picked up a photograph and was about to smash it on the floor when he realized it was Albert and his mother, either that or the world's oldest girlfriend. He dusted the frame and replaced it.

Sidestepping the spreading blood, he spotted Thumpet's turkey sandwich in pieces in the middle of it. All they gave him on the plane was a bag of peanuts. Then he saw the mayonnaise. *Gross.*

He wrestled Thumpet's wallet from his back pocket, which wasn't easy because his fat dead ass was on top of it. He unbuckled Thumpet's watch from his limp wrist. It was a cheap plastic job.

"Geesh, Albert. An Accountant of the Year should have a Rolex, at least a Seiko. Maybe we wouldn't have been pals after all."

He'd toss the watch with the gun and knife on the way to the airport, but hang on to the wallet. He might have to prove to someone he really was Albert Thumpet.

On the way out he stopped to stir the fire. The wrapper on the log said it was guaranteed to burn for three hours. *Purr-fect.*

He surveyed the crime scene.

"Definitely above average," he said, locking the door behind him.

# 2

"**MMM**, how'd you sleep?"

"Umph."

"*Ang-el ca-ake.*"

"Uh."

"I said how'd you sleep."

Danny's left eye broke a seal of mucus and pried open.
"Huh?"

Something heavy held him down. A jackhammer was attacking his brain. The bed reeked of tequila. He noticed a woman draped over him. She had black hair and a Guns N' Roses tattoo across her back.

She snuggled closer.

"Mmmm-mmm. I slept like a dream, sweetie."

Sweetie? Who was she? … It started coming back. Carol, Karen, something like that.

She fell back asleep and he wasn't ready to remember, so he wriggled out and sat on the edge of the bed. The hammering in his head grew seismically. His legs tingled with what felt like stun gun blasts as the blood returned. He closed his eyes, but that only made him dizzy.

He scooped on his boxers and wavered to the kitchen. Pieces of foam from the surfboard being constructed in his living room crunched underfoot. The air was toxic with epoxy resin and fiberglass. He barely avoided tripping over the Skil planer. He needed a real workshop.

A swimsuit shop down the boardwalk went belly-up last month. He thought about renting the space and opening his own surf shop. As if he could get his life together enough to do it.

He brewed a pot of coffee and carried a chipped mug from the Lost Wave Surf Shop out onto the balcony of the penthouse condo overlooking Hollywood Beach. A chameleon missing a tail skittered across the railing and disappeared. The Atlantic was a sheet of glass. No surfing today, not that he felt up to it. The bright sun forced him back inside.

Carol stirred in the bedroom. "Come back to bed."

If Danny could be a magician and know only one trick, it would be to make last night disappear. He'd sunk to a new low, a challenge these days. He didn't answer and she grew quiet again.

Except for Carol, it had been a typical night downstairs at the Tradewinds. Danny arrived early, as usual, to have a few beers and swap stories with the regulars, mostly men who made their living from the ocean.

They cooked up a pot of lobsters John the Diver brought in. Renewal of the Tradewinds' food service license had been negligently overlooked and Grady, the owner, was hollering they were going to get him shut down.

When his ragtag band—Scurvy—took the stage at ten, he switched to margaritas. They played their usual tropical mix. A few people danced. Danny kept turning up his guitar amp and the rest of the band kept shouting at him to turn it down. The more he drank and played, the better he felt.

Just another Friday night, until the band finished and he sat down with John the Diver and two women he never met, a blonde and Carol. Things got out of hand when they started drinking shots of tequila. John the Diver broke a tequila bottle over his head just because the blonde didn't believe he would do it and Grady threw them all out.

J.D. and the blonde took off in his pickup, leaving Carol behind. The next thing Danny knew he was waking up with no circulation in his legs.

He lowered himself unsteadily onto a wicker stool at the kitchen counter, sloshing coffee on the pile of mail that had been accumulating since his housekeeper, Rosalita, quit to become a real estate executive.

This year's lottery check was buried in there somewhere.

Until Danny won five million dollars in the Florida Lottery nine years ago, he lived in a one-room efficiency, working on a dive boat by day and bartending at night. It wasn't a bad life, but there's a lot of pressure to increase your standard of living when you win five million dollars.

The government took forty percent off the top, but that still left plenty. He opted for a ten-year payout plan and quit both jobs, one of his first mistakes

A classified ad for a condo promising *ocean vistas beyond imagination* drew him to the Seabreeze Towers penthouse. Danny never knew how it got the name *Towers* since there was only one of them, an eroding concrete rectangle standing on the Hollywood Beach boardwalk.

The condo needed work, but the ad didn't lie about the views. He grew up with the ocean, but one step onto the balcony and there it was all at once: limey shorewater turning dark over the barracuda-infested reefs before surrendering to the deep blue solitude stretching to the horizon.

His only other extravagances were a vintage Fender Telecaster he played at the Tradewinds every night and a custom nine-foot longboard that spent most of the time parked in a corner of the dining room because South Florida's waves were too puny for it.

A big chunk of each check went to a local charity, an anonymous attempt at penance that never cleansed his dirty conscience.

He didn't know what happened to the rest of the money, only that the check ran out each year. Grady estimated he spent thirty grand a year buying rounds of drinks at the Tradewinds and harangued him to get a financial advisor.

"You're pissing that money away faster than shit goes through a goose. What are you going to do when the checks stop coming?"

Danny never told him, but he didn't expect to live that long. Now here he was pouring coffee over the penultimate check. He sifted through the stack of mail. The first thing he picked up was the invitation.

Seminole High was holding a twenty-year reunion for the Class of 1975. He got the invitation a month ago and had no intention of going. He didn't know why he kept it, but every time he started to toss it, something held him back.

The same force compelled him to read it again:

## YOU'RE INVITED!

**Come join your *old* classmates for the 20th reunion
of the Seminole High School Class of 1975**

**Saturday, June 10, at the beautiful Island Hotel and Marina.**

**Rejoice, Reminisce and Rock n' Roll from 8:00 p.m. to ???**

**Presented by the Class of 1975
Reunion Organizing Committee:
Benjamin Finkel, Margie Santa Cruz Fisher,
Jan Remington Halsey, David Norton, Pattie Steinberg**

**Dress: Semiformal**

June 10. In Danny's unstructured world, days surfing and nights drinking passed hazily without demarcation. It took several seconds for it to sink in. The reunion was tonight.

The morning breeze off the ocean was warm and sticky, but he shivered. For twenty years, he'd done his best to forget high school. When a memory surfaced, he embalmed it in alcohol and stuffed it back in its crypt. Each time he thought he killed enough brain cells to lay the ghosts to rest, he would wake up to find them dancing above him.

Rejoicing wasn't an option and the reminiscence that dominated his thoughts was one of sadness and loss.

He reached for the bottle of Jack Daniels, changed his mind and lit the marijuana roach next to it. He took a toke and ground it out on the phone bill.

*Bennie Finkel.* The name on the invitation made him smile. What a pair. The lanky blond surfer boy and pudgy red-headed Jewish kid had little in common from the outside, but shared a mile-wide rebellious streak and willingness to go to any length for a joke. Like the time they forged a letter from the school superintendent notifying Principal Kostop of alarming new studies showing severe burnout in high school students. Henceforth, the letter instructed, Fridays would be reserved for student relaxation and meditation. She almost fell for it.

Fink went on to be voted *Best Sense of Humor* at the same time Danny was self-destructing. Good old Fink.

And then, of course, there was Sari. Would she be at the reunion? The thought jumped his heart rate, his battered skull suffering the pulsating consequences.

He had known Sari Hunter all his life it seemed. Through all the detritus in his toxic brain, he still remembered with illuminating clarity the summer day Sari and her family moved from New Jersey to the house next door on Sand Dollar Lane. He was ten years old.

He played basketball in the driveway all day as the movers unloaded furniture from a gargantuan orange truck. Whenever Sari came outside, he tried to draw her attention.

"He shoots, scores! The Knicks win the NBA championship. The crowd goes crazy." He danced in wild circles, fingers skyward. She rolled her eyes, but otherwise ignored him.

The next day he tried again, this time with his dog, Bam, pulling him up and down the sidewalk on his skateboard. Sari appeared in the front picture window, watched for a few seconds and walked away. That's the way it went day after day. Nothing seemed to impress her.

Then one afternoon the doorbell rang, and there she was. She was tall, taller than him, with shiny brown hair reaching down her back and high cheekbones he later learned came from her half-Cherokee father. But what he noticed most that first day were her brown eyes, eyes that through all the years he knew her told an entire story with just one look.

"Hello, I'm Sari."

"Hi! I'm Danny."

"My family just moved next door."

"Oh, okay. I hadn't really noticed. I've been busy, you know, just busy around and stuff like that."

Sari's eyes smiled. "How are old are you?"

"Ten."

"Me too. What school do you go to?"

"Eastbrook."

"That's where I'll be going. Do you like it?"

"It's alright. It's school."

"I love school."

"You love school? Why?"

"I love knowledge," Sari said, like it was the most obvious question in the world. "Don't you?"

"Knowledge is alright, but I'd rather know about important

stuff, like how to build a speargun or make gunpowder. Not fractions."

"Are you going into fifth?"

"Uh-huh."

"Me too. Maybe we'll be in the same class. Are the teachers good?"

"You'll probably like them. They love to talk about their knowledge."

"Are they nice?"

"Well, they don't hit you or anything, except Mrs. Matson. I never heard the name *Sari*. How do you spell it?"

"Like *scary* but without a *c* and an *i* instead of a *y*," she said too fast for Danny to absorb. "Just please don't mispronounce it like *sorry*. I don't like when people do that."

"Okay. I won't."

"Do you want to play?"

"If you wanna."

"What do you like to play?"

"I don't know. What do you like?"

"I like to write poetry."

"Poetry? What else do you like?"

Sari laughed. "My dad set up a ping-pong table in our garage."

"That sounds good!"

Their friendship grew quickly. When summer ended, they rode their bikes to school together on the first day. It turned out they were in the same class—Mrs. Matson's—and sat next to each other. An hour in, Danny noticed Sari fixated on a pencil box.

"Sari, what are you doing?" he whispered.

"Counting my pencils."

"I thought you counted them yesterday."

"I'm just checking."

"How many do you have?"

"Nineteen."

"Why so many?"

"In case I break one."

"Oh."

"Danny Teakwell." It was Mrs. Matson, stalking down the aisle slapping a ruler against her palm. "You're awfully chatty today. I'm sure it's because you're so excited to be back at school."

"Yes, ma'am."

"In that case, you can summarize for the class in fifty words or less what I was just explaining about the first periodic table of elements."

"Er, well, I'm not sure I can … because …" He stopped and shrugged.

"He's not sure he can because it's a trick question," Sari interrupted.

Mrs. Matson froze mid-step and stopped slapping her ruler. "And you are?"

"Sari, ma'am. Sari Hunter. I'm new. My family just moved here from New Jersey."

"Well, Sari from New Jersey, perhaps you—"

"No ma'am. It's not pronounced like *sorry*. It's *Sari*, like Mary or Larry."

"Fine, *Sari*. Perhaps you can explain why it's a trick question."

"Because there were sixty elements in the first periodic table, so it would be impossible to summarize it in less than fifty words. That would be like trying to summarize the solar system without naming the planets."

"I see. And that's what you were thinking, Danny?"

"Most definitely."

The class cracked up. Even Mrs. Matson let a smile slip.

"Very well."

They ate lunch together in the cafeteria, Danny scarfing down most of Sari's food because she was such a picky eater.

At recess, Danny made his friends let Sari play baseball with them. She struck out every time. Danny offered to teach her how to swing, but had already learned that stubbornness was one of Sari's defining qualities. She did things her way.

"Thanks," she said, "but I can do it myself."

The kids laughing at her *girly swing* didn't change her mind. Danny would cover his eyes and watch between his fingers as she whiffed again and again. Then one day she caught the ball just right and sailed it over the right fielder's head, Danny jumping and cheering even though he was on the other team.

After school, Sari's mom fed them snacks before they ran out to swim in Danny's pool or do experiments with Sari's chemistry set, Sari carefully studying the instructions while Danny advocated just mixing the chemicals together to see what happened.

On weekends, they packed sack lunches and a blanket and took long hikes in Echo Woods, pretending they were running away, the isolation pulling them even closer together.

Sari wasn't joking that first day. She loved writing poetry. She was shy about sharing it, but Danny cajoled her into reading it out loud on the blanket. In trade, Sari made Danny read poetry from the books she brought in her knapsack. Shelley, Keats, words he didn't understand, but it made Sari smile when he read them.

That blanket was like an island where nothing could touch them. They'd lie there for hours, playing *Name That Tune* with the dial set on WQAM in Miami, the Rick Shaw Show, spotting shapes in the clouds.

"Look at that one," Sari would say. "It's an old woman scolding her cat, and look at the cat's funny reaction." Danny saw a cotton ball.

South Florida's voracious developers bulldozed the woods long ago. Only the memories were left.

Carol stirred in the bedroom. He gulped coffee and steeled himself, but she resumed snoring.

When he tried to show Sari how he felt, the results were comical. If he mustered the courage to scoot closer while watching television, she'd remember she had to feed the dog. Once he even kissed her, but she kept reading her book, pretending not to notice. He accepted they were meant to be just friends.

Then one day he chased down some kids who stole her bike from school. He wheeled up on bent rims sporting a black eye.

"Danny, your eye! Are you okay?"

"I'm fine. It's nothing."

She traced the bruise, leaned forward and kissed him on the forehead. "Danny Teakwell, my guardian angel."

He cherished that kiss, but it wasn't long after that everything fell apart. Danny's father got laid off from his job. They had to sell the comfortable house with the swimming pool on Sand Dollar Lane and move east to a small rental house on the other side of town, in old Hollywood. Just a few miles away, but it might as well have been a galaxy for two immobile twelve-year-olds in the days before computers and mobile phones.

On moving day, they stood in Sari's backyard under a mango tree struggling for things to say.

"We'll write letters and talk on the phone every day," Sari said.

Danny nodded, but even as the words came out he somehow knew life didn't work out that way.

"Danny, let's go. Get in the car!" his mother yelled from the front driveway.

"Just a minute," he hollered back. He pulled a small silver box with a gold bow from behind his back.

"Here."

"Danny, you said no presents. Not fair."

"Don't worry about that. Just open it."

Sari began fastidiously unfastening one piece of tape then another. Danny's father was also yelling now.

"There's no time to be perfect, Hunter. Just rip it open."

She did, pulling out a rosewood box inlaid with abalone. "Danny, it's beautiful."

"Open it."

She lifted the top and music began playing. A tiny ceramic angel turned on a spindle.

"It's your guardian angel. For when I'm not around."

Sari's eyes welled. Now his parents yelled in unison.

"I gotta go."

"Wait!" She grabbed his arm. "I wrote you a poem." She held out an envelope made from red construction paper.

Danny pulled out a square of yellow paper. Blue letters cut with scissors spelled *The Heart of the Heart.*

"*The Heart of the Heart.* Is that the title?"

"No, silly. That's the poem. Sometimes less says more."

She threw her arms around his neck and Danny felt their tears smear. He knew the guardian angel should be strong.

"It'll be okay. Just like you said, we'll talk every day," he said and broke away.

They did talk on the phone at first and got together on several weekends, but they were going to different schools and making new friends. After a few months it became clear they were traveling down separate paths, the tie of familiarity unwinding.

Still, he would have fought to keep the connection alive had his parents not decided to divorce. Not long after the move, Danny learned the family secret that his dad was an alcoholic who got fired for drinking on the job. The trauma of family disintegration consumed his attention in his thirteenth year. By the time he started junior high, he and Sari had disconnected.

Entering Seminole High School three years later, it never

occurred to him Sari would be there, but on his first day as a tenth-grader, walking down a yellow corridor completely lost, there she was, standing at a locker.

He froze and got shoved aside, watching transfixed as Sari organized and then reorganized the locker. Good old Sari. They never heard of *OCD* back then, but in retrospect, there was little doubt Sari lived with it.

She was plainly dressed in a white teeshirt, denim shorts and sandals, more beautiful than ever.

His stomach churned. Watching her tape up a picture of her dog and cat, he realized he was afraid. Three years had passed. What if he didn't like her now? Worse, what if she didn't like him?

But when she turned and saw him, all the fear fell away, for there was no mistaking the joy in Sari's truth-telling eyes.

"Danny!" She slammed the locker and ran to him.

He dropped his books and lifted her off the ground. "You haven't changed. I can still pick you up."

"You've changed a lot," Sari said.

"I have?" he said apprehensively.

"Yes. You're finally taller than me."

The next two years were the best of Danny's life. The energy between them was still there, the palpable connection he knew as a kid. Maturity also exposed their differences more starkly. Sari was a straight-*A* student. Danny managed. Sari had ambition and defined goals. Danny took life day by day. Sometimes they clashed, but mostly they formed a symbiosis, each filling in parts the other lacked.

At the start of their junior year, on a moonlit night in the shadows of the abandoned Sunset Fishing Pier, the love they always knew turned tangible. They were on a blanket, just like in the old days at Echo Woods. Sari was reading a poem, just like at Echo Woods. But this time, she stopped in the middle of a line and leaned over and kissed him. It turned into a long kiss. In the warm garlicky air, they lost their virginity to a soundtrack of crashing waves.

"I feel scared," Sari said afterwards. "Is that weird?"

"I guess not because I feel it too."

"You do? What about?"

"I'm not sure exactly."

"Me either."

They both lay silent.

"The stars seem so big tonight," Sari said. "Like they're closer somehow."

"Maybe we're closer to them."

"Aw, Danny. That's like a poem."

"Ha, I must be learning from you. Hey, are you crying?"

"I have to ask you a question. It's a big one. Can I?"

"You know you can."

"Think about it hard before you answer."

"I will."

"Can we make a vow?"

"What kind of vow?"

"To always be true?"

He pulled her tight. "I vow to always be true to you, Sari Hunter."

She pressed her head against his heart. "And I vow to always be true to you, Danny Teakwell."

Danny broke away from the reunion invitation and stared at the wall of poetry books in his living room. *If only we really could go back in time.*

So young, so optimistic. Sari decided to be a veterinarian way back when they were kids, after her dog got hit by a car and a vet saved him. With Sari, it was just a matter of deciding. No one doubted she could be anything she wanted to be.

Danny, of course, had no clue. An ecology teacher who

understood his draw to the ocean encouraged him to think about marine science. His grades were average, but he stood a decent chance at an athletic scholarship.

As a Little Leaguer, Danny learned he was blessed with the ability to throw a baseball extremely hard. His control sucked, but when he got a fast ball near the plate, you could chalk up the strikeout in advance. He landed a spot as a starting pitcher at Seminole as a sophomore and they won the state championship.

Then came Sugar Lake and all the dreams were blown to pieces. In a single night, Danny managed to destroy everything that mattered.

He did it with the help of his two best friends: John Mangrum and Troy Stoddelmeyer.

Troy was the first kid he met when his family moved across town. They rode the heaven-and-hell roller coaster of adolescence together. Both blond, strangers mistook them for brothers, which they were of a sort. In the seventh grade, under the moonlight on a golf course, they cut their fingers and rubbed them together, proclaiming themselves *The Only True Brothers of the Night*.

In high school, John Mangrum moved from Brooklyn to Hollywood and forced his way into the brotherhood.

Mangrum and Troy, two more reasons not to go to the reunion. He crumpled the invitation and threw it at an overflowing trash can. It missed by two feet. His control still sucked.

He refilled the coffee. Out the window a lone surfer bobbed on the gentle water. It looked like Kenny Hooks, a regular at the Tradewinds. If it was Kenny, he was sitting on one of Danny's custom boards.

In twenty years he never let another woman come between him and his memories of Sari. He had relationships, and even lived with a woman for two years. Ellen Garcia, a lawyer of all things. She worked as a public defender representing rapists and murderers. Danny didn't understand how she did it, but admired her passion and conviction. If he had any sense he would have hung onto her, but he chased her away like all the others.

Devotion would be one way of looking at it. Most people would call it obsession. So did Danny on days like this.

The toilet flushed in the bedroom. Carol. Maybe no different from him, a lost ship seeking harbor in the comfort of a warm body. What could he say to dignify the night, make it seem like something other than a huge mistake? What would she say?

"Hey there, Mr. Big Stick."

Carol stood naked in the doorway, hands on hips.

Danny forced a smile. "Good morning, Carol."

"It's not Carol," she said.

"*Karen.*"

"Try again."

His anonymous lover with the Guns N' Roses tattoo on her back had a much larger one of a motorcycle across her chest, one spoked wheel centered on each breast. She appeared to be enjoying his idiocy.

"It's Donna," she said.

"I'm sorry. That really sucks."

"Don't sweat it. I never got your name either. J.D. kept calling you the Big Kahuna."

"I'm Danny."

They moved toward each other in slow motion. It might have ended like a television commercial, except Danny rammed his toes into the Skil planer halfway there. He choked back profanities and hopped on one foot to the center of the room, where they shook hands.

"Nice to meet you, Danny."

"Get you anything?" he said, squeezing his screaming toes. "Coffee?"

"Thanks, but my boyfriend's gonna be wondering where I am. I'll take a rain check." She headed back to the bedroom.

Danny started to ask a question but decided against it.

# 3

**AT NOON** Danny remembered he promised to help Grady fix the outboard motor on his sailboat. He made a peanut butter and jelly sandwich and took it with him in his corroded '76 Volkswagen Beetle to the marina at Sailor's Point. The sandwich and fresh air eased his hangover as he drove.

Grady already had the top off the outboard and was cursing at it when he arrived.

"Mornin', Captain," Danny said, ambling up the dock. Two kids in masks and snorkels paddled in the water scraping barnacles from the hull of a beat-up Boston Whaler floating next to a million-dollar yacht.

"Top of the morning to you, mate. Though a hot one it is." Grady tipped his grimy captain's cap, revealing a wiry patch of white hair. He smiled through teeth yellowed from forty years of smoking unfiltered cigarettes. He had one in his mouth now, filtered, his only concession to Danny's constant nagging to quit smoking.

"How's the Mrs?" Danny asked, referring to the thirty-two foot schooner officially known as *Lady Luck*.

"Being an old bitty. Might finally be time to junk this old Merc."

"Mind if I have a look?"

"Be my guest," Grady said, surrendering his seat as Danny hopped over the gunwale. Grady crossed the deck and reached into a dented cooler that usually held fish bait. "Beer?"

"Thanks, but I'm still recovering from last night."

"Yeah, sorry to have to throw you boys out, but you were out of control." Grady popped open a light beer and took a swallow.

"No problem. You did me a favor. After J.D. broke the bottle over his head, everyone was looking to me like it was my turn."

"You get to spend any time with your new lady friend?"

"Hand me a screwdriver."

"There's one right next to you. I asked you a question. What was her name?"

"I don't want to talk about it."

Grady started to say something, but lit another cigarette instead.

Two young men zoomed by in a power boat, sending out wakes that swelled into tidal waves by the time they hit the sailboat.

"Slow down!" Grady bellowed. The driver flipped him the finger. "Nouveau boaters," he muttered.

"Come over here and yank the starter rope while I hold the throttle," Danny said. "I don't think your carburetor's getting any gas."

Grady made his way across the still-pitching deck and bent over to grab the pull-rope.

"Jesus, Grady, would you mind putting out the cigarette? You're gonna blow us to hell."

"Not if your diagnosis about it getting no gas is right, smart ass."

Grady yanked the rope several times, punctuating the spaces in between with curse words.

"Nothing," he said, stopping to press the beer can to his sweating forehead and puff on the cigarette.

"No gas. It's probably the fuel filter." Danny traced the neoprene gas line to the filter. "If you won't quit smoking those nasty things to save your own life, how about doing it for me?" He used the screwdriver to chip rust from the clamps holding the filter.

"Enough about cigarettes. Let's talk about something important."

"Okay," Danny agreed. They bickered like an old married couple. The second clamp was worse than the first, the screw nothing but a crusty nugget. Danny tried to muscle it open. "What will it be today, professor? Politics? Theatre?"

"Are you going to the big reunion tonight?"

The screwdriver slipped off the clamp. "Ahhh." He stuck a bloody finger in his mouth. "How did you know about that?" he garbled.

"I overheard you telling Shannon in the bar."

Shannon Briley, the cocktail waitress at the Tradewinds, working her way through Broward Community College. Smart and funny. It didn't hurt her tips that she was a Miss Teen winner back in high school. Shannon was a good egg.

"I don't remember telling Shannon or anyone else about the reunion."

"Son, I've seen you at times I doubt you remember your own name."

Danny scowled. The truth hurt. The first time they met, Danny had just won the lottery. He sailed into the Tradewinds buying rounds for the house. Three hours later he was vomiting in the bathroom sink when Grady walked in.

"I noticed you're in an awfully good mood tonight, young man," he said.

"I just won the lottery," Danny said between wretches.

"Congratulations. I'm real happy for you. Now clean my damn sink and get your sorry ass out of here."

But when Danny moved into the Seabreeze Towers, the old sailor took him under his wing and had treated him like a son ever since.

"Well, I'm not going," Danny said.

"Why not? The triumphant Lotto winner. They'll be eating their hearts out. It could be fun."

"Three seconds of luck picking six random numbers between one and forty-nine is not exactly a lifetime to be proud of. Hand me a pair of pliers. This clamp is rusted solid."

Grady banged around in the toolbox and came up with a pair of greasy channel locks. "How did you ever happen to pick those numbers anyway?" he asked, lateralling the pliers.

"They were the jersey numbers of the six best running backs who ever played for the Dolphins."

"No kidding. You never told me that. That's kind of mystical if you think about it." Grady believed strongly in the supernatural. "So lemme guess, Csonka, Kick, Mercury Morris. Those are easy. Okay, number four would be … I know, Tony Nathan!"

"You got it."

"Yo-ho. Let's see. The last two are tough. I'm not sure the Dolphins ever had six good running backs." Their mutual love-hate for Miami's sports franchises was part of their bond. "I'll take a wild stab. Leroy Harris?"

"Yep."

"That fumblin' bastard," Grady cackled as if he and Harris were bosom buddies. "And …" He scratched his sagebrush head. "Damn, I'm stuck."

"Lorenzo Hampton," Danny said.

"Hampton?" He made a sound like a tire rupturing. "Hampton?"

"Well, I was like you. I ran out at the end so I went with a Florida Gator."

Grady nodded. "I guess that should count for something, but you should've picked a Miami Hurricane."

"Then I wouldn't have won the lottery."

"Decent point. Back to the subject. You have lots of other things to be proud of."

"Such as?"

"Things everyone around you sees except you, blockhead. Like your generosity, willingness to help your friends. Who do those ol' boys come to when they need someone to listen to their problems? Night after night, I watch 'em pouring out their sob stories like you're their last friend on the planet. Hell, the fact you're here right now says a lot. You gotta be hanging like a sick dog. Most people would've found a hundred excuses not to come today."

"Wow. I can hear them talking now. Not only did he win the lottery, he's always willing to tackle a friend's fuel filter in a pinch. What a guy."

Grady shook his head, took a long drag on the cigarette and dropped it in the beer can. Danny held the fuel filter up to the sunlight and shook it. He wiped it on his shorts and blew into the end.

"That's all it is," Danny said. "You just need a new fuel filter. This one's clogged. Let's rinse the tanks out with some gas. They probably have silt on the bottom."

"I think you should go to the reunion."

"What is it with you and this reunion? It's just a pathetic excuse for people to try to relive their spent youths and for the lucky few to flaunt their success over the rest."

Grady tapped another cigarette out of the hardpack. "Danny boy, you're an enigma to me. You know what an enigma is? I've always liked that word. *En-ig-ma*."

"The point?"

"In most ways I know you like a son, but there's still a part of you that's a complete stranger. Carefree surfer boy, so calm and cool on the outside. Oh yeah, you fool a lot of people, but not me. There are times, like last night, I see someone barely holding it together, like you're in a fight to the death to hide your *self*."

He lit the cigarette.

"I try to fit your life together, like a puzzle, you know, but the pieces don't fit. You're smart, got a heart of gold and ain't even bad looking. I can't keep count of the little gals who come up to the bar asking about the pretty blond boy playing guitar."

"The point?"

"With all you have going for you, I've just never been able to figure out why you're …"

"Such a washout? Why I don't have a job and waste all my days surfing and nights getting shit-faced?"

"Well, that's part of it, but what I'm really thinking about is why you're so … alone."

"Alone? As in not with a woman? Well, the truth is, I'm impotent, Grady. Completely one-hundred percent limp as a noodle."

Grady blew smoke above his head.

"The way I have it figured, something in your past is haunting you. And the way I've computed it, it must go back to high school. When I add up all the conversations we've ever had, there's a chunk missing. I know all about your life. Your year in college, the summer you spent surfing in Australia and all your crappy jobs from cleaning swimming pools to kissing tourists' asses as a cabana boy. But you've never mentioned one word about high school."

Danny slammed down the pliers.

"Damn, Grady. You wasted your whole life owning a shitty little bar. You could have gone to work for Interpol. But the truth is, you don't know what the hell you're talking about. There's some emotion for you. You like that?"

"Not bad," he said, unfazed. "Then there's the picture, the

snapshot in your bedroom of the handsome young surfer and pretty brown-haired girl standing in the shade of a coconut palm, both wearing thousand-watt smiles. I know that tree. Off the boardwalk near the paddleball courts."

He was right, of course. No one knew Hollywood Beach better than Grady Banyon. He could chart it in his sleep. The picture was him and Sari in the tenth grade. It was wedged in the corner of the mirror above his dresser. He fished it out of a box a month ago, after he got the reunion invitation.

"When did you see that?" he asked quietly.

"Last week, when you had everyone up for your shrimp-fest. I wasn't snooping. I went to use the head in the bedroom because the other one was *ocupado*. The picture caught my eye, the smiles actually. You can't fake smiles like that. That is you, I presume."

"A long, long time ago."

"Who's the girl?"

"An old friend."

"Whatever happened to her?"

"I'm not sure," he said absently. "I heard once she got married."

The picture was taken the first time he took Sari surfing. As usual, she resisted instruction.

"Sari, people die surfing. You're getting a lesson on dry land whether you want one or not." His determination must have showed because she relented.

The first wave pulled her bikini top down. It was before things got romantic and Sari caught him looking at her.

"Thanks for surfing lesson number one, coach," she said wryly, pulling up her bathing suit.

Grady put a weathered hand on Danny's sweat-soaked shoulder.

"Go to the reunion, son. Deal with your past. Fix it if it needs fixing. There's still time."

You don't understand, Grady. You can't fix the dead.

# 4

**HE ARRIVED** in West Palm Beach before noon, after a long night that took him from Bismarck to Los Angeles and finally back to Florida.

A pleasantly plump girl at the rental car counter told him to enjoy his stay.

"I bloody well will," he said in a cockney accent.

He sometimes fancied himself an Englishman despite being born and raised in North Florida. He practiced being warm and friendly with the girl before realizing she stuck him with a subcompact, after which he barely avoided being escorted from the premises.

*De-escalate confrontation.* One of Lazlo's favorites.

He unfolded a map of Palm Beach County, the route to the waterfront condos bleeding with red ink, straight as an arrow, except for a zag to the bus station where he stored a toolbox two weeks earlier.

*Hah! Cleanliness* is not the only thing next to *godliness.* So is *preparedness* … and *cunningness.* He started wondering whether maybe all *ness* words were next to godliness, but thought of *itchiness* and let it go.

The traveling and murdering had worn him down. No sleep in thirty-six hours. After he finished, he'd rent a motel room and take a nap before making the drive south to Fort Lauderdale for the reunion.

He passed a breakfast joint. *Pancakes.* Soft and warm as a woman's breast. Moist and yeasty like a woman's parking spot. Not that he'd ever tasted either, but he licked up a ton of pancakes and syrup to make up for it. Unfortunately, it was June 10th and ten isn't divisible by three. He did it once, but had to cheat on the math. He kept driving.

Lowering the window brought a welcome blast of hot humid Florida air. He rolled up his shirt sleeve and rested his wide arm out the window to show off his *MOMMY* tattoo. Good to be home, but he wished he had his own wheels—stuck back at the Orlando airport where the journey started.

He stopped at the bus station to get the toolbox and drove another thirty minutes to the King's Arms Condominiums on the intracoastal near the Flagler Bridge. King's Arms? Why not Baron's Balls? *Hah!* That's it. *Welcome to the Baron's Balls Condominiums, Where Everyone Bowls 300.*

He found this so amusing he wanted to share it with the man trimming the hibiscus bushes, but didn't because that would be stupid and no matter what else they say about … *Albert Thumpet*, they can't say he's stupid. Accountant of the Year!

Above average, by about a million miles.

He cruised past the parking lot and saw the black Porsche in slot 601. Just like always. He'd spent time observing the King's Arms on his last trip and determined the scum apparently doesn't work. How does a scum not work and own a Porsche and live in a luxury waterfront condominium? He'd find out.

He parked behind a chicken franchise and took the toolbox through the side door into the restroom, where he pulled a set of crisp blue coveralls over his clothes.

"Hi, I'm Ray," he said. "Came to check your AC."

Outside he lumbered over a six-foot wall and strolled casually to the front of the condos. The man with the hedge trimmer didn't even look up. In the lobby, he scanned the mailboxes. *No. 601, Mangrum.*

She was going to be so proud of him.

On the sixth-floor landing, he took in the harbor and waterway below. Nice view. Way too nice for scum. At 601 he reached for the bell but stopped and rapped instead. Repairmen would be more likely to knock than ring bells.

A short, stocky man with pale skin and long stringy black hair opened the door. He wore a white teeshirt, blue jeans and black pointy boots.

"Hi, I'm Ray. Came to check your AC."

"Nothin' wrong with it," John Mangrum replied.

"Routine maintenance. Only take a minute. They were supposed to call and let you know I was coming."

"They didn't."

"Those guys always screw something up. Do you find that in your line of work?"

Mangrum glared.

"Anyhoodle, sorry if I caught you at a bad time. I can come back. Do you mind if I use your phone to call my office and see if they can move up my next appointment?"

"Yes," Mangrum said, and shut the door in his face.

He smiled. Thank you, John About-To-Be-One-Dead-Fucker Mangrum. You are increasing my happiness about killing you at the speed of tri-light. He knocked again.

Mangrum jerked the door open, scowling. "Yeah?"

"I'm sorry, John Mangrum. I lied when we talked before. I'm not really here to look at your AC."

Annoyance gave way to bewilderment on Mangrum's face.

"I'm here to torture and kill you." He slammed the toolbox

into Mangrum's abdomen, knocking him into the living room over a cocktail table, stepped inside and locked the door.

*Honesty is the best policy.* Before Mangrum could recover, he delivered two sharp punches to the face, just enough to take the fight out of him.

Five minutes later, Mangrum sat bound with nylon rope to a dining room chair, duct tape across his mouth.

"Good afternoon *grrraduate.* I'm sorry I didn't have a chance to introduce myself before. My name might be Albert Thumpet. Do you remember me?"

Mangrum sat motionless, dark eyes glowering above the tape.

"No, of course not. It's been a long time since high school, hasn't it?" He opened his toolbox. "Boy, those were the days, weren't they?"

"Check out my quality toolbox," he said, pulling on a pair of surgical gloves. "I brought several above-average tools good for working on an air conditioner, but if you're above average like me, you know that most modern tools can be put to more than one use, preferably three. Take this drill."

He picked up a cordless drill and tapped the trigger, emitting several whirring bursts. Mangrum's eyes widened.

"Properly used, this drill is an above-average tool for working on air conditioners. Can you name at least two other uses for it?"

Mangrum shook his head.

"You must not be a very resourceful graduate. This drill would be excellent for drilling a hole in a scum's left eye. That's two. And also for drilling a hole in a scum's right eye. Three. Easy peasy."

Mangrum struggled against the ropes.

"Before we get started, John—do you mind if I call you John?—we'll need some music in case you can scream better than I can gag. Preferably from the old days. Call it nostalgia. It may come as a surprise to you, John, but I'm a very sentimental insane person."

He crossed the room to an expensive stereo system and ran his finger along rows of compact discs.

"Nice music collection. Any Carpenters? A friend of mine liked the Carpenters, but he's dead now."

His searching finger stopped above a CD like the selection arm on a jukebox.

"*Oh-man. O-men.* This is too perfect." He pulled out the CD and slipped it into the player. When he punched the play button, the Doobie Brothers started playing *Black Water.*

"Does this song bring back any memories, John?" Anger sharpened the words. He turned up the volume.

"I asked you a question, John. Do you remember listening to this song on a *black* night a long time ago?"

Mangrum shook his head again, vigorously this time.

"I think you're lying. I think you do remember you black-haired, black-hearted fucker."

"*Ummm-ummm-umm-um,*" Mangrum garbled.

"That so. Guess I'll have to go in and find out for myself."

He tapped the trigger again. Mangrum squeezed his eyes and whimpered.

"Almost forgot." He pulled a pair of goggles from the toolbox. "Always wear proper safety apparel when operating a power drill. It says so right here on the label. John, you can't see if you don't open your eyes."

Mangrum's eyes stayed tightly closed, squinting each time a bead of sweat rolled into them.

"Fine. Just take my word for it then. Consumers would lead happier and healthier lives if they would just read product warning labels. Let me ask you one more thing before we get started since you may not feel like talking later. Do you have a mother?"

Mangrum opened his eyes and nodded vigorously.

"You're lucky. I had one, but she wasn't built to last. No one is scum-proof," he said wistfully. "Of course you know that better than anyone." He started the drill once more.

When he finished, Mangrum drooped in the chair, held up by the rope, breathing but unconscious. He decided to hurry and extract the blood in case Mangrum left for Hell early. He was no doctor—although he did once perform an emergency tracheotomy on a pet gerbil he thought was choking on a seed—but he had a sneaking suspicion he might not be able to get any blood once his heart stopped.

He tied a piece of surgical tubing around Mangrum's bicep and assembled a syringe from the toolbox.

"Uh-oh. What do we have here?"

A constellation of track marks ran down Mangrum's forearm.

"Illegal narcotics or a bad case of thorns. Ninety-nine bucks says you drink hooch too."

He drew a syringe full of blood and pumped it into a glass vial. Mangrum remained unconscious. He tucked the vial carefully in his pocket and got out the pipe cutter.

"Don't know if this procedure is covered by your health insurance, John. I bought this size betting you weren't a manly sized man."

This was the one part of the day he hadn't been looking forward to, but symbolically it was the most important part. And symbols matter.

He scrunched his face and unbuttoned Mangrum's jeans.

"John! This is destiny. First you have *Black Water* by the Doobie Brothers and now you're wearing black bikini underwear. If I don't find a third black actor-factor before this visit is over, my name isn't Albert Thumpet."

Holding his nose with one hand, he tugged on Mangrum's pants with the other. They weren't going anywhere because his super-sized rear end was sitting on them. How come he never got to kill skinny people? *Du-uh!* Because life is unfair.

He gave in and used both hands, wrestling the pants down and maneuvering Mangrum's penis through the donut hole in the tool. It would be easier if the scum were erect, but he had to draw the line somewhere.

Mangrum stiffened and fought against the ropes as he tightened the blades. Yessiree. Cutting off a man's weenicker will bring him around every time.

Wrenching the tool back and forth he learned penises do not cut as neatly as pipes. He should have paid the extra ten bucks for the deluxe model with the rack and pinion blade-drive system. He finally lost patience and just ripped it off. What a mess.

He appraised the stub in his palm and considered what to do with it. Shoving it in the scum's mouth would be a neat trick, but no doubt had been done to death. He could stick it in one of Mangrum's hollow eye sockets. That would give the cops something to talk about for years. *I worked on a case where the stiff had a penis sticking out of his eye. I swear.* But again, it probably happened all the time.

A saltwater aquarium on a console in the dining room caught his eye. If he couldn't do anything original he could at least learn something. *Learn from your experiences.* Lazlo.

*Hah!* Lazlo was a little prick and here he was holding a little prick. He walked to the aquarium and tossed it in, curious whether it would sink or float. It floated. The fish attacked it in a frenzy.

"Very interesting."

When he returned to the living room, Mangrum was dead. Crap. The suffering was above average, but it bothered him that Mangrum may have missed the point of why his eyes were drilled out and penis cut off. He'd be sure not to make that mistake again.

He took off the coveralls and stuffed everything except the vial of blood and a clean pair of gloves in the toolbox. He'd dump it all off the bridge. Never leave a smoking toolbox lying around after a murder, a common mistake.

Donning the fresh gloves, he removed a slip of paper from his wallet and used a cordless phone to dial the number written on it.

An answering machine picked up: *Hey, this is Danny. Leave a message and I'll call you back.* He stared at the second hand on his watch. Three minutes would be an above-average amount of time for friends, or blood enemies, to chat. He waited and hung up.

One more job to do: find the missing black thing in John Mangrum's condo.

He nosed around, discovering that Mangrum owned a lot of black stuff. He examined and rejected a set of black coasters, black hair dryer, dirty black socks and a black ashtray before finding the black leather satchel on top of the closet in the bedroom.

Inside were three large bags of white powder. *Three.* He bobbed his head in unanimous agreement with his next thought. *Destiny!* Of course it was destiny. Anyone who called it luck would just be showing their ignorance of the universe. *Three* bags of *white* powder in a *black* suitcase. So that's how a scum can drive a Porsche and live in a luxury waterfront condo.

An above-average idea exploded in his brain. Ripping one of the bags with his teeth, he sprinkled the white powder around the condo, like it was fairy dust. He even skipped for a couple of steps, but the shuddering knocked over a floor lamp.

He thought about putting some in the aquarium to see if

the fish would eat it, but figured they would and didn't want to be responsible for turning a bunch of clownfish into dope fiends, especially after they had just lunched on their master's weenicker.

Each time he thought he spread enough, he gave it another go-around until the bag was empty. Too much, but it guaranteed even the lamest cop would notice. He didn't have high regard for the police since they never found the scums who hurt his mother.

He snatched up the toolbox and satchel of drugs and left in a cheerful mood, singing, *M is for the Major clue you gave me; O is for the Omen that you are; T is for the Trouble that you saved me. ... Put them all together they spell M-O-T-I-V-E ...*

# 5

**DANNY SPENT** most of the day helping Grady get *Lady Luck* up and running. It was late afternoon by the time he got back home. He sat on a bench on the boardwalk looking to the ocean for answers. A seagull stood in the tan sugar, studying him. The bird only had one eye, the other probably lost in a fight for a piece of popcorn.

The sun was behind him. Thunderclouds were rolling in fast from the horizon and a stiff breeze rustled the coconut palms. The smell of rain was in the air. It would hit and be gone in fifteen minutes, leaving a sunny sauna behind. You could set your watch by it.

Maybe he should listen to Grady. He couldn't fix the past by going to the reunion, but at least he could try to fix himself. Confronting the ghosts might be good for him. Trying to hide from them obviously hadn't worked. At the rate he was plummeting, he might not get another chance.

The seagull kept eyeing him. Danny sensed reproach, as if the bird were saying, "Hey, I've only got one eye and I'm making it okay. Why can't you get your shit together?"

Hell, he thought too much. The bird was just waiting for a handout.

"Oh Danny boy," crooned two-part harmony behind him.

It was Tony and Skip D'Angelo, two brothers who chartered deep-sea fishing trips, imitating one-half of a barbershop quartet. Tony was tall and lean, Skip was short and squat. They bore no resemblance other than that they both clowned around like little kids.

"Hey, guys. How's it going?"

"Slow," they said simultaneously.

"Which is something we need to talk to you about," Tony said, nudging Skip.

"Yeah, Danny," Skip said. "We don't quite have the money to pay you back that loan yet. We promised we'd have it for you today."

Danny loaned them five thousand dollars a month ago to have some work done on their boat. He had forgotten about it.

"But we'll have it for sure in a couple weeks."

"For sure," Tony confirmed. "School's out and the snowbirds will be pouring in for summer vacation."

"Don't worry about it. Pay it when you can."

"Thanks, Danny," Skip said, patting him on the shoulder. "It won't be long. This time next week we'll be bringing home the bacon."

"Yeah, and picking fish hooks out of fat white butts," added Tony. They looked at each other and burst into laughter.

"And holding blue hairs over the side of the boat while they feed their lunch to the fish," Skip said.

"Oh yeah," Tony whooped. "Hey Danny, we don't have the principal yet, but we have enough interest to buy you a couple of cold ones. How 'bout it? Join us at the Tradewinds?"

"I'd like to, but I have other plans."

"Other plans? Danny Teakwell not drinking with his buddies on a Saturday night at the Tradewinds? Has the world come to an end?" Skip looked genuinely shocked. "Say it ain't so."

"Yeah, say it ain't so," chimed Tony.

Their incredulity may have helped him make up his mind. "I'm going to … my high school reunion." He couldn't believe he said it.

"High school reunion? Lemme guess," Skip said, "You were a three letter man: B-U-D."

"No, dummy, he was an all-county shot putter. Pour *shot, put* here," Tony said, sticking his finger in his mouth and igniting a new round of laughter.

"Seriously," Skip said. "We're gonna miss ya. I can't remember a Saturday night at the Tradewinds without you. It won't be the same. Who's gonna take your place in the band?"

"Why don't you guys give it a go?"

They liked that idea and wandered off toward the bar singing *Cheeseburger in Paradise* barbershop style.

Upstairs, Danny opened the balcony doors to let in the rush of cool air tagging behind the thunderclouds. He called Koko Bartlett, their band leader, to explain he wasn't going to be at the Tradewinds and kicked back on the couch for a nap. He was still feeling the effects of his debauched night with Donna.

He slept until eight o'clock, which was fine because he definitely didn't want to be an early arriver. He went to the kitchen and microwaved some leftover spaghetti, washing it down with a beer. He grabbed another and took it with him to the shower.

Standing under the steaming water he tried to suppress the memories, but the harder he tried the more vivid the images became: Sari, Sugar Lake, Mangrum, Troy, *Enya McKenzie*. He hummed the *Pachabel Canon* to concentrate on something else, but it came out like a dirge. He stayed until the water turned cold.

Dressing posed a challenge. The invitation said semiformal, but the closest his wardrobe got to that was an off-white linen jacket, pair of khakis, teeshirt and sneakers. He looked for socks, but discovered he didn't own any. He considered using this as an excuse for staying home, but knew it was lame even by his low standards.

Brushing back his thinning hair, he studied his face in the mirror. Had it really been twenty years? Where had they all gone?

Nine o'clock. Now or never. He grabbed the jacket and headed for the door. He was almost past the threshold when he noticed the red light blinking on his answering machine in the foyer. He punched the button and waited for the tape to rewind. It took a long time. But when the tape started there was only silence.

Malfunction.

The Island Hotel and Marina was a thirty-minute drive north to Fort Lauderdale. His first trip through time occurred at the door to the Dolphin Ballroom, where he bought a ticket from Wendy Chappelle, a girl he sat next to in American History in the eleventh grade. He remembered her as thin with wild curly hair that frizzed in every direction. Twenty years later she weighed more and her hair was in a short perm.

"Oh my. Danny Teakwell. I haven't seen you in ages. You look great!" She sized up his outfit.

"You too, Wendy. Sorry about the clothes."

"No problem. You add a nice tropical look and that's the theme."

Wendy gave him a name tag and made him promise to dance with her later. Danny took a deep breath, tugged on the jacket lapels and entered a large ballroom filled with round tables covered by white tablecloths. Each one had a lit candle in the middle.

A disc jockey blasted *You're Sixteen* by Ringo Starr through a mammoth sound system. The song switched on a light in a dark chamber of his brain. There stood Danny, John Mangrum and Troy Stoddelmeyer, flipping quarters in the back room of the wood shop at Seminole High, sawdust-covered radio playing in the background.

Danny stayed near the entrance, hands in pockets, scanning the room. No Sari. He had no doubt he'd recognize her. But he didn't see Troy or Mangrum either. That was good.

He was surprised to see Illiad Mott. Mott was the classic geek who came to school every day in a short-sleeve white shirt and black trousers carrying an old-fashioned briefcase. Many childhood hours had been wasted making fun of him. Then in the sixth grade Mott asked him to join a secret club. In a clandestine candlelit meeting, Mott explained that he and five other kids were plotting to overthrow Castro. They had maps, two old rifles and held commando training sessions at night. They wanted Danny because of his scuba diving in case they needed underwater demolition work. Danny begged off, but stopped making fun of Mott after that. Illiad Mott, what do you know? Maybe he was still recruiting rebel fighters.

Laughing over the memory, he relaxed a little and set a course for a bar in the far corner.

"Danny Teakwell!"

"DeLisha Ferguson, I don't believe it." They worked together on the school newspaper. She had a baby during their senior year, but stayed in school.

"You look great," he said. "I guess we're supposed to say that to everyone, but you really do."

"You're lookin' pretty fine yourself. Let me guess. You have a beautiful wife and three towheaded rugrats?"

It suddenly struck him everyone else had grown up. "Oh, no, nothing like that. Not married and definitely no kids."

"How come? Just not the marrying kind?"

"I guess you could say that. Hey, I see your byline all the time in the *Miami Herald*. Figure it has to be you."

She laughed. "How many DeLisha Ferguson's are there in South Florida, right?"

"That and I remembered you always wanted to be a journalist. Police beat, right? That's really cool that you're living your dream. How is your son?"

"He's a junior in college, if you can believe it, and I personally can't. Seems like only yesterday we were all hanging out in the school parking lot."

"I know. It's crazy."

They promised to get together for lunch sometime soon.

At the bar he ordered a gin and tonic with extra lime. He sipped the drink and continued surveying the room.

There was lots of hugging and animated conversation as the graduates renewed ancient friendships. Most people had put on a few pounds. The ubiquitous long hair parted in the middle had been replaced by shorter, styled cuts and in the case of many of the men, had simply vanished. He didn't recognize everyone, but a lot of people looked almost the same.

The music switched to Steely Dan's *Reeling in the Years*. After twenty years, Danny still admired the song's guitar riffs, which he tried, but was never able to copy. He smiled in the surprising confirmation that he was enjoying the nostalgia.

The good feeling was rudely interrupted by a sharp object jabbing the base of his spine. He arched his back, spilling his drink.

"One move and you're a dead man," whispered a low voice.

Danny felt surprise but no fear. How could anyone get mugged in a crowded ballroom at their high school reunion?

He turned to find a grinning Bennie Finkel, adorned in a three-piece suit complete with watch fob, wielding a plastic fork. He was pudgier and seemed even shorter than in high school, with round gold-rimmed glasses and curly red hair that flared out at the sides.

"Fink!" Danny reached out and gave him a bear hug.

"You cocksucker," Fink said affectionately.

"I don't believe it. Man, you look—"

"Stop! Don't tell me I look great or that I haven't changed a bit or that it's been a long time. If I hear any more of that bull-shit I'm gonna puke. I swear I'll do it. I'll vomit all over you."

"Okay, okay. You're still a short little dork, but it has been a long time and it is great to see you."

"You too, Daniel, or is it Your Lordship since you won the lottery."

"You heard?"

"Oh yeah. I remember seeing it in the paper years ago. I've been meaning to borrow money ever since."

"You probably won't believe me, but there are a lot of times I wish I didn't win it."

"Sure, and there are times I wish I was three inches shorter and weighed thirty more pounds."

"So what the hell have you been up to?" Danny asked.

"For the last twenty years? Well, let's see, on the day after graduation, I slept in late. Then I got up and went out for a breakfast burrito—you're not in a hurry are you? This could take a while."

"Come on. What do you do?"

He hesitated before mumbling under his breath, "I'm a lawyer."

"A lawyer! You're kidding."

"You don't have to act so surprised."

"I didn't mean it as an insult. I just remember you laughing at me the day I signed up for community college. You said I'd be better off going to vo-tech and taking up sheet metal work. You swore you'd never go to college."

Fink reacted to the recollection with a pained expression, grousing something about fat white guys not standing a chance in this country without enough diplomas to build a bridge across Biscayne Bay.

"So what kind of law do you practice?"

"A little bit of everything," he said, recovering. "Divorces, personal injury, some criminal law." He pulled up his pants leg, showing off a three-inch scar on his knee. "See this?"

"Looks nasty."

"Got it climbing through a hospital window to visit an eighty-year-old accident victim in a coma. Left my card tucked in her brassiere."

Same old irreverent Fink.

"Hey, I probably shouldn't mix business and pleasure, but I've been thinking about starting a business and I'm gonna need to hire a lawyer."

"A business? What kind?"

"Just a little surf shop."

"You're still making surfboards?"

"Yeah, helps keep me out of trouble." Sometimes. He thought about last night. "You know, idle time being the devil's workshop and all. A small building opened up on the boardwalk near the paddleball courts. I checked it out and the rent's not too bad. What do you say? Can we get together next week and talk?"

Fink shifted his hips until he looked like a lopsided pear. "Sorry. That's not going to work because I'm going to be in, ah, depositions all week. Yeah, depositions."

"No hurry. I'll call you and we'll set up another time. You got a card?"

"Not on me."

"What kind of self-respecting ambulance chaser doesn't carry a card?"

"You know, Danny, business planning really isn't my specialty."

"I'm not talking anything fancy. I just need a lease and some incorporation papers. Don't they have forms for that kind of stuff?"

"Hey, look at Rhonda Gilliam." Fink pointed across the room at a woman in a tight, short white-sequined dress. "Now there's a woman who's changed."

"How so?"

"Her breasts. They're four inches bigger than they were in high school."

He studied Rhonda Gilliam's profile. She definitely did have some cleavage. "How do you know they aren't the same ones she had in high school?"

"I felt 'em one night. *Pequeño*," he said, holding up a pinched thumb and forefinger. "And lookee over there. Sam Hargrove."

"I remember Sam. All-State wrestler. Where is he? All I see is that woman in the black pants suit."

"That's Sam. Correction. Samantha. Transvestite."

"Huh. He's not bad looking."

"Yeah, if he doesn't get the prize for *Most Changed*, it's gotta be rigged. Check out Hobie Bernstein. *Most Likely to be Mistaken for a Gourd*. Does he have a single hair left? And look at Lisa Gotti. *Tidal Wave Bangs that Could Wipe Out a Nation*. She must buy hairspray in fifty-gallon drums."

Danny couldn't wait any longer.

"Say, Fink, you ever hear what happened to Sari Hunter?" He posed the question casually, or at least tried to.

"Just what it says in the graduate brochure," he said, sighing as Rhonda Gilliam passed.

"Brochure?"

"Yeah, the one we sent out with the tickets. You know, with all the thumbnail bios from the questionnaire. *Earth to Danny*."

"I bought my ticket at the door."

"I saw some outside on the ticket table. You should get one.

Very interesting, sort of a little tabloid about all the people we grew up with. You wouldn't believe how many of our childhood friends felt compelled to confess to the entire world that they're recovering alcoholics or drug addicts. There's all kinds of juicy stuff in there. Divorces, who's rich, who's a loser, who got knocked up the most times."

"It says something about Sari?"

"Yeah, she's in there. Hey, you're still interested in her, aren't you?"

"Just curious."

"Don't bullshit a bullshitter. What ever happened to you two? All I remember is one minute you were on your way to the chapel and the next it was over."

Danny emptied his glass. "Sore subject, Fink."

"Sorry. We all have our secrets." He coughed. "Anyway, cheer up, mope. It says she's divorced."

"Really?" He didn't know what to feel. "What else does it say?"

"She lives down in Coconut Grove."

"A veterinarian, I assume."

"No, believe it or not, I think it says she's a *struggling poet* and a jewelry maker."

"A poet?" Danny flashed back to the sixth grade. The teacher assigned everyone to write a poem and read it to the class. Sari's was light years ahead of the rest, but some kids laughed because the words didn't rhyme. Danny cheered her up as they rode home on their bikes, mocking the infantile rhymes of her worst critic, Nina Parella. "It is such a happy day, and if you ask me why I'll say, the kids are all outside at play, and the rain is far away." He got her laughing and they spent the afternoon making up silly poems that rhymed with *day*.

"Yo, homeboy," Fink said. "While you're standing there grinning like an idiot, I'm going to go talk to Rhonda Gilliam. Professional interest only. Those breast implant cases are big money. I'll catch up with you later."

"Wait! Is Sari coming tonight?"

"How would I know? I'm just a figurehead organizer. They asked to use my name on the invitation to bring in the babes. Go ask Margie Santa Cruz. They were always good friends. Maybe they stay in touch."

That was true. If anyone knew it would be Margie.

"One more thing," Danny said, "I still need your phone number."

Fink frowned and pulled a business card out of his lapel pocket. "Here."

"Benjamin P. Finkel, Attorney at Law," Danny read. "I thought you said you didn't have a card."

He shrugged. "I forgot."

Danny watched Fink walk away, wondering why he didn't want to be his lawyer. He drifted back to the bar, ordered another gin and tonic and went looking for Margie Santa Cruz.

* * *

He hummed as he relieved himself at the urinal. On the drive from West Palm Beach, he decided the Carpenters weren't so bad after all and that *Rainy Days and Mondays* in fact held special meaning because it had poured the last three Mondays in a row. By the time he got to Fort Lauderdale, the song was his new all-time favorite, knocking *Mama Told Me Not to Come* out of the top spot it held since 1970. His evolution was reaching staggering levels.

A short bald guy with tortoise-rim glasses urinating next to him glanced over. "Albert Thumpet?"

He stiffened. "Yeah, how ya doing, uh …?" He studied the yearbook pictures but didn't recognize the guy. He stretched to read the pee-stick's nametag but the angle was bad.

"Marty Oppenheimer," said the bald man.

"Marty! You old *grrraduate* you. How goes it?"

Was he supposed to know him? He worked the Luger down from his waistband until the silencer stuck out of his boxer shorts. If things went south, he could pump his old buddy Marty full of lead with his parabellum penis. But it would definitely throw off the night's plan. *De-escalate conflict.*

"This is a great time, isn't it?" he said. "Seeing all our old friends. Rejoicing and reminiscing, just like the invitation said. Boy-oh-boy, that's truth in advertising if I ever saw it."

"I didn't go to Seminole High. I'm a spouse. But I'm also a CPA and noticed in the graduate brochure that you're the only accountant in the graduating class."

He pulled the pistol back inside his boxers, which were green and covered with tiny sailboats.

"That's right," he said. "Accountant of the Year."

"When I saw your nametag, I wanted to introduce myself. We accountants have to stick together."

"Like fucking glue." He zipped up his pants and washed his hands thoroughly.

"I'm with Ashburner & Crack, Kansas City office."

Who gives a shit? He stuck his head in the sink, dousing it with cold water. Oppenheimer was getting on his nerves. He was tempted to shoot him on principle.

"Fine gentlemen," he said. "Know them both well." He reached for a towel but there was only a chrome hand-dryer mounted waist-high on the wall.

Oppenheimer looked confused. "They've both been dead a long time. The firm was established in 1892."

"Oh yeah. We go *wa-aa-ay* back." He stuck his head under the rushing dryer and brushed past Oppenheimer, water dripping from his chin.

Back in the ballroom, he went to the banquet table and filled a plastic cup with tropical fruit punch. Graduates were dancing to *That's the Way I Like It* by K.C. and the Sunshine Band and he became temporarily fixated on a woman with giant bazongas wearing a tight white-sequined dress. She was dancing with a short red-haired dweeb in a three-piece suit.

He moved to a corner and searched for Teakwell. He'd recognize him, having spent a whole weekend surveilling the scum at his oceanfront condominium, which was boring beyond death because Teakwell never went anywhere except to the ocean and the dive bar on the first floor.

Minutes passed and his tension grew. What if Teakwell didn't show up?

*Stop. Change course. Don't prepare yourself for failure.*

He concentrated on keeping his head perfectly still while letting his eyes roll around the ballroom. It was an above-average spy maneuver, but he had a hard time concentrating on two things at once and realized he was so preoccupied with keeping his head still that he wasn't rolling his eyes.

A couple strolled by, the woman craning to read his nametag. He raised his punch cup and withdrew into the darkness until his back pressed against the aquatic wallpaper. A sphere covered with tiny mirrors rotated above the dance floor, shooting dazzling stars of white light. He imagined the revolving ball was one of the sequined breasts of the woman in the white dress.

*Bingo! Bango! Bongo!* There he was across the room talking to a tough-looking woman in a sleeveless gown. Tall and dressed in crappy clothes, Teakwell stuck out like a sore thumb. *Hah! I spotted you. Ask me if I have a big surprise for you. Yes, I do.*

He removed the vial containing Mangrum's blood and carefully pinched off the plastic cap. *It's Radium 225, Professor Thumpet. One drop will blow the place to Kingdom Come.* He tipped the vial into the cup as a jovial man in a gray suit happened by.

"Spiking the old punch I see."

"I bloody well am," he said, laughing like a hyena.

But nothing came out of the vial. He shook it. Nothing came out. He pounded it against the wall. Nothing. He held it to his eye and twisted it like a tiny kaleidoscope.

Uh-oh.

*Coagulation.*

An anxiety monster rose up and put a hatchet in the back of his brain.

*Clotting.*

He bit his lip and tasted blood.

*Congealment!*

The triple Cs helped, but the possibility of his grand plan going off the rails because of congealment had him standing at the edge of an abyss staring ten thousand miles straight down into a pit of black fire.

He closed his eyes, tapped his heels three times and repeated *Thou art above average*, and just like that an above-average idea came to him.

He bought a shot of tequila and took it to the restroom. In a stall, he poured the tequila into the vial and shook it violently. This time when he poured a pinkish liquid oozed into the cup. Tiny clumps of red gel floated on the surface. They looked like chunks of strawberry, an excellent ingredient for tropical fruit punch.

* * *

"Danny, it's been so long." Margie Santa Cruz Fisher squeezed his neck, sleeveless gown showing off ripped biceps and shoulders. She was the former head varsity cheerleader, so it didn't surprise Danny she stayed in good shape.

"Guess what?" she blurted. "Sari's coming tonight."

His stomach did a triple axel. He looked to the clock, Margie's eyes following his. It was ten-thirty.

"Mm, I didn't realize it was getting so late. She should have been here by now. But I know for sure she was planning on coming. We talked just a couple of weeks ago."

He swallowed his disappointment. "Have you and Sari kept up much contact?"

"Not as much as I'd like, but isn't that the way it always goes? With me up here and her down in the Grove it's not very convenient to get together. My hubby and I used to have dinner once in a while with Sari and her husband before they got divorced, but it's been a while since I've seen her."

"What's she like, Margie? How'd she turn out?"

Margie always enjoyed having the inside scoop and warmed to the role. She twisted her black curls exactly like she did in high school.

"Sari's still Sari. She really hasn't changed that much. Wait, I take that back. She's still the sweet obsessive-compulsive we knew and loved in high school, but she loosened up a lot. Remember how serious and disciplined Sari was about everything? Everything had to be by the book."

*By the book.* The words brought back a painful memory from a letter Sari wrote long ago.

"Somewhere along the way she tore up the rules and just started living her own life."

"Fink said she's a poet," Danny said. "I guess that's a good sign of what you're talking about. Sari always loved to write poetry, but she was so practical about everything I wouldn't have guessed in a million years she would do it for a living."

Margie laughed. "I know, isn't it great? It's good stuff too. I've read all of it, or at least what's published. You can see Sari in it because even though a lot of her poems are sad, there's always a glimmer of hope tucked between the lines."

"Published?"

"Two whole books. *Night Songs* and *The Heart of the Heart*."

*The Heart of the Heart*. The poem Sari gave to Danny when they were twelve and his family moved away.

"I got mine from Sari. I doubt they're available in regular bookstores, but you might be able to get them from that new internet book seller."

"I'll look for them." Danny couldn't wait to get his hands on them. "Fink also said something about her making jewelry."

"That's how she supports herself. Poetry doesn't exactly make bestseller lists. She makes some wildly creative jewelry pieces, almost like she hammers her poetry into silver. She sells them at a sidewalk cart down in the Grove. I think she sells her poetry books there too."

Danny soaked up the information like a scorched field in a rainstorm. "What was her husband like?"

"He was a pilot stationed at Homestead, still is, I guess. Top Gun-type. Top of his class at the Air Force Academy. A real straight arrow."

The exact opposite of him.

"And maybe you don't want to hear this, but Rodney, that's his name, is a really great guy."

She was right. "So why'd they divorce?" he asked too smugly.

"Sari would probably kill me for saying this so you have to swear you'll never repeat it." She narrowed her eyes and bit her bottom lip.

"Back in high school you and Sari were the envy of everyone. Good looking, popular, but mostly people could see you really loved each other. It was just so obvious. I remember when you guys were named *Sweetheart Couple* of the junior class, even I was jealous."

She paused to sip her white wine and laid a strong hand on his arm.

"Danny, I never knew what went wrong. Sari never told me. But the main reason Sari was coming to the reunion was because she hoped to see you."

His brain cells froze, staring at each other waiting to see who would make the first move.

"It's true." She laughed. "I don't know if you're aware of it, but it doesn't take a psychic to tell you're still thinking about Sari. And while she never came out and said it, she thinks about you too. She still wears her heart on her sleeve, or in her eyes, I should say. Just like always. I think her husband knew it too because he asked me about you once. Who knows? Maybe that was part of the problem."

"Then why—" He stopped, buckling under the weight of twenty years.

"*Why* is something only you and Sari know. No one ever knew why you guys split up, although it was a juicy gossip topic. There was even a crazy rumor it had something to do with that girl killing herself."

Danny's stomach knotted. He looked for a hint of secret knowledge about Enya McKenzie, but saw none.

"Get this, people are still wondering. Ann Pallenberg and Cassie Hite—who's always had the hots for you by the way—started talking about it as soon as you walked in."

Margie looked at the clock again. "I'm sorry, Danny. I don't know why Sari didn't show up. Maybe she chickened out. Give her a call. Her number's in the graduate pamphlet they sent out."

She waved to someone behind him. "I gotta go rescue my husband. I left him at a table with a group of strangers and he's giving me the help sign. Nice to see you, Danny." She pecked him on the cheek.

"Promise you'll call Sari," she admonished.

"I will."

When she left he headed straight for the bar.

"Danny Teakwell?"

A large man with dark curly hair and pale blue eyes stood in his path. He wore a new black tuxedo a size too small. Danny didn't recognize him.

"How's it going," Danny said. He wasn't in the mood for small talk and tried to skirt around, but the man deftly sidestepped into his path.

Danny stopped and looked at the nametag. "Hi, Al. Or is it, Albert. Honestly, I've forgotten."

"Albert. Albert Thumpet. We sat next to each other in Boswell's biology class."

Danny remembered sitting next to Fink, but maybe this guy was on the other side.

"Good to see you again, Albert. You been getting along alright?"

"I have been getting along above average."

"Well, that's good. Nice to see you." He started moving again.

"Danny," the stranger called after him. "I was shocked and saddened to hear the news about John Mangrum. He was a good friend of yours, wasn't he?"

Danny stopped. "Mangrum? What news?"

"You know, about the murder."

"Murder? What murder?"

"John Mangrum. I'm sorry. I guess you didn't know. He was killed."

Mangrum dead. The news came as a shock, but no surprise. Mangrum always lived on the edge. It was only a matter of time before it all caught up with him.

"When did it happen?" Danny assumed it was old news. He hadn't seen or wanted to see Mangrum since high school.

"Earlier today apparently."

"Today? Are you sure?"

He studied the stranger for the first time, noticing the

anomalies: oily hair and skin to go with the crisp, undersized tuxedo, and a face of perfect calm, except for the eyes, blue lenses disguising feral activity behind them, like dirty windows on an asylum.

"I suppose it could be a different John Mangrum, but it's not a very common name. I heard the report on the radio driving over here. It happened in West Palm Beach. Is that where he lived?"

Danny had a vague memory of hearing that Mangrum did live in West Palm Beach. "How did it happen?"

"Ugh. Very savage. They said it was a mutilation murder. Guess that's why it made the news. The police think it was a revenge killing. They found a lot of drugs in his house."

That sounded like Mangrum. Danny stared beyond the stranger, focusing on nothing. Mangrum murdered, on the day of the reunion. He tried to kill him twenty years ago in the school cafeteria, and there were drunken nights since he would have tried again, but if this was real …

"I'm sorry to be the one to break the news to you. I remembered you guys were buddies in high school and figured you already heard about it."

The stranger placed his hand on Danny's shoulder in a friendly gesture. In the process, he spilled the punch he was holding all over Danny's linen jacket.

"*Oh-man*. Now look what I've done. I'm sorry. Let me pay to get it cleaned." He took out a wallet and Danny saw the driver's license name and address of Albert Thumpet, Bismarck, North Dakota, next to a wide jagged thumbnail.

"No, it's fine." He just wanted to get away from the guy.

"Are you sure? What a dope I am. First I shock you with the news about your best friend and then I spill punch on you. I hope I haven't ruined your reunion."

"Look, I gotta go." He strode away quickly. Glancing back he saw Thumpet rooted in the same spot. Was he smiling?

Danny straight-lined for the exit, but Fink caught up with him. "Danny, wait up. Where you going? You can't leave yet. The party's just getting started. Whoa, what happened to your jacket? It looks like someone had an abortion on it."

"Fink, you're still disgusting. You really haven't changed. Some weirdo named Thumpet spilled his punch on me. Do you remember him? Albert Thumpet."

He stroked his chin. "Thumpet. Doesn't ring a bell, but you know me, I only hung out with beautiful cheerleaders. Come on, a group of us are ditching the ballroom and going out to the marina bar."

"I'm not up for it. This has been one strange night. Did you hear that John Mangrum was murdered today?"

Fink blinked. "Today? Where?"

"West Palm Beach. That Thumpet dude told me. Said it was a mutilation murder."

"He's probably just pulling your chain. On the other hand, if it's true it couldn't have happened to a nicer guy."

"Damn, Fink. Mangrum might really be dead."

"The guy was a complete jerk, Danny. Why you were ever friends is a mystery to me. Come on. Now you have to come out to the bar with us. You can't let the demise of one of our classmates—real or not—be your last memory of your twentieth reunion. Could throw a curse. Besides Cassie Hite is coming and she just told me she wants to screw your brains out."

"Not interested."

"Well, I'm interested, so help me live the evening vicariously. I've had an erection ever since slow-dancing with Rhonda Gilliam. Do an old pal a favor."

Danny acquiesced and ended up sitting at a window table overlooking the intracoastal waterway with Fink, Cassie Hite, Ann Pallenberg and Dirk Forster, who Danny believed to be the largest human being ever to attend high school. He played SEC football and spent two years with the Pittsburgh Steelers as a backup nose tackle. They drank, laughed and applauded Dirk's ability to flatten an empty beer can to the width of a potato chip, a skill he mastered in high school. Cassie sat next to Danny, rubbing her bare shoulder against him.

Fighting to let go of the past, it was more alive than ever. The news of Sari wanting to see him and Mangrum being murdered imploded in a black hole, the nightmare of Sugar Lake and the death of Enya McKenzie.

"So the judge says …" Fink was telling a courtroom war story about a judge who acquitted a guy of DUI so he could consume the evidence, a bottle of fine single malt scotch.

"Right there at the counsel table, I'm not making this up, the judge, prosecutor, me and my client sat drinking the scotch out of paper cups the judge got from his water cooler. Wildest damn thing you ever saw."

Danny gazed absently out the window into the night. A well-dressed couple, probably reunited graduates, sat on the seawall making out passionately.

A sleek speed boat idled past, powerful inboard motor growling like a caged tiger. Danny watched it move beyond a safety buoy and disappear behind a sailboat moored to the dock.

Sometimes he thought about selling the condo, buying a sailboat and just taking off.

If everything Margie said was true, why didn't Sari come? *Sari's still Sari.* What could be better than that? But each time Margie's words came to rest they ran into Albert Thumpet's. *Very savage. They said it was a mutilation murder.*

Clouds obscured the moon and stars. A few rain drops chased away the amorous couple. Danny stared into a patch of blackness near the foot of the dock, lost in thoughts just as dark. All he could make out were the outlines of the boats and a dock piling that stood like a sentinel guarding them.

Then the piling moved. He blinked and focused.

Stillness.

*No, there.* It moved again.

It wasn't a piling. It was a person—*a woman.* She was watching them. He tried to make out her face, but she was hidden in the shadows.

Another boat approached, this one going much faster than the 5 mph speed limit in the marina.

"The cops are going to nail that sucker," Danny heard Dirk say, but he kept his eyes on the sentinel.

"What'd I tell you, here they come." From across the waterway a police patrol boat emerged, throttle open and blue light flashing.

The specter hadn't moved again and Danny concluded he was right the first time, that it was only part of the dock. In his charged state, he wanted to believe Sari had come to the reunion after all and was just apprehensive about coming inside. We delude ourselves about so much.

But just as he was about to rejoin the conversation a shaft of blue light from the police beacon illuminated the void at the foot of the dock.

*No! It wasn't possible.* Danny jumped up, knocking over the table. He pressed against the window.

"Danny!" Fink pulled at him while the others brushed colored liquids from their clothing. "What's wrong?"

He looked at Fink and back out the window. His legs were shaking.

Dirk picked up Danny's chair, but he stayed standing.

"Danny, you're hyperventilating." Fink pulled a vial of pills from his coat pocket. "Have a Xanax. It'll calm you down."

Danny waved him away.

"Well, I'll have one." He popped one of the orange tablets

like it was a breath mint and offered the jar to the others, who declined.

Fink and Dirk finally managed to press Danny into the chair.

"What happened?" Fink said. "You look like you saw a ghost."

He did. In a single pulse of blue light, he thought he saw Enya McKenzie.

# 6

**AT SUNRISE,** Danny straddled the longboard a hundred yards from shore, watching the gray-pink horizon burst into gold. Irradiated cloud puffs hung low against the chalky sky as if suspended on wires. The sweet smell of salt and surfboard wax stimulated a peaceful feeling of being home.

Even in June the early morning water was cool enough for his shorty wetsuit. He was too far out to catch a wave, not that there were any. Wind, a surfer's best friend, was absent. He might as well have been floating on a lake, which was fine because he went to the ocean seeking solitude. The early hour and smooth water practically guaranteed it.

Bobbing hypnotically on the swells, he gazed down Hollywood Beach. So different from when he was a kid.

Nothing ever stayed the same, except death.

The phantom from the night before turned out to be a barnacled dock piling crowned with pelican dung. He searched the marina for the woman with blonde hair but found no one.

Still, he got goosebumps under his wetsuit thinking about the haunting image of Enya McKenzie's face bathed in blue light. He'd dismiss it all as a hallucination induced by the trip back in time, except it wasn't Enya's high school face he saw, but the face of a woman twenty years older. Was the mind capable of such trickery?

He never would forget Enya's face. It was etched in his brain forever. She might say the same thing about his face if she were alive. But dammit, she's not alive. She committed suicide more than twenty years ago.

But did he really know that for sure? He never saw her after the suicide rumor, including the nights he parked outside her house on Myrtle Street. But he also never saw any actual proof she was dead.

The tide dragged him closer to shore. He wheeled the board and paddled out to sea.

He knew he was kidding himself, trying to reconstruct history to save his damned soul. Enya McKenzie killed herself twenty years ago. There's never been any reason to believe otherwise. And the accomplices to her death—John Mangrum, Troy Stoddelmeyer and Danny Teakwell—all escaped punishment, until yesterday, when some drug dealer apparently evened the score with Mangrum.

The *Sun-Sentinel* didn't mention Mangrum's murder. Thumpet said it happened in West Palm Beach. He'd get a copy of the Palm Beach paper later.

No punishment? That was a lie. He had flogged himself mercilessly for two decades, consumed by culpability for Enya's death and sorrow over the woman he lost because of it. Enya and Sari never even met, but were forever bound. They joined and vanished together over the Bermuda Triangle known as Sugar Lake.

Sugar Lake wasn't even a real lake, but a rock quarry. Dozens of them, excavated by developers for limestone to fill roadbeds and wetlands, dotted South Florida when he was growing up. At ten feet above sea level, it didn't take much of a hole to make an instant reservoir. Sugar Lake was a quarter-mile wide pit of deep clear water sheltered by pine trees in the woods off of Shepard Road.

Rumor had it the lake bottom was littered with dead bodies in cars dumped by the Mafia, giving Sugar Lake a certain legendary status among teenagers. Danny and his buddies went scuba diving there once looking for evidence, but all they found were a rusted bicycle and copy machine. Mostly, Sugar Lake was a place where Danny went with John Mangrum and Troy Stoddelmeyer to hang out and drink beer and smoke dope.

The Friday in late August 1974 that destroyed so much offered no hint in the morning of what it would bring when the sun went down. Danny was seventeen and about to finish his first week of the twelfth grade. He lived with his mother in a two-bedroom apartment behind an oceanfront hamburger grill. His sister was in Gainesville in her third year at the University of Florida.

In the morning Danny went skin-diving with Jeff Ballentine. Seminole High was overcrowded because of the transfer of ninth graders from junior to senior high. They were on a split schedule where freshmen and sophomores attended in the morning and juniors and seniors in the afternoon.

At school, he sat next to Sari in study hall, their only class together. She kept her nose buried in a book, not making eye contact.

"Sari," he whispered. "You alright?"

"Just worried about my calculus test on Monday."

"You'll ace it. You always do. What do you want to do tonight?"

"I'm sorry, Danny, I should have told you. Margie and I are getting together at her house to study. These differential equations are driving me crazy. Is that okay?"

"Sure." Danny would no more study on a Friday night than trade surfing as a hobby for colonic irrigation, but knew better than to try to talk Sari out of it.

He said he'd make other plans and call her from work on Saturday. Danny worked weekends at the Lost Wave Surf Shop where Ben Keahilani, a surf champion from Honolulu, taught him to make surfboards.

Mr. Caribe, the study hall teacher, shushed them and Danny went back to reading a surfing magazine tucked in his history book.

By the end of school, Danny still didn't have plans, so he went home and ate cheeseburgers with his mom and crashed on his bed reading a book of avant garde poetry Sari had given him. At eight he drove over to Ducky's, a convenience store near the high school that served as homing point for the *Dazed and Confused* crowd he ran with. Growing up in South Florida in the early seventies was an endless ritual of cruising in cars, jamming to power rock on the eight-track, drinking beer and smoking pot.

Danny and his friends spent most of their weekend nights searching for block parties, which were always happening somewhere. Some kid's parents would make the mistake of going out of town and the kid would invite a few people over. Word would spread and before anyone knew what was happening, throngs of teenagers were descending with beer, dope and loud instruments. Party news arrived at Ducky's faster than intruder alerts reach NORAD.

He sipped a beer in the parking lot with some other surfers, who hung together and looked like a distinct tribe with their sun-bleached hair, cocoa skin, baggies and flip-flops.

A bulletin came in of a bash cranking up at a house on South Lake a mile away. Danny left to check it out.

Dozens of kids were already mulling around the expensive home when he arrived. Two kegs had been tapped on the pool patio. A pick-up band was setting up poolside. All the makings of a good time.

Danny was filling a plastic beer cup when Kevin Minor, a kid he met in Driver's Ed, asked if he wanted to smoke a joint.

"Gold buds in a hash-oil paper," he whispered.

If Danny and his friends spent half as much time in high school studying math as they did developing their sophistication about marijuana they could have invented time travel.

They snaked into the house and found an unoccupied bedroom where Kevin pulled a sticky toothpick from a vial and held it up for display like a rare jewel.

By the time Danny returned to the pool patio, the killer joint was working its magic and he assimilated the surroundings through a warm glow. The band was jamming through a crude version of the Allman Brothers' *Southbound*. More kids streamed into the backyard. One was Rikki Anderson, a girl he kissed in the eighth grade.

"Hi Danny," she said radiantly.

"Rikki Tikki Tava." Danny called her the Kipling name in junior high and it stuck.

She peeked around furtively. "Sari's not here?"

"She's studying for a test."

Rikki was several inches shorter and wearing a tank top hanging open with no bra underneath. Danny fought the temptation to peer down her shirt.

"I guess that's why she gets *A*s and I get *D*s."

"That's probably it."

"That means I have you all to myself tonight." She skated glossy orange fingernails down his arm.

Danny pulled away, eyes darting at the informants lurking all around him. Rikki may not have invented flirting, but she exalted it to a level that might qualify for a patent. The last thing he needed were rumors flying that he was catting around with Rikki at a party while dedicated Sari slaved over a calculus book. He excused himself and fought his way back into the house looking for a phone to call Sari.

It was nine-thirty. Maybe he could talk her into taking a study break. He found a princess phone in the same bedroom where he and Kevin smoked the joint, now occupied by a couple making out on the bed.

"Sorry," Danny said, grabbing the phone and stretching the cord into an adjacent bathroom. Outside the band wailed through an unstructured blues jam, inside the stereo blasted Led Zeppelin. A cigarette smoldered in a deep black crease on the turquoise countertop. Someone's parents were going to be pissed. He doused the cigarette in the toilet and dialed Margie Santa Cruz's number. A woman's voice picked up that Danny couldn't identify through the din.

"Margie?"

"Deese is her modter," said a woman with a thick Hispanic accent. "Please hold. Marrr-gee!"

Margie picked up another phone. "I got it, Mom."

"Hi Margie. It's Danny. How's the studying going?"

"Torturously, but at least it's quiet. Where are you? Sounds like anarchy."

"It's getting close to it. That's why I called. I was wondering if you and Sari might be interested in taking a study break and coming over to join the insurrection. Everybody's down at South Lake."

"No thanks. Sari's not here and I've still got differential equations to conquer."

"Did she leave already?"

"Leave? She was never here."

"I thought she was coming over there to study."

"We talked about it earlier in the week, but she told me today she had other plans. I assumed they were with you."

"We must have got our wires crossed," Danny covered. "She's probably at home. I'll call her there. You're missing a jammin' party."

"If I flunk my calculus test, I won't be going to any parties for a long time. Good luck finding Sari."

Someone was hammering on the bathroom door. "Hurry up. I gotta *peeeee*, man."

"Just a minute," he shouted, dialing Sari's number. The distinctive contralto of Sari's mother, June, answered. Danny liked her ever since he was a kid, but the woman could talk. She asked questions about the baseball team and was transitioning to his college plans before Danny wedged in a request to speak to Sari.

"She's with Margie. They're studying for a math test. Try her over there. Do you have the number, Danny?"

"Uh, yeah. Thanks. Good night, Mrs. Hunter."

He hung up and stared into the brightly lit mirror. Where could she be? He had never known Sari to tell a lie, not to anyone. If she made up a story, there had to be a good reason. The guardian angel in him was concerned, but he shook it off and went back to the party.

A couple beers later, people were tossing each other into the pool, causing at least one shoving match to break out. It looked like things were about to get out of control. "Boys are so predictable," he could hear Sari, an early feminist, saying. "Always trying to prove their manhood. What they don't realize is that most of the time they only succeed in proving their inferiority to women." He never stuck up for his sex because he believed she was right. *Where was Sari?*

Danny was sipping his beer and watching the growing melee from a safe distance when unseen hands grabbed him and pulled him backward onto the grass. The beer flushed over him like a waterfall.

His muscles tensed, ready for a fight, but when he looked up he saw the grinning faces of John Mangrum and Troy Stoddelmeyer.

"You dicks," he said as they picked him off the ground. "What am I supposed to say when I get home?" he said, wringing beer from his Dewey Weber Surfboards teeshirt. "Beer? Gee, mom, I don't smell any beer."

"You don't have to worry about that, Sir Daniel," said Mangrum, "because we're all going"—he raised his arm and stabbed the darkness, a knight about to lead the Crusades—"to the lake!"

"To the lake!" Troy echoed.

"And we have a special surprise for you tonight," Mangrum said.

"Surprise!" Troy said.

"What kind of surprise?"

Troy piping, "A surprise wouldn't be a surprise if it was a surprise."

"Weren't, Troy. If it *weren't* a surprise," Mangrum snapped.

Poor Troy. Nice kid, but no mistaking him for Einstein.

"Accompany us, fellow soldier of the rebellion, to Sugar Lake, sanctuary of *The Only True Brothers of the Night*."

Mangrum looked wired. Danny could drink his fill and smoked some weed, but never did hard drugs, part of the surfer's credo. Mangrum, on the other hand, spent the major portion of his waking hours buying and selling candy-colored capsules and sinister-looking vials of powder. It was before cocaine caught on and, though Mangrum wouldn't admit it, Danny believed he didn't know what he was taking half the time.

"Sure, King Arthur. Let's go. This party is about to fall apart."

In the front yard, Mangrum told Danny to ride with them. They made their way past a string of automobiles parked chaotically along South Lake Drive until reaching Mangrum's red Chevy Z28 Camaro, freshly waxed as always, sitting like a showroom display model under a street light, angled onto a perfectly manicured St. Augustine lawn.

As they approached, Danny saw something with light hair move in the backseat. His first thought was shock that Mangrum would let Troy's Golden Lab inside his treasured automobile.

Then he saw a face. A girl. She had long fine blonde hair parted in the middle framing a creamy face dominated by immense blue eyes. She reminded him of one of the Hummel figures his sister used to collect. He thought he remembered seeing her at the party earlier. She was slumped against the side panel of the white vinyl interior with a bottle of Wild Turkey between her legs.

Mangrum slid in the driver's seat and Troy climbed in back with the girl, a surprise since he and Troy usually began disputing title to the shotgun seat fifty yards from the car.

"Sir Daniel," Mangrum said, "Meet the surprise: Enya."

Enya McKenzie smiled sweetly.

"Hi, Enya. I'm Danny," he said to the girl in the backseat.

She looked at him and parted her lips. Mangrum chortled as he wheeled the Camaro out of the parking space. He started to gun the motor when two police cars rounded the corner.

"The pigs have arrived," he proclaimed, backing off the accelerator and sliding down in his seat.

He slid a tape into the eight-track player as he pulled a joint out of the center console and somehow continued to drive perfectly. Mangrum's driving skills always amazed Danny. Whatever else could be said for him, the man could parallel park the Space Shuttle on Quaaludes. With Deep Purple blasting *Highway Star* from four speakers, he popped in the lighter and fired up the joint as soon as they turned a corner.

Danny glanced in the backseat to see Troy leaning on the pretty girl named Enya.

"So who is she?" Danny asked. "Looks kinda young."

Choking as he fought to hold in the cannabis smoke, "Enya McKenzie. She's a sophomore." He exhaled a mushroom cloud that filled the passenger compartment and handed the joint to Danny.

"Troy-boy, pass that bottle up here."

By the sheer force of his personality, Mangrum had not only forced his way into *The Only True Brothers of the Night*, but designated himself as leader.

"She's with Troy?"

"She's with *everyone*. She's a nymphomaniac. It's all over school."

"I think I saw her at the party. How'd she end up here?"

"Troy-boy flashed those big brown eyes at her and asked if she wanted to go for a ride. We've been cruising with her for a while—little smoke, little whiskey, some choice tunes. A pleasure drive. We came back to look for you. Wouldn't want to leave my best friend out of the fun. Here."

Mangrum passed him the whiskey bottle. Danny took a swig and handed it back.

"Give it to Enya," Mangrum said.

"I think she's probably had enough," Danny said.

"Bullshit. Enya, you want some more whiskey?"

"Umm."

"I'll take it," Troy chirped. He snatched the bottle, took a generous gulp and began nursing Enya with it.

Danny took a hit of the joint and passed it back to Mangrum. "Maybe you should ease up on Enya. She looks pretty fucked up."

Mangrum peeked in the rear view mirror. "Hey Enya, you fucked up?"

"Fucked up," she muttered.

Mangrum cackled. "You were right."

He cranked up the stereo, ending the discussion. They zoomed west on Shepard Road to the unmarked cutoff to Sugar Lake. Mangrum piloted slowly down the winding gravel road through the pine forest, cursing each time a rock bounced off the chassis of the Camaro. He pulled into a familiar clearing twenty yards from the lake. The wheels ground to a halt and the pounding music surrendered to silence.

"Skinny dipping!" he decreed.

"Skinny dipping!" mimicked Troy.

"Skinny dipping," slurred Enya.

Though he was suitably stoned and drunk, a bad feeling dogged Danny as he climbed out of the car. He wished he was with Sari, but where was she? He lagged behind as the group ascended a sloping limestone formation that glowed ghostly white in the light of the almost full moon.

The night air was warm, alive with the percussion of insects in the surrounding pine trees and palmetto scrub. A breath of wind rustled the trees, carrying the sweet scent of night-blooming jasmine.

Enya slipped on the gravel and toppled backwards into Danny's arms. Her upside-down face smiled as he boosted her back upright. Mangrum, leader of the pack, carried the supplies, the bottle of Wild Turkey and two unlit joints, hanging from his mouth like fangs.

At the pinnacle, Mangrum began shedding his clothes. Troy followed. Danny looked at them as they looked at Enya. Mangrum's smirk bothered him. Enya shrugged and pulled her teeshirt over her head, revealing compact breasts with areolas the color of ginger. All eyes were glued to her as she unbuttoned her jeans and wriggled them down boyish hips, revealing pink bikini panties with *Tuesday* embroidered in one corner.

She lifted a foot and teetered. Mangrum silently offered his shoulder for support. Danny felt himself getting aroused. Embarrassed for Enya and ashamed of himself, he forced his eyes away as she slipped off her panties. Mangrum and Troy were studying her like medical students.

After she was naked, Mangrum looked at Danny. "Let's go, bro. What are you waiting for?"

"Yeah," Troy chided.

"I don't feel like swimming. The water's too cold."

"Bullshit," Troy said. "We've swam in this lake in the winter."

Even Enya watched expectantly, as if saying *We're all in this together*. With the three of them ogling him like a stripper, he peeled off his teeshirt and hesitated before turning around to drop his shorts.

"Shit, Danny, your ass glows in the dark," Mangrum said, getting a laugh from everyone, including Danny. It was true. His surfer's tan accentuated a white ass that reflected the moonlight as brightly as the limestone they were standing on.

"At least I don't look like a marshmallow," Danny retorted without malice. This was also true. Mangrum was probably the only person in South Florida who had never been to the beach. The most strenuous activity Danny ever saw him undertake was washing his car, but only Enya laughed. Troy knew better. Mangrum could dish it out, but not take it.

He shot Danny a dirty look, swigged from the bottle and passed it around. After twenty years, Danny still retained the image of Enya's moonlit profile, blonde ponytail in one hand, inverted bottle of Wild Turkey in the other, whiskey drizzling down her delicate chin.

"Come on, Enya," Troy said. "Let's go swimming."

She peeked over the edge at the black surface of the water ten feet below and balked.

"Come on, it's safe. We've been diving off this ledge since we were little kids, haven't we Danny?"

Danny nodded, though he didn't think Enya had any business trying to swim in her present condition. But when Troy held out his hand, Enya took it. He coached her to the rim. When she got close, he wrapped both arms around her and jumped off, crying "Geronimo!"

Enya's piercing scream could be heard for the microsecond

before they hit the water. Danny rushed to the edge. Seeing no movement, he was about to leap in when they bobbed to the surface, Enya clutching Troy's neck, Troy laughing, Enya coughing. Danny watched Troy caress her head and stick his tongue in her mouth. She seemed to go along and all was quiet again, except for the insects.

Shaking his head, he walked back to Mangrum, who was sitting naked on a rock sifting through the contents of a tin box.

"I thought we lost 'em for a second," Danny said, lowering his butt onto a boulder, coral edges biting his cheeks like piranhas.

Mangrum extracted a razor blade and an orange pill from the tin box. He laid the pill on top and chopped it into fine dust like an expert chef mincing a garlic clove.

Danny sipped from the whiskey bottle. "What's that?" He recognized slurring in his voice.

"PCP."

"How do you know? They all look the same."

"Believe me, I *know*." Mangrum snorted half of the powder, held the box out to Danny who shook his head, then inhaled the rest. He set the box down and lit another joint.

"So where's her highness tonight?" he said, taking a toke and handing the joint to Danny.

For reasons he never understood, Mangrum liked to take jabs at Sari, nothing too strong, just enough to be annoying. "He's jealous of me, you know," Sari once said. Danny said that was crazy. "No it's not. I think he loves you, not necessarily in a sexual way, although you never know." He scoffed at the notion.

"I'm not sure," Danny admitted reluctantly.

"Well, you're with me and Troy. *The Only True Brothers of the Night*. What could be better than that?"

Danny laughed. "I've got news for you. I'd rather be with Sari than sittin' here naked on a rock with you."

Mangrum got quiet after that. He sat perfectly still, head tilted to the starlit sky.

Danny wasn't sure whether Mangrum had dozed off or was discovering new chemical insights in the cosmos. He wasn't far from the latter himself, as he looked up and saw two moons where there should have been only one.

Somewhere down the beach, Troy and Enya were laughing. Danny was wondering and worrying about Sari when Mangrum, still looking to the heavens, spoke.

"I don't know if I should tell you this, but as your best friend, I have to."

Danny waited for the newsbreak while Mangrum resuscitated the dying joint.

"I'm only telling you this for your own good," he finally said.

"What's the big mystery?"

Mangrum looked at him funny. "I saw Sari tonight when I was at the Lantern gettin' a pizza."

The Lantern was a pizza place that shared space with a grocery store in an old waterfront building on A1A. A lot of kids hung out there eating pizza and subs and playing pool. Those who were eighteen or had fake IDs drank pitchers of cheap beer.

"You saw Sari?"

"Uh-huh."

"What time?"

"Around eight."

Sari was okay. There was never any real reason to believe otherwise, but he still felt relieved. He wanted to go see her, but June and Dave, her parents, wouldn't appreciate a visit this time of night.

"Well, don't you want to know who she was with?"

"Sure, I guess."

Mangrum shot a sidelong glance. "Daryl Carpenter, the Golden Boy himself."

Carpenter was the quarterback for the Seminole Hurricanes. Good-looking, a damn good quarterback and dumb as a brick.

"Carpenter? I wonder what she was doing with him."

"You schmuck. She was *with* him. They were together."

"Huh?" Danny's brain was unable—or unwilling—to process the implication.

"Christ, how clear do I have to make it? They were sitting in a dark corner holding hands and practically fucking each other with their eyes. You get it?"

Somewhere a switch flipped, shutting off reason and opening a current of raw, primal emotion. Danny sprang from the rock and yanked Mangrum up by his fleshy arms.

"What are you talking about? You're lying. Tell me you're lying."

Mangrum looked at him through red slits and said calmly, "It's true, Danny. I'm not the one you should be mad at."

Danny let go. "I'm going to find Troy and if he says you're making this up, you're fucked."

"Troy wasn't with me. It was before I picked him up. And I didn't tell him about it because I wasn't even going to tell you." He rubbed his bare ass and sat back down on the rock, taking a hit from the whiskey bottle. "Here, you need this."

Danny reached mechanically for the bottle and drained it.

"Believe me, I was just as surprised as you," Mangrum said, untangling then replacing the hair band holding his curly black pony tail. "Then again, I don't know why. Let's face it, Sir Daniel, we all scratch where we itch."

This trivial proposition was offered with the solemnity of a philosophy professor defining the meaning of life.

"When you go beneath the surface, humans are no different from other animals. We're all savage, sexual beasts. Take Enya, for example. Here's a girl that, from what I hear, just can't get enough fucking. It doesn't mean she's a bad person, it's just instinctual. We'd be the same way, we just don't get as many opportunities."

He paused to relight the joint. "Trust me. If guys could get sex as easy as girls, we'd all be whores. I saw you when she was taking her clothes off. Your eyes were about to pop out. Troy-boy and I sit around wanting to puke listening to Sari-this and Sari-that, but as soon as Enya started gettin' naked it all went out the window."

"Fuck you," Danny said gloomily. "I still don't believe you." *Why did Sari lie to him?*

"Look, you can't even blame Sari. She's one of the best-looking chicks in the school and golden boy is used to having his way with the ladies, so big stud quarterback starts hitting on her and the hormones take over. Power's an aphrodisiac. It's always been that way. I'm sure the head caveman got all the babes."

"Sari's not like that," he said, disappointed with his weak defense.

"We're *all* like that—that's my point. In a state of nature we'd all be humpin' everything that walked by, but religion teaches us we'll go to hell if we do that, so instead we buy into the romantic fairy tale so we can feel good about fucking."

"Enough of your bullshit. Tell me exactly what you saw."

"You sure you wanna know?"

"Tell me."

"Okay, I go into the Lantern and order two slices of pizza from the takeout window. While I'm waiting for it, I look around to check out who's there. I almost didn't see 'em at first because like I said, they were in the back corner, same table we were sitting at that time you saved my ass from the big dude playing pool who went all crazy on me when I complimented his girlfriend's ass. There they were, Sari and Carpenter. They were holding hands across the table and leaning toward each other making those sickening gaga looks."

He tried to imitate one but succeeded only in looking like Charles Manson.

"Their faces were so close Sari's hair was about to catch on fire from the candle. I even left without my pizza because I didn't want her to notice me, but, you know, if you're dumb enough to screw around at the Lantern you deserve to get caught."

Danny wanted to smash Mangrum's smirking face. He wanted to cry. He wanted to kill Carpenter. He wanted to kill himself. But all he did was lower his head.

A school of shiners flashed beneath his surfboard, startling him back to the present. They shattered into glitter with a flick of his toe. Danny looked up to see three surfers wading into the water. One of them was waving to him. It was Ray Hartford, the surfing dermatologist, pasted white in nuclear-strength sunscreen. Danny waved back, but paddled north with the current to put distance between them. He didn't want company.

Troy emerged from the shadows that night just after Mangrum finished telling his story about Sari and Carpenter.

"What are you guys doin'?" he said.

"We're sitting around naked and talking, what does it look like we're doing?"

"I heard yellin'."

"We were howling at the moon. Where's Enya?"

"She's back on the beach."

"What's she doing?"

"Right now? Just lying there."

"You screw 'er?"

Troy, who to Danny's everlasting dismay had accepted the role of Mangrum's toady, shook his head. "I remembered you called first dibs when we picked her up."

A sound like a hissing tire escaped Danny's throat. "You assholes are disgusting. Take me back to my car."

"Take me back to my car," Mangrum mocked. Troy looked at Mangrum then Danny, wondering what he missed. "Sorry, can't do that yet, Danielsan. Don't you want to have some fun with Enya? A little payback?"

"Payback? What's going on?" Troy asked.

Mangrum ignored him. "Danny, let's all go visit Enya. Come on, you don't owe Sari anything now. Just think of that ripe body down there on the beach, naked under the moon, just waiting for it, itching for it."

If looks could kill, Mangrum would have died then. Danny turned and walked into the forest.

"Danny, wait," Troy shouted.

"Let him go, he's probably a faggot."

Danny stumbled along the rim of the lake, oblivious to the coral lacerating his feet. When he reached the far side, he sat on a ledge overlooking the water and stared at the mirror image of the moon in the center of the lake.

Through the insect buzz, he heard fragments of conversation, laughter and what might have been wailings of ecstasy.

Drunken tears wet his cheeks as he thought of the night he and Sari had made love on the same small beach. It was the same act, but seemed to come from two different universes.

Or was he just fooling himself? She lied to him about tonight, what if everything was a lie? Was Sari having sex with Daryl Carpenter right now? Was she on her back spreading her legs for him, letting him pound into her, moaning and asking for more?

It began deep in his gut as a low, rumbling snarl. As it expanded to fill his chest, the sound erupted into a savage wail that echoed across the lake, cowing the insects into momentary silence. He dove in and swam toward the opposite beach. People routinely drowned in Florida's rock quarries setting out to swim across and running out of gas halfway, but that night he could have made it to Cuba.

Everything was spookily quiet when he reached the shore and waded onto the sand. Mangrum and Troy were nowhere to be seen. Enya was on her back, lying still with her thin legs spread apart. Danny stood over her, silent tears merging with rivulets of lake water dripping from his face and hair onto her bare belly. He looked down at the tuft of blonde hair between her legs and swallowed hard.

He dropped to his knees and leaned forward, kissing her gently on the mouth. She moaned softly and parted her lips and whatever control Danny might have retained vanished. He pushed his tongue hungrily into her mouth and ran his hands up her thighs and across her ribs until they found her small breasts. Lowering his body weight against her, he kissed her harder. Before he knew what was happening, he was inside her wet vagina.

He never stopped to think about whether it was a consensual act, but if someone had asked the question right then, his frenzied, pickled brain would have insisted it was. Mangrum said she was a nymphomaniac, she parted her lips in the car, responded to Troy's kiss in the lake, took her clothes off to go skinny dipping. Mangrum and Troy had already taken their turns with her … she didn't resist.

It wasn't until the last moment, at the instant he climaxed inside her, when her blue lips murmured "No, please," that it hit him like a sledgehammer that he had just raped a drunken, unconscious fifteen-year-old girl. And the worst part of it was, *goddamn him*, he relished it. For those few minutes, he was exactly what Mangrum indicted them as—a brutal sexual animal, channeling his wrath and pain into Enya McKenzie.

*No, please.* The words had haunted him for twenty years.

Mangrum and Troy emerged from the brush like two wood nymphs, wearing only white cotton briefs.

"Virtuoso performance, Sir Daniel," Mangrum said. "I'd give it a 9.2. Of course, it didn't match my perfect ten."

Danny stood in silent shame, looking down. Enya stirred and opened her eyes. He forced his to meet them, a convicted criminal awaiting sentence, but where he expected hatred there was only a glazed look of noncomprehension.

"Troy only got a seven because he popped his cap in less than a minute."

"Did not," Troy protested.

While Mangrum was badgering Troy, Danny noticed a red stain on Mangrum's underwear. "What's that?" he said, pointing. "On your shorts?"

Mangrum's eyes darted to his groin and back to Danny. "Uh, I dunno. She must be having her period."

"That's not what you told me," Troy said. "You said you busted her cher—"

"Shut up!"

Danny exploded into Mangrum, sinewy arms drilling his chest, knocking him to the ground. He stepped forward and stood over him, hands balled into fists, breathing heavily. "She was a *virgin?*"

"How was I supposed to know?"

"You said she was a nymphomaniac."

Mangrum shrugged. "That's what I heard."

"That's what you heard. Troy, go get her clothes."

"Don't do it," Mangrum ordered.

Troy started then stopped, looking lost. Mangrum scrambled off the ground. "You self-righteous prick. We watched you take your turn and you rode her like a bucking bronco, so don't try to ease your dirty conscience blaming us."

The words bit like vipers. "Troy, get the clothes," he said evenly, eyes daring Mangrum to interfere. Troy looked at Mangrum, seething but silent, then ran up the hill and returned with Enya's clothes.

Mangrum spit on the ground at Danny's feet. "You got five minutes before we leave you here. Come on, Troy." Troy wavered helplessly until Danny nodded for him to follow Mangrum.

Danny helped Enya to her feet and coaxed her to walk with him to the lake to wash off, but she stood immobile, arms wrapped tightly, blue Hummel eyes staring catatonically. She was shaking. Danny held out his hand.

"Come on. It's okay. I won't hurt you anymore. I swear."

When he finally got her to move, she took one step and vomited all over herself. She collapsed to her knees. Danny wasn't sure what to do. He wanted to give her privacy, but there wasn't time. If Mangrum left they'd be stuck in the middle of nowhere, miles from anything. He picked her up and carried her down the beach, setting her down gently in shallow water.

She began rubbing herself with handfuls of sand, slowly at first, then harder and harder until Danny worried she might scour away her skin. He turned the other way, glancing back only to make sure she wasn't drowning. When he thought they couldn't wait any longer, he helped her out of the water and guided her listlessly back to her clothes.

"Put these on. I'm gonna go get dressed. I'll be right back to get you."

At the top of the ledge he was relieved to see the Camaro gleaming in the moonlight. He got his own clothes and dressed quickly, then went back for Enya and found her still struggling to pull her shirt over her wet skin. They were pressing their luck with a hothead like Mangrum. He helped her get dressed.

When they got to the Camaro, Mangrum and Troy were already in the front seats. Danny helped Enya climb in the back and slid in next to her. Mangrum brought the engine to life and peeled out of the clearing down the gravel road.

No one spoke as they drove back to Danny's car at the South Lake party house. Halfway there, Mangrum switched on the radio.

*Old black water, keep on rollin' ...*

The refrain tattooed Danny's brain and the Doobie Brothers song became a permanent part of the night at Sugar Lake.

# 7

**WITH THE MEMORIES** of Sugar Lake pressing on him like an anvil, Danny paddled to shore, catching a pitiful wave that took him only a few yards. He tucked the longboard under his arm and waded onto the beach. At the boardwalk, he ducked under a shower to rinse the salt off.

He was surprised to see Grady at work inside the Tradewinds and went in. Scratchy Irish folk music piped from a phonograph behind the bar.

"What are you doing here so early?"

"What does it look like? Cleaning fish."

Danny stood the longboard against a wall covered with fish nets and a mounted blue marlin under a thick layer of dust. Sure enough, Grady was gutting a fish on the oak bar.

"Nice looking mackerel."

"Caught it last night. Got eight more just like it. They're running."

Apart from cursing his boat motor, surfcasting was Grady's favorite hobby. Any time Danny looked over his balcony late afternoon, the chances were good the old conch would be sitting at the ocean's edge on a folding aluminum chair next to two twelve-foot fishing poles held in place by pieces of PVC pipe hammered in the sand. He didn't usually catch much, but that wasn't the point, just like catching the perfect wave wasn't the point of surfing or finding an unbroken sand dollar the true goal of shell collecting. The shore is church, the activities just diversions.

"How was your night?" Grady asked casually.

"Not bad."

"Missed you here."

"Yeah, well, I had something else to do."

"I see. Something fun, I hope."

Danny could tell Grady was toying with him, that he already knew he had gone to the reunion.

"I give. How'd you find out?"

"D'Angelo boys."

"Ahh." Secrets around the Tradewinds had lifespans shorter than a shot of rum.

"How was it?"

How do you sum up an evening of dashed hopes, rumors of murder and an apparition from the grave? He took a seat on a vinyl bar stool losing its foam stuffing through three layers of duct tape.

"Very strange."

Grady finished filleting the mackerel and pulled another from the refrigerator.

"Well, at least you renewed one acquaintance. I ran into a friend of yours in the parking lot this morning."

Danny sat at attention. "A woman?"

"Sorry, but nope. It was a man, big guy, name was Thumper or something like that. Said he saw you at the reunion."

"Thumpet?"

"That's it."

"What the hell did he want?"

"He said you two were old friends and he was stopping by to see if you were free for lunch."

"He's no friend of mine. I don't even remember him. What else did he say?"

"Not much. When I first saw him, he was standing by your car. He asked if I knew you and if it was your car."

"What'd you tell him?"

"What do you think I told him, blockhead? I said it was. What's going on?"

"I'm not sure. Something's not right about that guy. Have you heard anything about a murder yesterday in West Palm Beach?"

"Who can keep up with them?"

Danny told Grady about John Mangrum and his confrontation with Thumpet at the reunion.

"And this Mangrum, you say he was a close friend of yours?"

"Used to be."

"Funny, I don't remember you ever mentioning him. He must be part of that missing chapter we were talking about on the boat."

Danny dodged the subtle interrogation. "Did Thumpet say anything else?"

Grady scratched the white stubble on his chin. "Not really, except when I asked him how he enjoyed the reunion, he said it was *above average*. That's kind of a strange way to put it now that I think about it. You think this Thumpet is trouble?"

"I don't know. I need to check something. You got fifty cents?"

Grady gave him two quarters from the cash register which Danny took next door to the gift shop at the Treasure Cove Hotel to buy a *Palm Beach Post*. He found what he was looking for on page three of the county section, sandwiched between a story about beach erosion and an ad for surgical thigh reduction: a two-paragraph report of Mangrum's murder.

So Thumpet told the truth. Mangrum really was dead, murdered in his condo. Danny tossed the paper in a trash can outside the hotel entrance. He wasn't sure what to feel. Surrendering his enmity toward Mangrum wasn't easy, but it seemed indecent to hold a grudge against the dead.

Halfway back to the Seabreeze Towers, he remembered what Thumpet said at the reunion. He wheeled back to the hotel and fished the newspaper out of the trash, the doorman sniffing with disapproval. He studied the article again:

## *Palm Beach Man Found Slain In Condo*

Police found the body of a murdered Palm Beach man in his home at the King's Arms Condominiums yesterday. Police spokesperson Lt. Mara Reves identified the victim as 38-year-old John Mangrum. The body was discovered by a friend whose identity has not been released.

Reves said a substantial quantity of white powder believed to be cocaine was found on the premises and speculated that drugs were involved in the killing.

Details regarding the manner of death are being withheld pending investigation.

He reread the last sentence. *Very savage. They said it was a mutilation murder.* Thumpet's words. How would he know that?

A gnawing discomfort drew him to the parking lot where he found his Volkswagen at the same crooked angle he left it the night before. He tugged on the doors. Nothing seemed disturbed.

He walked to the front and popped the flimsy hood to the trunk. The latch had been busted for years. His spare tire had been stolen three times.

The spare was there, along with a flashlight, empty can of Budweiser, tattered Miami Dolphins cap and an oil-stained paperback edition of Byron poetry. He started to close the hood when he noticed the spare tire ajar in its recessed compartment.

The source of the latest bumping noise? The Beetle was falling apart. Probably time to break down and buy another car before the lottery money ran out.

He tried to wrestle the tire back into place, but it wouldn't go. He unscrewed the bracket and lifted the tire. A bulky brown paper bag was wedged at the bottom of the compartment. Whatever it held Danny had long forgotten.

He pulled it out and the bottom ripped open. Two packages of white powder wrapped in clear plastic landed at his feet with a thump.

"What the hell?"

He didn't understand what was happening, but knew it wasn't good. He unzipped the front of his wetsuit, stuffed in the bags and ran-walked back to the Seabreeze Towers.

He punched the elevator button five times. It had to be Thumpet, but why would he leave what looked like bags of drugs in his car? A set up?

No time to sort it out. Had to get rid of the powder.

Danny's phone was ringing when he barreled through the door. He ignored it. In the kitchen, he flipped on the garbage disposal and took out the bags. He tried to tear one open, but the plastic was too thick.

His answering machine clicked. It was Grady.

"Danny, I don't know what's going on, son, but there's a half-dozen cops headed for the elevator. Given our conversation this morning and my intuition, I didn't want to take any chances."

Danny locked the door and threw the bags in the sink, where he attacked them with a steak knife. The first bag spilled open, but the rubber flap blocked the flow and the powder piled up like a snow-covered mountain. He jerked out the stopper and watched gratefully as the mountain melted away.

He sliced the second bag open more precisely as the elevator pinged down the hall. The bag was still half full when a booming knock shook the door.

"Police! Open up. We have a search warrant."

He frantically shook the bag and swept a layer of white dust from the counter just before the front door exploded from its frame. He tried to stuff the empty bags down the disposal, but never made it.

"Freeze!"

Five cops in uniform filled his kitchen. One held a battering ram. The others pointed handguns at him. They formed a semi-circle around a mustachioed Latino dressed in a shiny suit, floral silk tie and Italian loafers that gleamed like exotic lizards.

"Grab those bags and cuff him," the man said. "And turn off that goddamned garbage disposal."

He examined the bags, swiping a finger across the powdered remnants and tasting it.

"Sonofabitch!" Flecks of spit showered the kitchen. He hammered his fist on the counter, sending a picture of surf-guru Duke Kahanamoku riding the nose at Oahu's North Shore off its hook onto the parquet floor where it shattered. Danny liked the picture and was tempted to complain, but kept his mouth shut. The uniformed officers stood around examining their shoes.

"My name is Detective Emilio Rodriguez," the man finally said, dark eyes glowing like coals. "Are you Daniel Teakwell?" He practically spit Danny's name.

"I am."

"How did you know we were coming, Mr. Teakwell?"

Not that Danny would tell him, but he sensed a truthful answer of a lucky guess might be too much for Rodriguez to bear. "I don't know what you're talking about."

The men in uniform leaned back as if afraid Danny's answer would ignite another conflagration, but Rodriguez stayed calm.

"We're here to search your premises. We have a warrant."

"Can I see it?"

He snapped his fingers. "Mullins, gimme the search warrant."
A cop with acne, who looked young enough to be in high school,
unfolded a sheet of paper and handed it to Rodriguez, who held
it in front of Danny. Hands cuffed behind him, he nosed in to
read it.

"It's just a form."

"So-oo sorry, Teakwell. I forgot you're such a special person.
Next time I'll ask the Chief Justice of the Florida Supreme Court
to handwrite a search warrant for you personally, maybe even
deliver it himself, with flowers and a box of candy."

"You got my middle name wrong," Danny said. Maybe that
made the warrant invalid.

"If you have some correction fluid, we'll fix it. In the meantime,
let me give you some friendly advice. There are two kinds of
criminals. Those who cooperate and those who don't. Reliable
statistics show those who do live happier, healthier lives."

"Are you threatening me?"

"Of course not. Just friendly advice, like I said."

"It would be easier to cooperate if I had some clue what this
is all about."

Rodriguez smiled, showing rows of perfect white teeth. "I
see. You don't know what it's all about."

He waved the empty bags and looked around at the other
officers. "He doesn't know what it's about."

They all laughed.

"It's about a white powder that's very popular in South
Florida. But mostly, it's about murder."

"Murder? You're crazy."

"No, Teakwell, what you did to John Mangrum—that's
crazy."

Mangrum! The drugs were a red herring or maybe part of
a bigger plan. Thumpet, whoever he was, must have set him
up for Mangrum's murder, which meant Thumpet must have

killed Mangrum. He struggled to make sense of it, but it was impossible.

"I know you probably aren't going to believe this, detective, but I'm being framed."

"You too? What a coincidence. You're the third person I've arrested this month who was framed. Isn't it terrible how the criminal justice system squanders taxpayer money arresting and convicting innocent people?"

Assigning acne-faced Mullins to watch Danny, Rodriguez barked search assignments to the others.

Danny slumped to the floor. There was probably enough cocaine residue in the bags to make out a possession charge, but he may have escaped a long prison sentence by emptying the bags in time. They'd also find some pot, but he was pretty sure that was only a misdemeanor. But Mangrum's murder? There couldn't be anything tying him to it since he didn't do it, unless Thumpet planted something else.

Rodriguez returned to the kitchen. "The search warrant covers your car. Would you like to give us the keys or would you prefer we break in?" Danny motioned to the keys on the counter.

"Oh boy, a surfboard keychain. That's really *bitchin'*." He tossed the keys to Mullins. "Go search the car."

Rodriguez produced a small tape recorder from his coat and ordered someone to fetch him a chair. Leaving Danny on the floor, Rodriguez parked in front of him and announced the date, time and location into the recorder.

"Mr. Teakwell, I'm going to read you your rights. Listen carefully." With his crotch practically in Danny's face, he read the *Miranda* warnings from a small white card. "Do you understand these rights?"

Danny nodded.

"You have to speak up."

"Yes."

"Are you willing to waive these rights and submit to questioning at this time?"

"I have nothing to hide."

Rodriguez smiled.

"Mr. Teakwell, did you know a gentleman named John Mangrum?"

"Yes." The cuffs were cutting into his wrists. He shifted position.

"In what capacity did you know Mr. Mangrum?"

"He was a friend of mine, a long time ago."

"When was the last time you spoke to him?"

"More than twenty years ago."

Rodriguez smiled again, more like a smirk. "More than twenty years ago. How about that?"

A cop walked into the kitchen carrying Danny's linen jacket, the one he wore to the reunion the night before, the one Thumpet spilled the punch on. Rodriguez nodded.

"Is that your jacket, Mr. Teakwell?"

"I change my mind. I want a lawyer."

He expected another verbal torrent, but Rodriguez switched off the recorder and said mildly, "That's your constitutional right. You're going to need a good one. You're under arrest."

"What charges?"

"Possession of cocaine with the intent to distribute, possession of marijuana with what I assume is the intent to get stoned and listen to loud rock music and," he paused to tug at the corner of his mustache, "for the murder of John Mangrum."

# 8

**"SO MY CLIENT TURNS** to me and says, 'If I knew what *adjudication withheld* meant, I wouldn't have said *Fuck you, Judge.*'"

In a windowless interview room, Fink sat across a metal table telling another war story and doodling on a legal pad. The only other furnishings were the metal chairs they sat on. Light came from a flickering florescent fixture hanging from two thin chains. Everything was painted gray. The room was hot as hell. Rings of sweat stained the collar and armpits of Fink's French-cuff shirt. Danny wore an orange jumpsuit smelling strongly of disinfectant.

"Get it? The judge was about to let him go, but he ended up in the slammer for saying *Fuck you, Judge*. It's hilarious."

Danny massaged his temples. "Maybe it would be funnier if I didn't have visions of being gang-sodomized dancing in my head."

"Just trying to lighten the mood. I'm a little nervous, alright? You're the only innocent client I've ever had."

When they first spoke, Fink refused to represent him. Arriving at the Broward jail, Danny remembered Fink's business card stashed in the linen jacket from the night before. When he asked Rodriguez for it, the detective immediately assumed it had evidentiary significance and sealed it in a plastic bag through which he grudgingly let Danny memorize the number.

"I've been thinking about it," Fink said when Danny called him from the jail phone. "I decided I can't help you with your surf shop. Sorry. Leases and incorporations just aren't my thing. You're better off with someone else."

Danny groaned and looked at the prisoners waiting behind him. He never went to law school, but it struck him that having to beg your lawyer to represent you was not the best way to start a murder defense.

"Bullshit," he whispered. "There's some reason you don't want to be my lawyer and it doesn't have anything to do with areas of specialty. Besides, this isn't about leases anymore. I just got arrested for murder."

"Murder!" Fink squawked loud enough to get the attention of the jail guard ten feet away.

Danny gave a thumbnail explanation of his arrest and Mangrum's murder, the sordid circumstances of which he learned reading the probable cause affidavit while being booked.

"You sawed off his cock?" said the inmate behind him. "That's cruel, bro."

Danny smiled and buried his face in the phone. "Hurry up, Fink. I only have five minutes."

"Damn, you're really putting me on the spot here."

"Look, I need someone I can trust. I intend on paying. I'm not asking for a freebie so it can't be about money. If it's something personal, tell me quick."

"It's personal, but … ah, alright. I'll be there as soon as I can. In the meantime, don't talk to the police."

Fink dropped his doughy forearms on the table. A plastic sapphire popped out of a gaudy cufflink and rolled off the edge.

"The first thing we need to concentrate on is getting you out of this dump," he declaimed in an impressive lawyerly voice, then slumped in his seat. "Unfortunately, the right to bail has changed a lot over the last decade. It used to be bail was practically guaranteed, but those fascists in the state legislature have made it a whole new ball game."

Danny hunched forward, anxious for the details following this introduction to the topic of bail, but Fink just sat picking orange paint from his pencil.

"Okay," Danny finally said. "So what's the bottom line?"

"I'm thinking, I'm thinking. You see, most of my criminal clients are DUIs. They get out no problem. But murder's different. I mean—you can appreciate that."

"So what are you saying? Just tell me. Do I get out?"

"Honestly? I don't have a clue. I've never handled a murder case."

"Yeah, yeah, I know. You're a specialist. Don't do leases. Don't do murders. What the hell do they teach you in law school?"

Fink's face pinched.

"You're the one who had to go get arrested for first-degree murder! Grand theft? Robbery? Oh no, too simple. Let's throw in cutting off a guy's dick and feeding it to his fish. Then add a bunch of venue problems because they arrested you in Broward County for a murder that happened in West Palm Beach. Bail? Your guess is as good as mine."

Scratched into the table top, Danny saw: *Bobby Pierce, Attorney at Law, Good and Cheap.* He memorized the number.

"But that's all going to change. Tonight I'll research it and be ready in the morning. Your first appearance is set before Trisha Kovacich at ten o'clock. She's supposed to be a good judge, tough but fair. We'll try to get you bailed out then."

Fink stretched back in the chair, blossoming belly straining for freedom against his shirt buttons.

"Let's talk about the charges. From what I can tell, they got you on the drug possession charges, but those aren't that big a deal because the amounts are small. Rodriguez is one pissed-off detective. It's driving him crazy that you dumped all that coke before he got there. He's convinced someone in the department tipped you off, even calling for an investigation by Internal Affairs. Thinks you're a big-time coke dealer and killed Mangrum over drugs."

"Do you think I did it?"

"It doesn't matter what I think, I'm your lawyer."

"So you think I did it."

"I didn't say that."

"I didn't kill Mangrum. And those weren't my drugs. I found them in the trunk of my car."

"I believe you, I believe you. But Rodriguez doesn't and he's not giving up on the drugs. Swears he can make an intent to distribute charge stick even though the coke is down the drain. That's a long-ass mandatory sentence."

"What'd you tell him?"

"I said if wishes were horses we'd all be riding."

"What exactly does that mean?"

"Not sure, but it pissed him off even more. The murder charge is weak. According to Rodriguez, this all got started by an anonymous tip."

"Thumpet," Danny said.

"Probably. An anonymous informant called claiming to be a fellow drug fiend of Mangrum's. Said Mangrum stiffed you on a deal and that he, the informant, was there when you threatened to kill him if he didn't pay up. That's what they used to get the search warrant, that and a phone call. When's the last time you talked to Mangrum?"

"Rodriguez asked the same question. I haven't seen or talked to him since high school. What's the big deal?"

"They have a phone company record showing a call from Mangrum's house to yours on the day Mangrum was murdered."

"Another part of the frame-up," Danny said disconsolately. "Just before I left for the reunion I found a long blank message on my answering machine."

Fink scribbled on the legal pad. "If we can narrow the time of death we might be able to deal with the phone call. It must have been made by the killer. You couldn't very well have been talking to Mangrum and killing him at the same time." He drew a big star on the pad.

"I also have an alibi for most of the day."

"Where were you?"

"Helping Grady."

"Who's that?"

"Grady Banyon. He owns the bar in the building I live in. I spent most of the afternoon helping him fix his boat."

"Grady Banyon. Got it. The tip itself isn't worth anything as evidence. It's hearsay. Inadmissible. The big thing they got now is your jacket, the one you wore to the reunion. They think it has Mangrum's blood on it. They're gonna test it."

Danny laughed. "It's fruit punch, unless you think Thumpet spiked it with Mangrum's blood."

Fink wasn't laughing.

"Come on, you don't really think he did that?"

"Right now, I wouldn't rule anything out. Rodriguez seems excited about the jacket. My guess is it came as part of the informant's tip. This guy Thumpet has gone through a lot of trouble to do you in. Which, of course, leads to the bazillion dollar question. Why?"

Danny had been asking himself that since the police led him away in shackles, a scene poor Grady had to watch. When he got in their face and demanded an explanation, Rodriguez threatened to arrest him for interfering with a murder investigation.

The old man was beside himself. "Gestapo!" he shouted as they loaded Danny in the back of a patrol car.

"I have no idea, Fink."

"Maybe you did something to piss Thumpet off back in high school. I mean *really* piss him off." He shook his head. "No, I guess that doesn't make sense."

"None of it makes sense. Go back to the jacket. Do they really think I'd murder someone then go to my high school reunion wearing a blood stain the size of an oil spill? I'm insulted they think I'm that stupid."

"You gotta look at it from a cop's mentality. It's hard for them to take the idea of a frame-up seriously. People just don't go through the time and effort it takes to frame someone except in the movies. If you're bent on doing someone in, it's a lot easier to just walk up and shoot 'em. Unless we can come up with a really good reason why someone would frame you for a murder you didn't commit, we're gonna be pissing in the wind on that defense."

Fink was right. It wasn't logical for a total stranger to frame him for murder. Danny didn't even remember Thumpet, much less doing anything to him that would lead to this nightmare. The only thing he ever did that might explain murder happened at Sugar Lake—with Mangrum. He needed to tell Fink about the connection, but wasn't ready yet. He'd only told one other person and had been paying the price ever since.

"Apparently, the only other evidence they have are witnesses to testify that you attacked Mangrum back in high school."

"That was twenty years ago. Surely that's not important."

"Like I said, their case is weak and they're grasping for everything they can."

"How did they find witnesses so fast? Mangrum's only been dead one day."

"The police have been all over the Island Hotel. A lot of our classmates spent the night there. Rodriquez showed me a stack of interview statements from people at the reunion. The word of your arrest spread like wildfire."

He stopped suddenly to scribble on his pad.

"New insight?"

"Huh? Oh, no. Just remembered I have to return some porn videos I rented. They kill you with late fees. Anyway, the cops told your high school chums that you're charged with murdering your former best friend, who—the last time they saw you together—was on his back on the cafeteria floor with you on top beating the shit out of him."

"Great."

"More bad news. When I went to Rodriguez's office, he was on the phone with a newspaper reporter chatting up your case. Depending how they play it, you might be big news in the morning. You know, *Lottery Winner Arrested for Psycho Killing*, that sort of thing."

Danny sagged. Sari would see it. He never cared much what people thought about him, another character flaw no doubt. If he did he might have more incentive to be a better person. But Sari believing he was a rapist-turned-murderer was almost too much to contemplate.

"Who are the witnesses?"

"What difference does it make? There were at least a hundred people in the cafeteria that day, including me."

An enormous guard with a head the size of a watermelon opened the door and said "Time's up."

Fink dropped his pad into a beat-up vinyl briefcase like he was in a hurry to leave.

"I'll see you in the morning. They'll transport you to the courthouse and I'll meet you there. We should have time to talk more before the hearing. In the meantime, I'll be researching your bail. Just make it through the night and we'll get you out of here tomorrow."

The confident assertion cheered Danny until Fink disguised *I hope* with a cough.

The watermelon head made impatient faces.

"One more thing," Fink warned. "Don't talk about your case to anyone. These places are crawling with snitches trying to cut a deal for themselves."

The guard took Danny to a room where a trustee issued him a pillow, blanket and some hygiene supplies that he had to sign for. He followed the guard down corridors between cells filled with prisoners. It wasn't like in the movies. No one hooted or banged metal cups on the bars. Most of the prisoners were reading or sleeping.

At the end of the corridor, the guard shouted at a video camera and a lock clicked. The guard waved Danny inside. The door clanked and he was officially incarcerated.

The cell was an eight-by-eight cube, painted gray like everything else, furnished with a stainless commode and sink and two concrete bunks, one on each side. Each bunk ledge had a vinyl mattress on top, more like a gym mat. A small window of thick plastic let in natural light, which Danny appreciated.

To his right sat a brooding man with dark hair and a long pale face punctuated by thin lips and a sharp nose. He waited for the man to look at him, but he kept staring straight ahead as if Danny wasn't there.

"Hi," Danny said. It came out like a greeting at cheerleader camp. He lowered his voice. "I'm, uh, Danny, your new, um, cellmate." He wished he had a tougher-sounding name. It turned out not to matter because he was talking to a statue. Fine, he could deal with brooding silence, just don't get any ideas about sodomizing.

"Nice to meet you," the man finally drawled. "Frank's the name. Frank Calhoun. Don't mean to be rude. Just admiring my lady," he said, gesturing to an eight-by-ten photo taped to the opposite wall, a glamour shot of a buxom woman with hair like broken straw and makeup thick as garage floor paint.

Danny relaxed. The guy didn't sound scary. He sounded sad. He laid his pillow and blanket on the empty bunk, careful not to obscure his cellmate's vision. "Pretty lady. Your wife?"

"Girlfriend. But not anymore." He started slobbering.

Unfamiliar with jail etiquette, Danny fell back on his pillow and stayed silent. Several minutes passed before Frank blew his nose and spoke again. "You ever really a loved a woman?"

"Once," Danny said. Etched in the gray paint was *If I'm such a criminal, why is God free?*

"I mean a woman you loved so bad it made your heart hurt. For real. A literally hurtin' heart."

"Mm-hm."

"Brenda was a woman like that," Frank said.

"The one in the picture?"

"Yup. Brenda Gulch. Best woman in the world. Best lover, best hair stylist, best everything. I still love 'er even though she put me here." He started blubbering again.

Just like a night at the Tradewinds. Only thing missing was a margarita, which he wouldn't mind having.

"She put you in jail?"

"For killing Leonard."

A murderer. Nice. This must be the waiting cell for death row.

"He pushed me over the edge. It was more than any man could take. Oh, they started out as just *friends*, you know how that goes. First, the three of us would do things together. Then more and more it was Leonard this and Leonard that and I was the odd man out."

"Did you tell her how you felt?"

"Hell, yes. I told her one of us had to go, Leonard or me. You know what she did? She leaned right over and kissed him."

"He was there?" Poor Frank.

"That was the problem. He was always there."

"What did you do?"

"I took my time planning it, which wasn't too smart from a legal standpoint according to my lawyer because it showed what they call *malice aforethought*. I was considering the usual means—shooting, stabbing and such—when one day a nature program came on the cable showing a mess of ants swarming over a cow and devourin' it. That gave me the idea. Seemed like poetic justice for Leonard since he was swarming all over my woman and devouring my life. Logical, right?"

"Well ..."

"One afternoon when Brenda was at work, I just flat out told him, Leonard, you ain't taking my woman."

"What'd he say?"

"Nothin'. I drugged his lunch and he was out cold. I dragged him to the backyard and staked him on one of them humongous red ant colonies."

Danny rubbed his forehead.

"My plan was to pour chocolate syrup down his throat and let the ants eat him from the inside, but just then Brenda pulled up in front. I ran out to shoo her away and guess what? She had just come home with a brand new lovey-dovey negligee she bought, just for me. I mean for her to wear, but me to look at. And I had a change of heart right there. I thought, you know, maybe I really didn't have nothin' to worry about, just like she always said. I starting regrettin' Leonard being staked to the anthill and ran back to save him, but it was too late."

"The ants got him."

"Nope. Sonofabitch died of a heart attack. Brenda was right behind me. When she saw Leonard she fainted. I had to call the ambulance for both of them. Hell of an afternoon."

"I'll say."

"Here's the real kick in the ass. A week later, guess what she did?"

Pessimistic about human nature, Danny said, "Found someone else?"

"You know it. With Leonard not even cold in the ground and me rotting in this jail cell, she ran right down to the Pet Palace and got herself another dog."

"Dog?"

"Yup. Rottweiler this time. Guess she wanted a pet better capable of defending itself. Leonard was just a little dachshund."

# 9

**DANNY SPENT** the afternoon playing Scrabble with Frank in the dayroom, a brightly lit recreation area painted pastel orange. A television, ping pong table, dated magazines and a few board games provided relief from the boredom of confinement. Frank was a terrible Scrabble player, obsessed with trying to spell *Brenda*.

Just before dinner, a large motorcycle enthusiast with a shaved head covered with tattoos told him he had pretty blond hair and asked he wanted to play husband and wife. Danny rose to defend his manhood, but Frank tugged him back down. "Sorry, I'm already engaged," he said and went back to Scrabble.

The night passed slowly. After the lights went out Danny lay awake on his bunk listening to Frank snore. Through the window wispy clouds drifted past like ghosts.

Images of Enya McKenzie shaded in blue light and John Mangrum tied to a chair with hollow eyes invaded his thoughts. Tomorrow he knew he had to tell Fink about Sugar Lake, the whole story, from beginning ... to end.

After they left Sugar Lake that night and got back to Danny's car, Danny took Enya home. She didn't object. They drove in silence to her block on Myrtle Street a couple miles from the South Lake party house. The night was hot and muggy, but Enya was shaking. He turned on the heater, but it didn't work. He struggled for something to say the entire way, but his mind was as blank as a mirror in a closet.

"That's where I live," Enya murmured as they approached a small pink cinder block house. A porch light shined in front, but the house was dark inside.

"I'll wait until you get inside," he said.

She couldn't get the car door open. Danny reached over to help and accidentally brushed her leg. She jerked so hard her head hit the window.

"I'm sorry. I didn't mean to touch you."

The double-meaning of the words sunk in and he kept going.

"Enya, I, uh, don't know what to say. There isn't anything to say ... except I'm sorry for what happened tonight." His face turned red with shame. "For everything. I wish I could change it."

He knew it sounded asinine. Gee, I'm sorry I raped you, but he *was* sorry. He would give anything to turn the world back two hours.

It might have helped him in life if she had hit him or spit in his face right then, but she just looked at him mournfully through watery eyes before getting out and running to the porch. He watched her get a key from under a planter and unlock the door. She closed it without looking back.

Danny didn't sleep that night. He twisted and turned and stared at the ceiling until the phone rang the next morning.

"Danny, it's for you," his mother yelled.

"Who is it?" he demanded from behind his bedroom door, heart pounding. No way was he ready to talk to Mangrum or Troy. What if it was Enya, or the cops?

"It's Sari."

He pulled the phone from the hallway into his room. "I got it." He waited until his mother hung up.

"Hi, Danny. It's me," Sari said.

"You don't sound like you."

"You don't sound the same either. Can I come over? I need to talk about something and don't want to do it over the phone."

During the night he had almost convinced himself Mangrum was lying about Sari and Carpenter, but this was obviously going to be the big breakup announcement. It seemed impossible his safe, happy world could fall apart so quickly. Yesterday morning his biggest concern was what kind of cereal to eat for breakfast. If she told him they could still be friends he'd go mad.

"Go ahead and just say it on the phone," Danny said sharply.

"Um, I don't think I can," Sari replied in a small voice.

He felt like a hypocritical ass, which he was. Any moral high ground he might have held was long gone.

"Sure, come on over. My mom's here, but we can take a walk on the beach."

Thunderclouds darkened the sky and the water below. Lightning flashes illuminated the horizon. The beach was empty. Wind gusts stung them with sand and water spray. Pieces of seaweed zipped by like tumbleweeds. They hiked for several minutes without speaking.

Ahead, pilings of the decaying Sunset Pier poked out of the water in disarray like broken flamingo legs.

Sari smiled sadly. "Do you remember our first time?"

"Of course. That's a silly question."

"I was so scared. I couldn't figure out why until the next day."

She turned to look at him for the first time, hair whipping her face. "It was because of what it meant to me, what you mean to me."

Danny noticed she was trembling, maybe from the water spray. He started to put his arm around her, but held back.

"We made a vow that night," she said. "Remember?"

"To always be true," Danny said, points on the words.

"I didn't go to Margie's last night, Danny."

Finally. "I know."

"You do?"

"I called over there from a party to see if you wanted to take a *study break*," he said sarcastically, "but you weren't there."

Sari's face flushed.

"I lied to you."

The confirmation seared his heart.

"But I've never done it before and I'll never do it again."

Again? *Again* sounded like the future.

"Everything was just so … complicated."

Enough beating around the bush. Just get it out. Tell her he knew she was at the Lantern with Carpenter, knew they were holding hands and—in Mangrum's words—fucking each other with their eyes.

He opened his mouth just as Sari blurted, "I was at the doctor."

He stared at her blankly. "Doctor?"

"I thought I was pregnant."

She pressed her face against his chest, luckily, because the anguish in her eyes had him on the verge of clawing his out. For the first time since they drove home from Sugar Lake, his new reality became clear. *What had he done?*

The damn open, Sari's words tumbled out like crashing waves. "I missed my period on Saturday and I never miss it. You know me. I can practically tell time by it, and when it didn't come by Thursday, I got so scared. I made an appointment for Friday night at a women's health clinic in Miami. I didn't want anyone to see me. That's where I was last night. I had to stay until midnight to get the results."

"Sari, why didn't you tell me?"

"I should have, but I was too scared. I didn't know what I would do if I was pregnant. I'm only seventeen and haven't lived hardly any of my life. And I didn't know what you would do. Parents always tell their daughters, if you get pregnant, he'll just run away. I didn't want you to run away, Danny."

Behind her a cargo ship pushed south on the horizon and he wished they were both on it, going somewhere far away, some place where she could never leave him, because he knew that's what was going to happen when she found out about Enya McKenzie.

Another shouting match erupted down the jail corridor. This time a guard and prisoner were going at it over the quality of the toilet paper. Frank stirred in the bunk next to him, making barking sounds. The ruckus died down and Danny returned to watching the sky through the window.

The Monday after Sugar Lake Danny tracked Mangrum down in the school cafeteria. Mangrum orchestrated everything. Without his lies, Danny never would have touched Enya. Hurt and anger drove him that night, not lust. He'd punish himself for the rest of his life, but for one day, Mangrum would pay.

He spotted him at a table with Troy and two other longhairs, gnawing on a hamburger. Their eyes locked. Danny's must have signaled his intentions because Mangrum dropped the burger and stood defensively.

Danny walked to the edge of the table.

"Why'd you do it?" He set his books down. "I want to know. Why did you do it?"

"Suck me."

Danny hurdled the table and landed on Mangrum with his full weight. They tumbled to the floor. Mangrum was no match. Danny pinned him easily and landed a punch that split his nose.

"Danny, stop!" Troy jumped on his back and grabbed his arm. Danny flipped him over his shoulder and aimed his fist at Troy's upside-down bewildered face, then lowered it.

It wouldn't have mattered because Coach Saxon flew in from the side and leveled him.

An ambulance took Mangrum to the hospital where he got seventeen stitches. The cops came and arrested Danny, handcuffing him and stuffing him in the back of a cruiser in front of the student body. They took him to the juvenile detention center where he spent the afternoon before his mother came to get him. She was not in a good mood.

Back in the days before high school students began regularly shooting each other, the event made the Hollywood newspaper complete with a picture of Danny sitting in the back of the police car. The article quoted Mrs. Kostop, the principal: "It doesn't make sense to any of us. Danny and John have always been good friends." A student named Megan Caprician stood up for him: "Danny Teakwell is the nicest boy I know. He'd give you his last penny if you needed it."

Sari was beside herself when she came over that night. Danny was confined to his bedroom indefinitely, but pleaded with his mom to let Sari in.

He shut the door behind them.

"Are you alright?" she asked.

"Um, not really."

"I've been trying to reach you all day."

She sat on the bed and held his face with both hands. He had no choice but to look straight into her penetrating eyes. "What happened?"

The question, obvious as it was, drew a blank. He hadn't planned the attack in terms of logically thinking it through. Was there any plausible explanation short of the truth for going postal on your best friend? Danny was a poor liar.

"He called me a faggot," he said, which at least was true. Mangrum said it at Sugar Lake. He tried to shift his gaze to meet Jimi Hendrix's on the poster behind her, but Sari held him firmly.

"I don't believe that explanation for one second. I've never seen you lose your temper, certainly not for something as trivial as name-calling. Tell me."

As the day's events wore on, beating up Mangrum seemed like less and less of a good idea. Here was the final nail. He couldn't lie to Sari.

He pulled her hands down and held them. "Okay. I'm going to tell you. It's bad. Really bad."

Apprehension filled her brown eyes, the weight of it in the room matched only by his own thickening dread.

"No matter what you think of me when I'm done—and it's not going to be good, I promise—I need you to know that I love you more than I've ever loved anyone or anything. I always will. It's like committing suicide telling you this, Sari, because I know what's going to happen."

Sari's fingers tightened as he began the tale of Sugar Lake. When he got to the part about the skinny dipping, her hands fell limp. As he neared the end, she pulled her arms away and wrapped them tightly around her shoulders.

He told the story truthfully, with one big omission. He left out Mangrum's lies about Sari and Daryl Carpenter. Danny wondered many times whether it was a mistake not telling her. The lies at least made what happened more comprehensible. But he thought it would sound like a cowardly excuse for a cowardly act. Mangrum's lies didn't mitigate what he did to Enya and he was ashamed for Sari to know he let someone like Mangrum override his trust in her.

"So that's about it," he said. There was no good way to put a good ending to the story, so he didn't try.

Sari sprang off the bed and backed toward the door.

"No," she said, wagging her head. "No, no, no!" she screamed.

"Sari, please. Wait."

But she opened the door and ran from the apartment.

From the bedroom window he watched as she climbed in her car and buried her face in her hands. He started after her, but it was too late. By the time he got outside all he could see were her tail lights.

"What was that all about?" Danny's mother asked from the kitchen. "Does it involve what happened today? Talk to me, Danny."

He retreated silently to his bedroom, locked the door and collapsed on the bed.

He called Sari every day for two weeks. At first her mother made excuses, but finally said, "Danny, I'm sorry. She just doesn't want to talk to you. Sometimes you kids squabble like you're still in the fifth grade. Why can't you just make up like you did back then?"

Because he wasn't a rapist in the fifth grade.

His mayhem got him suspended him from school for a month and grounded just as long. When he finally saw Sari, she was standing at her locker, just like on the first day at Seminole High, except this time when she looked up there was no joy in her eyes.

"Sari, can we talk?"

"Um, I can't. I'm late for class," she said and hurried away.

Two days later he found a letter stuffed through the vent in his locker.

*Dear Danny,*

*I apologize for avoiding you. I know I would just start crying again and I'm tired of crying. I don't want to spend this letter vilifying you, so I will keep it short because I know the more I write, the more my anger will come through.*

*You were everything to me, Danny Teakwell—my past, present, my life's hopes and dreams. I knew I loved you back on Sand Dollar Lane. It's so difficult to give that up, more than you could ever know, but I have to. I can't see you anymore.*

*That probably seems unfair to you, and maybe it is. You're probably thinking, "Stubborn Sari, always has to go by the book, can't even give a person a second chance." It's not like that. I know I can forgive. I just could never forget. Does that make sense?*

*I feel so sorry for Enya. What if that had been me? It can happen to anyone, Danny. Believe me. I know. I learned it a long time ago.*

*The whole thing seems like a bad dream. I'll never understand it, not in a million years.*

*I only want the best for you in life—always. I know you are hurting too. If I could take it away, I would.*

*Good-bye.*

*Love, Sari*

Learned what a long time ago? Danny never understood that part of the letter. It weighed on him for years.

He withdrew into a shell after that, spending as little time at school as possible. He avoided going anywhere he might run into Sari, not because he didn't want to see her, but because he wanted to see her too much. Every time he did, any occasion he caught a glimpse of her walking down the hall or talking in the parking lot, he plummeted into a funk he couldn't dig himself out of for days. He never saw Enya McKenzie, a blessing of the split school shift.

Before long he started skipping baseball practice. To his credit, Coach Malkoni tried hard to salvage him. In a heated lecture in his office, Malkoni tried to make Danny see what he was throwing away, even showing him a confidential inquiry from a college recruiting scout, but Danny was a lost cause.

After giving him more chances than he deserved, Malkoni stopped him one afternoon as he trotted onto the practice field.

"Danny," Malkoni said with the whole team watching. "You're off the team. Go clean out your locker. I'm sorry."

Danny nodded and walked back to the fieldhouse.

He tried to make distant memories of Mangrum and Troy. Whenever he approached their group in the hallway, they got quiet until he passed. Occasionally, when Danny was a safe distance down the hall he'd overhear Mangrum making fun of him. Danny ignored him. Sari was right that night in his bedroom. It took more than name-calling to make him lose his temper. Still, Danny listened each time, waiting for Mangrum to make the mistake of saying something about Sari or Enya, but he never did.

He spent most of his free time surfing and learning the art of shaping surfboards under Ben Keahilani's tutelage. Surfing was therapy for Danny, his mood lightening the moment he hit the water. Paddling out, he sometimes imagined himself never stopping, just stroking to the horizon never to be seen again.

When he socialized, it was with the surf crowd. He went to a few of their parties during the year, but never returned to Ducky's or the block party circuit. He spent a lot of lonely nights on his bed devouring poetry, amazed by the poet's gift for translating feelings *too deep for tears*, as Wordsworth said it, into words.

A few months after Sugar Lake he found another note in his locker. Thinking it was from Sari, his heart raced as he fumbled to unfold it. But it was from Troy:

*Danny — Heard something you should know. That Enya girl dropped out of school. Don't know if it's true. Troy*

Rumors spread quickly. Some of them even mentioned rape. No details or names were mentioned, but he stalked the halls of Seminole High feeling like *GANG RAPIST* was tattooed on his forehead. In the weeks following, he sometimes drove to Enya's house and parked in the shadows, thinking of things he would say if she came out, but she never did.

At Christmas he composed a letter to her, but hung onto it for weeks. He wanted her to know that what happened was their fault, not hers, wanted to give back some of the dignity they stole. He finally mailed it not knowing what to expect as a response. The letter was damning enough to be used against him, but by that point he didn't care and perhaps secretly craved punishment. As it turned out, he never heard anything.

In the new year he recovered a little. He met a girl named Jill at the beach who went to a different high school and they became friends. Jill was cute, fun and liked to surf. She made it clear she wanted to be more than friends, but he shied away from romance. In the story of his life, Jill earned a footnote as the first in a long line of relationships he sabotaged out of guilt about Enya and love for Sari.

As his senior year drew to an end, Danny's mother was all over him about applying to college. His grades were never great and got worse after Sugar Lake. The best he could manage was to get accepted to community college. Sitting in a recruiting trailer in the parking lot at Seminole High, a career counselor signed him up for freshman composition, college algebra, Western literature and men's softball. Nothing in his life had ever seemed more pointless.

In June, his mom and sister came to his graduation in the high school auditorium, but his dad hadn't been heard from in years and was a no-show. After the ceremony Danny went to the graduation bash at Rick's Armory, reluctantly because he assumed Sari would be there. A couple of buddies in the band coaxed him on stage to play a song with them. He was hammering out the riff to Alice Cooper's *School's Out*, which the crowd demanded over and over, when Sari walked in with Daryl Carpenter, clinging to her arm like it was the Super Bowl Trophy.

Carpenter. Fate's sick sense of humor.

Danny proceeded to get trashed and act out by succumbing to Rikki Anderson's flirtations. In the middle of this fiasco, someone set off a spark—a rumor—that ignited and roared through the cavernous armory.

*Remember that girl who got raped and dropped out of school. She committed suicide.*

Danny ran to the parking lot and threw up. He sat on the hood of his car staring vacantly at the moon, the same voyeur moon that shone over Sugar Lake, the same witness to crimes of the night since time began.

"Danny?"

The voice from behind startled him. It was the voice that read poetry to him and helped him learn long division.

Sari stood straight as an Oscar statuette, hands clasped, white sun dress clinging to her tan legs in the night breeze.

"I just heard the rumor about Enya."

He hung his head.

"It might not be true. You know how rumors are."

"And if it is?"

A pile of rowdy graduates poured from the armory, granting her a reprieve. The in-crowders. Carpenter's group.

"Come on, Sari," shouted Carpenter. "We're going down to Haulover Pier."

"Just a minute," she snapped. "Danny, I hope you don't think … I would never."

"You don't have to explain."

"Are you going to be alright?"

He nodded.

"Are you sure? I'm worried about you. I know how deep your feelings run. That's one way we've always been alike. You wouldn't … hurt yourself, would you?"

"No. I thought about it, before tonight. But I wouldn't do it."

"Sari," Carpenter yelled across the asphalt. "They're gonna leave without us."

"I guess it's time to go." As always, her eyes told the whole story. So much to say, but nothing to say. She started to leave.

"Sari?"

She stopped, silhouetted by the armory lights.

He wanted to tell her he was dying inside. He wanted to beg her forgiveness. He wanted to plead for her to come back to him.

"Happy graduation," he said. "It's been a long road."

Sari hesitated a few seconds before tearing away, walking quickly and then running across the parking lot. Carpenter waited to welcome her with open arms, but she brushed past him and disappeared into the night.

That was the last time Danny saw her.

He finally forced himself away from the cell window and turned over in the bunk to face the wall.

The only sound was a prisoner weeping in the next cell.

# 10

AT 8:30 Monday morning, June 12, Bennie Finkel sat in his third-floor law office, fretting. Nervously flipping his tie, he watched out the window as the man coming to visit him parked his car and got out and stretched. He took another swallow of coffee and waited.

A few minutes later, the receptionist he shared with the other two lawyers on the floor buzzed on the intercom.

"Bruno Hauptmann is here to see you." The man insisted on using the code name.

"Send him in," Fink said, removing his glasses and rubbing his eyes.

"Benjamin," the man said with mock comradeship as he burst across the threshold. Without waiting for an invitation, he seated himself in one of the two client chairs opposite Fink's desk. The sturdy chair screeched under the weight.

"Hello, Hauptmann. Here." He slid a white envelope across the glass desktop.

The man opened it, counted the bills inside, shook his head and frowned. "There's only fifteen hundred here. Where's the other five hundred?"

"That's all I have right now."

"Don't cross me," he said evenly. "I want the full two thousand."

"I don't have it. I swear to God. It's been a slow month."

The man made a kissing sound and slapped the envelope against his palm. "This is not acceptable. We had an agreement. I could sue you for breach of contract. Know any good lawyers, Benjamin?"

"You can't squeeze blood out of a turnip."

"Apt comparison." He scanned the room. "What can you give me for collateral?"

"Take anything you want," Fink said, hating himself as much as the man. Giving in to a bully, just like always. "Take the furniture. It's leather." It was also rented, but Hauptmann didn't know that.

"Furniture? What would I do with office furniture? No, I'm afraid it has to be something more portable."

They both looked around the room. There wasn't much else of value, except the fax machine, also rented. Fink was just about to suggest it when Hauptmann's eyes settled back on him.

"Give me that Rolex."

Fink frowned, but unclasped the silver band and handed the man his watch, noting the time as he did. He needed to get to the courthouse for Danny's bail hearing.

Hauptmann turned the watch over once in his thick fingers, dropped it on the turquoise carpet and stomped it with his boot heel. He tossed the remains on the desk where they exploded like shrapnel.

"Counterfeit."

"I never said it was real," Fink whinnied. "Look, I'll be getting a good chunk of money in a couple of days. You know that. Why are you picking on me? You'll have the other five hundred by the end of the week."

"Of course, our big case. I saw the paper this morning. Nice spread. I particularly enjoyed the insightful legal analysis you gave when the reporter asked if Teakwell was going to make bail. Let me see now, how did that go? I want to get it exactly right to do justice to your words. I remember: *I don't know.* Brilliant, Benjamin. Oliver Wendell Holmes couldn't have said it better."

Sometimes he wasn't sure which was more important to the man, the money or the torment. He wanted to throw the bastard out of his office, but knew he couldn't risk angering him. To his relief, Hauptmann stood up.

"A moment ago when you swore to God, did you mean it? Do you really believe in God, Benjamin?"

Christ, now he wanted to talk religion. "I suppose."

"Pray you don't screw this case up. You think life is hard now? Just wait. Your troubles will be much worse. But you already know that. Until next time, Benjamin."

Fink waited until he left the parking lot, grabbed his briefcase and took off for the courthouse.

# 11

**DANNY GROANED** as he read the six-column headline on the newspaper Fink planted in front of him: *LOTTO WINNER CHARGED IN GRISLY DRUG SLAYING*.

"You guessed it right," Danny said. "Front page of the Broward section. I'm gonna start getting the big head."

"It's the Lotto angle egging them on, that and the fact you— not you, I mean whoever did it—drilled holes in his eyes and cut off his cock. They're out there now. You're popular. The place is swarming with newspaper and TV people."

Fink, in a sky-blue seersucker suit and white bucks, bounced back and forth like a tennis ball in front of the table where Danny sat, wrists chained to his ankles. They were in a small interview room at the courthouse, nicer than the one at the jail, with peach walls and wood-veneer furniture, but there was no window and the eyewash couldn't disguise the thickness of confinement. A pot of African Violets withered on the table.

The newspaper photo showed his blond profile in the back of a police car as he arrived at the jail, an updated version of his high school arrest picture for battering Mangrum.

Fink breathed heavily as he paced. Red blotches covered his face and neck. He looked like he might have a heart attack.

"Have you found out anything about Thumpet?" he asked.

Fink stopped pacing. "Only what's in the reunion pamphlet. Did you know he came to the reunion all the way from Bismarck, North Dakota? I called the number he listed, but it just rang. I did find this though."

He extracted a large book from his briefcase. "It's our twelfth grade yearbook."

Danny wouldn't have recognized it. Mold had transformed the glorious purple and gold of Seminole High to mottled black. Fink opened it to a page marked with a sticky note and set the book in front of Danny.

"Check this out."

Danny scanned rows of hopeful faces with hair parted in the middle. "What am I looking for?"

"Third row, second from the left."

"Albert Thumpet. Huh. So that's the guy."

"Mm-hm. What do you think about the way he looks?"

"He's real cute, Fink. If my sister weren't married, I'd fix them up."

"*Du-uh.* Is it the same guy you saw at the reunion?"

Danny studied the twenty-year-old photo.

"He has the same dark curly hair, but the eyes look too dark. The guy at the reunion had really blue eyes. Hard to tell from this little picture. What are you thinking?"

"Just considering every angle. We both agreed it doesn't make sense that a guy from high school who you don't even remember would murder Mangrum and try to frame you for it, right?"

Danny nodded.

"What if it's someone just posing as Thumpet?"

"Why would he do that?"

"Hell, I don't know," he said, slamming the yearbook shut. The guard peered through the door window. Fink scowled at him.

"We need to find him," Danny said.

"Don't you think I know that? It's only been one day! I'm a sole practitioner."

"Relax. I was just making an observation."

"We'll find Thumpet, but I had to set priorities. We need to get you out of here first."

He pointed to the briefcase. "I did a lot of research," he said proudly. "I'm going to spring you this morning."

"Sounds good to me. How long before court?"

Fink grimaced, picturing the fake Rolex scattered across his desk. "Um, my watch broke." He stepped outside to ask the guard for the time.

"He says we have fifteen minutes."

"That should be long enough. Sit down and listen. I've got a story to tell you."

"Story? It's not story-time. It's bail-hearing time."

"This is about my case. It's important. At least it might be. I have a hunch."

"Alright. When you're finished," he paused to scratch his head with all ten fingers, "I have something important to tell you too."

"A long time ago, way back in high school, I was involved in something terrible, with Mangrum."

"And Thumpet?"

"No, at least not in any way I can figure out. I don't remember that guy at all. It was me, Mangrum and Troy Stoddelmeyer. You remember him?"

"Sure, I remember Stoddelmeyer."

"Good, because one thing we need to do is track down Troy. He may be in danger."

"Track down Thumpet, track down Stoddelmeyer. You may need a bloodhound more than a lawyer, but okay, I'm with you."

Danny proceeded to lay out the story of Sugar Lake, the secret he he had told only once before. Fink listened impassively.

"So you think this is all connected to Sugar Lake," Fink said when he finished.

"I do. It's the only thing tying high school, Mangrum and me to something that might justify murder. That's why you need to find Troy. He could be the next target."

Fink looked skeptical. "Okay, I know a good investigator. He's not cheap, but he can find people. But I'll be honest. I'm not buying the connection."

"I said it was just a hunch."

"You don't have enough even to qualify as a hunch. Not a single fact. Just your guilty conscience."

"There's one other thing I haven't told you. Remember what happened at the reunion, at the bar in the marina?"

"When you freaked out?"

"Yeah. The reason I freaked was …" He stopped to clean dust from a leaf on the African Violets with his thumb. Fink was going to think he flipped.

"Was? The reason you freaked was?"

"Because I saw—or at least thought I saw—Enya McKenzie standing on the dock."

"Enya McKenzie!" Fink jumped out of his seat. "Danny, settle down. This is all starting to get to you. Just sit down and relax."

"I am sitting."

"How about some water?"

"I don't need water. I'm telling you what I saw. I know it sounds strange. Believe me, I know it better than anyone."

"But that's impossible. Like you just said, she committed suicide. She's been dead for twenty years. I'm almost positive I remember reading her obit back in high school when she checked out. You were just stressin' because of the whole reunion and Mangrum thing."

He sighed. "You might be right. But it's something to think about."

"I agree with the first part."

"What about my story?" Danny asked.

"Are you spacing out on me? I just told you. It's sounds shaky."

"No, I mean, what do you think about what happened? About me … now that you know what I did."

"Ah, I see. I think it's a lot to carry around all these years. You're obviously still beating yourself up over it. In my opinion, it's not justified. A hundred other guys in your shoes would have done the same thing. I know it's not politically correct, but it sounds like she was asking for it. You don't go get drunk and naked with three guys in the woods not expecting something to happen."

Danny had considered that angle over the years, but rejected it. Enya never asked to be raped. As for the alcohol, that was part of the crime. How could she resist when she was practically passed out?

"In any event," Fink continued, "no matter how bad it was a normal person wouldn't snuf herself over it. You're not responsible for her suicide. My advice is to let it go."

A knock on the door. Fink jumped like he received an electric shock. "Court! It's time!"

"You said you had something important to tell me."

"It can wait. Let's go."

He hefted the briefcase and shot out the door.

"Hey!" the guard shouted after him. "You forgot your client."

But Fink was already gone. The guard helped Danny shuffle to the courtroom in his chains.

# 12

"ALL RISE," the bailiff called. "People of the State of Florida versus Daniel J. Teakwell, Case No. 95-2310TK, Honorable Trisha Kovacich presiding."

A regal fifty-ish woman, graying hair pulled in a bun, entered from a back door and sat at the bench. She greeted the prosecutor, a gangly fellow named Arlo Pickering, like they were old friends. Seated next to Pickering was Detective Rodriquez.

"Is the state ready to proceed?"

"Yes, you're honor."

"Defense ready?"

Fink nodded.

"Speak up, Counselor. The court reporter can't take down a nod."

Danny felt a headache starting.

"The defendant is ready," Fink whispered.

"Would you like to have the shackles removed from your client?" the judge asked.

Fink started to nod again, but caught himself. "That would be nice, Your Honor," he said. The bailiff unlocked Danny's chains.

Pickering unfolded his long body and asked permission to approach the bench. He handed the judge a document and glided over to give a copy to Fink. If he were any more relaxed he'd be asleep.

Counselor Finkel, on the other hand, looked like he was about to pass out. He set the document down without reading it. Danny gulped. It said *Motion for Pretrial Detention*.

The prosecutor proceeded to coolly and all too convincingly argue why Danny should be kept in jail awaiting trial for the murder of John Mangrum. The murder was particularly heinous and Danny presented a threat to the community. When he got to the part about Mangrum's penis, the bailiff grabbed his crotch.

"No conditions of pretrial release can guarantee protection of the public or assure the defendant will show up at trial," Pickering concluded and sat down.

Danny flashed nervous glances at Fink waiting for him to do something. Leap up and object, throw himself on the mercy of the court, anything, but he sat still as a block of granite, sweating copiously in the cool courtroom, eyes locked on the pile of papers in front of him.

He pictured himself a hunchbacked old man sitting in a cell scratching out petitions to the Supreme Court about his lawyer who got stage fright.

"Mr. Finkel, your response?" the judge said.

Fink lifted the pile of papers and waddled to the lectern.

"Hmm-hm-hm-hmm."

He removed his gold-rimmed glasses and cleaned them with his tie, the courtroom so quiet Danny could hear the silk squeaking on the lens.

"May it please the court," he said.

Then all hell broke loose.

"Danny Teakwell is an innocent man!"

In a great booming voice, he ripped into the state's case like a chainsaw through balsa wood. He chastised the police for their shoddy investigative work, maligned the prosecutor for misreading the bail statute and finally launched into the State of Florida itself with enough passion one could imagine it skulking off the map to South America.

Papers flew in a hurricane. There were cases for this and statutes for that. Danny didn't understand everything, but the basic points were that he had no prior criminal record and the state's case was, in Fink's words, "weaker than a geezer's thingy at an erectile dysfunction clinic."

The judge frowned.

"The prosecutor wants us to believe that Danny, I mean *Mr. Teakwell*, is a danger to the community. Preposterous. If Your Honor has the time and inclination, I have a dozen character witnesses here today willing to swear under oath they would trust my client with their money, their lives, their ... testicles!" He pointed to the gallery.

Danny looked back and saw Grady giving a thumbs-up. Clustered around him were the D'Angelo brothers, John the Diver, Kenny Hooks and an assortment of other miscreants from the Tradewinds. They smiled and waved like they were on a field trip.

Fink saw Shannon the cocktail waitress and held up a hand in apology. "And, of course, breasts for the ladies, Judge. No discrimination intended."

"Mr. Finkel," the judge said.

"Excuse me a moment, Your Honor." He paused to drain a full glass of water, wiping his chin on his searsucker suit jacket. "Yes?"

The judge sighed. "Never mind. Get on with it."

"On what evidence does the state base its case that Danny Teakwell is a criminal? That he deserves to be caged like a rabid dog, deprived of due process, liberty and the pursuit of happiness without a trial. Oh sure, a small amount of recreational cannabis for home use. Let's be real, Judge. Name me a law-abiding South Floridian who doesn't take a toke once in a while."

Again the judge started to speak, but stopped and waved him on.

"As I was saying, what evidence? A cowardly anonymous tip. A phone call to Mr. Teakwell's house that anyone could have made. And a jacket, a jacket they claim has blood on it. They haven't had time to test it, but promise us they will. In the meantime, it looks and smells like fruit punch."

The gallery chuckled.

"I saw Mr. Teakwell at his high school reunion wearing the very same jacket, before and after it got *tropical red punch* spilled on it. If forced to, I'll withdraw as his lawyer right now and take the stand under oath."

The judge looked tempted to take him up on the offer.

"And what about motive? Does the state have a motive for why Danny Teakwell, a kind, gentle soul who devotes his free time to helping the elderly, would commit such a terrible crime?"

Helping the elderly? Ah, fixing Grady's fuel filter on *Lady Luck*.

The crowd ate it up.

"Thank you, Mr. Teakwell," yelled an old lady with a walker and rolling oxygen tank.

"Order," cautioned Judge Kovacich.

"Why, why, why?" Fink continued. "They want you to believe it was a drug killing. They avoid the obvious question of why an intelligent person who won millions in the lottery and lives a modest lifestyle would get involved in the dirty, dangerous business of cocaine. My client doesn't even use cocaine. In fact, let's give him a drug test right now. Hand me that coffee cup and he'll pee in it right this second."

The judge rolled her eyes.

"Florida law is clear, as Mr. Pickering knows, that even for the charge of murder, pretrial detention is permitted only where the proof of guilt is substantial. The state hasn't come even close to bearing that burden at this hearing. We ask the court to set reasonable conditions for pretrial release. Thank you."

The gallery applauded as Fink returned to his seat. The judge banged her gavel and told everyone to pipe down.

Danny patted him on the back. "You were incredible, Fink."

"I think I'm gonna puke."

Pickering stood. "May I have a moment, Your Honor?" he requested tranquilly.

Judge Kovacich nodded and everyone watched as he leaned across the rail to confer with a bearded man in a tan poplin suit. Next to him Danny recognized Janet Traynor, star reporter for *Hard Bite*, a local tabloid television show dedicated to showcasing all that is unseemly in life.

"Your Honor, the state would like to call a witness. Detective Darren Stills. Detective Stills is with the Palm Beach Sheriff's Department. He possesses evidence highly relevant to the issue of motive in this case. We hadn't intended to disclose it at this time, but in light of Mr. Finkel's admittedly forceful argument I would like the court's permission to put Detective Stills on the stand to bolster the case for pretrial detention."

"Any objection, Mr. Finkel?"

Fink looked at Danny and shrugged. "No objection."

Stills, short with ears like teapot handles and eyes set deep in his skull, made his way to the witness box where the bailiff swore him in. Pickering asked some questions establishing Stills' credentials and involvement in the investigation then cut to the chase.

"Detective Stills, did you have occasion to conduct a search of the deceased's home at the King's Arms Condominiums?"

"I did."

"And did you bring with you to the courtroom today an item you seized during that search?"

"Yes."

"And what is that item?"

"I guess you'd call it a scrapbook."

"This scrapbook, you found it in the deceased's home?"

"Yes. It was in a box in the attic crawl space."

"What did you do with the scrapbook after you seized it?"

"I sealed it in an evidence bag and marked it for identification."

"Where has the scrapbook been since you seized it?"

"It's been locked in my office until I brought it here to court."

"May we see the scrapbook?"

Stills lifted a bag from his briefcase.

"With the court's permission, please remove the book from the evidence bag and open it to the first page. Tell us what you see there?"

"It's a clipping from the Hollywood newspaper dated March 5, 1973."

"Please read it to the court."

Fink stood. "Objection. Your Honor, what is the possible relevance of this testimony?"

"What's the relevance, Mr. Pickering?"

"If the court would allow the witness to respond, the relevance will become clear."

"Read the clipping. We'll see where it takes us. Objection overruled, but let's start connecting things up."

"Of course, Your Honor. Detective Stills, read the newspaper clipping."

"The headline says, *Sophomore Strikes Out Eleven in Hurricanes Win*, and the article reads, *Seminole High sophomore Danny Teakwell, in his first start as a varsity player, hurled eleven strikeouts yesterday as the Hurricanes beat Southwood 5–2.* That's the gist of it."

"Does it say anything else?"

"That Teakwell walked seven batters."

"My control always sucked," Danny whispered.

"Fine," Pickering said. "Please turn the page and describe the next item."

"It's another article about the defendant. The headline says *Hurricanes Pitcher Breaks Sophomore Strikeout Record.*"

"And the next page please."

Fink was on his feet again. "Your Honor, if the state is trying to prove my client was an outstanding baseball player, we'll gladly stipulate to that along with his many other fine qualities, but I still fail to see the relevance."

"Mr. Pickering?"

"Getting there now, Judge. Please describe what you see on the next page, Detective."

"It's a photograph of two young men, the deceased and the defendant, taken in the parking lot of Seminole High School. You can see the name of the school on a sign in the background. The men are dressed casually and one has his arm around the other."

Fink interrupted. "May we at least have a look?"

"Counselor, show the photograph to Mr. Finkel and his client."

Pickering bowed graciously and carried the book to the defense table.

"That's us, me and Mangrum," Danny whispered. "Probably tenth grade."

Returning the book to the witness, Pickering continued, "Detective Stills, what I'd like you to do is flip through the book and very briefly describe the contents." Turning to the judge, "With the understanding, of course, that the defense will have the opportunity to review the scrapbook and cross-examine."

There were more newspaper articles about Danny's baseball

accomplishments, including the infamous game in the county championships where he pitched a no-hitter, but walked eleven batters and lost, a surfing article from *Florida Now* magazine showing Danny shaping a surfboard at the Lost Wave Surf Shop, articles about Danny winning the lottery and a few more snapshots.

Pickering stopped him. "Thank you, detective, I think we get the picture. There's just one more item I'd like you to describe for the court. I believe it's on the last page."

Stills nodded eagerly and flipped to the back. "This is a weird one," he said.

Fink objected. "Judge, he's a witness, not a color commentator."

"Sustained. Stick to the facts, Detective."

"I apologize, Your Honor."

Emboldened, Fink kept going. "In fact, I object to this entire line of questioning."

"On what ground?"

"Relevance."

"Overruled."

"Inadequate foundation."

"Overruled."

"Hearsay?"

"Overruled."

Fink sat down.

Pickering asked, "Do you see a photograph on that page?"

"Yes."

"Describe it for the court."

Stills snorted and shook his head. "It's kind of hard to describe. It appears to be a clipping from a high school yearbook. It's a photograph of a couple below the caption *Sweetheart Couple of the Year*."

Danny straightened. He and Sari won that stupid thing their junior year. What could it have to do with Mangrum?

"And who does the photograph portray as the *Sweetheart Couple of the Year?*"

Stills smiled. "On the right side is the defendant."

"How do you know it's the defendant?"

"Well, it looks like him and his name is printed below the picture."

"And who is the other half of the *Sweetheart Couple of the Year?*"

"It's a woman in a tank top and shorts. Except it's, uh, not a woman."

"What do you mean it's not a woman?"

"Well, it's a woman's body, but someone else's face has been pasted over her face."

"Whose face?"

"The deceased's. John Mangrum."

Murmuring filled the courtroom. Judge Kovacich's eyes widened. *Hard Bite* reporter Janet Traynor took furious notes.

"Counsel for the defendant was looking for a motive," said Pickering. "We've given him two. He can take his pick. We have a drug deal and a love story, both gone bad. The state reiterates its request that the defendant be detained pending trial for this attrocious crime. He is extremely dangerous, most likely psychotic. On preliminary review, the State intends to seek the death penalty."

Danny almost fell out of his chair.

"Mr. Finkel, your response?"

"Death penalty? Judge, with all due respect to my worthy opponent, he is full of shit."

"One more profane outburst and you'll be the one wearing chains."

He bowed, trying to imitate Pickering, but injured his back. "*Aye-ee* ... apologize, but I can't sit idly by while Mr. Pickering slanders my client. Danny Teakwell is a perfectly normal human being. He's no more psychotic than I am."

The judge's face turned pale.

"May I cross-examine the witness?" he said, still bent over rubbing his vertebrae.

"You may, but please control yourself."

"Detective Stills, you represent the government, is that right?"

"That's right."

"Yes, it *is* right." Fink turned to the crowd. "*The government.*"

Scattered hissing.

"Detective, do you know the Florida criminal statutes well?"

"Reasonably well."

"Well, do you have an actual set of the Florida Statutes in your office?"

"As a matter of fact I do," Stills said smugly.

"You do? Well, that's nice. It's nice to know *the government*, using taxpayer dollars from freedom-loving people like the good citizens in this courtroom today, can afford to buy you a nice set of Florida Statutes."

Danny heard Grady grumble from the gallery.

"So tell us, Oh-Mister-Super-Great-Expert on the Florida Statutes, is it a crime in this state for one man to admire, respect and love another?"

"No."

"No more questions."

Fink wobbled to the bench, still squeezing his spine.

"Your Honor, this scrapbook does tell a story. The story of a red-blooded American boy who grew up on the mean streets of Hollywood with only one goal."

Mean streets? Hollywood?

"To play baseball. To live his life on the field of dreams. Good, wholesome Broward County dreams." Fink put his hand on his heart.

"God bless Broward County!" shouted the woman with the walker, voice muffled by her oxygen mask.

The judge hammered her gavel. "No more outbursts!"

Fink continued. "But in the twisted world of Mr. Pickering and Detective Stills, love is not honored. Talent is not respected. And scrapbooking, a hobby popular with millions of Americans, gets transformed into a sordid tale of murder."

The old woman ripped off the oxygen mask and yanked out her nasal tube. "Fight the Power!"

"Deputies, remove that woman." The deputies moved in, bringing a cascade of boos that intensified when the elder tripped over her walker and collapsed into the arms of a deputy, gasping "The government! The government!"

The judge pressed her temples with both hands. Janet Traynor had stopped taking notes and appeared to be making an illegal recording mumbling into a fake banana. Money, murder and now a sex angle. The case had all the hallmarks of a *Hard Bite* exclusive.

Judge Kovacich returned from a short recess to announce Danny's bond was set at five hundred thousand dollars, which he could satisfy by paying a ten percent surety to a bailbondsman who would be responsible for making sure he showed up for court. He had to surrender his passport before he could be released and was ordered not to leave Broward County.

She also ruled that venue on the murder charge belonged in Palm Beach County. Once the case was properly refiled up the coast, the state could renew its motion for pretrial detention if the evidence warranted—meaning, as Fink was in the process of explaining back in the interviewing room, if his jacket tested positive for Mangrum's blood.

Danny sat reshackled, waiting to be transported back to jail. The violets looked a little deader, but the prospect of imminent release pumped new life into him.

"Great job, Fink. You did it! How about that old lady? What a piece of work."

"My Aunt Sylvia. I paid her a hundred bucks. She'll show up on your bill as *litigation support staff.* And fifty bucks for the oxygen tank rental."

"Your aunt? But——"

"Pickering told me this case is his A-1 priority. He may seem mellow, but he hates to lose. Says he's going to get the case refiled and the jacket tested by the end of the week if he has to work day and night. That gives us three or four days max. If Thumpet did mix Mangrum's blood in the fruit punch, we should be able to attack it at trial. It's just so absurd. But in the meantime, if the jacket comes back positive for blood, you're probably back in the slammer."

Fink was pacing again, but with prowess now. "You know, that Judge Kovacich has a truly nice pair of breasts. For them to show under that robe means they must be huge."

He was a shrine to sexism and insensitivity, but Danny was glad to have the old Fink back. "I can't believe I'm getting out of here today. I could almost kiss you."

"Thanks, but hold the kiss. I don't want to end up in one of your love triangles."

"Man, that was weird. The whole scrapbook, but especially the picture."

"It clears up a few things. Doesn't it?"

"I guess. Sari used to say Mangrum was jealous of her, but I never believed it."

"Makes sense though. He lies to you about Sari and Carpenter to get between you. Oldest trick in the book. You know, I'm surprised Sari didn't give you a break in light of Mangrum's lies. After all, you're only human. People kill each other every day over jealousy and betrayal. All you did was have sex with a naked girl on a beach."

"I never told her about what Mangrum said."

"What? Why not?"

"It was no excuse for what happened. And I just couldn't bring myself to admit I trusted Mangrum over her. She detested him, swore he'd get me in trouble some day."

"I still think you should have told her. Might have made a difference. Anyway, we only have a few minutes before they take you back to the jail. I gotta talk to you about something. It's kind of embarrassing."

"Money, right?"

Fink's face scrunched.

"Nothing to be embarrassed about. Just charge me the going rate."

"Okay, but I have to warn you, legal representation in a murder case isn't cheap with all the … um, expenses. First there's your bond. We need fifty thousand for the bailbondsman. And another five for Dizbo Skaggs, my investigator, to look for Thumpet."

"And Troy. I don't want him getting hurt."

"Okay, and Troy. Skaggs is good, but he gets a hundred bucks an hour plus expenses."

"Whatever it takes. What about your fee?"

Fink squirmed.

"Fink, it's okay. How much would you usually charge? That's what I'll pay."

"To tell you the truth, I've never had a case this big, but it's customary to charge a retainer, sort of like a deposit. I'd bill my time against it."

"Just tell me how much."

Fink rocked back in his chair, almost losing his balance. "Twenty-five thousand?"

"Is that enough?"

"To get started."

"Let's do it. There's enough to cover all of that in this year's lottery check."

Fink's eyes shined. "Man, a twenty-five grand retainer. That's what some of the big shots charge."

"You're a big shot. You kicked the prosecutor's butt in there."

"I did, didn't I? Kicked it all the way to Lake Okeechobee." He giggled like a little kid.

Danny scribbled a phone number on Fink's legal pad. "Call this number and ask for Grady. Last time I was at my condo, it didn't have a door, but if it's been replaced, Grady will have a key. Tell him to go in there and find the lottery check. It should be on the kitchen counter. My passport is … I'm not sure. It might be propping up one of the sawhorses in my living room."

"You have sawhorses in your living room? You could at least spring for a futon."

"I shape surfboards on them. Anyway, just deposit the check and take what you need."

Fink drummed his fingers on the table. "Well, um, our banking system isn't quite that laidback. With you in here, the easiest way to handle things would be for you to give me a power of attorney. "I prepared one just in case."

He pulled a document from his briefcase and laid it facing Danny. The caption read *Durable Power of Attorney*.

"If you trust me enough to sign it, that is. You should read it first."

"I'm trusting you with my life, aren't I?"

Fink's hand twitched as he held out a pen. Danny skimmed the document. It appeared to give Fink total control over him.

"Fink, if I'm reading this thing right it says you have the power to pull the plug on me if I'm in a vegetative state. Is there something you're not telling me?"

"No, no. It's just a form."

Danny signed it. "One more thing. There's a guy in jail named Frank Calhoun. He's my cellmate. I want to bail him out."

Fink sighed. "Danny, you can't take care of everyone. As your lawyer, I'd advise to avoid consorting with known criminals. What's he charged with?"

"Killing a dachshund, but it was in the heat of passion and kind of an accident."

"Frank Calhoun, accidental dog killer. I'll take care of it." He flicked the ballpoint. "That wraps things up for us right now. It's going to take a few hours to get your check deposited and bail processed, longer if we can't find your passport. I'll get Dizbo Skaggs on Stoddelmeyer's trail and start checking into Thumpet. Let's meet at my office tomorrow morning at nine."

"I'll be there."

"What are you going to do when you get out?"

"I don't know," Danny said absently, but he knew exactly. He was going ghost hunting.

# 13

**EACH MINUTE** seemed to take an hour, but Danny was out by mid-afternoon. A guard ushered him out a side door. The instant it locked behind him, he stopped to face the sun and soak up the rays. A single cumulus cloud floated like a bloated spaceship across a blue drape of infinite space. A sparrow coasted in the breeze. He got to enjoy these pleasures for approximately three seconds.

"Mr. Teakwell!"

It was Janet Traynor, the *Hard Bite* reporter, running at him like a linebacker about to take somebody out, fluffy black mane pinned to her ears. She wore a bright red suit with a skirt that ended several inches above her not unattractive knees. A guy with a beer gut and ponytail carrying a large video camera struggled to keep up with her.

She stuck a microphone in Danny's face.

"Mr. Teakwell, Janet Traynor, *Hard Bite* news. Tell us, what was jail like?"

"Great. Lots of male bonding. All-inclusive, sort of like a cruise ship."

She smirked into the camera. "You're in fine spirits for someone facing the electric chair."

"That's because I'm innocent."

"Is it true you and John Mangrum were secret lovers as the prosecutor implied?"

"No. Absolutely not."

"So you're saying *maybe*."

"What?"

"The prosecutor said you assaulted Mangrum back in high school and sent him to the hospital. Why'd you do it? Did he make a pass at you?"

Danny darkened. "None of your business."

"As you prepare to fight for your life, what would you like to say to our viewers?"

Grady motored up behind her in the Beetle. He should have used the moment to score public relations points, but had never handled absurdity well.

He leaned into the camera. "First, I'd like to thank Grady Banyon and all the good folks down at the Tradewinds Lounge for their loyal support. That's the Tradewinds Lounge on Hollywood Beach, where happy hour runs every weekday from five to seven. Best margaritas on the Gold Coast. If you're not at the Tradewinds, you're not having fun.

"And of course I have to thank my lawyer for his excellent representation. I wouldn't be standing here talking to you if not for him. If you or your loved ones are ever falsely accused of murder, call Benjamin Finkel.

"I'd also like to give my sincere thanks to you, Janet, for taking time from your busy day exploiting lurid scandals and pain and misery to come down and chat with me."

The camera panned to Traynor, who was slashing a finger across her throat and mouthing *Cut!* Either the cameraman hated her or was high because he kept filming.

She tackled him just as Grady pulled up. Danny hopped in.

"What's her problem?" Grady asked, popping the clutch, leaving behind a trail of flatulent epithets from the sputtering rear-end motor.

"I guess she didn't like my answers. Did the Magic beat the Rockets in the NBA Finals?"

"You think the whole world changes just because you spend a night in jail? Olajuwon and Drexler murdered 'em. How's the old anus?"

"Jail wasn't as bad as I thought it would be. Don't get me wrong. It was bad. It just wasn't horrible. You know what I'm saying?"

"Sure, sure." He was engrossed in driving six inches behind the vehicle in front of them. Motoring with Grady was always exciting.

Danny raised the back of his hand and sniffed. "Ugh. The worst part is the smell. Urine, vomit, who knows what else. It sinks into your pores. Smell this."

"Generous offer, but I'll pass."

"I hope it comes out," Danny said, taking another quick whiff before parking the hand outside the window like a pair of dirty sneakers.

"Nothing a little salt water won't cure. Jump in the ocean when you get home."

They shared a great faith in the healing powers of the ocean. He would like nothing better than to grab his board and hit the water, but he had work to do. Fink said they only had three or four days before his case was transferred to Palm Beach County and the jacket analyzed for Mangrum's blood.

He knew it was up to him to figure out any connection to Sugar Lake. Fink didn't believe there was one. Why was he convinced otherwise?

Grady leaned on the horn.

"Outta the way, you little bastard!" he shouted at a kid on a bicycle who cut across their lane. "Here's some good news. I got a new door for your condo. Metal. Cost more, but they'll have a harder time breaking it down next time."

Danny took the hint. "You know I didn't do it, right? Except the marijuana. That was mine."

"I didn't think so."

"I'll tell you the whole story as soon as I figure it out. It's all a big mess. Can you trust me until then?"

"Your word's good enough for me. Hell, I never believed you were guilty. How could a softy who rescues beached starfish saw off a man's hardware?"

Danny gripped the door as Grady swerved onto Sheridan Street, directly into the path of a city bus.

"So, Grady, what's that you're reading? It must be pretty important *since you're driving.*"

"This?" He tossed a booklet in Danny's lap. "It's yours. You'll need it."

It was the graduate brochure from the reunion. Harry the Hurricane, Seminole High's mascot, ablaze in gold and purple, smiled at him from the cover above a caption. *Proud of what we were and who we are. Let the memories of yesteryear light the way to tomorrow.*

"Why will I need this?"

"To call Sari, of course."

"Alright, Sherlock. You got me again. How do you know about Sari?"

"It's like a wise friend once said to me. I could have worked for Interpol instead of wasting my life owning a shitty little bar."

A raspy laugh ignited a coughing jag that left him breathless. "I need to quit smoking," he said, pulling a cigarette from behind his ear and fumbling for matches on the dashboard.

"Sorry about that comment. But how did you know? I never told you about her."

"Easy. I already guessed there was a woman missing from your life. From the picture in your bedroom and the way you dodge talking about high school, I figured that's where she must fit. Smart, eh?"

"Not bad. But how'd you pick out Sari?"

"That took much deeper deductive reasoning."

"Such as?"

"You left the pamphlet folded open to the right page."

"Ah."

"I looked down the entries and, bingo, there she was: Sari Hunter, poet. That's a match, I said. You have a poet's soul, Danny boy."

"And what, pray tell, is that?"

"Aimless, head in the clouds, like you. Of course, the other clue was you own enough poetry books to build a tomb for Robert Frost. And I was right. You bet your ass, old Grady was right," he cackled. "So you're going to call her, right? Says she's divorced."

Danny frowned. "I don't know. I was planning to before I got embroiled in a murder scandal, but I kind of doubt she's waiting by the phone right now."

"But you're innocent!"

"True." There was a time Sari would have believed him.

Grady grabbed his arm. "Look at me. It's time. Call that woman. … You're right. You smell disgusting."

\* \* \*

Danny showered with water hot enough to boil lobsters, scrubbing to erase every subatomic trace of incarceration. Ravenous, he tied the towel to his waist and drew a bead on the refrigerator, which was empty except for a stick of moldy pepperoni. He took a bite and sat at the counter flipping through the graduate brochure.

Benjamin "Fink" Finkel. Divorced, twice. Attorney in North Miami. *Most Memorable High School Moment:* Getting to third base with ▬▬▬▬▬. *Favorite Song in High School:* "Dancing Machine" — Jackson 5. *Message to Graduates:* If you've been in an accident, you have important legal rights that need protecting. Call today for a free consultation. No recovery, no fee.

Danny laughed and gnawed off another piece of pepperoni before turning the page. There she was:

Sari Rae Hunter. Divorced, no kids. Jewelry maker and struggling poet in Coconut Grove. *Most Memorable High School Moment:* A night at the beach near the old Sunset fishing pier. You figure it out! *Favorite Song in High School:* "Heart of Gold" — Neil Young. *Message to Graduates:* I hope everyone is healthy and happy.

The brochure had an index with phone numbers in the back. He picked up the phone. Put it down. Picked it up again. Don't overthink. Just dial. It clicked after three rings.

"Hi, this is Sari. Leave a message and I'll call you back."

Amazing. Sari's voice. He hadn't heard it in twenty years. She sounded happy. The answering machine beeped.

"Hi, Sari. This is Danny. Um, Danny Teakwell. I'm sorry I missed you at the reunion. … I ran into Margie and she said I should call you." Chicken. "Actually, I've wanted to talk to you for, well, forever. I hope you'll call back." He gave the number.

The murder. He couldn't ignore it.

"You've probably heard about Mangrum. It's all over the news. I don't know what to say … but I'm innocent." He paused. "A poet, Sari. That's fantastic." He hung up with a sweaty hand.

He wanted to reanalyze his message and berate himself for the million ways it could have been better, but there wasn't time.

He flipped more pages:

Albert Roderick Thumpet. Single. Certified Public Accountant in Bismarck, ND. *Most Memorable High School Moment:* Mr. Boswell's Biology class. *Favorite Song in High School:* "We've Only Just Begun" — The Carpenters. *Message to Graduates:* None.

He tore off a last chunk of pepperoni and headed out his new metal door.

# 14

**THE HOUSE** on Myrtle Street didn't look much different from the night he drove Enya home from Sugar Lake. Same wrought iron porch railing. Same jalousie windows which, surprisingly given the heat, were cranked open. Even the color, flamingo pink, was the same as twenty years ago.

Danny got out and willed himself up the walkway. He didn't have a plan. A grapefruit tree panted for a drink next to the small porch. He pushed the doorbell and heard it buzz through the window slats. No answer. He buzzed again. Nothing.

A corroded mailbox hung next to the door. He reached in and pinched an envelope. It was addressed to *Current Resident*.

The door swung open as he was putting it back. A pencil-thin senior stood at the threshold. He wore navy blue trousers and a white short-sleeve dress shirt. His sturdy rectangular glasses looked like Buddy Holly's.

"Hi there!" Danny said, handing him the envelope.

"You're not the mailman," the man said in a cultured voice.

"No, I'm not. Sorry about the mail. I wasn't stealing it. I was just looking for ... are you Mr. McKenzie?" Danny towered over the man's vein-latticed scalp.

"Who wants to know?"

No one special. Just the guy who raped your daughter. "My name is Danny Teakwell, sir."

"I'm not buying any magazines."

"I'm not selling magazines."

"I'm not buying anything."

"I'm not here to sell anything. I was wondering if you might have a few minutes to talk … about your daughter."

"I don't have a daughter," the man said.

Danny lowered his head and addressed the weathered doormat. "I know, sir. I'd like to talk to you about Enya."

"Who's that?"

"Enya," Danny said, surprised. "Your daughter."

"Are you hard of hearing? I said I didn't have a daughter."

"Aren't you Mr. McKenzie?"

"No, I'm Myron Tamms."

Danny showered him with flecks of saliva that Tamms discreetly pretended not to notice.

"Sir, I'm looking for someone who used to live here. The name was McKenzie."

"McKenzie. I remember. He was the gentleman I bought the house from." Tamms appraised Danny's potential for preying on the graying. "Come on in."

Danny followed him inside where a blast of heat almost knocked him over. The house was a furnace. An icebox fan whirred uselessly in a window frame, pushing hot air against hotter air. The shades were drawn.

"Would you like some iced tea?" Tamms asked without turning back.

"I don't want to put you to any trouble."

"No trouble at all. I was just making some." He headed into the kitchen. "Had a brother named Daniel. Mind if I call you Daniel?"

"That's fine."

Tamms disappeared, leaving him alone in the living room.

*Enya's* living room. Her image assaulted him as his eyes adjusted to the darkness. He saw her on the couch doing homework and watching television, a young girl with an entire life in front of her. Tamms rescued him, returning with a tarnished silver tray carrying two tall glasses of tea, lollypop lemon slices clipped neatly to the rims. He set the tray on an old coffee table of dark wood.

"Have a seat, Daniel. Make yourself comfortable."

Suspicion allayed, Tamms seemed pleased to have a visitor. Danny sat in a dusty wingback chair. The house smelled musty, like all old people's houses.

"Sorry it's so damned hot in here. The air conditioner blew last week and a new one costs more than my Social Security check. But you didn't come to hear about my problems. You want to know about McKenzie."

"Yes, sir. If you don't mind. How long ago did you buy the house from the McKenzies?"

Tamms hummed an intricate classical melody that rose and fell in perfect pitch while he pondered the question. Danny spotted a viola standing in the corner.

"It's been a long time. And it wasn't the McKenzies."

"No? But you said—"

"You asked when I bought the house from the McKenzies. But there was just one gentleman. I believe his name was Aaron. Aaron McKenzie."

Enya's father. So she didn't have other family. He didn't know even that much about her.

"I don't suppose you have any idea where Mr. McKenzie moved to."

"Now you're really testing an old man's memory. It was out of state. I remember because I had to forward his mail for a while. Somewhere out west, I believe."

"Do you think you might still have the address?"

Tamms eased forward, humming again as he picked up the iced tea with steady hands.

"I'm afraid not. It may have been in the house-closing papers, but I threw those out years ago."

He knew the trip was a longshot. "Thank you for your time and hospitality, sir. Sorry to barge in on you."

"Don't run off, Daniel. You haven't even touched your iced tea. Stay and enjoy it. It's hot as Hades out there."

A plea tinted the words. Danny picked up the tea and took in a portrait of an elegant couple in a regal gold frame hanging above the couch. "Is that you and your wife?"

"That's my Martha. She died several years ago. Lung cancer. Terrible thing, cancer." The grief was palpable.

"I'm sorry. You sure were a nice-looking couple."

"Thank you. Martha was always the belle of the ball." He changed the subject. "So this McKenzie you're interested in, odd fellow."

"In what way?"

"Religious zealot," he said distastefully.

He held up a hand.

"Don't get me wrong, I have nothing against religion. It's zealotry I despise. Atheist or bible thumper, doesn't matter which. Me, I've always been one of those fence-sitters, although I suspect I'll be finding a lot more religion soon enough. A person has a way of reevaluating those things as the road narrows." He laughed a high-pitched wheeze.

He and Tamms could get along. "What makes you say he was a religious zealot?"

"When Martha and I first came to see the house it was like walking into a church. McKenzie had more crucifixes hanging on the walls than most people have family photos. All sizes and colors. Then when he was showing us the back yard, he started talking about morals and damnation and asked if I was a God-fearing man—like the buyer was going to have to qualify religiously as well as financially."

"What did you tell him?"

"I told him I feared man more than God. He didn't like that answer, but I cut him off and asked what the utility bills ran. But the strangest part was the girl's room."

Danny straightened. "Girl's room?"

"Yes, McKenzie had a daughter. But you knew that. That's why you're here. What did you say her name was? Enya?"

"That's right."

"Pretty name. You were friends?"

"Um, sort of. But I'm confused. You said there was only Mr. McKenzie when you bought the house."

"He was the only one living here. The house has three bedrooms. One of them was McKenzie's and one was filled with junk. The third belonged to a young girl, but there was no young girl. She apparently had been gone for quite some time."

"Gone?"

"The room was like a museum, frozen in time. McKenzie had to find a key to unlock it. Everything in the room was old, but perfectly preserved. I remember stuffed animals and a row of ceramic horses caked in dust. Whatever happened to your friend?"

"They think she died." *They? Think?*

"I'm sorry about that. Makes me feel kind of guilty."

"Why would you feel guilty?" Danny asked, putting too much emphasis on *you*.

"For being so hard on McKenzie about his religion. Martha and I didn't take well to the crucifixes in the girl's room. A big one at the foot of the bed was four or five feet long, plastic Jesus hanging from it, crown of thorns, spiked wrists, blood, the whole nine yards. Martha was a woman with strong opinions.

She was appalled, couldn't imagine a young girl having to wake up to such a sight every morning."

Tamms pulled a folded handkerchief from his shirt pocket and mopped perspiration.

"Then there was the open bible on the pillow. Martha picked it up and started reading it out loud. McKenzie was somewhere else in the house. I had to tell her to keep her voice down. It was a dreadful passage about how all the sinners of the world— which includes all of us one way or another—are going to burn in a lake of fire and sulphur."

Danny still hadn't resolved his own feelings about religion. He and Sari spent a lot of time debating it growing up, her always trying to get him to see the light. He believed in a higher power, felt it out on the ocean, but wasn't sure what it actually did. The last time he prayed was for Enya. It didn't help.

"We raked McKenzie over the coals for that. Martha and I believed children should be spared religion until they're old enough to decide for themselves. But if his daughter's dead, I suppose that changes things."

Tamms wiped his forehead again. "This heat is something. Global warming. I read a persuasive article about it in *Scientific American*."

Danny fidgeted. Each minute that passed was one less minute to find answers before landing back in jail. He was about to bolt when Tamms said, "I'm really enjoying our visit, Daniel. We make friends in the strangest places."

Danny picked up the tea again. He could spare a few minutes for an old man.

"Do you play that viola?"

"I did for many years. As a much younger man I played with a small symphony in New York. That's where I met Martha. She was a music student from Arkansas who came to intern with the symphony in the summer of 1949."

"You played in a symphony? That's really cool, Mr. Tamms."

"Call me Myron. I haven't played in a long time. Damned arthritis. Do you like music, Daniel?"

"I do. I play some guitar. Very badly."

"Guitar! One of those electric models?"

Danny laughed his first real laugh since before the cops busted down his door. "Yeah, one of those."

He fielded several questions about electric guitars, but when Tamms offered to refill their glasses, Danny insisted he had to go.

"Are you sure you can't stay for dinner? I have a decent little pot roast cooking."

"I'd really like to, but I have some work to do. Maybe some other time."

"Okay. Some other time then. Sorry about the air conditioning," he said dispiritedly.

"I really would like to come back."

"Maybe you could bring your guitar over and play it for me."

"I'd be embarrassed to play for you. How about we play something together?"

"A duet? Oh my. Now you've challenged me. I will have to see what I can do."

Back in his car, Danny burned his hands on the scorched steering wheel. Poor Myron Tamms. No air conditioning. Just last week there was a news report about an old woman dying from the heat. He made a mental note to see about getting it fixed. He'd have to handle it delicately.

No wonder the lottery money always ran out. He never stopped trying to buy salvation with it. A good chunk of every check went to a rape crisis center.

Heading home down Hollywood Boulevard, his thoughts cycled to the revelations about Enya's room. Her father must have preserved it after her suicide, a shrine to a dead daughter.

Why was he still unconvinced there was a suicide? The evidence was stacking up. All he had to contradict it was a hallucination in a drunken haze minutes after being told that one of his coconspirators in her death had been murdered.

*Give it up!* But of course, he couldn't, so he made an illegal U-turn and headed west toward the public library. He wanted— *needed*—proof Enya was dead. Fink said he remembered seeing her obituary. The library would be a good place to look for it.

# 15

FINK HID behind a pair of bug-eyed sunglasses, stirring a piña colada the size of a flower vase with a paper parasol glued to an oversized toothpick. He watched the boats move up and down the intracoastal, fantasizing about taking charge of his life.

Hauptmann demanded the meeting when Fink called to say he had the five hundred dollars. He gave instructions to meet on the restaurant deck at exactly two. It was almost three according to his new watch, $2.99 at Walmart. So where was Hauptmann?

"Benjamin! How good of you to make it." The man walked up from his blind side and took the opposite seat. "Lovely out here, isn't it?"

"Let's cut the civility crap, Hauptmann."

"Ooh. Feisty today. Got that testosterone pumping from your big courtroom victory, I suppose. That was quite a performance."

"You were there?"

"Of course not, but I was around. I saw Teakwell on television with that Traynor woman afterwards. He seemed to be in an awfully good mood, certainly much too good for all the trouble he's in." He laughed wickedly. "More trouble than he knows. Thanks to you."

Fink speared a chunk of pineapple with the toothpick, imagining it was Hauptmann's eyeball. He popped the pineapple in his mouth and pulled an envelope from his back pocket.

"Here's your money. Gotta go. I've got work to do." He started to rise.

"Sit, Benjamin. Sit, boy." His taunting eyes dared Fink to disobey.

Fink glared, but sat. That was the bottom line. When it came down to it, he had no choice. Hauptmann knew it and knew *he* knew it. "What do you want? You have your money."

"I've been thinking we need to renegotiate our contract."

He knew this was going to happen. "And what would the new terms be?"

"One hundred thousand dollars. A final payment and we're done."

"A hundred thousand!" Fink snorted. "You're nuts."

The couple at the next table turned to stare. He hunched forward and whispered stridently, "There's no way I have that kind of money. You know that. You might as well just do what you want. Go ahead and kill me right here."

"Don't be so melodramatic. Teakwell has the money. Take it from him. He signed the power of attorney."

"How did you know about that?"

"I have friends in commerce who, like you, owe me favors. One of them works at Teakwell's bank."

"I can't steal his money."

"You can and will, unless you value Teakwell's money more than your own skin. Teakwell is going down. Money will be the least of his concerns. If he raises questions, just engage in some creative billing. You lawyers are experts at that."

Fink slapped a twenty on the table. "I'm outta here."

"Let me know when you get the money."

"Yeah, yeah."

# 16

**"IT'S EASY,"** said Laurie Winfield, assistant reference librarian, a tall, slender woman with dull auburn hair and stooped shoulders.

She pulled a chair up to the microfiche reader and motioned for Danny to sit in it. She wore granny glasses, no makeup and a faded print dress that fell below her knees.

"Have you ever used one of these?"

"A couple of times in high school."

"You insert the film here and move it around with this handle." She tapped two plastic rings beneath a cathode ray tube monitor. "These adjust your view. One for zoom, one for focus. If you need a copy of something, push this print button. Copies are ten cents a page. You pay at the front desk. We operate under the honor system. Got it?"

"I'll give it a shot."

"Okay, now what are you interested in looking at?"

"Some old editions of the *Sun-Sentinel*."

"How old? We have them going back to 1963."

"June, 1975, I don't know the exact day." School usually ended in May which meant the graduation party where he heard about Enya's suicide must have happened in early June.

But his memory could be wrong.

"And May," he added. "May and June."

"May and June '75. Follow me." Danny did, taking long strides to keep up with her clipped pace as she navigated between rows of tall file cabinets. She found the one she wanted and ran her finger down a column of thin drawers, stopping at the second from the bottom.

"Here we go," she said. "*Fort Lauderdale News and Sun-Sentinel*. 1973 to 1976. They changed the name to just *Sun-Sentinel* in 1982."

She removed the drawer and flipped through postcard-sized envelopes of photographic film. Frowning, she pressed an unpolished fingernail against her lips. She flipped forward then backward, paused, went forward and back again, and stopped again.

"May and June of 1975 are missing."

"Missing? Where could they be?"

"I don't know. They're supposed to be in this drawer. Were you in here earlier?" she said accusingly.

"No!" Danny said, overreacting to another baseless charge.

"Well, microfiche doesn't just disappear."

"Maybe they got misfiled. Everyone makes mistakes," he said charitably.

"Not me. I keep my microfiche in order. It has to be here somewhere."

She scanned the room.

"And what is this?" she said, strutting to a microfiche reader on the far wall. "Well, well. What do you know? *Fort Lauderdale News and Sun-Sentinel*, May and June 1975. Are you sure you weren't in here earlier?"

"Positive. How often do people use this stuff?"

"Not as often as they should. Hardly ever, in fact. Everything's getting computerized. Soon I won't have a job. Anyway, here's the film. Call me if you need help."

He sat at the microfiche reader. It took him a couple of tries to get the film right-side up, but then it was easy.

Uncharacteristically, he decided to approach things in an organized fashion. He'd start with May 15 and go day by day through June 15. He felt certain the graduation party was sandwiched in between.

The possibility that someone else was interested in the same pieces of microfiche pecked at him as he worked. Were they looking for the same thing?

He located the obituaries at the back of the Broward section, but not all of the slides were in order, which slowed the work. It took an hour to make it to June 10.

He stopped to rub his eyes. Five more days to go. Unless he had missed it, the odds were shrinking quickly that Enya's obituary existed. He wanted so desperately to believe she was alive and that he saw her standing on the dock of the Island Hotel marina in June of *this* year. He forged ahead.

On June 11, 1975, Greece adopted a new constitution and the first oil was pumped from the North Sea. There were twelve obituaries. Most of the dead were elderly, but there was also a child and a twenty-year-old man.

Laurie Winfield stepped in to announce the library was closing in ten minutes. Physically and emotionally exhausted from the past two days, he was tempted to call it quits, but knew that would leave him wondering. He'd continue through June 15. So organized. Sari wouldn't believe it.

He raced through the twelfth and thirteenth. Nothing. Winfield returned.

"It's closing time."

"I'm almost done."

She stood behind him, tapping a shoe. He hit the gas on June 14 and missed the obituaries, ending up in the classifieds. As he backtracked, Winfield complained about the unfairness of not getting paid overtime even though she deserved it.

Emily Johns, Ida Hornbrook, Sol Goldberg … It had been a bad day for the living. More than twenty obituaries. Clark Collinsworth, Nora Valdez …

Winfield reached to switch off the machine. He put his hand on the button to block her. Harry Fontaine, Shirley Halbersham …

"Oh no," he murmured.

"What? What? Did you find something? What is it?"

There it was, painfully short. He fumbled for the zoom knob and screwed the lens closer:

> Enya Kay McKenzie, 16, of Hollywood, died June 10. She is survived by her father, Aaron McKenzie, sister, Sabrina, and brother, Adam. Graveyard services will be held tomorrow, 4 p.m., Westbrook Cemetery. Arrangements by Slagger-Jewell Funeral Home.

"Was she a relative?"

Winfield's head was practically resting on his shoulder. He ignored her and stabbed the print button.

She backed away. "The library is *closed*."

The copy from the printer fed straight into Danny's hands. He switched off the machine and started to gather the film sheets, but Winfield held up a hand.

"I'll take those," she said curtly.

Danny handed her the microfiche and walked away.

"Hold it! That will be ten cents."

# 17

**DRAINED AND DROOPING**, he stood in the library parking lot watching the remnants of the long day melt like orange sherbet in the western sky. The wish that Enya was still alive had sustained him. Now she was unequivocally dead. It was time to give up.

But as soon as he resolved to surrender, her image outside the marina bar pushed the compass in the opposite direction.

He bargained with his compulsion, lost again, and jumped into the VW, steering it west, chasing the disappearing sun.

If his bearings were right, the Westbrook Cemetery was a few miles west off of State Road 822. He reread the obituary at a stoplight. June 10. Same date as the reunion. Same date Mangrum was murdered. The obituary said Enya had a brother and sister, but Myron Tamms was clear about there being only the one girl's bedroom. He'd call him in the morning.

Simple Minds sang *Don't You Forget About Me* on the radio. Had Sari called him back? Would she?

Thirty minutes and three wrong turns later, he pulled up in front of a wide set of gates with cursive iron letters forming *Westbrook Cemetery* in an arc across the top. The gates connected the ends of a high, white cinder block wall that stretched beyond his view in both directions. A heavy chain and padlock secured the gates. A sign said the cemetery closed at sundown.

The sky grew darker by the minute. He sat idling, considering what to do. Go home and get some sleep was the rational answer, but instead he accelerated and swung right down a deserted side street until he came to a bulbous ficus tree. He wedged the Beetle between the tree and cemetery wall and turned off the motor.

Twilight had surrendered to night. He remembered seeing the flashlight in his trunk when he discovered the cocaine bricks, a seemingly distant event that happened only yesterday. Testing it, he was surprised it worked. He stuck the flashlight in the waist band of his shorts, climbed on the roof of his car and pulled himself up onto a branch, which he used to scoot over the wall into the cemetery.

Dropping onto soft-packed sandy soil, he heard Judge Kovacich firmly instructing him that any violation of the law would result in his bail being yanked.

The shadows of grave markers yawned in the moonlight like open graves. Assembled in neat rows, they gave the impression of a giant haunted chess board. The cemetery had been carved out of a tropical hammock, but several islands of trees were left undisturbed, tangled velvet mushrooms dotting the landscape. The air was breathless, insect chatter the only sound.

As his pupils dilated, the most conspicuous aspect of the cemetery became apparent: it was enormous. He would need luck finding Enya's grave.

He moved forward along a manicured footpath that organized the graves into sections like auditorium seating. At the first row of graves, he switched on the flashlight. The monuments were old, pock-marked and blackened with mold.

The light traced an elaborate marble kiosk guarded by an

iron fence with spear points. *Greta Livulet, Mother, Sister, Friend*. She died seventy years ago. He checked several more graves. He was in the old, original part of the cemetery.

The grave would be the final punctuation to Enya's story, he swore as he walked, the crucial piece of evidence his troubled mind needed to put the ghosts to rest once and for all.

He migrated through generations in minutes, the ornate monuments giving way to bland slabs of marble and granite. A burst from the flashlight confirmed the passage through time. Norman Detweiler died in 1966, the same year a stroke took Danny's grandmother.

He was in the open, next to a paved road, considering whether to go right or left, when a sound in the distance brought him to a halt. It occurred to him he was trepassing in the center of an active, ongoing business. There were probably security guards or caretakers living on the grounds.

Treading more cautiously and relying on the moon for light, he moved up and down corridors between graves, frustrated by their erratic chronological organization.

He was trying to figure out what the hell Bernadette Monroe, who died in 1941, was doing over here, when he shined the light on the plain rectangular granite marker next to hers and froze: *Born: 1959, Died 1975*. A sixteen-year-old who died the same year as Enya.

But it was a name he didn't recognize. Another young victim of something or someone.

An hour of fruitless searching later, he concluded the effort was hopeless. Better to come back in the morning and get a map, but questions might be asked. He couldn't afford letting anyone know that celebrated murder suspect Danny Teakwell had an interest in anything dead. He continued walking.

Another sound. This one nearby. He fell to the ground. Something crawled across his bare leg. He shut it out. Listen to the sound. *Clunk, scrape, thump.*

It came from behind a copse of trees not twenty yards away. Rythmic now. *Clunk, scrape, thump. Clunk, scrape, thump.*

He loped to the edge of the trees and wormed his way into the tangled growth. The farther into the hammock he went, the dryer the undergrowth became until it crunched loudly each time he put a foot down. Should have gone around the trees, but he was stuck now. The only quiet way out was up. He shimmied up the knotty trunk of a strangler fig.

Arms muscled by a lifetime of paddling surfboards allowed him to move quickly through the tangle of incestuously woven branches. He made a midair transition to a towering cypress that reached all the way to the other side. Just as he got there, the sound stopped.

He edged out on a limb until he overlooked a moonlit clearing. Halfway down a row of grave markers, he made out the source of the noise: a freshly dug grave.

Grave digging at night? Maybe day visitors didn't want to be reminded their loved ones were decaying under several feet of wormy soil. He watched the still scene until satisfied the workers weren't coming back, swung down and dropped, farther than he realized.

The impact rattled his teeth and knocked the flashlight loose. It clattered loudly against a tree root. So much for stealth.

He approached the pit. Dust to dust. Tomorrow's light would see another human vessel returned to Mother Earth.

Next to the grave a gleaming shovel stuck like a flagpole in a mound of freshly turned dirt. It seemed out of place. Surely modern grave diggers used machinery, but the shovel was the only tool in sight.

The grave marker was already in place. That didn't seem right either. When his dad died, the monument wasn't ready until weeks after the burial.

He pointed the flashlight and slipped the switch, but nothing happened. Jockeying the switch back and forth didn't help. Neither did tightening the lens cap. Electrical engineering skills exhausted, he pounded the flashlight against his thigh and it sprang to life.

He aimed the beam at the tombstone, gasped and fell to his knees, sinking into the piles of dirt.

*Enya Kay McKenzie*
*Born April 13, 1959, Died June 10, 1975*
*In God's Hands*

The flashlight slipped from his hands and tumbled into the pit where it landed with a clatter.

Enya's grave. *Open!* What the hell?

Danny kneeled and peered into the excavation. The flashlight, suddenly indestructible, still shined. But something blocked the light. Something red.

He moved closer for a better view. The beam painted a tight circle of red, but he still couldn't make it out. Edging nearer started a landslide from the piles of dirt surrounding the grave. When he backed up, his hand raked against something hard. He pulled a crowbar from the dirt.

Leaning in more carefully he waited as the *f*-stops of his pupils dialed in on the illumination. An outline took shape. Lines, corners, shiny red fabric.

He was staring into an open casket. It was metallic and lined with red satin. Except for the flashlight, it was *empty*.

Commotion in the distance. Men's voices, excited and urgent. Shafts of light criss-crossed the edges of the thicket he had just passed through.

"Tarney, go call the cops," shouted a high-pitched voice.

A second, deeper voice concurred, "Go, Tarney, run!"

They were headed his way. He'd have to process things later.

If they caught him, he'd be right back in jail. The flashlight. It had his fingerprints on it. Evidence left behind.

He got up to run, pivoting directly into the path of a meaty forearm that crashed into his skull and knocked him on his back. A hulking silhouette blocked the moonlight.

"Imagine meeting you out here," the figure said. "It must be fate."

Danny scrambled to his knees and reached for the crowbar. He never had a chance. The shovel was already in motion. It hit him square on the ribs, which snapped like stalks of celery.

He tumbled sideways, into Enya's grave. *Into hell.*

"See you soon!" the attacker said, then fled.

Danny tried to sit, but collapsed from the agonizing pain. He thought he might pass out. The men with the flashlights were almost upon him.

"Over there. I see something." The deep voice.

He could hear their footsteps now. The flashlight beams passed over the grave. Trapped.

"Holy Mother of Christ!" shrieked the high-pitched voice.

A desperate idea took shape. Begging forgiveness, he rolled into the coffin and bit his shirt as he stretched to pull the lid down. Light streaked the dirt wall as it closed the last inch.

"Lord have mercy. The grave's been dug up." The alto voice.

"We got here just in time."

"In time for what?"

"In time to see he didn't steal the goddamned casket. You think he was looking for buried treasure?"

"Grave robbers? Wow."

Danny pointed the flashlight at the red satin ceiling four inches above his eyes. If it failed him now he might go mad.

"Get in there and check it out, Ted," said the deep voice.

"No way."

"What, you afraid the stiff's gonna jump up and grab you? Boo!" he laughed.

Danny held his breath.

"Let's see you go down there," Ted said.

Pause.

"Ah hell, let the cops do it. They don't pay us enough to crawl around in the muck. Tarney should have reached 'em by now. Come on, let's go look for the perv. He's gotta be around here somewhere. You cover the west side, I'll take the east."

"The hell you will," Ted whined. "The west is swamp. The east is where the cops are coming. You take the swamp. I'm going east."

"Fine, fine. You can be a real pussy, you know that, Ted?"

Danny got ready to move.

"Oh, Ted?"

"Yeah?"

"Better get out your gun. If the crazy doesn't get you, the zombies will."

"Screw you."

Danny counted to ten and pushed the casket lid up. He gulped for fresh air, then stopped just as quickly. Each breath felt like a knife in his side. He eased himself to his feet and shined the flashlight the length of Enya's casket.

The smooth shiny satin glowed blood-red.

His aching heart temporarily obscured the nauseating pain in his side. More tumult in the distance. The police.

He closed the casket and stepped gingerly on top of it. Including the loose piles of dirt, he had six feet to scale, with nothing to grab or climb on.

Something shiny in the dirt. The shovel. The grave robber left it behind. Danny stretched for it and fell back onto the casket under buckets of collapsing dirt. He chomped his shirt and tried again. Again the pain caused him to collapse, but this time he had the shovel in his hand.

Jamming the blade in a corner of the grave, he used the handle as a step and boosted himself up and out, landing face-first in the soft dirt. Coughing and spitting, he got up and headed in the direction he thought would take him back to his car.

He moved as quickly as his rattling ribcage allowed, staying in the shadows. If they found his car, it was over.

The farther he got from Enya's grave, the more his thinking cleared. Some abstraction nagged at the fringe of his consciousness. Some relevant fact.

More light beams ahead. He ducked behind a tall crucifix. *Darby Brandenburg, 1890-1962.* He was back to the old quadrant. The wall couldn't be very far, but two cops stood in the way. They were walking straight for him.

A radio squawked.

"Turn that thing down. You wanna wake the dead?"

"Grave robbing. What's the world coming to? It's not enough to prey on the living anymore. Now they go after corpses."

The marble cross was too narrow to hide behind. His ass stuck out a mile. They'd see him for sure. He sized up the crucifix.

The radio crackled to life: "You guys find anything on your side?"

"Not yet. He's probably gone."

They were twenty feet away. Making another plea for forgiveness, he slithered up the crucifix, stretching his arms out as his shadow disappeared. He looked skyward and made the vow of all desperate people. If he got out of this jam, he'd go to church.

The cops came in view. Their belts jangled with enough gear to fight a war.

"Man, these tombstones are sumpin', aren't they?"

"Whaddaya mean sumpin'?"

"Fancy, you know. Expensive. That sonofabitch over there probably cost more than a three-two in Opa Locka. Rich people really know how to live when they die."

Danny pressed against the cool stone. If they looked back, he was busted. But they marched straight ahead, toward Enya's grave.

When the darkness consumed them, Danny took off for the wall. He didn't stop until he spotted the ficus tree that had carried him into this nightmare. He reached the wall and fell gasping against the bricks, bent over holding his shorts to ease the miserable pain. Muddy sweat ran in his eyes.

The ficus was on the other side of the wall. It was a one-way ticket in. He spotted a shadowy gumbo-limbo tree on his side of the wall, half a football field away.

As he made his way to it, he replayed the grave scene frame by frame. Someone crazy dug up Enya's grave and blindsided him with a forearm.

Thumpet? It had to be. The man was big, like the guy at the reunion party, the events too bizarre to be coincidental. Mangrum's murder, the trumped up charges, and now digging up a young girl's grave and stealing the body … or remains. What would be left after twenty years?

*That was it.* He rewound the tape. There he was on his back in the closed coffin, staring at the red fabric. No stench of death or decay, only a mild musty scent. Then standing in the casket with the flashlight, staring at *the shiny satin that glowed blood red.*

Unblemished. No stains. No imprint.

He reached the tree and climbed it, the rush of discovery distracting from the pain. He humped a limb across the wall and scanned the road. Everything was quiet. His car was still hidden in the shadow of the ficus. Grabbing the limb, he swung down like he did in the graveyard, except this time the jolt to his ribs made him let go too soon and he landed with a jarring crash. He lay still catching his breath.

*Unblemished.*
As if no dead person had ever laid in it.

# 18

**DANNY LIMPED** into Fink's office the next morning at nine. He had woken up on the couch with a head full of graveyard dirt cuddling an empty bottle of Jack Daniels.

He found his lawyer glued to a computer monitor, a blue glow illuminating his face. The image touched a frazzled nerve, transporting him back to the night at the reunion and another face lit in blue.

"Hey, hey," Fink said without looking up. "Check out my new computer. Like it?"

"Very nice."

"Now that I'm in the big leagues, I figured I should start acting like it. Legal research is going from books to bytes. I subscribed to a computer-research service. I have every court decision ever issued right at my fingertips. Every word Lord Fartus wrote in the House of Lords five hundred years ago, right here. Is that not incredible?"

"Pretty neat."

"Now I even have the money to pay for it, thanks to you."

"Glad I could help."

"There," Fink said, stamping a few more keys. "I'm logged on.

We're almost ready." He glanced up for the first time. "Whoa, what happened to you? You look like hell."

"I'll explain in a minute. What are we ready for?"

"To watch this baby work its magic. Pull up that chair and I'll show you."

Danny nudged the heavy client chair around the desk and eased into it.

"Remember at the courthouse, I said I called Thumpet's number in Bismarck and the phone just rang? Same thing last night. So I start thinking, maybe my new friend here can tell us something about Thumpet. This database has a ton of news libraries in addition to court documents. Most people make it into the newspaper sometime in their lives, right? Hell, you're in there practically every day. I thought, why not Thumpet?"

He turned to the computer keyboard. "Talk to me, sweetheart. Tell us all about …"

Danny watched him type *Albert Thumpet* and press a key. The computer hummed before flashing, *Your search has found 2 ARTICLES.*

"Ready?"

"And waiting."

Fink hit the key again and the blank screen filled with text. "It's an article from the Bismarck paper, the day after the reunion. Read it."

## *Accountant Found Fatally Stabbed In Apartment*

A cleaning woman discovered the body of Bismarck accountant Albert Thumpet, 38, in his apartment Friday where he had been fatally stabbed. Police said the apartment showed signs of being ransacked and believe Thumpet arrived home during a burglary.

"It looks like a case of pure bad luck," Homicide

Detective Edward Dampier said. "If he had come home fifteen minutes later, the burglar probably would have been gone and he'd still be alive."

Thumpet was a respected certified public accountant. In 1993 he was named Accountant of the Year.

Louise Rousette, the apartment manager, described Thumpet as an excellent tenant.

"He was a nice guy. Kind of shy. Never had any problem with him, except that once in a while he played his stereo too loud. He loved the Carpenters."

Thumpet was single and has no known family in the Bismarck area. No murder weapon has been found and the police have no suspects.

Danny let out a whistle.

"Exactly," Fink said.

"So Thumpet isn't Thumpet. Your theory was right. But then who?"

"Beats me. The article answers one question, but raises a hundred others. Now we know you didn't do anything to piss off Thumpet back in high school. We just have to figure out who killed him so they could go around murdering and framing people in his name."

"You're convinced that's what happened?"

"Unless you believe in incredible coincidences. What better way to infiltrate the reunion and the lives of the people around it than to become part of them? But to accomplish that, the killer had to get rid of Thumpet."

"I'd believe anything at this point. What's the other article?"

"Huh?"

"Your magic computer said there are two stories. What's the other one?"

"Just a blurb in the business section about Thumpet being recognized as Accountant of the Year. Now tell me what happened to you? You look like you're gonna lose your lunch every time you take a breath."

"I had an interesting night, but before I get into it, do you have any kind of pain reliever around here?"

"Are you kidding? What do you need?" Fink yanked open a desk drawer filled with plastic cylinders wrapped in white labels. "Name your poison. Got some oxycodone, hydrocodone …"

"How about a couple of aspirin?"

"Mm, don't see anything like that."

"What are you doing with so many drugs?"

"I've been sickly since I was a kid," he sniffed. "You remember that. Now I'm an adult and it's a lot worse. Bad women, bad debts and this lousy profession! People think it's easy being a lawyer, think we sit around all day drinking martinis and having sex with our clients while the bucks roll in. It's nothing like that. It's stress, stress and more stress."

He continued sorting vials.

"So what the hell, I need a little help every now and—ahh, here we go. Acetaminophen and codeine. Safe and effective. Got two hundred of 'em in Mexico, right over the counter at the *farmacia*."

Danny chugged down the pills with the coffee he picked up on the way over.

"Okay," Fink said, "Let's hear about your latest disaster."

Danny explained the previous day's cast and storylines chronologically: Laurie Winfield, Myron Tamms and finally the unfriendly grave robber with the shovel.

He handed over Enya's damp, dirt-stained obituary.

"Holy crap, Danny. When you get in a jam, you don't screw around. You were really in her grave? You're not shitting me?"

"It really happened."

"Wow. Wow, wow, wow."

"I know," Danny said. "So where do we go from here?"

"Wow, wow, wow, wow, wow."

"Enough! I get it. What should we do now?"

"Well, we've been sitting around moaning about how much we don't know. Let's take a different approach and start with what we do know. We'll make a list."

He picked up a pen and wrote *What We Know* on a legal pad. "Alright. What do we know?"

"Nothing," Danny said.

"Quit being such a pessimist. We know lots of things." He started writing. "First, we know this guy posing as Thumpet killed Mangrum. We also know the same person is trying to frame you for the murder. See? We're getting somewhere. Third, I'm beginning to believe you that this has something to do with Enya McKenzie."

"Good."

"Fourth, we know that Enya McKenzie committed suicide twenty years ago."

"We don't know that for sure."

"Danny, I'm holding her obituary and you just said you were in her coffin. I know you don't want to accept it, but don't you think the evidence is making it a little weird to stay in denial?"

"But I told you, I don't think there was ever a dead body in that coffin. It was—"

"Yeah, I know. Unblemished. Fine, I'll rephrase for your benefit. Fourth, we *strongly believe* Enya committed suicide. You like that better? Fifth, someone, probably the Thumpet impersonator, robbed her grave last night."

"But there may not have been anything in it to rob."

"Did you happen to notice whether he was carrying anything when he left, like maybe a bag of bones?"

"It was dark and I was busy falling into the grave."

"Alright. We know someone, most likely the Thumpet

impersonator, *visited* her grave last night. You know what that gives us?"

"Still nothing," Danny said bleakly.

"Wrong! Added up, it gives us the answer."

"Which is?"

Fink scratched furiously on the legal pad, tore off the page and threw it at Danny.

"*R-E-V-E-N-G-E,*" Danny read.

"That's it. Here's the theory. You guys had sex with Enya. She killed herself and now someone's trying to get even. So he kills Mangrum and tries to make it look like you did it."

"Why not kill me too?"

"It's not too late. Maybe he wants you to suffer first."

"Why wait twenty years?"

"He's a procrastinator?"

Danny groaned.

"I don't have all the answers. Probably something to do with the reunion. You could be right about Stoddelmeyer too. He might be in danger."

"Is your investigator looking for him? I don't want anything to happen to Troy."

"He's on the case. Nothing motivates Skaggs like a paying customer and I told him I already got the money from you. The good news is, if we don't know where Stoddelmeyer is, the killer probably doesn't either. Skaggs is shady, but good. He'll find him."

"Why do you think the guy dug up the grave?"

"He's obviously a psycho. Maybe he's in love with Enya and obsessed with having her. I doubt you could do that though, after twenty years."

"Do what?"

"Have sex with a corpse. I wonder if there'd still be a vagina? It'd be nasty, wouldn't it?"

"Shut the fuck up."

"You asked!"

"Let's move on. Notice anything interesting about the obituary?"

"Yeah, it says she had a brother and sister. Did you know that?"

"No. In fact I left her house yesterday with the definite impression she was an only child. Myron Tamms may know. Let me have your phone."

Fink pushed it across the desk. A pink *While You Were Out* message was taped to the top.

"And I thought you said you never handled big cases?" Danny said, peeling off the message.

"What are you talking about?"

"Here's a phone message from Bruno Hauptmann. Didn't he kidnap the Lindberg baby?"

"Hauptmann?"

"It says *Call when you get the money.*"

Fink's freckles turned scarlet. "Let me see that. Someone's idea of a joke. You run into all kinds of loonies in this business." Fink tucked the message in his pocket.

"You got a phone book? Look up Tamms," Danny said, spelling it. "Myron Tamms in Hollywood."

Fink lifted a phone book out of a drawer and thumbed pages. "Myrtle Street?"

"That's him. What's the number?"

Danny punched it in. Tamms answered after four rings.

"Mr. Tamms, hello. This is Danny Teakwell. I stopped by your house yesterday afternoon asking about the McKenzie family."

"Yes, Daniel," Tamms said. "I recall our visit fondly. How are you?"

"I'm fine, sir. I—"

"Have you killed anyone since we last met?"

Danny closed his eyes.

"I'm getting old and my memory fails me now and again, but I'm almost certain you neglected to mention that you're an accused murderer."

Danny covered the mouthpiece. "Was my picture in the paper again this morning?" he whispered.

Fink nodded. "Above the fold. They have a nickname for you. *Lottery Lunatic.*"

"Sonofabitch," Danny muttered. "No, not you, Mr. Tamms. I don't know what to say. I'm sure it sounds lame, but I'm innocent. I'm working hard trying to clear myself. That's why I came over yesterday. But I apologize for bothering you." Danny started to hang up.

"Hold on, Daniel. You haven't told me why you're calling."

"You'll still talk to me?"

"I'll listen. You didn't strike me as the cold-blooded type. I'm half deaf and blind, but my internal senses still function quite well. How may I be of assistance?"

"Well, Mr. Tamms—"

"Please call me Myron."

"Okay. When I was there yesterday, you told me about the young girl's bedroom and said when you bought the house only Mr. McKenzie lived there. Yesterday at the library I found an obituary for Enya McKenzie, the girl, and—"

"Did you kill her too?"

"I didn't kill anyone, Mr. Tamms."

"Myron."

"I didn't kill anyone, Myron. Enya died a long time ago."

"She has something to do with your case?"

"She might. I don't know for sure."

"Okay, sorry to interrupt. Go ahead."

"The obituary said Enya had a brother and a sister. Did you know Mr. McKenzie had more than one child?"

Tamms hummed a piece Danny recognized as Handel's *Water Music.*

"No," he finally said. "There was just the one girl's bedroom. No sign of other children. Does that mean something?"

"I don't know. I still don't know much of anything to tell you the truth. Thanks for your help." He started to hang up but remembered the broken air conditioner. "There's one more thing I wanted to talk to you about. How's your air conditioner?"

"Deader than opera."

"I have some good news about that. My cousin owns an air conditioning business. He's new in the business, so he's running a special, trying to drum up customers. I talked to him this morning and he said he could replace your unit for … three hundred dollars."

"Three hundred! The estimate I got was for fifteen hundred."

"Well, like I said, my cousin's running a special."

"That's quite a deal. Has your cousin done any hard time?"

"No, sir."

"Sounds too good to be true. But I suppose a special is a special. I could have that much by the end of the month."

When the Social Security check arrives. "I was thinking I could lend you the money so you could get it fixed now."

"That's very kind of you, Daniel, but I don't take charity."

"It wouldn't be charity. You'd have to pay me back. When you can."

A pause. "Well, only with the understanding that it's a valid and enforceable loan with interest at the market rate."

"Absolutely. I'll call my cousin and he'll take care of it. Thanks again for the help, Mr.—Myron."

"Thank you, Daniel. Stay out of trouble and don't forget to come back and visit. Bring that guitar of yours. I actually managed to tune up the old viola today. I'm going to take you up on your duet proposal."

"Okay," Danny laughed. "Pick an easy song." He hung up.

"Cousin in the air conditioning business?"

"Just trying to help a nice old man. Gimme the yellow pages."

Danny found the number for Chambers & Son Air Conditioning. The son was Roy Chambers, who turned up frequently at the Tradewinds to swap fish stories. Danny got Roy on the line and explained the situation. Chambers expressed sympathy for the old man and said he had a crew available that could head out there after lunch.

"Just be sure you send the bill to me. Don't let the old man see it. And remember, you're my cousin." He hung up and turned to Fink. "Tamms doesn't know anything about any siblings."

"I gathered." Fink was smirking.

"What's so funny?"

"Danny the do-gooder."

"Just trying to save my tarnished soul."

"Bullshit. You've been a soft touch as long as I've known you."

"You know, Fink, this is a really nice office you have here."

"Thanks. I decorated it myself. Ha, not really. The office comes with everything. Furniture, fax machine, even a receptionist with big breasts. All I had to buy was the computer."

"What about that handgun?" Danny pointed to a large blue-steel pistol in the open drawer from where Fink pulled the phone books. "Did that come with the office?"

"Oh, that? It's for protection."

"Really. How long have you had it?"

"Got it last night, actually."

"Last night? What motivated that purchase?"

"Well, uh, you know, with Mangrum getting his cock sawed off and you being framed for murder and me being your lawyer and all, I figured why take chances? It's a dangerous world. I bought it from Skaggs. He owns an arsenal. Could run his own militia. Probably does."

"Fink, do you know anything about guns?" Danny hated them.

"Of course," he said defensively. He picked up the pistol and tossed it hand to hand. "This baby is a nine-millimeter semiautomatic that holds thirteen rounds in the magazine and one more in the chamber. Single-action, meaning you gotta pull back the hammer for it to fire. Skaggs says it's a classic."

He stretched his arm out and aimed down the sight. *"Pick-ew."*

"Put it down. You're making me nervous."

"Since when have you become such a worrywart?" He bent back the hammer. "It's okay. It can only fire if there's a round in the chamber. See?" He pulled the trigger.

Danny saw the muzzle flash before he heard the sound, a loud pop that erased the air from the room. Purple spots filled his eyes.

Across the desk, Fink's pale lips formed an *O* big enough to toss a beanbag through. They both stared at the framed picture of Lady Justice on the wall, bullet hole in her forehead.

"You better make sure the receptionist isn't slumped over her desk," Danny said.

Fink bounced up and out the door.

When he returned, he went straight to his desk-drawer pharmacy and rifled through jars of pills until he found one that made his eyes light up, but the beam faded when he couldn't get the top off.

"Childproof caps! Kids! I hate 'em. Don't they ever think about people having panic attacks when they design these things?" He gnawed on the lid until the vial cracked.

"Can you help me?" he whimpered, holding out the jar.

Danny hesitated, but opened it and handed it back. Fink shook out three orange tablets.

"What are those?"

"Xanax," he said, popping them in his mouth. "Alprazolam, technically. Generic version. My doctor recommends them. He's an excellent physician."

"Are you supposed to chew them?"

"Wurt fatter dis way," he said, orange powder caking his teeth. He swallowed, licked his lips and leaned his chair back. "Everybody's okay. Lucky shot really. Hit the copy machine. I've wanted to shoot that damn thing a hundred times."

Fifteen minutes later Fink was serenely explaining his planned legal attack on the search of Danny's condo. He didn't understand all the mumbo jumbo, but it centered on whether the police had probable cause to get a search warrant based on the anonymous tip.

"If we can get the search warrant thrown out, the prosecutor won't be able to use any evidence they found, including, if it turns up, Mangrum's blood on your jacket."

"I don't want to win on a legal technicality. Everyone will think I'm guilty."

"You win these things any way you can—if you're lucky."

Danny recognized his lawyer had made an excellent point.

The phone rang. "Law offices of Benjamin Finkel. Yes, there was a minor firearms incident up here, but everything's fine." He mouthed *Building Security*.

"Yeah, I'll be more careful, but if you'd provide better security I wouldn't need a gun in the first place." He rammed the receiver down.

Fink's emotional outbreaks weren't doing his own nerves any good.

"So what's next for you?" Fink asked.

"I still have to confirm Enya's death."

Fink slapped the desk. "Here we go again."

"Where do they keep death certificates?" Danny said.

"Office of Vital Statistics."

Danny found the number in the blue pages. It rang six times before a nasal male voice answered.

"Hi, I'm calling about a death certificate. How does a person go about getting one?"

"You generally have to die first. Sorry, office humor. Whose certificate are you seeking?"

"A person named Enya McKenzie. She died in 1975, I think. I'm trying to find out the exact date and cause of death."

"Are you a relative or legal representative?"

"No."

"Then you can't obtain a certificate that lists the cause of death. Florida Statutes section—"

"Can I get one without the cause of death?"

"Death is a vital public statistic. Any member of the public can request a death certificate."

"How do I get it?"

"Mail in a request with all the pertinent info. Include a self-addressed envelope and a check for seven dollars made payable to the State of Florida. Processing takes two to three weeks."

"Any way to speed it up?"

"Honestly, you'll be lucky if you get it in a month."

Danny didn't have that long to wait, but took down the address. He stood up. "I gotta go."

"Where to?"

"First, to eat. I haven't had a real meal since before they arrested me."

"Then what?"

"Um, just a few errands."

Fink was already convinced he was nuts. He didn't want to make it a slamdunk case by confessing he was headed straight to the Slagger-Jewell Funeral Home after lunch.

"So what are you doing tonight?"

"Why do you want to know?" Fink said suspiciously.

"Thought I'd drop in at the Tradewinds for some R and R. Come join me for happy hour."

Fink laughed nervously. "Me? Hanging with the sun and fun crowd? I don't think I'd fit in."

"We welcome all body types and skintones. It's a friendly group."

"Mm, I don't think so."

"Perhaps I should mention that several of the women who frequent the establishment devote their lives to looking good in bikinis and would be thrilled to meet someone with a real job who doesn't smell like dead fish."

"I'll be there at six."

He left his glassy-eyed lawyer staring into his new computer monitor, handgun perched on top of a thick legal dictionary.

# 19

**DANNY DROVE** back to the beach and pulled into Luno's Lobster Trap. Still early. Not many cars. Good.

Slipping on sunglasses and the Dolphins cap from the trunk, he tried to slink in incognito only to be greeted loudly by Luno, who'd known him since he was a kid selling lobsters he caught scuba-diving.

He sat at a table in the corner. A teenager named Tori, who loved to surf, capered over and pleaded for quarters to feed the jukebox. He found four and gave her three, saving one for the phone.

"Yay! Thanks, Danny," she cooed. "Any requests?"

"How about *Brown-Eyed Girl*?"

Tori smiled with her pretty brown eyes and danced off to the juke box. Today he'd dedicate the song to Tori, but it always belonged to Sari.

He feasted on a fried grouper sandwich, the fish so fresh it fell apart before he could bite it. The hush puppies and fries were hot and greasy, right out of the fryer. He ordered a piece of Luno's famous homemade key lime pie for dessert then said, "Make it two."

When he finished he went to the payphone in back, found the funeral home number in the hanging phone book and fed in the quarter.

"Slagger-Jewell Funeral Home," said a stern-sounding woman.

"Hello, I'd like to speak to Mr. Slagger or Mr. Jewell," Danny said. Tori cranked up the jukebox, drowning out the reply. "I'm sorry, could you repeat that?"

"I said that Mr. Slagger is deceased and Mr. Jewell is unavailable. May I help you?"

"I really need to speak with Mr. Jewell. It's important."

"Of course, sir. These matters are of the utmost importance. I'll put you through to one of our assistant directors who will be pleased to assist you."

"No one died. I just want to talk to Mr. Jewell."

"May I ask what it's about?"

"No. It's private."

"If you'd like to leave your name and number, I'm sure Mr. Jewell will be happy to return your call."

"Listen carefully. Go find Mr. Jewell. Tell him this is about improprieties in his business. Improprieties that could be very bad for business if they became public."

He had no idea whether that was true, but burying a casket without a body—if that's what happened—couldn't be standard operating procedure.

"Please hold." He listened to a symphonic slaughtering of *Hey Jude* before she returned.

"Mr. Jewell can meet with you at noon, Mr.?"

"Calhoun. Frank Calhoun." He hoped his cellmate wouldn't mind him borrowing his name.

"Please be on time. Mr. Jewell is very busy."

"I'm sure he is. I'll be on time."

Danny stopped at a convenience store to buy some ibuprofen and a bottle of water. His ribs were still killing him. A stack of newspapers sat on the counter next to the register. He was curious what the press was saying about him, but knew it would only make him depressed.

A tan kid with acne and blond bangs took his money. A grommet. Danny could spot a surfer a mile away.

The kid counted out his change. "Seven, eight—whoa! Wait a minute. I'm looking at you and thinking, like, I *know* this dude. I don't believe it. You're Danny Teakwell."

The publicity was worse than he thought.

"I'm right, aren't I? Come on, admit it."

Danny shrugged.

"Never mind, I know I'm right. *Doo-ood*. This is awesome. You're, like, a legend."

Right up there with Manson and Hinkley. Danny's palm hovered above the counter waiting for the rest of his change, but the transaction was a faded memory to the clerk.

"Can I get your autograph?" He snapped up a pen and looked around for something to write on. "I know!" He took a dollar bill from the register. "This is perfect, all that money and everything."

*Lottery Lunatic.* Isn't that what Fink said the papers were calling him? "Look," Danny said.

"How much was that trophy money? A thousand bucks, I think."

Trophy money?

"First prize at the Sun-Coast Surf Championships. Man, that's my dream. I was there. You ripped that last wave. I remember two judges gave you a ten. But admit it, dude, you were lucky to get that wave."

Danny relaxed. The kid had no idea he was an alleged psycho killer. He'd notched a few wins on the Florida surf circuit over the years, including the Sun-Coast contest up the coast at Sebastian. The kid was right. Wave selection is everything and Danny was patient as usual. He donated the prize money to a gadfly named Bartro Sabilinas who carried on a campaign to save Florida's barrier reefs, the only living coral reefs in the continental United States.

The kid looked so damned earnest holding out the pen. Feeling ridiculous, Danny took it and scribbled his initials across George Washington's forehead, grabbed his change and exited quickly.

Back in the car, he got stuck at the light waiting to cross the intracoastal. A couple of kids were fishing off the seawall near the bridge, bringing back memories of summers with Troy. They'd spend all day sitting in that same spot, perfectly content to catch fish never worth keeping, drink cream sodas and tell stupid jokes. He hoped Troy was okay.

# 20

THE SLAGGER-JEWELL Funeral Home stood as a stately edifice to death. With a marble facade marked by four towering columns, it resembled a federal reserve bank. Danny snugged his sunglasses tight and pulled down the ballcap. He took a deep breath, did a couple of shoulder rolls and entered a wide reception area covered with thick burgundy carpet.

His sneakers made no sound as he approached the receptionist, one Norma Pollinuk according to a brass plate on her polished desk. Everything about the place was first class. He bet it cost a lot to die here.

Dressed conservatively in a silk dress and string of pearls, Pollinuk sat with perfect posture, hands crossed on the desk. Her frown said she already pegged Danny as the muckraking caller.

"Good afternoon. May I help you?"

"Hi. I'm Frank Calhoun." The sound echoed off the high ceiling like he was introducing the Rolling Stones at Madison Square Garden.

"Ah, Mr. Calhoun," she indicted with a malignant stare over her half-frame glasses. "I'll tell Mr. Jewell you're here.

Sit down over there." She pointed to a waiting room of dark-burnished wood.

He plowed through the carpet and sat on a red-velvet sofa resembling a church pew, an ecclesiastical touch he supposed was intentional.

A round-faced child, maybe six or seven, sat directly in front of him, sunk into a tall leather chair. She held a *Southern Living* magazine, but her hazel eyes were fixed on Danny.

"Hi," Danny said.

"Hello," she said somberly. "Do you know you have your sunglasses on?"

"Um, yes, I do."

"Why? It's dark in here."

"Well, I—you know, you're right. It is dark in here." Danny took the sunglasses off and folded them up.

"Can you see better now?"

"Yes, I can. Thank you."

"You're welcome."

Her solemnity was unnerving. Dwarfed by the chair, she reminded Danny of Lily Tomlin as Edith Anne on the old *Laugh-In* shows. Her knee joints didn't reach the front, so her white-stockinged legs capped with shiny white shoes stuck out like tiny stilts. She wore a short-sleeve navy blue dress with a white collar and white buttons down the front. A matching white plastic purse sat propped beside her.

The child continued to stare. Danny took an interest in the ornate mirrors and paintings covering the walls, but there was no ignoring her. When he looked again, she was tugging at her ears.

"I like your earrings."

"They're real gold. Eighteen carrots. More than Bugs Bunny."

"Very nice."

"I got my ears pierced yesterday for my seventh birthday."

"Wow, birthday and ears pierced. Two big events in one day."

She bobbed her head, warming.

Kids and the elderly. Danny had always enjoyed popularity with both groups, probably because he took the time to listen to them. If everyone on the planet were under eight or over eighty, his life would be easier.

"Do you like to sing?" she asked.

"As a matter of fact, I do."

"I thought so. Me too. My mother gave me singing lessons for my birthday. I'm not sure why. I already sing really good."

She opened her mouth as if about to deliver proof, glanced at Pollinuk and thought better of it. "So did someone die or are you here to make pre-need arrangements?"

"What?"

"I asked if someone had departed or if you were here to make preparations for the future."

Danny looked at her magazine again. It wasn't *Southern Living*, but *Southern Mortuary*. The lovely floral display on the cover was resting on a coffin.

"Actually, I just stopped by to talk to the owner."

"Mr. Jewell?"

"That's right."

"He's my father."

"Is he really?" That explained a lot.

"Do you have an appointment? He's very busy."

"I've heard that. I do have an appointment."

"He's probably embalming someone. You might want to wait until he's done unless you're used to it. Have you ever seen anyone get embalmed?"

"I can't say I have."

"It's very interesting."

"I'll bet."

"It's an old practice. *Centuries* old. That's hundreds of years. It's pretty yucky, but it's gotten a lot better."

Danny laughed. "That's good to know."

"In the old days, they used to have to *e-vis-er-ate* you." She sounded the word out carefully. "That means take out your brains and intestines and junk. Then they'd stuff you with Herb to make you smell good."

"Good ol' Herb."

"Yeah. But it was messy, messy, messy. They don't do it like that anymore. Do you know what they do now?"

"I have a feeling I'm about to find out."

"Yep." A smile slipped. "First, they cut open your neck and pump out your blood. Then you get filled up with embalming fluid."

"Formaldehyde?"

"Very good. Actually, it's called formalin. It's formaldehyde and water put together. After that, they stick this long needle in your stomach. It's like a shishkabob thing except a lot bigger. A little pump sucks all the juices out of you and they fill you back up with some real pretty blue stuff. That part's called *aspiration*."

The kid obviously knew what she was talking about. He might learn more from her than her father. Danny doubted Jewell was going to be eager to help.

He lowered his voice so Pollinuk couldn't hear. "Do you know how long a body lasts after it's been embalmed?"

She crossed her arms and kicked her legs against the chair, a rare clue she really was a child.

"That depends what you mean by *lasts*. It'll last a long time, but it won't look very nice. There's a guy named Lenin. Not the one in the Beatles. My father told me about him. He's been dead a long time and the Russians keep his body out for everyone to look at. I don't know for the life of me why they would do that. Do you?"

"I guess he was kind of a hero."

"Whatever. My father showed me his picture and he looked pretty good, but Dad said that's only because they keep re-embalming him."

What a fascinating kid. Following in her father's footsteps in her size two patent leather shoes. "What's your name?" Danny asked.

"Jessica. I know your name. You're Frank Calhoun. I heard you tell Mrs. Pollinuk."

"My friends call me Danny." He couldn't lie to a kid. "What did you do for your birthday?"

"We had a party. Right here," she waved airily at the funereal surroundings. "But it ended early. I got caught hiding in a casket while we were playing hide and seek and some kid's mom pitched a fit. It was fun until then. My boyfriend came. Brandon Bickles, except I call him *Pickles*. He's the smartest boy I know. Not smarter than me, but smart for a boy. Are you married?"

"Married? Um, no."

"My dad's married. To my mom. Do you have a girlfriend?"

"No, I don't."

She pursed her lips. "Don't girls like you?"

"Well, some do, I guess."

"Do you have a pet?"

"No, don't have one of those either."

"Huh. What do you have?"

From the mouths of babes. "Not much, I guess."

"You should get a pet. Then you won't be all alone."

"I live in a condo. I'm not sure what kind of pet I could get."

"Get a hamster. They're real easy to take care of and don't take up much room."

"A hamster. I'll think about that."

"Mr. Calhoun."

Norma Pollinuk stood beside him, hands on hips.

"His friends call him Danny," Jessica said.

Pollinuk scowled. "Mr. Jewell will see you now."

"His friends call him Jarrod," Jessica yelled after them.

Danny followed Norma Pollinuk across the reception area and down a white corridor lined with offices. Six men and one woman held the title of Assistant Funeral Director. At the back corner they came to a door with a heavy brass name plate proclaiming in ostentatious script, *Jarrod Jewell, Jr., Funeral Director.*

Pollinuk knocked.

"Come in," said a nasal voice.

The door skidded open to reveal a stocky, rosy-faced man sitting behind an antique desk big enough to play ping pong on.

"Mr. Jewell. This is Mr. Calhoun. The one who *called.*"

"Yes, yes, come in, Calhoun," Jewell said with a tired affability that surprised Danny.

His clothes looked expensive, but were disheveled. His monogrammed shirt was so wrinkled it looked like a batik. Pink blotches stained his yellow silk tie.

"Have a seat. Want some coffee?"

"No thanks."

"I'll have some, Norma."

"Certainly, Mr. Jewell."

"And shut the door."

Pollinuk gave Danny a sour look and high-stepped out while Jewell scratched his belly and scrutinized him.

"You look familiar. Do I know you?"

Not unless you watch television or read the newspaper.

"Nope. We've never met."

"Are you sure? I spend a lot of time studying faces and don't usually forget one."

"I'm pretty sure."

"If you say so."

A photograph on the desk featured Jewell and an attractive redheaded wife with Jessica scrunched in between, all posing with cheesy smiles in front of a gold casket.

"So what's this about? I run a clean operation. By the book. No scams, no preying on widows—and believe me, plenty of that goes on in this industry. I learned the business from my father. He taught me that if you treat people right, the business will come to you. Good will. Word of mouth. Just like any other well-run enterprise. And he was right. We've been very successful at it."

Danny scanned the rows of certificates and plaques behind him. Every respectable organization in America apparently agreed Jewell was a saint. He couldn't just launch into accusing him of crimes against nature.

"I may have overstated my case on the phone. It was important to see you immediately."

"You mentioned improprieties."

"I might be wrong. It could be my question involves no impropriety at all."

Relief bloomed on Jewell's face like a sunflower. Pollinuk returned with coffee in a souvenir mug from the *Raise the Dead Ball*. Jewell relaxed and put his feet on the desk. "Alright, so what is it?" he said, sipping the coffee.

"Is it normal to bury a casket without a body in it?"

Coffee projectiles in a spread formation hit multiple targets, including Danny.

"A casket with no corpse?" he wheezed. "We did that?"

"I'm not sure. If I could just ask a few questions you can probably clear things up for me. I'm not here to cause trouble."

"You could have fooled me, but okay. I'll answer your questions, then you answer mine."

"Fair enough."

Danny waved to the photo on the desk.

"Nice family." How did he explain why he was prowling around the graveyard last night inspecting Jewell's dug-up coffins?

"To start with," he said breezily, "if a person was buried for twenty years, what would be left of her body?"

Jewell sprung to attention. "So that's what this is about. The cops called first thing this morning. You're sick, buddy." He plucked up the phone receiver and punched a button. "Norma, call the police."

Danny leaped up. "Wait, don't do that!"

Jewell waved the receiver in front of him for protection.

"Listen to me. I didn't have anything to do with digging up that grave. I swear. Publicity is just going to hurt both of us."

Jewell grunted. "Never mind, Norma. All right, stay near the phone. That'll be fine. Yes, I'm sure." He set the receiver down, but pulled the phone closer.

"Nobody even knows if that was our casket. The police contacted all the funeral homes this morning and asked us to check our records."

"It's your casket." He handed Enya's obituary to Jewell, which caused his cheeks to inflate like a blowfish.

"Assuming it was our casket, which I'm not conceding, we're not legally responsible because some wacko decided to go out and rob a grave."

"I'm not here to sue you. I'm just looking for information that could help us both. What would be left of a body that was buried in a casket for twenty years?"

"Was the alleged casket in a proper burial vault?"

"What's that?"

"A concrete box, lowered into the ground, the casket goes inside."

There was no concrete vault. Danny would have used it to stand on. "No. The only box in the grave was the casket."

Jewell's injured expression said he didn't like that answer. "Hmph. Was the alleged casket sealed or unsealed?"

"What's the difference?"

"Big. If the casket was sealed and the body properly embalmed, the corpse would be intact. It wouldn't be pretty but, structurally speaking, you'd still have a body."

Basically the same thing his daughter said.

"What if it was unsealed?"

"A pile of dried bones would be my guess. Now are you going to tell me what this is all about?"

"One more question. Suppose someone removed the contents of this casket that had been buried for twenty years."

"Someone, huh? Are you aware that defacing a corpse is a serious felony?"

"I told you, I didn't dig up that grave."

"Then why do you know so much about it?"

Danny's turn to wheeze. "Please, just answer this one question and I'll explain everything to you." Not exactly everything. "If a body was buried in a casket for twenty years and someone removed the, uh, contents, what would it look like inside?"

"Look like? What are you talking about?"

"I mean, would the casket look, um, lived in? You know, stains on the fabric, residue, whatever."

"I don't know what it would look like. We're in the business of putting people to rest, not digging them up." His rosy cheeks darkened two shades.

"Could you make an educated guess?"

"To use your words, I'm sure it would look *lived in*. A putrefying human body is going to leave its mark."

"Even if it was sealed like you were talking about?"

"Anaerobic bacteria don't require oxygen."

"What would that do?"

"Turn everything to mold. Leave the dearly departed looking like cottage cheese left in a refrigerator too long. There'd be stains, residue, debris. And the corpse would leave an imprint in the padding. Even the good stuff. I know because my old man takes a nap in a casket every day. Swears it's more comfortable than his bed. A little eccentric."

No wonder little Jessica plays hide and seek in coffins.

"There'd also be hair and skin tissue. We embalm as well as anyone, but it can only last so long."

Danny closed his eyes, resurrecting the image of Enya's casket. There was no stain or residue, no imprint, nothing on *the shiny satin that glowed blood red.* "That's what I was hoping you'd say."

"So let's hear your story."

He felt bad about lying after making a deal, but the unvarnished truth wasn't going to cut it. "Here's my situation …" Danny explained that Enya was a friend from high school. The twenty-year reunion brought back her memory and he couldn't resist visiting her grave to pay his respects after drinking a pint of whiskey. When he arrived, the grave was already dug up.

"The grave was dug up," Jewell said flatly.

"I know it sounds fishy, but it's true. The casket was in the grave with the top open. The fabric looked clean—no remains. No residue or imprint, no skin, no hair. It looked almost new."

"Let me make sure I have this straight. In a moment of nostalgia, you broke into a locked cemetery, crime number one, to visit an old friend, whose grave—whose one little grave out of more than two thousand—just happened to have been dug up by a different intruder the same night. Is that about it?"

"That's what happened," Danny said. Crazy as it sounded, except for the part about why he was there, it was true.

Jewell grabbed the phone again. "Norma, it's me."

Danny spoke firmly, but with more control. "You don't want

to do that. Even if I did dig up that grave—which I didn't—it doesn't change the fact there was never a corpse in that casket. That means you could be in trouble too."

Foiled again, Jewell growled and drummed his pudgy fingers on the desk. "Get me some aspirin, Norma. Yes, I'm fine. Just get me the aspirin." He set the phone down again. "What do you want from me?"

"Just what I said. Some understanding, same thing you should want. Help me figure out why that casket was buried without a body in it and I'll become a distant memory. You'll never hear from me again."

Jewell twisted a bulging University of Miami class ring with a green stone. "Okay, but we'll have to go see the old man. My father, Jarrod Jewell, Sr. The co-founder of this institution."

"He'll know?"

"If he doesn't, no one will. He ran this place for forty years."

"Did he keep records?"

Jewell just laughed. "He's out in the embalming room, making up a corpse. Retired ten years ago, but could he take up golf or shuffleboard? Not a chance. Putting makeup on dead faces, that's my father's hobby. You ready?"

Danny stood and waited because Jewell chose that moment to straighten his desktop.

He sighed. "Okay, let's do it."

"Let's do it," Danny said encouragingly.

He duck-walked out the door and Danny followed him. They passed a casket display room behind a pair of glass doors, Jessica's playground. A variety of models, including one in a psychedelic paisley print, were perched on Corinthian pedestals.

Jewell stopped at a metal door and sorted through keys on a Mercedes-Benz ring. He muttered something that sounded like *Please* as he led them into a windowless room the size of a warehouse, bathed in florescent light. The air was pungent with bleach.

Angled stainless tables lined the nearest wall, bolted to the concrete floor. Danny wondered why they were tilted until he saw the drains. Next to each table was a sink from which coiled hoses extended and a credenza topped with rows of chromium instruments, a dental nightmare multiplied by a thousand. One table had a lump under a sheet.

He shivered, although the room wasn't cold, which surprised him. He expected to walk into a freezer.

In the far corner, a stick figure wearing a lab coat stood working over one of the tables.

Jewell coughed and jangled his keys, but the man didn't look up. He was talking to a corpse.

"You look lovely today, my little chickadee," he said as they approached.

Jewell groaned. "Dad, we have a visitor."

The old man ignored him. He was waving a crystal decanter over the dead body.

"How 'bout a little drink, just you and me? Come on, dollface. One little brandy never hurt anybody. Don't make an old man drink alo—"

"Dad!"

The old man finally looked up, smiling impishly through toothless gums. He had to be in his nineties. His head was a shrunken globe covered with liver spots, hairless except for a few white strands standing straight in the center. The brandy decanter trembled in his gloved hands.

"Hello, Junior." A bead of spit hung tenuously from one side of his mouth.

"Dad, where are your dentures?"

"Got 'em soaking." He waved to a shelf.

Danny zeroed in on a row of glass jars filled with clear liquid and something else. His stomach twitched as he recognized a human heart in the first container. All down the row, the jars held what appeared to be human organs, except the one at the end, where a set of yellowed dentures rested on the bottom like a sea creature waiting to pounce.

"Dad, I told you to get rid of those. Remember our deal? I hired Lila for your birthday party and you were supposed to dispose of the … things in the jars."

The geezer's face drooped. "I tried, but I just couldn't do it. They're my mementos. Everyone keeps mementos." He turned to Danny. "Don't you?"

"Dad, these aren't ticket stubs. They're human organs!"

The geezer looked wounded. "He says that like they're just any old organs, but these belonged to some of my dearest friends."

He set down the brandy and reached for a jar containing a gray slab.

"This liver belonged to Harry Pendelbright. We were in World War II together. This very liver metabolized three bottles of vintage burgundy the night we liberated Paris in August of 1944. That's history!"

He lifted another jar. "And this here is Bert Freemer's brain. Bert was my poker buddy. Good ol' Bert. He'd go all in with a pair of deuces. You can see why," he whispered to Danny. "Brain's a little on the small side." He stroked the canister like a newborn before returning it to the shelf. "I knew and loved Bert for fifty years."

Junior grimaced, but gave up the contest he obviously had fought and lost before.

"Dad, meet Frank Calhoun. Frank, this is my father, Jarrod Jewell, Sr."

"Hello, Frank." He stuck out his spindly hand.

"Dad, I don't think Mr. Calhoun wants to shake your hand when you've been … working." He bobbed at the corpse, which Danny had been trying not to look at. It was covered with a sheet except for the head. A multitiered tackle box spilled open like stadium bleachers on the table next to it, cubby holes jammed with cosmetics.

"You're right, Junior. Where are my manners?" He peeled off the glove and stuck the hand out again, knuckles protruding like rivets under tracing paper skin. Danny shook it gently.

"Pleasure to meet you, Frank." He turned back to the corpse. "And this here is Sally Orfingdahl. Poor little gal had a heart attack in her sleep. Sally, this is my son, Junior, and his friend, Frank."

Junior's expression screamed *Why me?*

The old man picked up a *Vogue* magazine from the table and stabbed the cover with his finger. "When I'm finished, Sally here is going to look just this supermodel."

"Dad studies fashion magazines to stay current," Junior explained.

"Gotta stay in touch with the times. Time'll leave you behind in a hurry, Frank. Don't ever forget it. I wouldn't be doing Sally much of a service if I made her up to look like your Aunt Bessie, would I?"

"I guess not." He felt ridiculous with everyone calling him Frank, but it was too late to change now.

"Gotta have the right look, right texture, and of course, the right products." He picked up a checkerboard of eye shadow. "Read this label."

"Lancôme."

"That's it," he cackled. "Sally deserves the best. Got all the top brands here, even some rouge I bought from a sales lady in a pink Cadillac. I treat 'em all like supermodels. Of course, makeup can't work magic by itself. That takes talent. Frank, you look like you have a keen eye for the ladies. Come over here and take a good gander at Sally."

"Thanks, but I—"

"Don't be shy," he said, shoving him in the ribs. Danny yelped.

"Nonsense. It's not that bad. Look her right in the eyes. Ignore that excess glue around the lids. I'm not finished yet. And don't pay attention to the cotton in her nostrils. Block it out of your mental picture."

Danny saw his hand coming again and leaned in preemptively.

"Attaboy. Get right in there up close and personal. Tell me what you see."

Danny stared into Sally Orphingdahl's dead face.

"Check out that smile. Smiles have always been my specialty. Hell, truth be told, a teenage girl can put on makeup with a little practice, but it takes an artist to make a corpse smile. She's perfect, isn't she?"

Junior rocked impatiently.

"Very nice work."

"Nice? No, no. *Perfect*. Tell me one thing that's not perfect. One thing."

"Really. It's fantastic. Perfect."

"Frank, you're lying. Man to man, tell me one thing that's not perfect about her."

Danny saw the hand coming in again. "Too much blush?"

"What? Move over." He wrapped a pair of glasses with lenses thick as airplane windshields around his ears and pulled in a spotlight mounted on a swivel. "I'll be damned. He's right. Too much blush!"

He slapped Danny on the back, causing him to double over. "*Oww-ahhh*."

"*Oww-ahhh* is right!" said the old man. "Too much blush. That calls for a drink." He picked up a bottle labeled *Formaldo-Zaz! Arterial for Problem Cases*. "Brandy?"

"Da-ad," Junior said.

"Oops." He found the brandy decanter and poured some into a lab beaker, handing it to Danny.

"Is that beaker clean?"

"Is that beaker clean? I love this kid. A little arterial never hurt anyone, Frankie. Have one, Junior?"

Junior shook his head, dismayed the meeting was turning into happy hour.

"He's always been kind of a party pooper. Too much blush. Sally never would have forgiven me if I sent her off to the everafter looking like a hoochie-coochie girl. I owe you one, Frankie-boy."

"Fine, then maybe you can help him out," Jewell said crisply.

"Any-ting," he said, gargling brandy. "Any-ting at all."

Jewell tipped his palms. "He's all yours. Good luck."

Danny raised the beaker and knocked back the brandy.

"Mr. Jewell, I'm looking for information about a burial you handled. It was a long time ago, twenty years to be exact."

The old man tried to whistle between his toothless gums, but no sound came out. "Long time. Put a lot of folks to rest in twenty years."

"I was hoping you might remember it because it was, or might have been, kind of unusual."

Jewell butted in, "Dad, did you ever bury an empty casket?"

"Empty casket?"

"That's right. Did you ever bury an empty casket? It's a simple question."

"Why would I do a thing like that?"

"That's what I want to know, because if you did it was probably illegal and we could be in a lot of trouble."

"Empty casket," the old man repeated.

"It would have been for the funeral of a young girl, a high school girl," Danny said. "There was no burial vault, if that helps."

Jarrod Jewell, Sr. stared into space mashing his gums.

"Her name was—"

"McKenzie!"

"That's it! I don't believe it," Danny said.

"That calls for another drink." He poured more brandy into Danny's beaker and helped himself to a double.

"McKenzie!" he repeated, as if the name would start a party each time uttered. "Of course I remember. It's not every day you bury an empty casket."

"You did it?" Jewell said. "You buried an empty casket? I don't believe it. How could you?"

"Because the girl's father asked me to."

"Was she dead?" Danny asked.

The old man eyed him curiously.

"'Course she was dead, Frankie. That's the way things work in this business."

"Then where was the deceased?" Junior said, in the prestages of an anxiety attack. Danny's case had been causing a lot of them.

He closed his eyes and waited for the game-ending answer.

The old man took another hit of brandy. They waited while he gargled again.

"She committed suicide," he finally said.

The words hung in the air, suddenly thick with the stench of death.

"Then why wasn't she in the casket?" Junior asked.

"She drowned. Jumped off a bridge one night, down in the Keys as I recall. They never found the body."

"I assume you saw a death certificate?"

"No, I didn't and I'll ask you, sonny, to stop talking to me in that tone of voice. Frank, do you talk to your father like that?"

Danny stood cemented under the weight of the revelation.

"No death certificate? Then how did you get a burial permit? You can't get a burial permit without a death certificate."

"I didn't."

Voice rising an octave, "You didn't get a burial permit?"

"I didn't need one."

"Of course you needed one. It's a crime to not have a permit. You know that."

"Let's not forget who taught this business to who." The old man turned to Danny. "Is it *who* or *whom*?"

Danny shook his head.

"Whichever. The *law*, sonny, says you need a burial permit to bury human remains. We just buried an empty box. It was perfectly legal." The impish smile again, a senior version of *MAD* magazine's Alfred E. Neuman.

"Can I ask a question?" Danny said.

"'Course you can, Frank."

"Why would someone bury a casket with no body in it?"

"Good question," Junior sputtered.

"It is a good question. Only time I remember it happening. Frank, you'd be surprised how many people want to pay for a funeral service and monument even when there's no body. But a casket? No point. McKenzie bought a nice one too. Silver Eldorado. Only thing he scrimped on was the pillow. No need, of course, in an empty casket."

There was no pillow in Enya's casket.

"So answer the question, Dad. Why did the gentleman bury an empty casket?"

"Wanted to protect his family." He took another swallow of brandy, most of which missed his mouth. "Let's see, how did that go? I believe the deceased had some family coming from out of town. McKenzie wanted to spare them the additional trauma of knowing the girl's body wasn't recovered.

"As Junior here can tell you, Frank, people get awfully prickly when it comes to the remains of their loved ones. If we treated everyone as well when they're alive as we do when they're dead, the world would be a far better place. McKenzie didn't want the rest of the family knowing that poor little ..."

"Enya," Danny said.

"That poor little Enya was fish bait."

"The family thought the deceased was in the casket?" Junior shrieked. "And you went along with it?"

"Seemed like a reasonable request. McKenzie was a nice fellow. Religious, decent type."

"So that explains why no burial vault," Danny said.

"Exactly. Just like the pillow. No need. Save a chunk of change right there."

Danny measured his words carefully. "So the bottom line is you have no way of knowing for sure that Enya, the deceased, was actually dead."

"Run that by me again, Frankie."

"I mean it's possible she was still alive at the time of the funeral since you never saw a body or a death certificate."

The old man poked a latex finger in his nostril. "Well, anything's possible, but why hold a funeral for someone who's not dead? What would be the point?"

Danny shook his head. "I don't know."

Drowned. What a scary way to die. But no body in the casket—no proof she actually did die. He turned down another drink and shook the old man's hand again. On the way out, he and Jewell exchanged promises to keep each other's secrets.

Norma Pollinuk sent ocular death rays at him as he passed through the reception area. Jessica was lying perfectly still on the carpet in the waiting room, hands folded across her chest. When she heard Danny, she jumped up.

"Are you leaving?"

"Yeah, I gotta get going. It sure was great to meet you. You're one impressive young lady."

Jessica beamed. "Did my father help you with what you needed?"

"He was very helpful. So were you."

"Did you meet my grandpa?"

"I did."

"Isn't he wonderful?"

"He's pretty cool."

"Yeah, real cool."

Pollinuk cleared her throat loudly. Danny winked at Jessica and turned to go.

"Bye, Danny. Don't forget that hamster!"

# 21

DANNY DIDN'T KNOW what to think as he drove home. Each time one piece of the puzzle fit into place, the others moved or changed shape. He had an obituary in his pocket. He saw the grave—was *in* the grave! The family held a funeral. Jewell, Sr. heard it straight from Enya's father that she committed suicide. But still no body.

Back at the Seabreeze Towers he ran into Grady standing on the boardwalk smoking a cigar.

"Cigarettes *and* cigars? When did you start smoking cigars?"

"At least I don't smoke *reefers*. I guess that's one good thing about your arrest. Now I get to harass you about your smoking."

"Yeah, well …"

"Anyway, I decided to quit. The cigars are just occasional to help me beat the habit."

"You're quitting smoking. Seriously?"

"Might as well give it a try, at least while you're in this jam."

"You old coot. Thanks, Grady."

"I'm not doing it for you. I did it because I need a break from your nagging."

"Well, thanks anyway."

"On another subject, I need to warn you. Rumors are afoot the lads plan on kicking your ass tonight," he said.

"Come again?"

"That little television promotion you did with the Traynor gal on leaving the jail brought in a big crowd of strangers last night. They were all asking when the *Lottery Lunatic* would arrive."

"You're kidding."

"I'm not. John the Diver mentioned something about castration, so I hid the big knives. Me, I'm not complaining. The cash register rang all night."

"This world is insane."

"Tell me something I don't know. Speaking of insane, how is your life going? Where were you last night?"

Lying in a coffin in a dug-up grave. "Just resting," he said.

"That right? Didn't see your car."

He prepared for another interrogation, but Grady dropped it. "Anyhoo, come see us tonight. Your fans await you."

Danny said he would be there and was bringing his lawyer.

Upstairs, the answering machine blinked. Sari?

*Beep.* "Danny, Roy Chambers here. Wanted to let you know my guys made it out to Tamms' house. Whole AC was shot. Thing was twenty years old. Whoever installed it was a friggin' moron. Put it too far from the house, practically in the middle of the backyard. We moved it closer. Couple of hours extra labor moving the concrete pad and redoing the lines. Will run you a grand with the brother-in-law discount."

Myron Tamms would have air conditioning. A morsel of good news. He was almost in the bedroom when the machine beeped again.

"Danny, this is Margie Fisher, *Santa Cruz* to you. I've been hearing about your case. I don't know what to say except that

I don't believe a word of it. This is probably the last thing on your mind, but have you talked to Sari? You said at the reunion you were going to call her. I've been trying to reach her, but she hasn't called back. That's not like Sari. With this whole crazy thing going on and the Seminole High connection, I started worrying. If you talk to her, will you tell her to call me? Also, let me know if there's anything I can do to help you."

She left a number.

Danny replayed the message. *I've been trying to reach her, but she hasn't called back. That's not like Sari.*

A sick feeling bubbled in his stomach. For the first time since the calamity started, he considered the possibility Sari had somehow gotten caught up in the madness.

He tried to shake it off. He was just being paranoid. Sari didn't have anything to do with Sugar Lake. How would the killer even know about her? But if Fink was right, if it really was about revenge, what better way to punish him than hurt Sari?

He called Margie back. The machine picked up. "Hi, you've reached the Fisher residence …" A man's voice. He hung up and rushed out the door. In the parking lot, he cranked up the Beetle and sped toward I-95, the quickest way south to Coconut Grove.

Carved out of a hardwood hammock, the Grove occupied five square miles on Biscayne Bay in South Miami. Born as a winter haven for literati and tycoons, it retained a bohemian vibe, but like the rest of Miami, crass development threatened its identity.

Danny's destination was the economic epicenter: the Cocowalk, an enclave of restaurants and shops a block from the bay. Margie said Sari sold her jewelry from a sidewalk cart. Any sidewalk vendors had to be nearby.

He should have searched for Sari a long time ago. Why hadn't he? It wasn't because of pride, one of the only deadly sins he lacked. Guilt played a big role. But mainly, he was honoring

Sari's wishes. Had they ever changed? Did she ever regret the decision to break up?

When he saw her, he'd say … he had no clue, but she would know his feelings by the time he left. He'd also set the record straight on Mangrum's twenty-year-old lies at Sugar Lake, just in case it mattered. The wisdom of Jarrod Jewell, Sr. came to him. *Time'll leave you behind in a hurry, Frank. Don't ever forget it.*

Danny cruised in on South Bayshore, passing Monty's seafood restaurant and Dinner Key Marina, pale green water of Biscayne Bay luminous behind them.

Then he got stuck in traffic. An art festival, meaning there would be a lot more vendor carts and booths around than usual. He parked illegally at Bayside Park and hiked in. He approached the first vendor he reached, a woman selling hand-painted wind chimes.

"Hi. Cool wind chimes. I'm looking for someone who operates a sidewalk cart in the Grove. She sells jewelry. Her name is Sari Hunter. Do you happen to know her?"

"I'm from Georgia. I'm just here for the festival."

The scene repeated itself over and over. Forty-five minutes later, gripping his aching side, he climbed the hill from the bay to the Cocowalk, stopping to rest at the top. He was leaning against the storefront of Paula's Fine Women's Clothing when a taut voice interrupted him.

"Loitering is illegal in Coconut Grove!"

A skeletal, pasty-faced woman in a filmy black pants suit stood in the threshold.

"I'll only be here a minute," he said.

"You've already been here for," she looked at her watch, "two minutes and twenty-three seconds. Move along or I'll call the police."

"Go ahead and call. They'll have to take a number."

He saw a payphone across the street. Margie Santa Cruz might have Sari's address.

"Are you saying you're not going to move?"

"No, I'm saying go to hell," he said.

"Profanity is illegal in Coconut Grove!" she yelled.

After remembering to change the last name from Santa Cruz to Fisher, he got Margie's number from directory assistance. The machine answered again. He hung up and sat on a bench outside a skate shop, watching the afternoon rain clouds gather above the bay and hoping for a brainstorm. A commotion erupted across the street.

Paula was arguing with a short, athletic-looking black woman in denim shorts and a yellow tank top. The debate appeared to extend beyond loitering. Paula was shaking a sheet of paper in the woman's face, ruby lips stretched in a snarl over thin porcelain teeth.

"Don't you dare talk to me in that tone of voice," she shrieked. "I pay obscene property taxes just so you and your ilk can live on the sidewalks."

"*You're* obscene. I pay vendor taxes and work my ass off so people have a reason to come to the Grove. Your Euro-trash rags sure ain't doin' it."

Paula's mouth opened wide enough to need stitches. "I'm calling the police!"

Danny wondered how many times a day Paula threatened the citizenry with police action. The cops must hate her.

"You go right ahead and call the *po*lice. I'll call your clueless husband and tell him about the Cuban boy-toy who comes visiting at Paula's Fine Women's Clothing three days a week after closing time."

Danny stifled a laugh.

"It's people like you who have ruined this community," Paula said with teary eyes. She crumpled the paper and threw it on the sidewalk. The door slammed and the *Open* sign flipped to *Sorry, We're Closed.*

"Yadee, yada," the black woman muttered, stooping to pick up the crumpled paper. She smoothed it against her thigh and crossed the street to Danny.

She saw him watching. "You got a problem?" she said.

"Me? I've got lots of problems."

"Shoot, I'm sorry. That snooty woman just ticks me off. She's been ripping people off in that overpriced store forever. Do you believe she has dresses in there that cost ten thousand dollars? You'd think she'd be willing to give something back to the village. It wasn't like I was asking her to actually do anything, just let me tape up a damned flyer."

She stuck out her hand. "I'm Sondra," she said.

"Danny," he said, shaking it.

"I've never seen you around here before, but you obviously aren't a tourist."

"Just looking for a friend."

"Yeah," she said dispiritedly. "Me too. My best friend."

Thunder rumbled overhead. The paper in her hand flapped like a storm warning flag.

"How does someone just disappear?" she said.

She held up the flyer. "I can't believe we've been friends for five years and this is my only picture of her. So much for all the Kodak moments."

"What happened to your friend?"

"She's missing. More than a week. The police, who Miss Paula has so much faith in, say they can't do anything because there's no evidence of a crime. I tell them, what do you call *missing*? That's evidence. But no, people are missing all the time, they say, and almost always turn up *un*-missing. Well, screw them. My friend is more dependable than green on grass. If she's missing, something happened.

The fire faded. "But they don't listen. They just don't listen."

A tremor in Danny's gut was spreading. He pointed at the flyer. "Could I see that?"

She smoothed the paper again and handed it to him.

Danny looked down and the world dissolved into a blur except for the block printing:

## MISSING: SARI HUNTER

*Last seen June 6 at her sidewalk jewelry cart in Coconut Grove.*

*Description: 5' 7", brown hair and eyes. Last seen wearing blue shorts, white teeshirt and athletic shoes.*

*If you know ANYTHING, contact Sondra Carmice day or night, 555-9132. Leave message if no answer.*

*REWARD for information.*

At the bottom was a picture taken at the beach, rough surf in the background. Sari clutched a Marlins baseball cap to her head. It must have been unusually cool because she wore a long-sleeve teeshirt and sweat pants.

When he finally looked up, Sondra Carmice was eyeing him suspiciously. "Why'd you do that?" she asked.

"Huh?"

"You made a sound when you saw the flyer, like a gasp. Why'd you do that?"

"I ... I know Sari."

"You know her?"

He nodded. "All my life."

"What are you talking about—*all your life*? Who the hell are you?"

"Most of it," he said. "Since the fifth grade."

"No way. You said your name's Danny? Don't tell me you're Danny Teakwell."

"You know me?"

"I feel like I do." She grabbed his arm, change in demeanor dramatic. "Sari told me everything about you."

"Everything?"

She nodded. "There's not much to do but talk when you spend every day on the sidewalk together. I'm a wood sculptor. Masks and figurines. My cart is next to Sari's, has been for five years. I know her story and she knows mine. You're a big part of hers. Everything she said about you was great, except for, well, you know."

"Yeah, I know."

"You broke her heart."

On perfect cue, a fat raindrop splattered on his forehead. More followed. They ducked under a striped awning as the bottom fell out of the sky.

"What are you doing down here?" she shouted above the rushing rain.

"I was worried about her. We had our twentieth high school reunion a few days ago. A friend of Sari's told me she was planning to come, but she didn't show up. I thought she just changed her mind, but ... a lot has happened over the past few days."

He left the cryptic words hanging. Across the street, Paula spied on them through the blinds.

"The friend called this morning. Said she's been leaving messages for Sari, but hasn't heard back. Said it wasn't like Sari not to return calls. That's the way I remember her too."

"You're both right."

The rain drenched their legs.

"She was excited about the reunion. We were supposed to go shopping for a dress the afternoon she disappeared. I hate to use that word, *disappeared*, but I don't know what else to call it."

She looked at the picture and shook her head. "We tried to be so careful. But it's such a damned dangerous world. If someone makes up their mind to hurt you ..." Her voice dissipated in a gust of wind.

"Couldn't she have just gone on vacation?"

Sondra shook her head. "Impossible. She would never do that without letting me know. I'm telling you, we're like sisters."

"When's the last time you saw her?"

"Just like the flyer says. Tuesday, June 6th. Seven days ago. We worked that day, but it was slow. Tuesdays always are. I closed up before lunch. Sari was still there when I left, organizing her jewelry. She spends as much time counting and organizing it as making it."

A memory flashed of Sari counting her pencils on their first day of school together.

"We talked about going shopping for a dress later. She said she'd call, but never did. Even that's not like Sari, but we didn't have a firm plan and sometimes we keep our carts open late, when we need extra money. But I knew something was wrong the next morning when she didn't show up.

"I went to her apartment. It's only a few blocks from here. The newspaper was on the porch and mail from the day before was still in her mailbox. I have a key and went inside. Everything looked normal. I went back and studied her cart. Locked up and normal.

"I wasted a day thinking like the police. She'll turn up. You're silly for worrying. I didn't report her missing until the next morning. Now I've wasted a whole week being dangled along."

"Maybe someone around here saw something," Danny said.

"I've asked everywhere. No one saw a thing." She glared across the street. Paula snapped the blinds shut.

"It was like one minute she was here and the next minute she was gone, without a trace. I finally decided to forget the police and do something on my own." She pointed to the flyer.

"Too little, too late. I shouldn't have waited so long."

She started to cry. Danny put an arm on her shoulder. She leaned into him.

"I have some resources I can put to work," he said. "I have some friends who can help put up flyers. If you have an extra one, I can get more made. I also have access to a private investigator. I'll get him looking for Sari."

"Okay," she said dully, handing him a fresh flyer and business card from her backpack: *Sondra Carmice, Sculptor of Wood.* "That's my number. It's on the flyer too. I'll be at my cart tomorrow. My rent's due."

"I have some money if you need it. And the police, I don't know exactly how, but I'll get their attention. I promise."

She pulled back and studied him with one eye closed. "I think I finally get it."

"Get what?"

"Why Sari still talks about you. It never made sense. Twenty years is a long time to carry a torch, especially for a man. But I see it now. I can see your heart, Danny Teakwell."

"Um, thanks, I guess."

"I can see the crack in it too."

Danny turned red.

She patted his arm. "Look at the fine print on my business card, in the corner."

"*Tarot readings.* So you're a psychic?"

"I don't call it that. It's more like a kind of advanced insight. I have to tell you something. Last night I did a Tarot reading about Sari. ... I drew the Death card."

Shannon at the Tradewinds sometimes played around with Tarot cards. He'd seen the armored skeleton on the Death card.

"No, wait. Don't look like that. The Death card is the most misunderstood card. It can mean that something's about to end and a new chapter started, a transformation. That's what

I believe. Sari's coming back," she said uncertainly. "Say you know it's true, even if it's a lie."

"I know it's true."

He tucked the flyer inside his shorts and fled into the storm.

Sondra shouted after him. The steel raindrops drowned out the words, but his wishful thinking heard *She loves you.*

# 22

JAXON KEMPLER—Albert Thumpet of late—nudged the motor on the behemoth Chrysler New Yorker until the speedometer needle hit sixty-six, where he kept it steady as he drove up the Florida Turnpike from Orlando. Just a couple hours from home.

He couldn't wait to get back to Ocala, world of rolling hills, giant oaks and horses by the boatload. A different world from South Florida, land of the lotioned idolaters. A better world, at least when people weren't killing his mother.

Dialing in an oldies station, he relaxed in the worn leather seat with a toothy grin and his eyes popped wide open. There's no bliss like psychotic bliss. Such a special day. He couldn't wait to see her. She was going to be so proud of him.

Simply having his own wheels back improved his mood, although the clozapine tablets probably helped some.

The rental cars of the past week were an annoying but necessary precaution. As much as he loved the New Yorker, it was old and prone to leaving him stranded roadside—exactly the wrong place to be when you have a murder kit or body in the trunk. Yet another avoidable error made by below-average killers. He should write a book, *Murdering for Dumb-Asses*.

But he hated rental cars, especially the tiny subcompacts he'd been crammed in. They were suffocating, like being in a coffin.

*Damn.* Why did he have to think coffin? He hated that coffin even more than tiny rental cars. If it wasn't already in a graveyard, he'd kill it.

*Think positively. Live in the moment.* Dr. Lazlo and his henchmen were lying sickies, but even a diseased oyster spits out a pearl once in a while.

Think about the bouquet of daisies on the passenger seat. They are *today. Fresh! Alive!* True, they've been decaying by the second since their necks got snipped, but—*think positively*—they are the perfect gift for the perfect girl.

Positive or negative, too many things to think about challenged his concentration and he lost control of the New Yorker, which swerved onto the shoulder, leaving a cloud of burning rubber as he wrestled it back on the road.

It was June 13. He wasn't sure what time. His watch said nine-thirty, which didn't mean anything because it hadn't moved since the night before when he smashed it on a gravestone.

A sign showed a Pancake Palace at the next exit at the *exact* moment the Carpenters came on the radio singing *Top of the World.* An obvious omen, one so clear and powerful he took it as a sign to break with the past and change the future by stopping for pancakes. Thirteen wasn't divisible by three, but it did have a three in it and he needed food. Not just for him. His houseguest would be starving.

He'd get a triple-order to compensate for the violation. Exceptions were made for special days like this.

Too bad the judge had to rain on it by letting Teakwell out of jail. That required a major change in plans, including an all-night drive from Hollywood to Jacksonville in the north corner of the state—in a car the size of a friggin' grapefruit—then all the way back to Orlando to pick up the New Yorker at the airport. He left it there a week ago when he flew to Bismarck to kill Thumpet.

But he had finally taken care of business and could relax and concentrate on *her*.

He pulled off the exit and picked up a triple stack of buttermilk pancakes with extra syrup.

Back on the highway, Stevie Wonder's funky synthesizer launched into *Superstition* on the radio. The song creeped him out, not only because he was superstitious. He could swear he heard his mom singing high harmony with Stevie. He turned it off.

Strange. Usually he only heard her at home. He believed she lived in the walls, although he couldn't pinpoint the exact spot. Lazlo told him that was impossible.

"Take your clozapine, Jaxon," he said, "and the voices will get better."

What Lazlo didn't understand was that he liked hearing his mom's voice. It helped him remember her. The clozapine dulled his memory, one reason he didn't take the medication like he was supposed to, that and it made him constipated and drool a lot.

He caved and refilled the prescription that morning, having recognized the withdrawal symptom of feeling off his rocker even more than usual.

*Good old mom*. He was eight years old the last night he saw her. She left him alone, saying she had to work, but he knew she was going to the Shady Grove Bar because he'd followed her there many times.

He didn't know exactly what went on inside because the windows were painted black, but it sounded like a party that never ended. Laughter and loud music poured out every time the door opened.

His mother always came home with a man. It was never the same man and Jaxon didn't like the way they looked. They were nothing like the men married to the respectable ladies on television. He wished that just once she would come home with someone like Donna Reed's husband, or even better, the Beav's dad, Ward Cleaver. He never met his real father. When he was in the nuthouse, he wrote a letter to Hugh Beaumont asking if it was him, but never heard back.

They'd go in her bedroom with a bottle of alcohol and lock the door. Inside they made horrible noises. One night Jaxon was convinced the man was hurting his mother, so he got a big knife from the kitchen, went to the door and gave it a booming kick. His feet were already huge.

"Come out with your hands up," he yelled.

But when the door swung open, it was his mother, holding a towel over her. He asked if she was alright, which turned out to be a bad question because she smacked him in the face and told him to get his little ass back to bed.

After that, Jaxon just hid in his room when his mother brought men home. That's what he planned to do the night she brought *three* men home, except this time they didn't go in the bedroom. They stayed in the living room. Jaxon crawled under his bed, where he sometimes slept, and held his ears.

The sounds were louder and meaner. The more his mother screamed, the harder he pressed his hands against his ears, until he thought his skull would crack. He bit his lip and tasted his blood for the first time.

When the screaming stopped, he heard only the three men. He crept from under the bed, careful not to step on the squeaky board, and cracked open the door.

He saw three naked men gathered around his mother's bare backside which was hanging over the couch. His mother acted like she was asleep, but how could anyone sleep with all that going on?

Jaxon crawled back under the bed, which turned out to be lucky because a few minutes later one of the men came into the room, turned the light on and stepped on the squeaky board. Jaxon followed a pair of scuffed snakeskin boots around the bedroom until the light went out and the house got quiet.

He stayed under the bed for a long time before deciding he didn't really care if his mother slapped him again because it didn't hurt that much the first time and he wanted to make sure she was okay.

"Mommy," he said, slipping into the living room. "Are you asleep?" He walked around the couch and discovered his mother wasn't asleep after all, but dead, with a broken neck and the left side of her head caved in.

A pewter bookend shaped like a clown that Jaxon bought her for Christmas lay on the floor covered in blood.

He sat on the couch next to her and watched television for seventeen hours until his Aunt Grace came and found both of them. They sent him to a hospital for three months where he refused to speak, after which he went back to the house to live with Aunt Grace and Uncle Nick. The stupid cops never found the men who killed his mother. They even accused him of doing it.

He thought he found them once at a topless bar in Daytona Beach, but it wasn't them and he ended up killing three innocent lawyers with a tire iron. One of them wore snakeskin boots. The court found him not guilty by reason of insanity and sent him to the state mental hospital. He stayed there for twelve years.

They let him out a year ago. During his exit interview, he asked Lazlo what he should do when he got out.

"Do?" Lazlo said with his annoying habit of answering questions with questions. "You do whatever you want to do. As long as you obey the law, of course."

"No, I mean what should I *do*? I've spent twelve years locked in a room while you and your cronies shoved pills down my throat. You told me when to eat, when to sleep and when to take a dump. What do I *do*? It's a jungle out there, Lazlo. Or so I've heard."

Lazlo smiled patronizingly.

"Just relax and have confidence in yourself, Jaxon. I know patients in your shoes who have gone on to lead happy and productive lives—provided they take their medication regularly. Remember our talks about that. The social worker will be checking on you."

"How many?"

"I beg your pardon."

"How many patients in my shoes do you know who have gone on to lead happy and productive lives?"

"I'm not sure. A few."

"A few? How many patients in my shoes have you actually known, Dr. Lazlo?"

"Enough."

"A thousand?"

"Not that many."

"A hundred."

"Perhaps," he sighed.

"So out of that hundred, a few have gone on to lead happy and productive lives? Is that *three*? Excellent number, but not very fucking many."

Lazlo threatened to put him in restraints if he used profanity, commenting that maybe Jaxon wasn't ready to get out.

Well, of course he wasn't. They both knew that. But they also knew it was the only way for Lazlo to be rid of him.

The interview ended with a pep talk.

"Just remember, Jaxon, as these things go, you're way above average."

He figured Lazlo told that to all his patients, but in his case it was true.

On release, he went back to the house. When they heard he was getting out, Aunt Grace and Uncle Nick moved without leaving a forwarding address.

It wasn't always easy being on his own. People out here didn't act the same as people in the hospital, which caused friction. Like the time he threatened the bank teller for saying "How are you today?" He thought she was mocking his mental illness. Lazlo said he had difficulties *relating*.

But that was all before he met *her*. He was doing so much better since then.

Jaxon knew powerful forces brought them together so he could make amends for not protecting his mother and maybe some other things, like killing the three lawyers and setting his high school on fire. They were bound together by the *Chain of Pain*. That's what he called it—the connection of suffering shared by all victims of The Crime.

At first he thought everyone could see the *Chain of Pain*. He learned otherwise while floating in a world famous glass bottom boat at Silver Springs, east of Ocala. He was feeling hostility in the gaze of a school of fish when he moved his leg and heard a scraping against the famous glass bottom.

When he looked down, what to his wondering eyes should appear but a silver chain with thick, gleaming links binding his leg to the ankle of a lady sitting across from him.

"Can you go to the bathroom with me?" he asked the woman when they returned to the dock.

He wasn't suggesting anything dirty. He just had to pee and figured he couldn't get to the bathroom unless she went too because of the chain. But her husband told the security guard, who called the police, and he almost ended up back in the mental hospital.

Lazlo bitched a blue streak about that one.

After that, he kept it to himself when he saw the *Chain of*

*Pain*, including a little while ago at the Orlando Airport when he dropped off the rental car to retrieve the New Yorker. The girl behind the counter had the *Chain of Pain* around her neck. It was gold this time, but there was no mistaking it. Jaxon just closed his eyes and boasted about the incredible mileage he racked up on the rental car.

A gas station sign said it was four o'clock and ninety-four degrees. The pancakes next to him smelled heavenly. He nudged the accelerator. He needed to get home and feed his guest to prepare for his visitor.

# 23

**DANNY PLOWED** the Beetle through torrents that turned the streets into rivers. The toy wipers were useless. He drove back to Hollywood from Coconut Grove at a crawl under the weight of a suffocating depression. At each step during the past two days, he swore things couldn't get any worse, only to find that they not only could, but did, with a ruthless regularity.

Now the very worst had happened. Sari was missing. And there wasn't a damn thing he could do about it. He'd get the flyers distributed and put Fink's investigator on her trail, a dozen investigators if that would help, but when all was said and done, he knew he was essentially helpless.

The fallen guardian angel had failed again.

Sari, the only true innocent of everyone involved in the whole mess.

Back at the Seabreeze Towers, a galvanized sky covered the beach like a helmet, but the rain had slackened. A rusty pickup truck occupied his reserved space. He motored in circles looking for a spot, but the lot was jammed. He parked next door at the Treasure Cove Hotel and hustled to the Seabreeze elevators.

Upstairs, he locked himself behind the metal door and

called Phil Drexler, a print shop owner and regular at the Tradewinds. He answered on the first ring. Danny gave a heavily censored explanation that a friend was missing and asked if Phil could print some flyers. "No problem," he said. "Bring it to the Tradewinds tonight and I'll have as many as you want first thing in the morning."

He entered Fink's number. He wanted Dizbo Skaggs in Coconut Grove as fast as possible. Troy was important, but this was Sari. He also needed Fink to pressure the cops to start searching for her. They weren't going to listen to the *Lottery Lunatic*.

The receptionist said Fink left for the day. He called his house, but got an answering machine reminding *No recovery, no fee.*

"Fink, it's me. Make sure you come to the Tradewinds today at happy hour. It's important."

He hung up, deflated. All that lottery money and he never bought any clout.

*Clout.* No one had more of it in South Florida than the *Miami Herald*. He got the graduate pamphlet from the kitchen counter and looked up DeLisha Ferguson, his high school journalism chum turned police reporter. The operator put him through to her at the City Desk.

"Ferguson."

In the background Danny could hear the barely restrained chaos of a city newsroom. "Dee, it's Danny Teakwell. Bet you didn't expect to be talking to me again so soon."

"Danny! Are you alright? I was just asking the Broward reporter about your case. What in the world happened? Is that the kind of thing you can ask someone charged with murder? What's the proper etiquette here?"

"I wish more people would ask. Most of them just look at you funny and run the other way, but since you did ask, none of it's true. Right now I don't understand it well enough to explain it."

He was tired of repeating that to friends. "I need your help. I don't know who else to ask."

"Ask away."

"Are you sure?"

"Damn right. I still owe you for staging that boycott when they tried to kick me out of Seminole when I got pregnant. I remember they threatened to kick you out too."

He remembered the boycott. They almost shut down the school.

"Do you remember Sari Hunter?"

"Your sweetie? Sure. I didn't know her well, but what I knew, I liked."

"She's missing." Danny explained how Sari disappeared a week earlier from her vending cart in Coconut Grove. "The police won't do anything because there's no actual proof of a crime."

"Well, it is true that most missing persons turn up okay."

"I know Sari. She wouldn't go away without telling her friends because she's such a worrier herself. Dee, I'm pretty sure something bad's happened."

If he told her everything he knew, he could present a stronger case, but he stayed vague. "I have some reasons. I just can't explain them right now. They're complicated. I was hoping you could …"

"Write a story about her being missing."

"Yeah. I know it's a lot to ask."

"I might be able to. I'll have to check it out first, but it sounds like a legitimate story."

"I'm sorry to put you on the spot, but I was thinking some media attention might pressure the police to do something, or maybe bring someone out of the woodwork who saw or knows something."

"It's happened before. Where do I get the details?"

He gave her Sondra Carmice's name and number. "She's Sari's best friend. They work together as sidewalk vendors. She can tell you everything."

"Sondra *C-a-r-m-i-c-e*. Okay. If I can get through to her tonight I might be able to get something in for tomorrow. Don't expect much. Check the Metro section. My editor isn't going to give it much room. It's not really big news. I mean, oh hell, there I go puttin' my foot in it."

"I know what you mean. Thanks, Dee. Your friendship means a lot."

"You mean a lot. Besides, this isn't a favor. I liked Sari. If she's missing, somebody should be doing something about it. In full disclosure, if this turns into a story involving you, I won't be able to keep you out of it."

"I wouldn't expect it. You're the good journalist you were meant to be. Don't worry about me. Write whatever you need to."

Danny clicked off the phone and felt a little better, like he had accomplished something. He went to the bedroom, stripped off his wet clothes and laid the damp flyer out to dry, so exhausted he could barely stand. He set the alarm for six and climbed in bed.

His eyes came to rest on his old acoustic guitar leaning in the closet. A memory crept across the boundary of long ago, sitting on the bed with Sari in high school, giving her a guitar lesson. They were playing rock star, hamming it up and laughing, until Sari carefully fingered and strummed an *E*-minor chord and looked up seriously.

"I want to play a song. I wrote it. Really it's a poem, but I kind of made it into a song using the chords you taught me. Don't laugh. Swear."

"I wouldn't laugh."

"Swear."

"I swear," he said, and crossed his heart.

"Okay. It's called *Forever Yesterday.*"

She began singing in a tentative voice. The words were cryptic as with all of Sari's poetry, but there was no mistake that it was about the night at the foot of the Sunset Pier when they lost their virginity together.

Danny still remembered the melody, a thousand chords away.

Maybe the air conditioner was turned too low because his teeth were chattering. He pulled the comforter over his head and curled into a fetal position, trying to restrain the terror spreading inside.

# 24

**THAT SONG AGAIN!** So weird the things you think about when your brain doesn't have anything to do. Even the words came back. *There's a song in the sky, a melody so wide, and when the night comes, on the wind, it sings forever.*

Sitting on the bed and playing the guitar. What a funny picture.

The clarity of the memory brought comfort that her brain cells still functioned. She hadn't eaten in three days.

Sari lay on the basement floor, staring up at the hole in the ceiling. It looked small from the floor, but she estimated it to be sixteen inches wide. At the rate she was shrinking, she calculated two more inches would give her a chance. That's all it would be, a chance. She still hadn't figured out how to raise herself closer to the ceiling, one reason she just took another spill.

She climbed up and back onto the aluminum ice chest. Either she had become immune to pain or her blistered toes had simply turned numb. If someone had asked her two weeks ago the top five things a person would need if abducted, shoes never would have come to mind. If she made it through this, she'd never take a pair for granted again.

She'd been standing on the cooler carving the escape hole with the rusty nail for seven ... she looked at the marks on the wall ... eight days.

Eight days since the monster approached her sidewalk cart and introduced himself as Detective Albert Thumpet of the Miami Police Department. Figures it would happen just when her life was going well again.

A week earlier she got an offer to publish her third poetry book from a small academic press. Publishing poetry didn't pay any bills, but it gave her more satisfaction than anything else. She never regretted ditching veterinary school after getting a biology degree.

She called it quits after lunch, anxious to get home and freshen up to go shopping for a dress for the high school reunion. She'd been acting like a school girl prepping for the prom, getting her hair cut and even trying to stop biting her nails. No expectations. Her only hope was that if she happened to lay eyes on the boy she'd loved since the fifth grade, he'd smile when he saw her.

The noise from behind startled her as she latched the padlock on the cart. She turned to find a large man with dark curly hair framing pale blue eyes, standing too close. Intuition buzzing, she snatched her bag and took off in the other direction.

"Sari Hunter?"

She stopped. "Who wants to know?"

"Miami P.D.," the man said, flashing a gold badge. "My name is Detective Thumpet. We need to talk. It might be better if we have a seat."

He waved a meaty hand at a shaded bench usually occupied by tourists eating ice cream.

Sari followed him, but remained standing. "What's this about?"

"Danny Teakwell."

She sat down. "Danny? What is it? Is he hurt?"

The imposter shook his head and smiled. "Mr. Teakwell's health is way above average. You, on the other hand, were almost toast."

"Excuse me?"

"We nabbed Teakwell a block from here an hour ago. A patrol officer observed him acting suspiciously and stopped to ask questions. A frisk turned up a loaded gun."

"Danny with a gun?" She laughed. "That's ridiculous."

"He was also carrying a suicide note. The note laid out a plan that had Teakwell shooting you and then offing himself. It took us a little while to nose around and find you."

"This is crazy, Detective …"

"Thumpet. Albert Thumpet."

She started to ask for his identification again, but the man kept talking.

"Apparently, his plan had something to do with someone named, let's see." He pulled a notepad from the pocket of a herringbone suit jacket. "Enya McKenzie. You know 'er?"

Enya's name sent a jolt. She feigned nonrecognition.

"Danny wouldn't hurt a fly. Maybe you arrested someone posing as Danny."

"'Fraid not. It's him. We're impounding his car around the corner right now if you want to see it. Volkswagen Beetle with a surfer sticker on the back."

That sounded like Danny. She walked with the man until they rounded the corner. She didn't see a car being impounded. Nothing was right. Who wears herringbone in Miami?

"Hey, can I see your identification again?"

"Absolutely. It's good for a pretty lady like you to be careful. The world is filled with wackos. You never know who you'll run into."

He reached in his jacket, but pulled out a black handgun instead of the badge. Putting his arm around her shoulder, he drew her close and stuck the gun in her ribs.

"Walk to that blue car and don't make a sound. One peep, I kill you, then Teakwell, then your whole family."

He moved her across the street to the car. When he popped the trunk, she tried to bolt, but he punched her in the stomach and threw her in. They drove for hours. She didn't know how many. When he finally stopped and the trunk opened, she was inside a house garage. He pushed her along a hallway and down some stairs to the basement.

"Now you and me are gonna have some fun," he said. "Take off your belt."

"No."

It came out firm and brave even though she was scared witless. But she knew from long ago what her response would be to sexual assault, ever since a scary afternoon in the fourth grade back in New Jersey.

The man closed in, waving the weapon in crazy circles. She backpedaled.

"*Hah!* I've got news for you, Sari Hunter. Two feet behind you is a wall made of high-quality cinder blocks. They're oldies, but goodies. Built to last. You're gonna be here a while, so you might as well relax. You're my new roommate."

She backed into the wall. Nowhere to go. She raised her fists.

He laughed like a hyena. "Scary Sari, if you have an above-average brain like I think you do, you know there's no point fighting. You'd be lucky to last ten seconds. But don't take my word for it. Decide for yourself, smart or dumb. The facts. One, I am six-four and weigh two-sixty, although I've been trying to lose a few pounds, and you I would guess are around five-seven, one-thirty. Is that right?"

Sari didn't answer.

"Close enough. So let's see, the math is kind of complicated, but if you subtract five-seven from six-four and one-thirty from two-sixty, then multiply by *three*, it means I could easily snap your scrawny neck without even getting a spot on my new herringbone jacket.

"Two, I'm holding a nine millimeter pistol loaded with fifteen rounds of ammunition that will make your insides look like a monkey that got hit by a tractor trailer. And three, hmm."

He scratched a pimple with the gun barrel. "Three, I have a track record, a résumé. I'm the man for the job when only the best in killing will do. Now take off your belt."

Sari turned over the choices. She knew he was right. Fighting wasn't going to save her. He'd already subdued her once and that was on a public street. But it didn't matter.

"You're not going to rape me. You'll have to kill me first."

She tensed, preparing for attack. Go for the balls!

Her captor bared yellow, crooked teeth and howled the hyena laugh. "Rape you? That's a good one, God. That's another good one on me. *Oh-man.*"

He pointed the gun at the ceiling like he was going to fire it, but pulled it back down.

"Scrary, raping you is not the point. Nothing personal. If I were a rapist, you'd be my first victim, and I mean that as a compliment. But I'm not."

"Then why do you want me to undress? Why are you pointing that gun at me?"

"This? I didn't say I wasn't going to kill you, but rape is an entirely different bad ending. I could hardly rape you and be *Enya's Avenger.*"

Enya's name again.

"And think what my mother would say. *Are you out of your fucking mind, son? After what the scums did to your mother?* No, rape isn't part of the plan, not even Plan B. I need your belt because, properly used, belts make above-average weapons and escape tools. Shoes too. And whatever's in your pockets."

When she hesitated, he pointed the gun at her head.

"I'm not going to rape you, but if you don't do what I say in three seconds, you'll be nothing but an unraped fucking memory."

She undid her belt and dropped it on the floor, then forked over her keys and wallet.

"Shoes."

She kicked them off.

"And socks."

"Why socks? They can't be used for anything."

"Do you have any idea how many bodies are found every single day with socks stuffed down their throats?"

"But that's ridiculous. How would I—"

He raised the gun again. "One, two—"

She glared, lifting one foot then another to pull off the socks, disgusted at having to put her bare feet on the grimy floor.

"Very good," he said. "Now like I said, we're gonna have some fun." He nodded to a torn, stained mattress behind her.

She stiffened. Liar.

"Have you ever played the *Game of Life*?"

In the center of the mattress sat a shrink-wrapped rectangular box. It really was the *Game of Life*, the classic board game.

"Family fun for more than thirty years. I thought you might want to learn a few things about Life while you're here. The entire wisdom of the universe is in that little box. I have some errands to run. That'll give you time to bone up on the rules. I'll bring food back and we'll play our first game.

"Study the instructions, but don't get your hopes up. I'm the best player of Life in the universe, unless you count God. Satan's good too. That's a match-up I'd like to see. Can you imagine the pay-per-view? Be ready to play when I get back."

He gathered her belongings and retreated up the stairs, the thick boards bowing under his weight.

"Don't be So-Sad-Sari," he said at the top. "I spent twelve years in a room a lot smaller than this. It wasn't always fun, but I became an expert on Life."

The door closed and a lock latched. Then another one. Then a third. The door had three shiny gold deadbolt locks, each spaced a foot apart.

She immediately began searching for a way out. The door was metal. The cinder block walls were solid, like he said.

Two small windows with no glass sat like cat eyes on the longest wall, but they were three feet below ground inside a window well and pegged with sturdy bars in fresh cement. Through a door was a tiny bathroom with a filthy sink and a toilet with no top or lid. No window.

A rusted coal-burning furnace took up space under the stairs. Soot rained down when she stuck her head in. The vent was too narrow for escape, but the furnace did give a clue about her location. North Florida, maybe Georgia. That would coincide with the long drive.

The floor was poured concrete. No tunneling.

That left only the ceiling. The boards were old. Some had water stains and spots where the wood looked rotted.

The room contained only three movable objects: the mattress, board game and an old aluminum ice chest, like the one her family used to take camping. Standing on top of it, she could barely reach the ceiling on her toes. The sides of the cooler were slanted, making it impossible to get extra height by flipping it vertically. The mattress was a queen-size, too big to put on top of the cooler and too mushy to put under it. She tried both.

Probing the boards with her fingernails she found a soft spot near the corner. She searched for something to use as a tool, but discovered only a rusty nail sticking halfway out of a floor joist.

It took a while to wiggle it loose. Her fingers were bleeding even before she chipped the first sliver from the ceiling. She only got to pry away a few more before the putt-putt car returned.

So began her daily ritual of sweeping up the wood chips from the ceiling and hiding them in the furnace. At last count, not including the small splinters, she had twelve hundred and forty-seven of them. She knew keeping count was nutty, but it was a tangible measure of progress, and there was nothing else to do each day when the room darkened.

He returned that first day with a bag of food.

"Black's a good color for you," he said gesturing at the soot. "Good funeral color too. Now let's play *Life*."

He strutted to the mattress. "Wait a minute! This game hasn't even been opened. Unless you have x-ray vision you didn't listen and study the instructions. Too bad for you. Your first lesson in Life."

He dangled the bag of food in front of her.

"The problem with you and a lot of other people is you don't take Life seriously enough. Unless you want to spend your last days getting as skinny as that spider crawling up your leg, you'll be ready to play when I come back in the morning."

He stalked out and slammed the door. The locks latched again.

She slapped away the spider. That bag smelled good. She was hungry. If playing the game was the only way to get food, she didn't see another choice until she found a way out.

At the window she tugged on the bars and craned to see the band of blue sky above the window well. The sun was setting behind the house. Not much, but it helped with her directional bearings. Disorienting not to know where she was.

She went back to the mattress, tore off the shrinkwrap, and read the game instructions in the fading light. Not complicated. Same game she loved as a kid. She played it all the time with her family, and Danny. Cruise through life in a plastic car, choose a career, marry, have kids and try to make more money than your opponents before retiring rich or poor.

It started to rain as darkness approached. Water ran down the wall through the barred windows to a drain in the middle of the floor. She dragged the mattress to one side to keep it dry and curled up on it. Invisible creatures scratched and scurried around her.

She curled tighter and shut them out by trying to think of a better escape plan than carving a hole in the ceiling. But she couldn't come up with anything. The only other way out was through the metal door with the three locks.

She'd stay alert for other opportunities, but in the meantime needed a plan she could invest her faith and energy in, something to give her hope. He said he planned to keep her there a while.

Early the next morning the monster unlocked the door and came down to play the game.

They sat on the mattress with the game board between them. He brought breakfast, at least that's what he called it. Twinkies and a liter of root beer. She didn't complain. Her last food was a banana she had for breakfast the day before. She insisted she had to eat before she could properly focus on the game. No way was she taking the chance of him leaving with the food again.

When she was ready, Sari instinctively picked up the blue car, same one she always used as a kid.

"Hey, don't be such a Grabby Gary, Scary Sari," he said, then waved it off. "You want blue? Fine, but I have news. Car color rarely figures into game strategy."

Next they chose a destiny: college or career.

"I choose college, obviously," he said. "Usually, we spin for high number to see who goes first, but since you're my guest, you go."

"Thank you, um, I don't know your name." She would learn as much as possible.

"You can call me Albert. Albert Thumpet. We might have gone to high school together."

"Is that your real name?"

"Real enough. Quit asking questions and play the game." The big black gun stuck from a holster in his waistband.

She twirled the spinner. It landed on seven.

"*Hah!* You lose your turn."

"What?"

"You spun counterclockwise. You have to spin clockwise." He rubbed his hands. "Ha ha. It's in the rules."

"No way." She picked up the instructions. "I read these twice. It doesn't say anything about—"

"First page, right column. Game Play. All players spin for the highest number and play continues *clockwise*."

"They're not talking about the spin. They're talking about the order of the players."

"*Du-uh*. The *players* go clockwise because the *spins* go clockwise. They go together. The whole universe goes clockwise, except when it goes backwards of course. My turn and I spin a ... three! *O-men*. Good for me, bad for you."

He pulled a *Life* tile, the best way to clean up in the game, and set it face down. "You go."

She spun and got a ten.

"Say no to drugs," he said for no apparent reason, until she counted out the spaces and saw the words on the square.

"I've been saying no to them for years, but they keep cramming them down my throat anyway."

On his next move, he chose a career. "One problem with this game is it doesn't have any cards for what I really want to be."

"What's that?" Any insight could be useful.

"Race car driver. Or Pope. Here we go. *Accountant*. Yes, it is definitely my day to be an accountant."

Sari spun and counted four spaces.

"You lose your turn again."

"I can read."

As the game progressed, Sari made a little money, bought a cabin and invested in a stock certificate, but gambled by not buying insurance, which was a mistake because a tornado hit the cabin. That sent the monster into a fit.

"You've got to have insurance! It's a simple fact of Life. The worst always happens. If you don't know that by now, you'll find out soon enough."

"What does that mean?"

"No reason to ruin the game for you. Play on."

When it came time for him to get married, he launched into singing *Here Comes the Bride*.

She wasn't learning anything except that he was insane, which she had already figured out. "How long am I going to be here, Albert?"

"None of your business. Play."

"Why did you bring me here?"

"Because I have exciting plans for you and your boyfriend."

"I don't have a boyfriend."

"And I don't know a scum named Danny Teakwell."

"Danny's not my boyfriend."

"Close enough."

"What are your plans?"

"My secret. We all have secrets. Even you, Scary Sari. Settled. Now play."

By the end of the game he amassed a fortune and she was in debt. He congratulated her on playing hard and never giving up. Then he said he had more errands to run.

"Here." Blushing, he handed her a bag with a travel pack of tampons, three bars of hotel soap and a sawed-off toothbrush and toothpaste.

"Where's the rest of the toothbrush."

"Sorry. Above-average weapon."

"Could I, um, get a razor to shave my legs?"

"Nice try, but *wa-ay* above-average weapon."

"How about some books? Could you bring me some books to read, since you said I'm going to be here a while?"

She was already thinking of ways to raise herself closer to the ceiling. She could stack the books on the cooler.

"Books? Well, a mind is a terrible waste. I'll think about it," he said, then left.

She immediately went to work on the ceiling, prying away toothpicks of wood with the rusty nail.

The next day he insisted on playing the game again. His game face was intense, but he looked up suddenly and said, "Answer this. Are you in love with Teakwell?"

"You don't answer my questions so why should I answer yours?"

"Because I will kill you easy as an ant. Answer the question."

"No, I'm definitely not in love with Danny Teakwell."

"Liar," he said, and went back to the game.

From his repeated comments about Danny and Enya, his obsession became apparent. He had some tie to Enya McKenzie and blamed Danny for her death. *Enya's Avenger*, that's what he called himself.

But what was the connection? He said he went to Seminole High. Maybe he was Enya's boyfriend, although she had a hard time picturing it. He was more like the weird guy carrying on a secret crush from a distance. Could he be a relative? Did Enya have a brother?

"How do you know Danny and Enya?"

"What I know could fill a room bigger than this. It could fill your head and more."

He stayed silent after that. When they added up the money

at the end of the game, Sari won. He stomped up the stairs in a snit.

The morning of day four he came down carrying a paper sack and dripping bag of ice.

"I'm taking a trip. Be back tomorrow. There's a cooler over … Hey, where's my cooler?"

Sari's heart jumped. "That one over there?" She pointed to the other side of the room.

"What's it doing over there? I always keep it over here."

"I use it to sit on."

"Hmph. I guess that's okay. Just don't damage it. It belonged to my mother. Put this food in it. Here's some ice."

She accepted the bags, careful to hide the damage to her fingers.

The sack held two boxes, each one containing two pieces of fried chicken and a bisquit. She ate one meal after he left and saved the second for lunch the next day.

But he didn't come back that day like he said. Or the next day or the next one. He'd been gone four days.

She had worked on the escape hole the entire time, stopping only when it got too dark to see. What seemed fanciful at the beginning appeared more plausible by the hour as the hole slowly widened, but the intense effort and lack of fuel finally overcame her.

The sun was settling lower behind the house, shadowing her view of the moldy boards. She stretched her neck and felt lightheaded.

Too many falls already. She stepped off the cooler, gathered the splinters and put them in the furnace. The dizziness didn't go away. She went to the mattress to lie down. So hungry.

# 25

THE ALARM nagged Danny awake at six. He splashed water on his face and rode the elevator down to the Tradewinds to meet Fink.

A loud buzzing shook the Tradewinds as he approached, drowning out the whoosh of the ocean. Danny scrubbed a portal in the salt-glazed glass. The place was swarming with complete strangers. He couldn't spot Fink or even Grady. Tabloid revelers?

*That's the Tradewinds Lounge on Hollywood Beach, where happy hour runs every weekday from five to seven.*

His televised spiel to Janet Traynor. He'd rather get repeatedly punched in the face than go in, but had to talk to Fink about Sari and get the flyer to Phil Drexler. Maybe no one would recognize him.

Keeping his head low, he skirted the crowd. He spotted John the Diver and Kenny Hooks at a corner table and tacked through the swarm in their direction. Along the way he passed Ray Hartford, the surfing dermatologist, expounding on the dangers of skin cancer to a group of tourists with lobster flesh. He reached the table after shouldering between two overweight men in skintight pants.

"Hi guys."

"You iguana-sucking sonofabitch," John the Diver said.

Kenny Hooks was either too blitzed or depressed to speak.

Danny shrugged. "I was just trying to give Grady some free advertising. How was I supposed to know so many people watched Janet Traynor?"

J.D. waved morosely. "These people have invaded my sanctuary. They're in my living room."

"Don't be so selfish. Think of Grady. This must be like heaven for him."

Glass splintered behind the bar. "Dammit to hell." Grady's unmistakable brogue.

A light blinded Danny from the side. He almost tripped over a guy in an Elvis costume pointing a camcorder.

"Turn that damn thing off," Danny shouted, but the man kept filming.

J.D. stood up and accidentally knocked the camera to the floor after which Kenny Hooks, attempting to assist, negligently knocked a bar stool on top of it.

"Thanks, guys," Danny whispered. "Appreciate that."

"Shove it," J.D. said, and sat back down.

Danny patted his shoulder. When this was over, he'd make it up to them with a big party—assuming he was alive and not in prison.

"Danny!" Grady bellowed from behind the bar. The utterance had a hypnotic effect on the rowdy crowd, which fell silent, all eyes on Danny.

Grady shrugged sheepishly. "May I have a word?"

The throng parted as Danny made his way to the bar.

Somewhere in the back a slurred voice shouted *Speech!* The request sparked a chorus of *Speech! Speech!* accompanied by a foot-stomping, hand-clapping rhythm section.

Grady wrung his apron, mouthing apologies.

*Speech! Speech!* Even the marlin on the wall seemed to be flapping its lips.

Danny reached the bar and sat on a stool. The chant continued.

"I was just gonna say hello," Grady said. "How about a beer? On the house."

"Sure, Grady. That would be nice."

The partiers let out a hurrah as Grady popped open a Red Stripe and handed it to Danny.

"Cheers!" declaimed a foursome dressed in pastel golf jackets.

Above the chanting, Danny heard the high-pitched voice of Larry Dworkin, a timeshare salesman who insisted on calling everyone by nicknames. "Teekie, Teekie, Teekie."

"Grady, don't these people realize I'm accused of torturing and murdering someone?"

"Ah, well, the people who know you can't take it seriously and the rest of these folks are probably just insane."

A fat guy in Bermuda shorts chewing a cigar shushed the hoard. Someone pulled the plug on the jukebox. Danny set the beer bottle on the bar with a clink. He spotted Shannon across the bar, a hand clasped to her mouth. A few feet in front of her a woman in her nineties crouched expectantly in a miniskirt, flashing two thumbs up.

He couldn't stand any more. He twirled the bar stool.

"You are all a bunch of sick bastards!"

Applause and cheers. The guy in the Bermuda shorts slapped him on the back, sending his ribs into pain-zone nine.

Appeased, the crowd backed off and resumed partying. Danny rubbed his eyes.

Shannon came over to place a lengthy drink order and kissed him on the neck.

"The natives may be restless, but I still love ya. I've already made enough in tips to pay for my books this semester."

"Don't let the boys bother you," Grady said. "They're grousing now, but this will give 'em something to talk about for the next five years."

Larry Dworkin ponied up to the bar and summoned *El Grando* to pour him another draft.

Danny spotted Fink's flaring red hair and three-piece suit across the room, at a table with a well-endowed brunette in white cutoffs and a bikini top.

He saluted the barkeep and maneuvered through the congestion, dodging pats along the way.

"Danny!" Fink said. "Pull up a chair. This is Marisa. Marisa, this is my friend and client, Danny Teakwell."

"You're even cuter in person than on TV," Marisa burbled.

Fink frowned.

"Wanna dance?" she asked.

Fink's frown turned to a pout.

"So, Marisa, how were you lucky enough to land the table here with Counselor Finkel? The owner just told me women have been asking about his availability all night. I said I'd check to see if there was anything going on between you two."

"No kidding?" Fink said. "Asking about me?"

"Oh yeah." It was a lie, but had its intended effect as Marisa studied Fink in a new light. "Of course, it's understandable. Mr. Finkel is one of the most prominent attorneys and bachelors in Broward County."

Marisa put her hand on Fink. "Wanna dance?" she asked.

"Some other time, honey."

She made a face and excused herself.

"So which ones were asking about me?" Fink asked giddily. "Point some of them out."

"I'm not sure. I think you should go dance with Marisa, but first we need to talk. Sari's disappeared."

"Disappeared? What are you talking about?"

Danny explained his trip to Coconut Grove in a measured voice. There was no in-between on this one.

"Her friend says she's been gone a whole week."

"I don't know what to say. How are you handling it?"

He shook his head. "I need your help. We need to get Skaggs down to the Grove looking for Sari. Tonight if possible."

"What about Thumpet and Troy? Maybe I can hire someone else to look for Sari. We need Skaggs."

"Hire someone else to look for them. You said Skaggs was good and I want him looking for Sari. Can you call him?"

"I'll try, but I have to warn you, he's never home. I don't even know where he lives. He's like a shadow. Gives me a new phone number almost every month. I leave messages and he gets back to me. But I'll call. Sari missing. Damn."

Danny drained the beer. At the next table, the D'Angelo brothers were doing their goofy shtick for a pair of women wearing Tradewinds teeshirts that had been fading on a shelf for five years.

"And you need to talk to the police about it. Try to get them looking for Sari. Do anything you can. I think her disappearance has something to do with my case."

"Not another conspiracy theory."

"Think about it. If you were right that this is all about revenge over what happened to Enya, it's not implausible. The killer evens the score with Mangrum by killing him. With me, he takes a different approach, prolongs the agony by framing me for Mangrum's death and taking Sari. There'd be no better way to hurt me than hurting Sari."

Fink sucked on his piña colada, frowning.

"How would he even know about you and Sari? You said you haven't had contact with her since high school."

"That's true. So it would have to be someone with information dating back that far. Maybe another member of our class is in on it, a real one."

"I know you're on edge here, and I feel for you, but don't you think the odds are better that if something happened to Sari, it was some random act of ... some random act that has nothing to do with your situation? Better yet, she probably just snuck off for a vacation without telling anyone. She'll be back tomorrow wondering what the excitement is all about."

Someone grabbed his shoulder. Danny turned to bawl out another intruder before recognizing Shannon's tell-tale purple fingernails.

"There's a phone call for you," she said.

"Here? It's probably another reporter. Tell them I'm not home."

"Grady thinks it might be important."

He looked and saw Grady stabbing a finger emphatically at the phone.

"I'll be right back, Fink. Call Skaggs while I'm gone. There's a payphone in the back."

Fink pulled a cellular telephone from his lapel pocket.

"Got it taken care of right here. I told you I was joining the big leagues. This is the new thing. Some day everyone will have one of these babies, but as of right now, I am not everyone."

"Whatever. Just call Skaggs."

Danny snaked through the dancers as Bob Marley sang *Buffalo Soldier* on the jukebox. Grady held the phone to his chest, tapping ice tongs on the bar. Danny joined him in the middle of the oak rectangle through the swinging door.

"Who is it?" he asked above the din.

"Says he's an old friend, but wouldn't give his name. I thought he might be another crackpot. Told him you weren't here, offered to take a message. He said, *Tell him it's about Sari Hunter.* That got my attention."

Danny's too. "Hello? This is Danny Teakwell. Who is this?"

An incoherent rumble.

"Speak up. I can't hear you."

"Danny. It's Troy."

"Troy?"

"Yeah, it's me."

"Are you okay?"

"Right now, but I need to see you. Right away."

"Where are you?"

"Up in Jacksonville, where I live. You need to come up here tonight."

"Tonight? What's going on? Did you say something about Sari?"

"I can't talk about it over the phone. I need to see you."

Danny thought he detected quavering in his voice, but couldn't be sure through the noise.

"I booked you a flight at the Fort Lauderdale airport. It leaves at eight. Your ticket's waiting at the counter."

Danny looked at the neon beer clock. Already quarter to seven. "I don't know if you've heard about my situation, but I have kind of a full plate down here right now. I can't just pick up and leave for Jacksonville. Let's talk over the phone. What's this all about?"

"Danger. For everyone."

"Who's everyone?"

"You, me … and Sari Hunter."

"Tell me what you know about Sari."

"There's no time. You can't miss that plane. I'll explain it all when you get here. Listen carefully. Take a cab from the airport to the Riverwalk. It's downtown on the St. John's River. The taxi driver will know it. Just tell him you want to be let off where it starts, near the big fountain. Go right. Follow the walkway. I'll meet you along the way. Come alone, and don't tell anyone. It would only make things worse."

"I'll come, but first tell me if Sari's okay. Troy! Troy!"

The line went dead.

*There's no time.* What did that mean?

He dumped the phone in Grady's hands and pulled out Sondra Carmice's flyer.

"I have to go out of town for the night," he said, handing over the paper.

"You can't do that! You'd violate your bail. I was sitting right there in the courtroom when the judge read it to you. She said you can't leave the county."

Danny grabbed his shoulders. "There's no time to explain. Look at the flyer."

"Flyer, schmy—" Grady glanced down and stiffened. "Danny, no."

A man wearing sandals over black socks tapped Grady's shoulder, requesting a beer.

"Have you no decency, man?" Grady ranted. "A woman's missing!"

The man skulked away.

"I need your help," Danny said.

"Say it."

"Get this flyer to Phil Drexler. He's gonna make copies. In the morning, see if you can get some of the boys to take them down to Coconut Grove. Tell them to post and hand out as many as they can."

"It's done. But what about you? What's in Jacksonville? Who was that on the phone?"

"Troy Stoddelmeyer. An old friend from high school and a big part of the puzzle. This could turn out to be a good thing, a breakthrough. I have to find out."

Hunched in his soaked apron, Grady Banyon, the strongest person he ever knew, looked old and fragile.

"Danny boy." He couldn't disguise the hoarseness. "Be careful. Even an alley cat only has nine lives."

"I have two left, Grady. I've been keeping track. I'm gonna be okay. Tell Fink I found Troy and went to see him. I'll call both of you as soon as I can. I promise. Take care of that flyer."

Grady tightened his grip.

"See if you can fix Fink up with a date, someone not too high-strung." He hugged him and sprinted for the door, dodging the drunken patrons like a punt returner.

# 26

**THE SOUND** of the car brought her head off the mattress. It wasn't the same compact he took her in. She lived in the trunk of that car for hours with nothing to do but listen to the putt-putt motor. Since then, she'd heard it come and go from the house many times. The motor coming up the driveway roared.

She went to the barred windows and was about to shout for help when she heard him. Singing.

The Carpenters? He better have food.

Several minutes passed. She sat on the mattress blowing on her fingers, listening to his heavy footsteps plod back and forth. What was he waiting for? Did he forget she was there? She wanted to scream, but wouldn't.

Finally the triple deadbolts clanked open and he bounded down the stairs.

"Well, if it isn't Scary Sari. Look what I brought you."

He held up two plastic bags. She caught a whiff of something sweet, buttery. It took all her will not to reach out and try to grab them.

"Sorry about the wait. Despite careful planning, I ran into some snags on my trip. But *I'm ba-ack*. Hungry?"

She glared.

"You're in luck because I brought way more than enough food to fill that little stomach of yours."

"So let's have it."

"There's a catch."

She tried to hide her disappointment, but couldn't.

"Don't be So-Sad-Sari. There's always a catch. Surely you've learned at least that much from Life. Before I give you this scrumptulicious lunch, you have to guess what's in the bags. We'll play *Let's Make a Meal*. I'll be the host. Guess what's behind Bag Number One."

Exhaustion combined with hunger and humiliation to bring tears. She lowered her head so he couldn't see them.

"Go ahead, guess."

"I'm not guessing," she said.

"I said guess!"

She shook her head, not looking up.

"Suit yourself," he said and started to leave.

"Muffins?"

"*Hah!* I thought you'd change your mind. Not bad, but *wrong*. Guess again."

The smell was familiar, but she wasn't thinking clearly. She studied the bags. No markings. "Donuts?"

"Wrong again. One more chance. Will it be third time's a charm or three strikes and you're out? Hurry. Time's running out. Dink-donk, dink-donk."

"Give me a hint."

"Say please."

"No."

"Fine, I was talking to the raccoons on the way in and they mentioned how much they would enjoy a high-quality franchise restaurant meal if the stubborn prisoner in the basement didn't want it." He started for the stairs again.

"Please."

"Okay. Here's the clue. It's the kind of food that when you get really mad at someone, you want to pound him into one."

"Pancakes?"

"Easy clue, but congratulations anyway."

He gave her the bags. Unpacking them, she found two styrafoam containers and a quart of milk. Each container held a stack of pancakes. She salivated.

"I kept one stack for myself. I love pancakes. My mother used to make them for me every Sunday."

She took several swigs of the milk. It tasted luxurious. She searched the bags for utensils, aware the monster was studying her.

"Where are the utensils?"

"So-Sorry-Sari. Utensils can be used to hurt people. My best friend at the nuthouse, Cracky Glimicker, used a plastic spoon from a yogurt snack to scoop out an attendant's eyeball. We never give them to our patients, er, *clients*." He laughed the hyena laugh. "You have to eat with your hands."

More debasement. He usually wasn't this bad. Something must have happened.

Powdered sugar covered the pancakes. Adding butter and syrup she folded them like a sandwich and took a bite. So smooth and creamy.

She forced herself to chew slowly. When she picked up the milk again, she noticed him ogling between her legs and twisted away.

"What happened to your fingers and toes?"

She froze mid-bite.

"Looks like a bear's been gnawing on them. But there aren't any bears in this basement. At least I don't think so. I know what's going on."

She held the pancakes in front of her face to hide her panic.

"Trying to claw through the cinder blocks. Not too smart."

"Wouldn't you try to escape?"

"Of course. I tried every day in the mental hospital, but this is a maximum security basement. You're not going anywhere."

"Albert," she said, taking another bite. "Could you tell me how much longer I'll be here?"

"From now on it's Mr. Thumpet. You may be here long or short. This is just a suggestion, Scalaria, but if I were you I'd worry less about how long I was going to be here and more about whether I'll be breathing when I leave."

"The reason I'm asking is that it gets really boring down here all day. Before, I asked for some books and you said you'd think about it."

Even if she finished the escape hole, there was no way to grab the boards without something higher to stand on.

"I've thought about it and don't really see how they could be used as above-average weapons."

He tapped his forehead. "Books, books, books. Okay."

"Thank you." She finished the first stack of pancakes and spread syrup over the the second. She'd never eaten so many pancakes in her life.

"I ran into a couple of your old friends on my trip. Remember a scum named John Mangrum?"

*Mangrum.* "I knew him once."

"Well, you don't know him anymore. He had some repair work done and it didn't turn out too good. He's a deadhead now, and I'm not talking about driving that train high on cocaine."

"John Mangrum is dead?"

"And guess who did it?"

"You."

"Your boyfriend!"

"I told you I don't have a boyfriend." She already felt strength returning.

"You know who I'm talking about. Teakwell killed Mang-scum. The corrupt judge let him out on bail, but he's on his way to getting squashed by the wheels of justice. With any luck, he'll end up strapped to Old Sparky. In the meantime, he's becoming a major pain in my ass. I had a fight with him in a graveyard last night."

Raving looney. "Why do you want to hurt Danny? Is it about Enya?"

He leaped to his feet and began circling. "Is it about Enya? *Du-uh!* Everything is about Enya. If you can't ask smarter questions than that, forget it."

"Danny's a good person. He didn't mean to hurt Enya."

Her head snapped back. He had her by the hair. The pancakes fell to the floor.

"And the scums didn't mean to hurt my mother," he screamed in her face.

"Enya didn't deserve to have bad things done to her any more than my mother did—probably less. But maybe you do, Sari Hunter. Maybe I was wrong. Maybe you'd like to be introduced to my above-average weenicker."

A disgusting sound erupted in his throat. She tried to pull away, but he held her in an iron grip. She closed her eyes just as the wad of spit pelted her cheek. He pushed her head down sharply and resumed circling.

"Let's get one thing straight, Scar—"

Sari clamped both arms around his ankles and hammered her shoulder into his legs, getting traction digging her feet into the mattress. The monster toppled forward like a stone statue.

Before he could react, she scrabbled up his legs and across his back until her teeth—her only weapon—were even with his neck. His broad shoulders started to rise.

She closed her eyes and sunk her teeth in. He roared. The blood sickened her. She spit and tried to bite again. But before she could, he rolled onto his back, crushing her beneath him, then rolled again and stood up with her hanging on as if she weighed nothing at all.

She let go with one arm and pawed his face. A fingertip found a socket and dug in. He howled. *She had him*. She pushed and … the room started spinning. What was happening?

Her fingers unclenched, flailing uselessly against the stale air. She couldn't fight off the feeling. Her head dipped like a bird with a broken neck. She let loose and slid to the floor. Someone threw a black curtain around her.

"*Hah!*"

The slur echoed in darkness. Eyes welded shut, on her back. Sinking.

"Good news and bad news," said the monster from far away. "I'm not going to kill you for giving me the hickey of the century. I've tasted my own blood many times, so you're lucky I'm probably the most understanding person in the world when it comes to that.

"The bad news is that the powder on your pancakes wasn't sugar. I have an important visitor coming and she'd get jealous if she knew about you, so you have to go to sleep for a while. Sweet dreams!"

\* \* \*

Sari was tied to a long table in a ballroom, surrounded by platters of exotic, aromatic food. Masked men and women in gowns and tuxedoes twirled to a discordant pipe organ playing crazy carnival music.

The music stopped suddenly and a man in a black cape leaned over her. "Are you hungry, Sari?" Yellow eyes glowed behind the holes in his mask.

Sari shrunk away. Murmuring filled the room.

A forked tongue flicked his lips.

"Are you sure?"

Her back felt hot. She smelled smoke.

The man picked up a knife and an apple. "Then say good-bye, Sari."

The haunting music started again and everyone sang. *Say good-bye, Sari. Say good-bye, Sari. Say good-bye, Sari.*

Her eyes opened.

"Do you have to say good-bye so soon?"

"Yes, I have to go."

Voices. Outside. She tried to lift her head, but her neck was an iron fence post. Moving her lips brought no sound. Through the medicated fog she struggled to concentrate on the words.

"When will I see you again?" The monster.

"I'll be back next week." A woman's voice.

"I don't want to wait until next week."

"You'll be fine."

"Easy for you to say."

"Just remember what we talked about."

"Alright. Good-bye, Enya."

Even in her sedated condition, the name caused Sari to twitch.

"I told you, never call me that name."

A car door slammed. The engine started and the car accelerated rapidly down the driveway.

"Hey, you forgot your flowers!"

# 27

**IN THE BACK** of a deathtrap taxi rattling south on I-95 from the Jacksonville airport, Danny's brain swirled with questions. The driver fiddled with a staticky radio until he found a country station. They sliced into the heart of the city on a narrow bridge. Geometric highrise buildings made of glass marked downtown on the left. Night had fallen. The wide, dark waters of the St. Johns River moved beneath him.

What did Troy know about Sari? Did he know Thumpet? How? Questions big and small. How could Troy Stoddelmeyer, slacker of the century, afford to buy him a first-class plane ticket?

The taxi veered right off the interstate under another bridge, hooked and coasted to a circular drive.

"There it is," the driver drawled. "Riverwalk. Ain't nothing happening here on a Tuesday night though."

Danny saw the outline of a large fountain, dark and silent. Troy said there would be a big fountain. He pulled out a wad of bills and paid the driver, glad he had the presence of mind to grab his cash stash from the condo before heading to the airport.

His sneakers spanked conspicuously as he rounded the

fountain, passed a sculpture of circular metal pipes and came to the entrance to the Riverwalk, a meandering riverside path constructed of rough-hewn timber.

A map under plexiglass said it was 1.2 miles long. Troy said he'd meet him along the way. Why all the cloak and dagger?

Senses on high alert, he started walking. He passed under another bridge. A klieg light made it impossible to miss a sign offering tips for protecting manatees. The path zagged right. He followed and almost ran into three teenagers wearing ball caps turned sideways. "Wazzup?" one said. They kept walking. After that, it was still and quiet.

The taxi driver was right. Whatever sightseers came to the Riverwalk on a Tuesday were gone. He didn't see another soul.

So where was Troy? He recreated their conversation. He hadn't talked to Troy in twenty years. The killer had impersonated Thumpet. Could he mimic Troy? No, he decided. Troy's voice was imprinted at an early age. So where was he?

He walked for several minutes, ribs throbbing. Nothing. He stopped at another sign. A *You Are Here* arrow showed he was already at the halfway point.

The more he walked, the farther the living world got left behind. The lights on the opposite bank disappeared. He could smell the coffee from the Maxwell House factory. The Gator Bowl's light stanchions spread like pterodactyl skeletons.

The path jinked again. The lamp poles were older and there were fewer of them. He passed a sidewalk exiting the Riverwalk next to a row of shops.

The lights were out up ahead. The only thing he could make out was the outline of warehouses in the moonlight. He must be near the end.

He waded into the darkness until a scuffing sound brought him to a halt. A shadow occupied the path ahead, darker than the darkness around it. At first he thought it was a trash can.

He took a couple more steps and saw it was a person, huddled against the wall, knees pulled to his chest.

"Troy?" The figure didn't move. "Troy! Is that you?"

No movement. He edged forward, half-expecting the thing to spring to life like something from a low-budget horror flick. The shops were built to the edge of the walkway, blocking the moonlight and any avenue of escape. On the other side, nothing but water.

He got close enough to make out a hooded parka, camouflaged, the kind hunters wear.

"Hello?" No response.

Finally close enough to touch the parka, he saw a paper bag holding a bottle between the thing's legs. Gentle snoring fluttered from under the hood.

Just a wino. He laughed at his jitteriness, but the instant he relaxed and refocused on the path, hands clamped his ankle.

A trap! The camouflaged man was sprawled across the deck, tugging at his leg with both hands. Danny slammed his loose foot onto the man's exposed wrists. He shrieked.

He was about to deliver another stomp, but didn't need it. The attacker let go, moaning, fingers twitching on the planking. Danny grabbed the parka and rolled him over. Fist raised, he yanked back the hood.

A pasty face stared up through rheumy eyes. "Don't hurt me. Please don't hurt me."

"Who the hell are you?"

"I ain't no one. I'm just Vernon. Vernon Stack. I didn't mean no harm. My hand, my hand."

"Why did you grab my ankle?"

"I just wanted a cigarette. I woke up and saw you going by. No one passes here at night and I—I just wanted a cigarette, that's all. My hand," he blubbered.

Danny let go of the parka.

"Jesus, you scared me."

He pulled out his cash and dropped a twenty in the panhandler's lap.

"Here, go buy a carton, but try just asking next time. You're going to get hurt a lot worse if you go around grabbing people in the dark."

But the man had already forgotten the injury. "God bless you," he said, studying the bill with wonderment.

Danny frowned and shook his head. He'd had enough of the Riverwalk. But he made it this far, might as well go to the finish line. When did his return flight leave? He was in such a rush he never checked.

"You got a lighter, Vernon?"

"Yeah, but no ciggies."

Danny uncrumpled the ticket stuffed in his back pocket. "Could you give me some light?"

Vernon flicked on a disposable lighter and held out the flame.

It was a one-way ticket.

Fighting to calm his rattled nerves, Danny left Vernon Stack behind, still holding up the twenty and giving thanks to the Almighty.

A chain-link fence topped with barbed wire announced an unceremonious end to the Riverwalk. The fence followed the sloping terrain into the river, separating the tourist attraction from a graveyard of industrial buildings behind it.

The final platform turned out over the water, the far edges masked by darkness. A payphone rose incongruously from the dock. He picked up the receiver. It was dead.

He slammed it down. Three hundred miles. Precious wasted time. Bail violation. All for nothing. He turned to head back.

"*Pssst.*"

# 28

**DANNY STARED** into the void.

"Out here," a voice said.

"Who is it?" Indistinct shadows stared back at him.

"It's me."

"Troy?"

"Out here."

Danny walked blindly toward the river. A human outline seated on the timbers at the water's edge took shape. It stood up. A shock of blond hair flashed.

Troy. Incredible.

"Twenty years and we meet like this?" Danny said. He leaned forward for an embrace at the same time Troy stuck out his hand. They reversed roles, missed again and ended up patting each other's shoulders.

Danny couldn't help gawking. The image of Troy that flashed in his mind was a Little League shortstop two sizes too long for his uniform, bangs hanging in his eyes, chanting *Hey batter, hey batter* while Danny wound up on the pitcher's mound. The updated version was a grown man wearing an expensive suit and power tie, a matching handkerchief tucked into a lapel pocket.

"You grew up," Danny said, unable to hide his surprise.

"Yeah, I guess I did."

"I mean, you look great." Physically he was still Troy. Same dirty-blond hair and puppy dog eyes. They looked swollen. "It's just that I never expected ..."

"I know. You expected me to be a loser."

"I didn't mean that."

Did he? Troy was one of the most unmotivated people he'd ever known, never taking initiative, content to be pulled through life by other forces, like John Mangrum.

"It's okay. I would have predicted that for myself. I always figured I'd end up working in my old man's concrete business, but it's funny, I haven't had dirt under my fingernails in years."

He held them up as proof. They were smooth and manicured. "I'm a stock trader. Live in a big house right on the river, not far from here. Got a wife and three kids. Drive a Mercedes."

"That's impressive."

"Not really. Being a stockbroker doesn't take much. Don't even have to go to college. I was managing a fast-food restaurant before I got into it. The company gives you the products to sell and information on how to sell them. Mostly you just need some good luck, or even better, an inside tip."

"Don't put it down, Troy. It's a lot better than I did." The small talk seemed out of place, but the twenty-year distance seemed to require it.

"I take it for granted now, like my life has always been this way, but seeing you makes me remember when it wasn't." He sat back down, tasseled loafers dangling over the dark water.

Danny sat beside him. If he closed his eyes, he could imagine them sitting in the dark at the end of the Sunset Pier, back before it shut down, baiting hooks with frozen shrimp from Publix and sharing their confederation as *The Only True Brothers of the Night*, which they were until Mangrum forced himself in. Part of the blow of Sugar Lake was losing Troy. He always blamed Mangrum, but knew it was his own fault. He pushed them both away in an unsuccessful effort to disassociate himself from the crime.

"Dark night. Dark water. Brings back a lot of dark memories," Troy said.

Danny smelled alcohol.

"You know, when I get home from work and my three-year-old throws her arms around me and tells me she loves me, I forget I even have a dark side. But we all do. Savage animals. That's what Mangrum called us the night at Sugar Lake."

Danny remembered the same speech. "What's going on, Troy? Why did you make me walk the whole damn Riverwalk?"

"I had to make sure you were alone and weren't being followed."

"Followed? By who? I have a lot of questions that need answers. Number one is Sari."

"Sari."

It came out a one-word sentence.

"There were so many messed-up things about that night at Sugar Lake. I knew Mangrum was up to something. I just I didn't know what. We were cruising around with Enya and he asked where you were. I said you were probably at the party by yourself because Sari was studying. You told me that earlier at school."

Troy loosened his tie.

"He got this weird look and turned the car around to go find you. Then I remember how strange things were when I came up from the beach and you two were arguing, Mangrum talking about you paying back Sari. When you beat the shit out of him in the cafeteria and broke up with Sari, even I started figuring it out. I'm not as dumb as you guys always thought."

Danny started to protest, but held back.

"Mangrum finally admitted everything one night when he was stoned on Quaaludes. Told me how he lied to you about Sari being out with Daryl Carpenter. He said he did it for your own good, that Sari was ruining your life, but I knew that was bullshit. He did it because he was jealous of Sari."

Was Danny the only person on the planet to not figure that out?

Troy slipped a silver flask from his coat pocket.

"Good scotch. A long way from the Boone's Farm Apple Wine we got drunk on the first time. Have some. It'll be like the old days." He laughed nervously.

"I'll pass. Tell me about Sari. You said on the phone she was in danger."

"In a minute. She's okay. Don't worry."

*She's okay.* The two best words Danny could have hoped for.

Troy took a stiff hit from the flask.

"There were a lot of times I wanted to do what you did to Mangrum that day in the cafeteria. Hell, I know how he treated me. I pretended to blow it off when you tried to talk to me about it because I knew it was true. I wondered for years why I let him get away with it."

He took another gulp.

"I finally figured out I was chicken, afraid to be my own man because I didn't know who that was supposed to be. I wanted so much to fit in, to belong. Even that night at Sugar Lake. We all acted for different reasons. You were mad at Sari. I did it because I wanted to be like Mangrum. The sad part is that none of it had anything to do with Enya."

Enya's name evaporated any trace of nostalgia. Troy sat fiddling with the empty flask, staring out at the water as if searching for something.

"I've been a coward my whole life. I covered it up by being reckless. I remember driving my motorcycle ninety miles an hour down Sheridan Street, pulling wheelies coming off the bridge. You remember that?"

Danny was on the back half the time. "It scared the crap out of me."

"I thought I was brave, thought it made me a man. What a joke. Well, that's about to change." Troy reached into his suit jacket. "This is where I turn things around."

Danny followed his disappearing hand. It emerged clutching a folded sheet of paper.

"What's that?"

"My confession," Troy said without emotion.

"Confession? For what?"

"For raping Enya McKenzie and causing her suicide. Do you want me to read it to you? It's not that long."

"No, I don't want you to read it to me. I want you to tell me what the fuck is going on."

"I'm making amends. Finally standing up and taking responsibility for what we did."

"Amends? It's a little too late for that. Enya's gone. Her family too. A confession doesn't make any sense. Why now?"

"John Mangrum's death."

The words were spoken like the official death pronouncement. Danny felt momentarily detached as he absorbed their full import. *The Only True Brothers of the Night*, minus one. Like it or not, Mangrum was almost as much a part of his childhood as Troy.

"I've changed a lot since you knew me, Danny. Not just the clothes and the job. I found an important piece that had been missing from my life. The Lord."

Danny couldn't hold back a laugh. "The Lord? You used to hide in my closet to get out of going to church."

"I told you, I've changed. I joined my wife's church. She's been talking to me about it for years, but I wasn't listening because I knew I'd have to confront myself and wasn't ready. But the time is right. You can't find righteousness until you acknowledge your sins. All He asks is that we seek forgiveness. It's a good deal."

If Troy didn't sound so dead serious, Danny would swear it was a joke. Troy Stoddelmeyer, fundamentalist stock broker, wasted on fine scotch and quoting the bible on a dark dock. Camus got it right.

"Confession really is good for the soul, Danny. Mine ... and yours." Troy stuffed his hand in his coat pocket again and pulled out another folded square of white paper.

"I have one for you too," he said.

"One what?"

"A confession."

"A confession. For me." Danny waited for the punch line.

Troy shifted. "You need to sign it. It's why you had to come to Jacksonville." He took out a pen and laid it on the dock between them.

Danny snatched the paper. "Troy, I'm going to tell you something. Then I'm going to ask you one more time what you know about Sari. And I'm warning you in advance that it's the last time I'm going to ask. I don't have time for any more preaching. So listen carefully."

He tried to lock in on Troy's eyes, but the darkness made it impossible.

"I made my confession twenty years ago. I wrote a letter to Enya taking responsibility for what I did. It wasn't much, not nearly enough, but I did it. So I really don't need to listen to your holy-roller bullshit. I carry my guilt about Enya around every day. It's always there. Signing some piece of paper isn't going to save your soul or mine. Also, in case you haven't heard, I'm in a bit of jam down south right now. I don't plan to add to it by signing a confession that I raped Enya."

"Your confession isn't about Enya. It's for killing Mangrum."

"What?" Danny held the paper up to the moonlight.

### Confession of Danny Teekwell

*I, Danny Teekwell, confess that on June 10, 1995, I murdered John Mangrum at his condomineum in West Palm Beach. I did it because he robed me of drugs and money.*

"Jesus, Troy. Don't you have to know how to spell to be a stockbroker? At least you could have got my name right."

"Sign it, Danny. You'll feel better."

"No way."

Troy reached in his coat a third time. Danny wondered whose confession would appear this time, but when the hand showed again, it was gripping a snub-nosed revolver. He pointed it at Danny's stomach.

"You must have some interesting sermons at that church of yours. Is this how they teach you to save your brother's soul? At gunpoint?"

"Please, Danny." He started crying. "Don't make this hard. Just sign it."

"I didn't kill Mangrum."

He looked to the stars. "He says you did."

"God?"

"Albert Thumpet."

The name dropped like a brick on the planks. So everything was tied together. "What do you know about Thumpet?"

Voice cracking, "Enough to know he's dangerous."

"There is no Albert Thumpet. The real Thumpet is dead. This guy is an imposter. He's the one who killed Mangrum."

"He could be fucking Elvis for all I care. I just know I need you to sign that confession or he's going to destroy me."

"So all that stuff about standing up and finding religion was just a trick? How could you do it, Troy? I would have bet my life you'd never sell me out."

"I had to. He said he had proof I raped Enya and would show it to my wife unless I got this confession signed."

"So let him. Sugar Lake happened twenty years ago. Surely that wouldn't be as bad as this."

"You don't know my wife. The part I said about the church stuff is true. Our mailbox says *Thou Shalt Repent.* If she knew, I'd be finished. I'd lose my family. My kids. They're everything to me, Danny. Everything. Todd, my oldest, looks exactly like me. Jacob is a natural baseball player, just like you were. My little girl is only three. You'd kill for her if you knew her. They think I'm a big deal. They need me. And I need them. They're the only thing I've ever done right. I'm not giving them up."

"I'm sorry, Troy. I hope you're wrong about losing your family, but I'm not signing that confession."

"I'm desperate, Danny. Don't rely on what you knew as a kid. I'm not the same person."

"We're always the same person. That's part of the problem with life. We can't change who we are. Before you think about pulling that trigger, think about the night on the golf course when we cut our fingers and rubbed our blood together. You can't shoot me, Troy. I'm Danny."

The gun lowered. Danny exhaled relief, but it didn't last long. The revolver was in motion again, to Troy's temple, where he pressed the barrel and tightened the trigger.

"You're right. You are Danny. I should have thought of that first. Danny the do-gooder. Sign the confession, Danny, or I'll blow my brains all over this dock. I've got nothing left to lose if you don't sign that piece of paper. You're right. I can't shoot you, but I can do it to myself. And you won't let it happen because you *are* Danny. Sign it."

Keeping the revolver at his head, he held out the pen. Danny didn't move.

"I'll do it. I swear." His body heaved between sobs.

The anguish was real. Troy was practically hysterical. The way he was jerking up and down the gun might go off even if he didn't want it to.

He laid the paper on the dock and scribbled. "The pen won't work. The wood's too rough." He braced his foot on a boat cleat for leverage.

"Make it work, Danny!"

He scratched some more, waiting for an opportunity. It came when Troy's puffy eyes fluttered closed.

Danny shot-put his hand into Troy's forearm. The weapon came to life. A burst of white light blinded him, evoking a surreal memory of a Fourth of July night when they were kids and Troy lit a firecracker that blew up in Danny's hands.

The revolver clattered on the deck. Troy's arm fell limp. He collapsed onto Danny's lap, dead weight.

"Troy!"

Silence until a faint whisper said, "I'm sorry, Danny. You should have let me do it."

No time for hurt feelings. Troy knew Thumpet. He pushed him upright.

"You gotta get it together. I need information." He pulled the handkerchief from Troy's pocket. "Wipe your face. It's covered with snot."

Troy obeyed woodenly.

"Tell me about Thumpet."

"I met him a month ago, in a parking garage downtown. I was getting into my Mercedes when this huge fucker with crazy blue eyes walks up. He says, *Nice car—too nice for scum.* I ignored him, but the top was down and he reached in and yanked the keys out. He's strong as an ox. I grabbed his arm with both hands, but he broke away like it was nothing. Before I could get my seatbelt undone, he had my neck pinned against the headrest. When I yelled for security, he pinched my neck and cut off my windpipe. Then he laughed this crazy laugh. You know what he said?"

Danny shook his head.

*"Did Enya call for security?* He knows everything. He knew who I was, where I live, he knows about you and Mangrum. He talked about you and Sari being *Sweethearts of the Year* or whatever it was called. He knows every detail about Sugar Lake, almost like he was there. Get this. He even claims to know the song that was playing on the radio the night we drove Enya back from the lake."

"*Black Water*," Danny said flatly.

Troy looked surprised. "That's what he said. I didn't remember that. I asked who he was and he said *Enya's Avenger.*"

So it really was all about revenge.

"He said he wanted money to keep quiet about it.

"How much?"

"Close to twenty grand so far."

"What about these confessions? Where'd they come from?"

"He came to my house early this morning."

"What time?" Danny thought about the night before and instinctively touched his ribs. It must have been Thumpet in the graveyard. To get to Jacksonville, he'd have to drive all night.

"Early. Around dawn. We were asleep when someone started pounding on the door screaming. My kids woke up crying and my wife was yelling at me to call the police. I knew it was Thumpet, or whoever he is, because he was hollering about Sugar Lake. I told my wife it was a pissed-off client who lost money in a real estate investment.

"When I got downstairs, he was agitated, rambling on about coffins and graveyards, all kinds of crazy shit. He was furious you got out on bail. I took him out back to my boathouse so he wouldn't wake up the neighbors and tried to calm him down.

That's where he gave me these confessions and told me I had to sign mine and get you to sign yours. *Or else*, he said."

"What about Sari? What do you know about her?"

Troy shook his head and blew his nose. "Don't worry about that. Last night at my house, he said my life depended on getting you here tonight to sign the confession. Like I said, he was freaking out that you got out of jail. I made him promise not to hurt you. He told me he just wanted the confession. Said you deserved to die, but that it wasn't part of Plan A. That's what he said, *Plan A*. I knew you didn't kill Mangrum."

He bowed his head. "I'm sorry, Danny."

"Keep going."

"I told him you weren't stupid enough to rush up here to sign a confession. He said to mention Sari, to say she was in danger. I knew he was right. I knew that would bring you here faster than anything. But it was just a ruse."

"It's no ruse. Sari's gone. She disappeared."

Troy's eyes widened. "He never let on, I swear."

"Where can I find him?"

Troy ran his hands through his hair. "I don't know that either. Hell, I don't know anything. The second he mentioned Sugar Lake he had me hooked. I never asked any questions. He'd call me at work when he needed money and tell me where to leave it. The only times I saw him in person were that first day in the parking garage and last night at my house."

"He must have said something, let some clue slip. Think. Did he ever say where he came from? Any hint?"

Troy frowned. "Nothing. Except … forget it. It's too much of a long shot."

"Forget nothing. A long shot's better than no shot, which is what I have now."

"Last night when we were in the boathouse, he asked me where to find an all-night pharmacy. He was super-hyped, practically delirious. He must be on some kind of medication. To ask that question means he must not live in Jacksonville, so I was thinking that—"

"To get a prescription filled he'd have to show ID and give his name and address," Danny finished. If Danny could track down the pharmacy, maybe he could beg or buy the information. "Did you tell him where to go?"

Troy laughed the way he always did when he thought he got caught saying something stupid. "I just wanted him to leave. I told him to look for an all-night Brisco's."

"What's that?"

"A drug store chain."

"How many are there?"

"A bunch. I watched him drive away though—to make sure he really left—and he went south on San Jose Boulevard. That cuts off the north half of the city. And he'd have to go all the way to Mandarin to cross the river, so that leaves out the west side too."

Danny frowned and closed his eyes.

"I said it was a long shot."

It was all he had. He'd hire a cab to take him to the all-night drugstores in that part of the city and see what he could find out.

A loud knock against wood startled him, but it was only Troy climbing off the timbers.

"I need to get home and talk to my wife. You better get out of here too. That gunshot might bring the cops."

Danny stood, feeling old and arthritic. He picked up the revolver and handed it to Troy.

"Keep it and call the police. He killed Mangrum, and an accountant in North Dakota. Take your family to a safe place."

Troy nodded and took the gun. "The confession wouldn't have held up in court," Troy said. "Hell, I knew your name was misspelled."

Danny couldn't shake the betrayal, but the look in Troy's docile brown eyes stirred reverberations of a bond stamped long ago. He saw a shy, bored kid throwing rocks at land crabs on the bank of South Lake—the day they met.

Troy must have felt it too because he leaned forward and grabbed Danny around the neck, pulling their heads together. Behind Troy's shoulder, a cargo ship powered down the river against the current.

"*The Only True Brothers of the Night,*" Troy said as they detached.

Danny offered a weak smile as a puffing sound erupted from somewhere in the night and a mass of red debris showered him. Troy fell forward into his arms. He'd been shot in the face.

# 29

"TROY!"

Danny struggled to hold on, but the slippery blood made him lose his grip. Troy slumped to the planks.

"No!" He dropped to his knees as two more bullets jolted Troy's torso. A dark stain flowed in rivulets through the creases in the boards.

He eased Troy onto his back. The bottom half of his face was gone, lazy brown eyes staring hollowly into space. "Please don't die, Troy." But he knew it was already too late.

Where was the shooter? Nothing moved on the Riverwalk or behind the barbed wire fence. The cargo ship was halfway across the river. A sniper?

No sound except the wakes from the ship knock, knock, knocking against the pilings. Whoever shot Troy somehow managed a quick getaway. He turned his attention back to his dead friend, lowering his head to say a prayer. That's when he saw the three holes in the deck planking.

Under the dock. He'd been there the whole time.

Twenty yards away a large figure climbed from under the beams back onto the Riverwalk.

"Stop!" he shouted. *You bastard. I'll get you this time.* He searched Troy's coat, grabbed the revolver and took off. The shooter was running fast, but his sequoia legs were no match for Danny's stilts. Even slowed by the broken ribs, the gap started to close. He got near enough to make out a red polo shirt just as the man disappeared into the part of the walkway where the lights were out.

Danny sprinted in behind him. Suddenly, there he stood, an opaque outline, dead still in the middle of the path.

Danny didn't slow. He'd hit him full bore. It would help make up for the size difference. The man kneeled and by the time he realized what was happening, it was too late. A needle point of light and the *thupt* of the silencer punctured the night and his left leg gave way, sending him sledding to the deck.

Footsteps approached. Face down, Danny could feel the killer looming above him. He heard a gun click.

"This is a moment I've been waiting for," he said.

Danny wondered if he would hear the shot before the bullet entered his brain.

"Unfortunately," he sighed, "I have to keep waiting." The gun clicked again and the shadow vanished. Danny twisted to see the man loping down the Riverwalk.

Clutching his leg, he rolled over. Orion looked down on him. The revolver lay uselessly on the other side of the walkway.

Troy dead, Mangrum dead, Sari missing and here he was, alone and helpless, a stranger in a strange place. He wondered how long it took to bleed to death. He closed his eyes.

A sudden clamor down the walkway brought them back open, a loud thud followed by shouting and profanity. He pushed himself off the timbers, grabbed the gun and gimped toward the source of the tumult. His wet jeans stuck to his leg. When he looked down, he couldn't tell his blood from Troy's.

No more sound up ahead. Whatever the commotion was, it was over.

He was stumbling like a drunk, dizzy and disoriented, when he got back to the row of shops abutting the path. The blood had run down his leg, filling his shoe. Each step left a bloody heel print.

Something moved to his left. He raised the revolver and tightened the trigger.

"You!"

Vernon Stack sat on a doorstep rubbing his jaw.

"It's me alright. Ol' Vernon."

"What are you doing here?"

"Oh, not a lot. Just waiting to see if my teeth fall out."

"I heard noise. What happened"

"I was about to ask you the same thing. You look like you been out slaughtering pigs. And that red stump you're limping on doesn't look too good either. Had a friend once with a leg like that. Got run over by a train. He's gone now. Just like your friend."

Danny grabbed him by the parka. "What do you know about Troy?"

"Troy? Was that his name? We didn't have a chance to exchange greetings. He wasn't in a very good mood when I grabbed hold of his ankle. Probably woulda killed me if his gun didn't fall in the river."

Vernon Stack wasn't talking about Troy. He was talking about Thumpet.

"You grabbed onto the guy that just ran past here? The big guy?"

"Yep. He was quite a load, and in a hurry, although he did take the time to kick me in the jaw before he left."

"I said you were gonna get hurt grabbing onto people's ankles."

"Well, I did it for a good cause. I wasn't grubbin' cigarettes this time. I did it for you."

"Me? What are you talking about?"

"Son, I've been down on my luck a long time, travelin' the country looking for a better life. Boston, Philly, New York—finally got smart enough to move down here where it's warm. In all my years of panhandling, ain't no one ever give me twenty dollars, 'specially after I grabbed his leg. I heard a bunch of clatter and you shoutin' at someone to stop. The big fella came running by, so I figured why not?

"I grabbed his ankle just like I done yours. 'Cept he was a lot bigger and goin' a lot faster, so he fell down. Can't say I'd have been so charitable if I knew about the gun. Lucky for me it slid into the water.

"He wasn't happy about that. No sir. Apparently had a real fondness for that gun. Even had a name for it. *Lugi.* But his wallet fell out too. That maybe saved me. He was too busy gathering up his belongins' to bother with old Vernon."

He stroked his chin again. "Other than that one kick."

All his struggles, and a panhandling stranger had waged a more successful battle against his enemy than he'd been able to manage. He patted Vernon on the shoulder.

"I don't know what to say. Thanks, Vernon. Thanks for trying."

"Don't mention it, uh, I never got your name."

"Danny."

"Well, Danny, you'd better get a tourniquet on that leg damn fast. I don't want to go around God-blessing folks who end up bleeding to death. It would shake my faith."

He pulled a frayed scarf from his neck. "You can use this. I won't be needin' it in the Sunshine State. It ain't too clean, but then this ain't exactly General Hospital."

Danny sat next to Vernon and pulled up his pants leg, revealing a red sticky mess. He probed for the point of entry, fighting off faintness as his finger slipped into a soft warm hole. The back felt worse, torn and ragged. The bullet passed all the way through.

As he wrapped the scarf, sirens in the distance grew in volume. He tied the scarf with a sailor's knot. It didn't look pretty, but would have to do for now.

"I gotta go, Vernon."

"Adios, amigo." He was sorting through pieces of paper, holding them fanned like a poker hand.

"What are those?"

"My business cards. *Vernon Stack, Professional Panhandler, No Coin Too Small.*"

He chuckled. "Only kidding. The big fellow left them behind. Like I said, his wallet came out when he hit the ground. Big old fat thing. All kinds of paper fell out. He collected everything but these. I was just checking to see if they were anything useful, like United States currency, but it's just junk. I used to carry a wallet like that, when I owned a wallet. Had everything in it from my first library card to—"

The sirens fizzled out near the end of the Riverwalk, where Troy lay dead.

"Let me see those." Danny tore the scraps from Vernon's hands.

"Be careful! Those are the fingers you were tap dancing on."

Three slips of paper.

"Can I keep these?"

"No value to me."

"Do you know where that sidewalk goes, the one just past these shops?"

"Out to a parking lot in front of the stores. There's a bus stop on the street. That's how I got here."

Danny started for the sidewalk just as tires screeched behind the shops. A police radio belched. Now they'd be coming from both directions. Not a lot of options.

"Vernon, could you do me a big favor?"

"Your wish is my command."

"Would you mind pointing the police in a different direction from where I'm going?"

"All that blood didn't come from your leg, did it?"

Danny shook his head. "Someone got killed, but I didn't do it."

"Well, hell, it's none of my business. Which way you plannin' on going?"

"That way," he said, pointing to the fast-moving water.

Vernon let out a low whistle. "Hope you're a good swimmer."

Danny limped to the water's edge and looked down. The trash from Thumpet's wallet would never survive the river. If the scraps contained any clues, now was the time to find out. He held them up close, but couldn't make them out in the darkness.

"Vernon."

"I know." He flicked his lighter.

The first item was a picture that looked like Beaver Cleaver's dad. Must have come with the wallet. Beneath it was a cardboard square embossed with a smiling reindeer. A Christmas tag, faded message barely visible. *Love, Mom.*

The last item was a receipt for something that cost fifty-six dollars. From ... he squinted to read the faint purple ink.

A pharmacy! But not Brisco's. A place called The Little Town Drugstore. He could have searched forever. The prescription was for something called *clozapine*. Danny never heard of it, but committed it to memory.

He scanned for an address. Vernon must have read his mind because he moved the lighter in closer. There it was: *The Little Town Drugstore, 9376 Thoroughbred Way, Ocala, FL.*

Ocala? South of Jacksonville in the middle of the state.

Flashlight beams were moving down the sidewalk. He stuffed the debris in his pocket.

"Bye, Vernon." He climbed over the timber benches and rappelled down the tar-blackened pilings. His good foot slipped and he fell backwards with a splash. The current picked him up and began sailing him north.

"Don't move!" he heard a cop yell at Vernon.

The bullet hole burned in the briny water. He tried not to think about the gaping pipes pouring raw sewage into the polluted river.

Ocala. A hundred miles away. Why travel so far to refill a prescription? Then he remembered seeing it, in the bottom corner: *Refills: 2.*

*Ocala was home.*

# 30

THE SCRATCHING inside the fried chicken box surprised her. The trap, baited with a chicken bone, actually worked. Her father, a half-Cherokee who regaled her with ancestral narratives growing up, would be proud. Sari Hunter had finally become one.

She cornered the prey and grabbed it. The mouse bit her finger. Please don't have rabies. She took it back to the triangle of moonlight peeking through the barred windows and sat cross-legged on the mattress.

The house above was still. The monster had driven away in his rumbling car shortly after the woman he called Enya left. Sari slipped back into unconsciousness soon after.

When she woke the second time, it was dark. The first thing she did was check herself. He could have done anything to her after she blacked out. The zipper on her shorts was halfway down, but it might have been already. She seemed okay.

Then she heard the clawing in the box. She set the trap the night before and forgot about it.

The mouse stopped squirming. She kept a firm grip and raised it in the light. The creature looked terrified, goggling her through pop-eyes, nose twitching spasmodically. Sari used to have a pet mouse when she was a little girl, a white one named Fire. She went to the barred window and set the mouse free.

She adjusted the mattress to stay in the patch of light. The light kept moving, but she couldn't remember if it was because the earth rotated or the moon revolved.

Tugging again on her zipper, images of her fourth-grade teacher invaded her brain and her stomach knotted. The monster's words came back. *We all have secrets. Even you, Scary Sari.*

She hadn't thought about Brian Caberly in a long time, but his memory had been with her every day since the abduction. The shock, fear, confusion, the feeling of being trapped—all the same emotions she experienced that day in New Jersey when she was nine and in the fourth grade.

Brian Caberly, the school's new teacher, was handsome and charming. All the girls in her class had a crush on him, but Caberly made it clear he favored Sari. She assumed it was because she was such a dedicated student. What other fourth-grader footnoted her book reports?

At first she enjoyed the extra attention. That changed the day he gave her a present, a heart-shaped gold locket, and told her not to tell anyone where she got it. Not knowing what to do with it she buried the locket in her backyard.

Then on the Friday before the last week of school, Caberly asked her to stay after class to talk about her math test. Sari worried, thinking she must have messed it up. Math was more difficult for her than other subjects, but she always worked harder on it and did well. What was there to talk about unless it was bad?

She stayed at her desk when the afternoon bell rang as the other kids ran to retrieve their jackets and lunchboxes from the coat closet, a tunnel at the back of the room with doors at each end. Mandy Taylor, her seat neighbor and arch enemy, asked what she was doing.

"Waiting to talk to Mr. Caberly."

"Teacher's pet! Teacher's pet!" Mandy taunted, and ran from the room.

When the classroom emptied, Sari waited and watched as Caberly marked papers at his desk. He finally looked up and smiled.

"You're still here," he said.

"Yes, sir."

"Good."

"Did I goof up my math test?"

"No, no. Is that why you thought I asked you to stay? I'm sorry. Just the opposite. I wanted to tell you that you got a perfect score, only one in the class."

Sari forced a smile.

"Being a teacher is a hard job, much harder than people realize, but students like you make it a lot easier."

Why wasn't the praise making her feel good?

"I'm going to miss you when school gets out next week. What are your plans for the summer?" He came over and planted himself on Mandy's desk.

"Um, I don't know. Just play, I guess. I'm supposed to go to Space Camp."

"At Cape Kennedy?"

"Yes, sir."

"That sounds great. I can see it now, Sari Hunter, first female astronaut. And I'll be able to say I knew her when she was just a pretty little fourth-grader."

Sari didn't say anything.

"By the way, whatever happened to that locket I gave you? I never see you wear it. Didn't you like it? It would look really nice with the dress you're wearing."

"I lost it. I'm sorry."

"Don't worry about it. I'll get you another one."

"No, really. I don't need a locket."

"It's no problem at all. Like I said, I like you."

He got up and clapped his hands.

"Look, I was wondering if you could help me out. I found out this morning that we teachers are supposed to have everything in our classrooms neat and tidy when we break for summer vacation. Order from the Commandant! That's what I call Principal Brewer."

He laughed. Sari didn't.

"The art supplies in the coat closet are an absolute mess. I could really use a helper and who's better-suited than the most organized girl in the class? Would you mind giving me a hand?"

"Um, I'm supposed to be home in a while. I have to help my mom … wash the dog."

"It'll only take a few minutes. You'd really be helping me out."

Sari didn't want to help, but how do you say no to a teacher? She followed him between rows of stairstep desks to the cloakroom. The art supplies filled a stack of shelves in the middle of the tunnel. The closet had a light, but Caberly didn't turn it on. Illumination came from the openings at each end. It was enough to work by, but it would be easier with the light on.

"Here we go. You take the top two shelves and I'll take the bottom two. We'll have it done in a jiff."

It made more sense to Sari for him to take the top rows since he was a lot taller, but she didn't argue. She wordlessly set about stacking boxes of pencils and lining up jars of paint and paste pots.

Caberly kneeled beside her, straightening piles of colored construction paper. She glanced down at his sandy brown hair and thought it was weird to be able to see the top of her teacher's head.

Organizing the two shelves wasn't a very big job. She worked quickly.

At first she thought it was an accident when Caberly's hand brushed against her bare leg below the hem of her dress. She scooted to her right. When it happened again, she didn't know what to think. She stopped working and looked down. Caberly was busy gathering up broken crayons. She arranged a few boxes of chalk and stepped back.

"I think I'm finished, Mr. Caberly. I really need to go."

He looked up and smiled with nice teeth. "No more of this Mr. Caberly stuff, Sari. Now that school is almost out, just call me Brian. Do me one more favor."

He pointed to a pile of rags on the floor. "Gather those smocks and hang them up. Then we'll be done."

When she bent over to pick up the smocks, she felt warm flesh press the inside of her thigh, under her dress. She jerked away so quickly she hit her head on a shelf and fell to the floor. When she turned, Caberly hovered over her, hands clasped, looking surprised.

"What happened? Are you okay?"

She rubbed the knot on her head with one hand and pulled her dress down with the other. The situation was becoming clearer, although she had no idea what to do about it. The closest she had come to learning about sexual abuse was the cheesy black and white movie they watched in the third grade, where the hideous man with no teeth offered the kids candy to go for a ride. Sari knew not to take candy from strangers, but no one ever told her to be afraid of teachers. She lobster-crawled away, brown eyes locked onto Caberly's blue ones.

Caberly held out a hand.

She didn't take it, continuing to scoot backwards until she was cornered in a nook.

"Relax, Sari. Here, let me help you up." He leaned down and

wrapped his arms around her, pulling her body against his. His stubble scraped her cheek. She could feel his warm breath and smell his cologne. Then he started moving his hands down.

"Get away!" she screamed into his ear as loudly as she could.

"Augh!" Caberly released his grip and clasped his ear. "You little …"

Sari pulled a drawing compass from the shelf and stabbed the air with the sharp point. "Stay away! Don't touch me!"

Caberly raised his hands in surrender. "Whoa, young lady, I think there's been a misunderstanding here."

"Move back!"

Caberly gave up the game. The smile disappeared.

"Don't be a tattletale, Sari," he said threateningly. "You could get in a lot of trouble. Who do you think people are going to believe? You or me? Besides, you asked for it. Flirty, pretty little Sari."

The classroom door opened. Alarm spread across Caberly's face.

"*Sar-ee.*"

Mandy Taylor! Sari never thought she'd be happy to hear that voice.

"I'm back here," she yelled. Mandy skipped into the coat closet and came upon Sari pointing the compass at Caberly.

"Sar—" She stopped. Caberly gave a half-hearted wave. "Hi, Mr. Caberly," she said haltingly. "Sari, your mom's waiting for you."

"Thanks!" Sari dropped the compass, grabbed Mandy's hand and ran out the door.

Mandy yanked to a halt when they exited the classroom. "What are you doing?"

"Just go home, Mandy. Go home *now.*"

Sari fled to the parking lot, not stopping until she reached her mother's car. She stayed silent all the way home. Her mom asked what was wrong. She said she had a stomachache, which was true. Saturday morning at breakfast, she almost told her mother what happened, but held back and never again came close to telling anyone, not even Danny.

On Monday, she went to school and toughed out the last week before summer vacation. Caberly didn't look at or speak to her. That summer her father got transferred to Florida and their family moved to the house on Sand Dollar Lane. She never saw or heard from Caberly again.

The triangle of moonlight was only a shard now. It would disappear in thirty seconds. She counted them down each night.

How much had the incident with Caberly affected her? She never really knew. For years she battled with anger and guilt, wondering if she really had done something to lead Caberly on. Only adulthood and psychotherapy cast a true light.

After it happened, she always held something back. Her life became a never-ending struggle to exert control over her surroundings. Part of that was never fully trusting, especially men. Except for Danny.

Then came Sugar Lake and she tangled up what happened with Caberly with what happened to Enya, letting it overshadow everything she knew about Danny. It wasn't the same situation. She knew that. But to this day she'd never come up with an explanation for Sugar Lake.

At the time, breaking up seemed like the only possible decision. Growing up, everything in her head was good or bad, black or white. Danny always insisted life was shades in between. She wished she could have seen it then.

*Regret.* It was the name of her new poetry book.

The sliver of light shrunk away. She lay on the mattress. Still feeling the drug, she fell back asleep quickly.

# 31

**THE MURDER GROUPIES** were gone, the juke-box dead. Shannon mopped tables with a wet towel as Grady washed glasses in a sink behind the bar. Fink sat at the bar sipping a vodka martini from a beer stein. Shaken, not stirred, like James Bond. Men who made decisions like the one he just made didn't drink piña coladas.

"Excuse the beer mug," Grady said vacantly. "It's the only clean glass left."

"It's fine," Fink said.

"Sorry things didn't work out between you and Coral."

"That's okay. Thanks for introducing me to her. It was my fault. I come on too strong sometimes. I get nervous around women ever since Jenny Stetweiler beat me up in the second grade. I never should have told Coral her breasts reminded me of cantaloupes, but I meant it as a compliment."

Grady wasn't listening. He was washing the same glass for the third time, gazing stoically at the ocean.

"Danny's gonna be alright," Fink said. "You gotta keep believing that. I've known Danny a long time and he's got a gift for getting himself out of jams. I remember one time in the tenth grade he got caught chewing gum in Mrs. McClellan's math class and … no, I guess that wasn't really the same as this. But there was another time …"

He gave up and took another swallow from the martini. His new cellular phone sat on the bar looking like a toy tank, stubby rubber antenna ready to fire. When was it going to ring?

"So you knew Danny back when he was with this Sari gal?"

"Oh yeah," Fink boasted. "Sari was something special. Looks, smarts, had it all. Great girl."

"What ever happened between them?"

Fink mulled attorney-client confidentiality. "They had a falling out."

"Was Danny happy back then?"

"Sure, but we all were. We didn't know enough not to be. Why?"

"Just wondering."

Shannon came over and wilted against the bar, running a hand through bedraggled curls. "Can I go home? I'm about to drop. I'll come in early tomorrow to finish cleaning up."

"Sure, sweetheart," Grady said. "We'll see you tomorrow."

She retrieved her purse from the back-bar and stopped to peck Grady on the cheek. "You gonna be okay?"

"Of course," he said with false bravado. "By this time tomorrow, Danny will be sitting here regaling us with tales of his adventures in the Great North."

"You'll call me if you hear anything?" she said.

"I will."

She gave Fink a shoulder pat. "It was good to meet you, Bennie. Any friend of Danny's is a friend of mine. And don't worry too much about Coral. I'm sure she didn't mean it when she called you a …"

"Fat little fuck. That's okay. Good meeting you too, Sha—" The cell phone beeped.

"There's your call," Grady said. "Must be awfully important

the way you've been watching that phone the last hour. Does it have anything to do with Danny's case?"

"Danny's case? Of course not. Whatever gave you that idea?"

"Just asking. Aren't you going to answer it?"

The phone beeped again, but Fink didn't move.

"I'll tell you what," Grady said, unfastening his wet apron and draping it on a barstool. "I'm calling it quits too. We'll let you talk in private. Go out the front door when you leave and make sure it closes all the way behind you. It'll lock by itself. You gonna be okay driving home or should I call you a cab?"

"I'll be fine. Thanks."

Grady and Shannon disappeared through the back and the lights clicked off. Fink stared at the beeping phone.

*Dammit, you're drinking a vodka martini!* He drained the beer stein and snatched the phone.

"Hello," he barked. Silence. He forgot to push the talk button. "Hello," he said again.

"Greetings, Benjamin."

"Yeah, whatever."

"I got your message. Why the new phone number?"

"You mind your business and I'll mind mine."

"My, my. Touchy."

"Cut the crap. Let's just meet and get this over with."

"I'm looking forward to it. I knew you'd come around. I had faith in your cowardliness. It was the right decision. Think of the trouble and embarrassment it will save you. Do you have the money?"

"I'll get it tomorrow when the bank opens."

"Alright. We'll meet at your office at four."

"No more office visits. No offense, Hauptmann, but we haven't exactly established a relationship based on trust. Let's meet in public. Alligator Paradise. And make it three."

"The tourist attraction?"

"That's right. Main pavilion, next to the roller coaster, where they feed the gators."

"I see. Safety in numbers. Just be certain you have the full one hundred thousand—in cash. And don't worry about Teakwell. He'll be out of the way soon enough. In the meantime, don't even fantasize about double-crossing me. I'm always prepared in case you ever wonder about those things. I'll expect to see the cash as soon as I arrive. If you don't have it, well, I'll leave that to your imagination."

"Three o'clock at Alligator Paradise," Fink said and clicked off the phone.

# 32

## THE CONFESSION.

As Danny drove west on I-10 in his newly acquired junk-heap, he tried to reconstruct the chaos on the dock, but couldn't account for the confession Troy tried to make him sign. He intended to destroy it, but must have let go of it when Troy got shot, meaning the cops might have found it, placing him at the scene.

Another dead friend. Another possible murder charge. Another bad night.

The image of Troy's face bursting into red haunted him mile by mile, but he shoved it aside. Only one thought mattered: finding the man posing as Albert Thumpet. Now, for the first time since the nightmare began, that was at least a possibility.

He'd find the Little Town Drugstore in Ocala and do whatever necessary to get Thumpet's real name and address, assuming the bucket of bolts he was driving made it that far.

After Danny landed in the river, he let the current carry him until he spotted signs of life. He remembered his boast to Grady that he still had two lives left. He lowered it to one. He was damned lucky to get away.

317

He limped two blocks to a gas station, relieved that the money roll was still in his pocket. Troy's gun slipped out and sank to the bottom of the river. The stuff from Thumpet's wallet dissolved to mush.

Inside the convenience store, he laid down wet bills for two Jacksonville Jaguars teeshirts, ibuprofen, hydrogen peroxide, antibacterial ointment, Gatorade, cheese puffs and a map of Florida.

In the restroom, he put on one of the teeshirts and tore the other into strips, which he used to wrap his calf after dousing the wound with the first-aid supplies. The pain was excruti-ating. He swallowed three of the ibuprofen and devoured the cheese puffs. He buried his bloodstained teeshirt and Vernon's scarf in the trash can and counted his money. Just over eight hundred bucks.

He went out front and loitered in the shadows, profiling motorists as they came and went, searching for someone who might be willing to sell a cheap car to a stranger for cash.

When a kid with long hair in a ponytail pulled up to the far pump in a dilapidated Dodge Dart belching plumes of smoke, Danny stepped from the shadows.

"Hey, how's it going?"

"Alright."

"Nice car."

The kid looked at him suspiciously. The car was scrap-metal on wheels. The forest-green body was full of rusty holes. The tires were bald. A piece of rope held the passenger side door closed. A coat hanger did the same for the trunk. Duct tape filled the space where one of the rear windows used to be.

"I mean, it needs some work, but I'm a big fan of classic Dodge Darts. You wanna sell it?"

"Sell it?"

"Yeah, for cash. Right now."

"How much?"

"I'll give you three hundred bucks."

His desperation must have shown.

"No can do. This car has a 360 cubic-inch V-8 engine with serious power and an awesome FM radio with four speakers. I'll sell it for a thousand. I'll even leave you my lucky charm. Looks like you could use it."

"What is it?"

"Not *what*. *Who*. James Garfield."

"The actor? Maverick?"

"No, man. That was James Garner. This is James A. Garfield. Our twentieth president."

He pointed to a plastic figurine of a balding man with a bushy beard, stuck to the dashboard. The man had a dour look and wore a suit with wide lapels.

"Probably a silly question, but why do you have an, uh, action figure of President James Garfield in your car?"

"Like I said, for good luck."

"Didn't Garfield get assassinated?"

"Dude, he was *president*. How much luckier can you get?"

"Yeah, okay. Let's talk about that price."

Danny could only get him down to seven hundred. He didn't want to part with that much cash. His wallet survived the river, but it would be too easy to trace his credit cards or a rental car. For all he knew, he was already the subject of a statewide manhunt. He reluctantly traded the cash for the keys, leaving him with one hundred and six dollars.

"Where do you want me to send the title?"

He gave the only address that came to mind other than his own: The Slagger-Jewell Funeral Home.

The kid was recounting the money as Danny drove away. "Don't worry," he shouted. "James Garfield's gonna take care of you, man."

That was half an hour ago. He spread the map across the steering wheel and studied it as he drove, concentrating on keeping the speedometer at sixty-five. He wouldn't survive a traffic stop.

The kid wasn't lying. The V-8 had some serious horsepower. It would have more if not for the bad piston rings. The car burned oil like a sonofabitch, leaving a trail of thick smog behind him.

Blue Oyster Cult's *Don't Fear the Reaper* played on the radio, which actually did have good sound. He cranked it up.

U.S. 301 looked like the best route south to Ocala, but Danny passed it by. Too much traffic, and it cut through Starke, home to the Florida State Prison and Old Sparky, Danny's future home if he didn't find answers quickly. He aimed instead at an obscure red line on the map called State Road 121 twelve miles farther.

State Road 121 was a dark, deserted two-lane strip of asphalt winding through the rural Florida that never showed up on postcards. Lots of churches, junk cars and tacky lawn ornaments. In Lake Butler, he cruised past a bank clock: 2:00 a.m.

An hour of driving landed him in Gainesville, home to the University of Florida. He pulled into the drive-thru of an all-night Taco Bell on Thirteenth Street and bought a burrito and large coffee. He drove on, eating and listening to Widespread Panic on a college radio station.

When he graduated from high school, he used to come to Gainesville to visit Jeff Bennis, a pre-med student, one of his few career-minded friends. They'd drink cheap beer at the campus Rathskeller and hike over to the stadium to watch the Gators play football. If he remembered right, Thirteenth Street turned into U.S. 441 up ahead and went straight to Ocala.

It began drizzling. He flipped on the wipers. Only one worked, but at least it was on the driver's side. The college station started fading out, so he found a blues station playing Muddy Waters. *Got my mojo working, but it just won't work on you.*

On the outskirts of Ocala he stopped at a convenience store to fill up with gas and check the oil. Two quarts low. No surprise. But the car didn't have to last much longer.

The store was empty except for the clerk, a hard-looking woman in tight jeans and a Daytona 500 teeshirt. It was almost three according to a Marlboro clock above the counter. Danny asked for directions to Thoroughbred Way. The clerk said she never heard of it.

He coughed up three dollars for an Ocala map. Along with the gas and oil, he'd already spent close to half of his remaining cash, the first time in nine years he had to worry about money. The irony wasn't lost on him. He pointed to a rank-smelling carafe smoldering on a hot plate. "How much is the coffee?"

"Dollar for small, two for large."

"I'll take a small."

Back in the car, he sipped the bitter brew and found Thoroughbred Way on the map. Only three blocks long, near the town square.

Twenty minutes later he rolled up across the street from the Little Town Drugstore. An awning with candy-cane stripes adorned the front. Inside was an old-fashioned soda fountain. A *Sorry, We're Closed* sign hung on the door. Another sign said the store opened at seven.

Weary with no place to go, he considered staying there until morning, but it was too risky. He could probably afford a room at one of the truck stops he passed on the way in, but that would leave him flat busted, and even a motel presented perils. The image of a swat team breaking down the door sent him driving east on Highway 40 into the bowels of the Ocala National Forest.

A small green sign with a triangle on it, the National Park camping symbol, pointed him down a gravel road that ended at a pond called Spring Moon Lake. There were plenty of empty sites, but Danny passed them by and drove to the far edge of the grounds where he eased the car into the brush.

He collected branches to camouflage the back. No one was going to mistake him for a member of the Good Sam camping club.

Satisfied the Dart was concealed, he climbed in back and tried to get comfortable on the shredded upholstery, bare springs poking through. It was impossible, but he finally found a position where both his leg and ribs were at rest.

A collage of gruesome images from the bloody night flooded his brain as he fell into a fitful sleep.

# 33

**AN ORANGE SUNRISE** filtering through the window bars opened Sari's eyes. The first thing she saw was the *Life* game board set up next to the mattress. He must have snuck into the basement during the night. The drug made her sleep like a zombie.

The game was ready to play. The blue and green plastic cars were parked in the starting block, a pink peg-driver for her, blue for him. The decks of cards were laid out. He'd even dealt out the starting cash for each player.

The nerve of him to think she was going to keep playing the stupid game after he drugged her.

Then she noticed the books. He brought them!

*1984, Catcher in the Rye, Shock Treatment: Crime or Cure, Moby Dick, How to Get Anything on Anybody, The Giving Tree* and three Danielle Steele paperbacks. The paperbacks were too small, but the other books formed a platform six inches high, enough for her to reach the ceiling. One successful pull-up would pay for a lifetime spent at the gym.

She was sorting the books when she spotted the white bag at the top of the stairs and ran for it. A kid's meal with soggy chicken chunks, fries and a drink made her forget everything else.

Returning to the mattress, she inspected the food carefully, said grace and began nibbling on a french fry. Out of habit programmed from days and nights of boredom, she lackadaisically spun the game spinner and moved her blue car down the path.

She knew the game board as well as he did now. When she spun a six, she didn't have to count the spaces to know she just had a ski accident that cost five thousand dollars. But when she landed, she saw the words had been crossed out with a marker. Block letters were printed below: *ENYA'S AVENGER SAYS GO BACK 3 SPACES*.

She knew that space too. Funeral expenses.

Sari examined the board for more messages. Everything else looked normal. She sorted through the job cards. All were normal until she came to the *Doctor* card. *Doctor* was blotted out. Below the cartoon characters in white coats it now said *Coroner*.

The stack of cardboard tiles on the winner's space drew her attention. The millionaire's space. His favorite space. She lifted them apprehensively and turned the first tile over. Obliterating the original message in thick letters was a single word: *YOU*.

The second tile said only *ARE*.

She hesitated before turning over the third. *ALMOST*.

Closing her eyes, she traced the rounded corners of the last tile. She just wouldn't look at it. Let him play his mind games with himself. Her stubbornness was her last vestige of self. She felt close to losing Sari.

She skidded the game piece across the damp floor and stared at it for ten minutes. She was crying before she reached it. It wasn't even the word itself, which was *DEAD*.

Finishing the meal quickly, she shifted back into work mode. The chipping went faster standing on the books, but her perch was more precarious. The first time she leaned for leverage the middle books squirted out and she tumbled off the cooler.

An envelope fell from one of the books. Printed on the front was *SO-SAD-SARI*. She tore it open.

*Deer Scary Sari,*

*I enjoyed having you as my house gest, but your time is almost done. I know you are Teekwell's luver in his heart if nowhere else and that he wood come save you if I needed him to. Thats why I kidnaped you and brought you to my humble home.*

*You must be knowing by now that I am always extra prepared. For every Plan A, theres a Plan B and so on. INSURANCE! It helps make up for misteaks. Rememory about how your log cabin got wiped out by the tornado.*

*Teekwell tried to ruin the game, but I won as usual. That's LIFE. Stoddelmeyer got what he deserved and your boyfriend left his DNA squirting on the crime scene.*

*I probly should have killed Teekwell like the others, but I can't. Killing is too good for him, but also too bad for him. His child woodn't like it, and his mother neither. Life imprison will be worse for him anyway. I know you agree.*

*I Owned a shovel with a lifetime guarantee, but lost it in a graveyard down in your nek of the woods so I have to buy a new one. When I do I'll dig a nice hole for you in the backyard.*

*Here are the books I promised. Hope your a fast reader.*

*Excuse this cheep pen. So-Sorry-Sari.*

*Your fiend and Enya's Avenger,*

*Jaxon Kempler*

*p.s. That's my real name. Youl be dead soon so you can know it.*

*psssss. Enjoy your last super. I kept the toy.*

She set the letter aside and rebuilt the book stack. He liked to scare her, but had never gone to such lengths. That he defaced his beloved game made her think the threat might be real.

The escape hole was almost ready. Maybe it *was* ready. So hard to tell. She had to be sure her shoulders and hips would fit through. Getting stuck halfway was one of her worst fears, the final humiliation. But she also worried that she was being too careful, being her obsessive-compulsive self, increasing the risk. No way to know how long he'd be gone from the house.

She tore a cardboard strip from the game box and used it to measure herself, then the hole. Close. She'd work for one more inch.

Carpet covered the hole on the other side. The monster hadn't fallen through it. His loud clomping rarely approached this corner of the house. She fretted constantly about what was on the other side of the carpet. She wanted desperately to pierce it and see, but there could be no clues until she was ready to go.

The letter confused as much as frightened her. *Should have killed Teekwell like the others.* Had the monster been telling the truth when he said John Mangrum was dead? And now Troy Stoddelmeyer? Troy was at Sugar Lake too.

*Killing is too good for him, but also too bad for him.* What did that mean?

And what in the world was the stuff about *his child* not liking it if Danny got killed? Or *his mother.* Danny's mother? The child's? What child?

The part about Danny and the DNA was too much to contemplate. She shifted to the strange conversation she overheard yesterday through the fog of the drug.

*Good-bye Enya.*

*I told you, don't call me that.*

Who was the woman who came to visit? It couldn't be Enya. Could it?

*Chip, chip, chip.*

None of the questions mattered unless she got out of the basement. She'd work until she escaped or collapsed, or he came back to kill her.

# 34

DANNY EASED into a parking space across the street from the Little Town Drugstore, the same space he had occupied several hours earlier.

He checked himself in the rearview mirror, startled by his graveyard face. His skin had gone sallow and his eyes looked like they were filled with epoxy. His shirt was still wet from the pond of sweat he woke up in.

Raking his fingers through his doormat hair, he exited the Dart and leadfooted across the street. His appearance wasn't going to make things any easier.

The store was empty except for a well-dressed brunette and her young son sharing a milkshake at the soda fountain. He needed to be alone with the pharmacist, so he waited, pretending to look at magazines.

When they left, he approached the pharmacy counter. The kid behind it didn't look old enough to be breaking curfew much less dispensing controlled substances. He had expected the Little Town Drugstore to be run by a Marcus Welby-type, but this could prove lucky. Youth carried so many shortcomings, inexperience and gullibility to name two Danny was counting on.

A shiny new pharmacy diploma for one Travis Nichols hung behind the counter.

"Mr. Nichols?"

"That's right."

"My name's Stu Sutcliffe," he said, spitting out a new alias. Frank Calhoun had enough problems. The name of the original Beatle was the first one that came to him. "I'm looking for my brother."

"I don't see anyone here except you and me."

Smart ass.

Chuckling, "That's funny. What I mean is I've been looking for him the past few weeks. He disappeared from Jacksonville. He's mentally ill and our family is really worried about him. We got a tip he might be in Ocala."

"I just moved here. I'm sure I don't know your brother."

"I'm not explaining myself well. My brother takes a medication called clozapine," Danny said, remembering the receipt and trying to pronounce the name smoothly. "I'm checking out the pharmacies in town trying to get a lead on his whereabouts."

"Clozapine. They give that to schizophrenics."

That was news to Danny. "Yeah, that's his diagnosis. I was hoping you could help me track him down by checking your records to see if he's getting his medication here."

"Sorry. Prescription records are confidential by law."

"I know that, but I thought you might make an exception. My brother's too ill to survive on his own. You could be helping to save a life."

"I also would be committing a crime and risking loss of my license. I can't do anything for you. Check the community mental health center. If your brother's that wacked out, he's probably already had a run-in with them."

That might be true of Thumpet as well, but he couldn't

keep chasing rainbows forever. Nichols' tone made it clear he intended to play it by the book. If he had any money, he'd try to bribe him.

"Okay, I'll check with them. I also need to buy some first-aid supplies."

"Over there, against the wall."

Danny crossed the store, considering his options. He already knew there was only one. He scooped up three rolls of gauze, adhesive tape, more hydrogen peroxide and a bottle of rubbing alcohol. He had no idea whether he was nursing the leg correctly, but couldn't very well ask Nichols the best way to treat a gunshot wound.

On his way back to the counter he caught Nichols staring at the leg. No point wasting time. Danny was a pacifist by nature. The last time he physically attacked anyone was in the twelfth grade when he took out Mangrum, but it wasn't a hard decision when he thought about Sari. He dropped the supplies on the counter. Nichols rang them up.

"Comes to $16.65."

Danny counted out the money while Nichols put the merchandise in a bag. Overwhelming force, he told himself, the best strategy for avoiding real violence.

When Nichols leaned down to get a bag, Danny hoisted himself over the counter. Before Nichols could react, Danny slammed him against a wall of shelves. Pill bottles rained on top of them. He pressed his forearm against the pharmacist's throat.

"Take the money, take the drugs," Nichols croaked. "I just work here."

"*Shsssh*," Danny said, heart pounding through his chest. "Calm down. I don't want money or drugs. I just need information. I don't want to hurt you, but I will if I have to. I'm desperate. Do you understand?"

Nichols whimpered. The boy pharmacist was six inches shorter than him.

"Okay, I'm going to let go. If you move or scream I'll … kill you."

Nichols stood still except for his trembling. "I don't want any trouble," he said. "I just graduated. I have sixty thousand dollars in student loans to pay back."

Danny checked the store again.

"It's this simple. All I want is a list of your customers who have prescriptions for clozapine. Names and addresses. That's it. Give it to me and I'll go. There can't be very many."

"I don't have any list like that."

"Get it off your computer."

"There is no computer. This is just a little mom and pop operation. The records are a mess. That's one of the reasons they hired me, to clean things up. It's the only job I could get when I graduated. I barely passed my boards. They even make me fix the milkshakes."

No computer. Unbelievable. Even Fink had a computer. He thought everything would be easy if he could just get the pharmacist to talk. "What kind of records do you have?"

"File cabinets of manila folders, alphabetical by patient, but they're not complete."

"How many?"

"I don't know. Thousands probably. This place has been here a long time. They're over there."

A row of tall, battleship-gray filing cabinets filled a back wall. It would take days to go through them. "What can you do for me? I know he gets his medication here."

"If you give me his name, I'll try to find his file."

"I don't know his name," Danny said dejectedly.

"I thought he was your brother?" Indignant courage seeping into his voice.

"I lied! Question me again and I'll cut your balls off with that letter opener." He couldn't let the kid get too brave. One of them might get hurt.

"The guy I'm looking for is big, probably six-four, weighs at least two-fifty. Has bright blue eyes and dark curly hair. Have you seen him in here?"

"I don't remember anyone like that, but I only work mornings and weekends. Look, I was serious about the community mental health center. If the guy you're looking for is really a schizophrenic and lives in Ocala, that's probably where he get his prescriptions. Private shrinks don't usually treat the worst cases. They don't have health insurance. You could check with the docs over there."

"While you're calling the cops? Do I look stupid?" He suddenly felt very stupid and almost laughed. He was standing behind the counter threatening to kill a pharmacist and had no way out.

"I won't tell anyone. I mean, you'd kill me, right?"

"Right," Danny said unconvincingly.

"Trust me. Like I said, I'm just getting started. I don't want any trouble on my record. Just go and I swear it'll be like you were never here."

The kid sounded sincere, but even if he was lying there was nothing Danny could do to keep him quiet short of actually killing him. "All right," he said. "I was never here. Where's the mental health center?"

Nichols gave detailed directions that made it sound like he was shooting straight. Danny apologized for assaulting him, raised the hinged countertop and hitched out carrying the bag of medical supplies.

By the time he reached the car, he was swiping feverish sweat from his face and neck. He should have snagged some antibiotics when he was behind the counter. He weighed going back to get some until he looked through the glass and saw Travis Nichols speaking frantically into the telephone.

He squealed out of the parking space and hit the gas.

# 35

**HE PUSHED** the Dart south on 441 until he came to a truck stop advertising hot showers for five dollars. His dwindling assets totaled forty bucks, but he needed to clean up and change his appearance before heading to the mental health center. He had to operate on the assumption Nichols called the cops.

His leg also needed tending to. The sharp pain had turned to a dull throb. It didn't hurt as much, but somehow hurt worse. Locked in the shower stall, he removed the teeshirt strips. They were saturated with cloudy drainage. The calf had swelled, painfully stretching the skin, which felt tender and hot. The puffy fringes of the entry and exit holes were dark red.

*Infected.* He knew it.

Gagging, he stretched the wound open and poured the hydrogen peroxide and alcohol into it. The trucker in the next stall must have thought he was being sodomized by an elephant. He caulked the holes with the leftover ointment and wrapped his calf in several layers of gauze. It looked a lot better, but felt the same.

He shaved in a steamy mirror with a disposable plastic razor and travel-size can of shaving cream, expensive at five bucks, then arranged his hair with his new pocket comb. Another dollar. He thought about shaving his head to help disguise his appearance, but didn't think the plastic razor could finish the job.

His new wardrobe started with a black teeshirt that screamed *I Love Big Trucks* across the front in red letters. The only other choices were *Bad Mother Trucker* and *I Just Dropped a Load*. The cheap dungarees were a better investment. A size too small, but they hid the bullet wound.

He evaluated himself in the mirror. Definite improvement except for the ridiculous shirt. He tore off the label and turned it inside-out.

At the mental health center, he'd use the mentally ill brother routine again. He hadn't come up with any better explanation for wanting to track down a schizophrenic. If they asked for the patient's name, he'd explain his brother always used fake names, part of his paranoia issues. They could try looking up Albert Thumpet, one of his favorites.

In the truck stop diner, he bought a hot dog and took the only empty seat at a row of payphones. Each of them had a chair and small café table. He needed to update Fink and had promised to call Grady.

He dialed Fink collect.

"Hi Fink," he said when the call went through.

"Hi Fink? Hi Fink? That's all you have to say is *Hi Fink*?"

Another stormy day at the law offices of Benjamin P. Finkel.

"You've got everyone going out of their minds down here. Where are you? No! Don't answer that. This phone could be tapped."

"Tapped?" Danny squawked. "What's going on?"

Next to him, a barrel-chested trucker in a tank-top that showed off his bulging U.S. Marines tattoo scowled at the outburst.

"You don't know?"

"I've been kind of out of pocket. What's up?"

"*What's up* is the cops think you shot Stoddelmeyer on a dock in Jacksonville and your bail down here has been revoked because you skipped town and that punch on your jacket turned out to be loaded with Mangrum's blood, and to top everything off they found a written confession that you killed Mangrum next to Stoddelmeyer's corpse. That's *what's up!*"

About what he expected. "I didn't shoot Troy. Thumpet did it, or whatever his name is. I don't have much time. It's another crazy story ..."

He synopsized the events, leaving out details like the bullet hole in his leg—he didn't want Grady to know—and location in case Fink was right about the tap.

"So now I'm getting ready to go over to the mental health center. It's my last option."

"That sounds like a nowheres-ville option."

"Really, Fink? I thought it was the plan of the century."

"Sorry, sorry. What can I do?"

"Not much. Keep your fingers crossed. If I make it out of there, I may need you to wire me some money."

"Money? From your bank?"

"That's where it would be."

"I, um, would advise against that. It would leave a trail and add a federal felony to your list of crimes for using an instrumentality of interstate commerce to aid and abet your flight."

"Alright. No money. How's Grady holding up?"

"Not good."

"I'm calling him next."

"That reminds me. That geezer called looking for you. The one who lives in Enya's house."

"Myron Tamms?"

"Yeah. Said it was an emergency, about your case. The guy was really agitated. Said you *absolutely must* call him back. What do you think that's about?"

"No clue. Gotta run now. I'll check in again if I can."

Danny hung up to call Grady.

"Collect call from Danny Teakwell. Will you accept the charges?" the operator said.

"Yes, I will." Grady's gravelly voice.

"Ahoy, it's me."

"Hello," Grady said.

Fink's soundtrack played in his head. "Hello? That's all you can say? It's me, Danny."

"Yes, it's good to hear from you. This afternoon will be fine. Delivery at the dock at two."

"Grady, it's Danny. Are you okay? Is somebody there?"

He heard scuffling before Grady shouted, "Get your hands off me."

The voice of Detective Emilio Rodriguez pierced the line. "Handcuff him. Hello, Teakwell. Nice of you to call. We're all missing you down here, especially your bail bondsman."

"What happened to Grady? Let me talk to him."

"He's indisposed."

"You'd better not hurt him. I swear. I'll hire lawyers to sue your ass all the way to the Supreme Court if you lay a finger on him. Let him go."

"Teakwell, this may come as a surprise to you—lost as you are in your mad, homicidal frame of mind—but your opinions don't carry a lot of weight right now."

"Make sure you remember that when you're giving your tenth deposition in the litigation of the century. I mean it. The second I put down the phone, I'm writing out a dying declaration. *Use every penny of my estate to hire lawyers to sue Detective Emilio Rodriguez.* Let him go."

A pause. "Escort Mr. Banyon outside and take off the cuffs. Tell him he can come back when he's ready to behave. Inform him that if he acts up again he'll be arrested for obstructing a police investigation."

"Real tough guy, Rodriguez. Picking on old men."

"No reason for you and me to squabble, Teakwell. Tell me where you are and I'll come get you. No charge."

"Thanks, but I'm kind of enjoying liberty. I know you aren't interested in technicalities, but I'm innocent—of everything. I'm gonna prove it." Or go down trying. He knew he wouldn't survive captivity.

"That's what the county pays me to do. Let your lottery tax dollars work for you. If you didn't commit these barbaric crimes, the system will prove it."

"Presumption of innocence, huh."

"That's it."

"I don't have a lot of faith in the system right now. It kind of failed me."

"It could fail you a lot worse. You're a dangerous fugitive now, already chalked up two murders. The system says we're allowed to shoot you if you flee. *Tennessee v. Garner*, United States Supreme Court, 1985. I've read it carefully."

"You have to find me fir—" Danny heard a click buried in the phone lines. A trace? "Nice talking to you, Rodriguez." He hung up.

He pondered Grady's words. Delivery this afternoon at two on the dock. A code? Sure, the payphone at the marina where Grady keeps *Lady Luck*. He'd call him there if he could.

He was to the door when he remembered Fink's message about Myron Tamms. What would get the old guy so excited? Tamms didn't seem like the type to fly off the handle over nothing. More important, Tamms stuck by him even after finding out about the murder charge. The least he could do is call him back.

His previous seat was occupied by a man wearing an eye patch and stroking a guinea pig, but the Marine's seat was open. He dialed Broward information, memorized Tamms' number and fed some change into the phone.

A soft feminine voice answered. Did he waste his money on a wrong number?

"Is Mr. Tamms home?"

"He had to step out."

"Okay, well, I—"

"Is this Danny Teakwell?"

"Who's this?" he said suspiciously.

"My name is Natalie Jesch. I'm Myron's … friend. He asked me to come over and wait in case you called. He had to go to the doctor."

"Is he okay?"

"He was doing better before you came around. He has a heart condition and his blood pressure is up."

She sounded pissed. Natalie Jesch must be Myron Tamms' girlfriend. Good for him.

"Myron said he must speak with you."

"What's it about?"

"He wouldn't tell me. He's stubborn as a mule. But he said it was urgent and about your case. *A tragic mystery.* That's what he called it."

"A tragic mystery?"

"Myron will be back in a couple of hours. He's going to be upset he missed you. He was adamant I come over and mind the phone. Made me miss my book club meeting."

"Thank you for helping. I'm sorry you missed your meeting."

"I didn't do it for you, Mr. Teakwell. I did it for Myron. He's a beautiful man. He trusts you. I don't know why. You had better not be what the newspapers say you are."

"I'm not, but I can't guarantee anyone will ever know it. I wouldn't do anything to hurt Mr. Tamms."

"You just call him back. I've known Myron a long time and I've never seen him in such a state."

He was a plague on everyone he came in contact with. "I'll call back when I can," he said, and hung up.

Exiting the truck stop, he ran into a force field of hot, humid air. His sneakers stuck to the tacky blacktop as he hobbled to the Dart, hidden behind a line of tractor trailers.

A state trooper cruised by on 441. Danny ducked his head. Time was running out.

# 36

**THE MENTAL HEALTH CENTER** was a modern, multi-tiered building of painted brick surrounded by fresh asphalt. Danny drove by scanning for cops. If the pharmacist called them, this would be the logical place to be waiting.

He tried to evaluate the situation from a police mentality, like Fink suggested back at the jail. Nichols didn't know he was public enemy number one. A dispatcher would get a call that a man climbed over the counter at a drugstore and threatened the pharmacist. Did he take anything? No. Did he hurt you? No. We'll check it out. Thanks for calling. That might be the end of it in South Florida. But Ocala was a small town.

The lot looked clear. He parked in an outpatient space near the front. Farther away and out of sight would have been smarter, but walking was becoming a real problem. He could no longer raise the front of his foot. On each step, his toes beat his heel to the ground.

An automatic door slid open and he entered an art-decoish waiting area with chrome chairs, black speckled carpet and pink walls. And lots of people. The place was packed.

He didn't expect that. Head down, he drop-footed to one of the only empty seats. Had to be careful not to squander his last chance. He'd take in the surroundings, observe how the place functioned.

The man next to him adjusted a hat made of aluminum foil. They made eye contact.

"Are you trying to read my mind?" he accused loudly.

Perfect. "No, of course not," Danny whispered.

"Don't lie. I know you."

"I swear I wouldn't do that." *Please don't start freaking out on me.*

"It's not working, is it?" He tapped the aluminum foil hat.

Danny took a chance. "No, it's not."

"Aha! Can't go through this can you?"

"Nope. Can't read a single thought."

"That means the government x-rays in that blinking light can't get through either," he said, pointing at the smoke detector.

He sat back satisfied. Danny disengaged, twisting away and picking up a newspaper from a side table. He opened it and pretended to read while scanning the room.

Three women sat behind glass partitions checking people in and out. Hallways split off in a T formation. A harried woman in a lab coat passed by waving a clipboard and speaking rapidly to an orderly running to keep up.

Danny spotted a security guard in the corner and tensed, but the guard looked relaxed, not like he was on alert for a fugitive. Still, the radio on his belt meant the cops were only one click away.

The women behind the partitions were busy. He didn't picture them having the time or inclination to listen to a family sob story. And if the cops had called, they might be waiting for a limping guy asking questions about a missing mentally ill brother. Maybe he'd be better off in motion, try to find an isolated doctor or nurse to plead his case to. But that would require more walking.

He made up his mind when he glanced down at the newspaper and saw his unsmiling mugshot staring back at him. Above it a headline said, *LOTTERY LUNATIC KILLS LOCAL STOCKBROKER, ON THE RUN.* It was the Jacksonville newspaper.

Danny pulled the paper up to cover his face. Everything was as Fink said on the phone. The Jacksonville cops found his confession to killing Mangrum on the dock covered in Troy's blood. The reporter pieced together that Troy, like Mangrum, was Danny's high school classmate and former friend.

Detective Rodriguez contributed generously to the story. He downplayed the dope angle now.

"Apparently, what we have is a maniac bent on wiping out his high school class. But we'll find him. We're tracking airlines, rental cars, credit cards, everything. He can't make a move without us knowing."

One good decision at least, sticking to a cash economy.

Scanning the page, Sari's picture from the flyer smacked him in the face.

"Teakwell's former high school girlfriend, Sari Hunter, 37, has been reported missing from her home in Coconut Grove. Rodriguez said Teakwell is considered to be the prime suspect in her disappearance."

He winced. At least they'd finally be looking for Sari.

Lab tests found Mangrum's blood on Danny's jacket. No mention of fruit punch. Judge Kovacich revoked Danny's bond. Law enforcement agencies throughout Florida were cooperating in the investigation.

It closed with a description of Troy and his family. His three-year-old's name was Greta. The last line came from Troy's wife. "He might be able to hide from the police, but not from God.

Vengeance will be the Lord's."

A disturbance broke out down the hall in the direction where the woman in the lab coat had run. She stepped out of a room and called the security guard to come help.

Danny boosted out of the chair and scuffed down the hall in the other direction, dropping the newspaper in a trash can.

Two men in blue scrubs conferred up ahead. He kneeled and retied his shoe. Would they challenge him? He looked more like a patient than an employee. Were they allowed to roam the halls?

A door on his right said *Authorized Staff Only*. Fourth down, time running out. Time for the Hail Mary. If he strolled into the weekly staff meeting, it could all be over. He opened the door.

Empty. The room was a lounge outfitted with a fridge, sink and microwave. Foam coffee cups littered tables surrounded by folding chairs. Across the back of one of them lay a white labcoat … and a new plan.

He put on the coat. The sleeves were a little short, but otherwise not a bad fit. Buttoning the front, he studied his reflection in the microwave glass. "I'm Dr. Sutcliffe," he said.

No, that was pushing it. Medical student Sutcliffe. From just up the road at Shands Teaching Hospital at the University of Florida, working as a research assistant for one of his professors doing clinical studies of schizophrenics.

Danny kept in touch with his buddy Jeff Bennis through med school and had picked up a few factoids he could toss around. With a little luck, it could work. It had to.

First he had to do something about the swelling in his leg, which was stretching his bandages and the new jeans painfully tight. He found scissors in a drawer and cut a slit in the back of the pants and through the outer bandages. His calf expanded to fill the new space.

On the way out he grabbed a jelly donut from a tray.

\* \* \*

"Quite an interesting case," fourth-year medical student Stu Sutcliffe explained to medical records employee Mimi Sloane as she sat at her computer terminal.

Medical Records was a windowless room lined with shell-colored horizontal filing drawers. The only adornments were some framed photos on Sloane's desk, including several of a cocker spaniel.

Danny sat in a plastic bucket chair pulled close to the desk to hide his leg.

"He apparently has this obsession with a girl he knew from high school, out to get revenge against anybody he thinks mistreated her. Anything like that sound familiar?"

She shook her head. "No, but that's nothing. I could tell you stories that even your Professor—what's his name?"

"Banyon. Professor Grady Banyon."

"Even your Professor Banyon wouldn't believe."

Danny's ruse was working so far. After heisting the lab coat, he stumbled through corridors until he came to the medical records room on the second floor where he encountered Sloane, gold-rim glasses circling pretty green eyes, nice skin, and hair cut short like a boy's. She seemed pleased to have someone to talk to, especially a medical student.

The professor he worked for, Danny prevaricated, was conducting clinical studies of schizophrenics. Danny got paid ten bucks an hour as a research assistant to interview subjects and write up reports. He was supposed to meet a patient down here today.

"Like a moron, I forgot to bring his file. Do you think you could help me track him down? It would save me a lot of embarrassment."

"No problem. Where do you live in Gainesville?" she asked as she typed on the computer.

"The, uh, dorms near the medical school."

"You still live in a dorm? Yuck."

"They're cheap. I'm trying to keep my student loans down so I can afford to set up shop in a small town somewhere, a nice little family practice. A lot of my classmates have to sell their souls to the big city just to pay back their loans." Bennis's spiel before moving to Tampa and making a fortune doing boob jobs and tummy tucks.

Stu Sutcliffe, small-town boy, dedicated humanitarian.

Mimi Sloane smiled. "Ever think about Ocala? It's a nice town."

"It does seem nice."

The computer beeped it was ready. "Okay, what do you know about this patient?"

"That's the problem, I don't know much. I forget his real name, but I know he likes to use an alias. Albert Thumpet."

"Albert Thumpet. We'll start with that." She typed it in. "No Albert Thumpet. Got anything else?"

"I know what he looks like. I interviewed him once before."

"You interviewed him and don't know his name?"

The tangled web. "He insisted on using that alias all through the interview. Kept calling himself Albert Thumpet. That's the only name that stuck with me. He's tall and big, really big, with dark curly hair and blue eyes."

"Oh, I think I know who you're talking about! Real pale blue?"

"Almost translucent. You know him?"

"I think so. I mean, I don't know his name, but I've seen him around the hospital."

He was in the right place. The bastard was somewhere nearby. Was Sari too?

Sloane studied his face.

"Ever been to Hijinks?"

"Where?"

"Hijinks. The club in Gainesville. The hot spot. I used to work there as a waitress. Just wondered if maybe we ran into each other. You look familiar."

"Never been there. I heard it's a fun place. I'm pretty boring. Spend most of my time in the hospital or at the library."

Sloane rolled back her chair, showing off nice legs in white pantyhose under a short skirt.

"Is it possible to locate a patient by a physical description?"

"Yes and no. The hard copies of the patient files have photos and physical descriptions. So it is possible. But they're not on the computer and we have hundreds of patients. Can't you just call someone back at Shands and get the guy's name?"

"The only person I could call would be Professor Banyon. Then he'd know I screwed up. He's a terror. Goes through research assistants like a tank of gas. I really need this job. The guy takes clozapine, I know that much."

"Hey, that helps. We cross-index patients by prescriptions to track what meds are being used in what amounts. I can pull up a list of all our patients on chlozapine."

"Could you?" Mimi Sloane was a nice person. He felt like a jerk for misrepresenting himself.

"Sure." She fiddled with the computer as Danny shifted his aching leg.

Rapid footsteps in the hallway drew his attention. He'd been expecting the cops to descend at any second, ever since the current carried him from Troy's murder scene. But it was only a light-haired woman in a white blouse and dark skirt. She passed quickly.

Danny was turning back to Mimi when a spark lit up a locked memory vault.

Something about the woman.

*That profile!* Enya at Sugar Lake holding her ponytail in one hand and the upside-down whiskey bottle in the other, the image he swore he'd never forget.

He jumped up, but his leg buckled. He regained his balance and scooted to the doorway.

"What's wrong?" Sloane said. "Was that him?"

He leaned across the threshold in time to see the back of a slender blonde woman disappearing around the corner at the end of the corridor. He was losing his mind. Must be the fever.

"Are you okay?" Mimi said as he returned to his seat.

"Yeah, sorry. I thought I saw someone I know from the medical school."

"I mean your leg."

"Oh, this?"

He waved to the bloody gauze erupting through the back of his pants like it was a scraped knee.

"Had a little trouble trying to restrain a meth addict in the emergency room at Shands last night. That's my night job. The guy grabbed a scalpel and was threatening a nurse. I tried to kick it out of his hand, without success, obviously."

Lying bastard.

Mimi Sloane looked like she wanted to cradle him.

"Poor boy. Anyway, here's the list. You can come back around here and look at it if you want."

Danny gimped around the desk and leaned over her. Her satin blouse angled open exposing a pink bra strap and freckled shoulder.

"Only eight?" he said, staring at the monitor, stunned by his sudden reversal in fortune.

"That's just the first screen."

He knew it was too good to be true. She hit *Next Page* and Danny watched the names roll over.

"Thirteen in all," she said.

Still a manageable list.

"This is a huge request. Is there any way you could possibly go through the files to help me find him?"

"What's in it for me?"

"Oh. Well, um, what do you want?"

"I'm just teasing you. Of course I'll help. But it could take a while. Do you have time?"

"Absolutely," he lied again.

# 37

**FINK STARED** at the restroom mirror with flared nostrils, baring his teeth.

"You talking to me?" He whipped the pistol from his waistband, but it got caught on the microphone wire taped to his belly and clattered to the floor, cracking one of the ceramic tiles. He swept it up in a smooth motion like it was all part of the plan and pointed it at the mirror. "Are you talking to me?"

Move over De Niro. Motherfucker, he was getting badder by the second.

He laid the gun on the counter and refastened the wire to the microphone disguised as a shirt button. He retested the recorder taped to his groin. Still worked. He got the recorder and button mic from the *Spy All Day* store at the mall. Only sixty bucks. He rebuttoned his shirt and tucked the gun back in.

Tight fit. He'd join a gym when this mess was over.

The raggedy vinyl briefcase stuffed with cash stood at his side. He deserved a better case, like the sweet soft leather bag he saw in the window at the Lincoln Road mall in South Beach. If everything worked out, he'd buy one.

The bank wouldn't let him withdraw a hundred thousand dollars from Danny's account. Said they didn't have that much cash on hand. He got twenty grand in twenty-dollar bills, which he taped in stacks to a layer of paperback books, hoping Hauptmann wouldn't dig beneath them too soon.

Fink unscrewed the cap on his new tube of styling gel, squeezed a generous amount on his palm and combed it through his hair.

He was hoping to look smooth and tough like New York Knicks Coach Pat Riley. He'd heard a rumor that Riley might be coming to coach the Heat. That would rock.

But when he stopped to appraise the results, Riley looked a lot cooler. Probably used more goop. He squirted a winding trail down the center of his scalp and worked it in.

He might as well have used a caulking gun. His head looked like an oil spill. He mopped it with paper towels and recombed his hair.

Still didn't look like Pat. Maybe it was the red hair. And the glasses. He'd look into laser surgery when this was over.

He left the restroom feeling in control, but was already shaking by the time he got to the reception area.

"You use your head to clean the toilet while you were in there?" the receptionist said.

Bitch. He'd fire her except she was married to one lawyer on the floor and having an affair with the other.

Back in his office, he gazed at the pile of shrapnel in the center of his desk. The decimated Rolex. Hauptmann really crossed the line on that one. So what if it was counterfeit? It was still his, dammit. Besides, his parents gave it to him.

He patted his groin, tracing the outlines of the gun and recorder.

Only a few hours to go. He popped another alprazolam. His last one.

# 38

IT WAS the seventh file, thick with chart notes and court documents he couldn't decipher, but the first page had a typed summary with a picture stapled to it. It was him. No doubt about it.

> *Jaxon (No middle name) Kempler, D.O.B. 3-3-56. Race: Caucasian. Sex: Male. Marital Status: Single. Height: 6' 4".*
> *Weight: 264. Hair: brown. Eyes: blue. Address: Rural Route 3, Box 12, Ocala, FL. Diagnosis: Schizophrenia.*
>
> *Born and raised near Ocala. Mother deceased (see below). Father unknown. Discipline issues growing up. Fights, truancy. Progressively worse in high school. Expelled in tenth grade for setting fire to school. High intelligence.*

He read about the death of Kempler's mother and his arrest in Daytona in 1983 for killing three lawyers outside a topless bar.

"Damn."

"Is he the one?"

"Yeah. It's him."

The psychiatrists testified at trial that Kempler was suffering from a psychotic delusion at the time of the murders, believing the men were the ones who killed his mother.

*Disposition: Not Guilty By Reason of Insanity. Committed indefinitely to Florida State Mental Hospital. Released after twelve years. Prognosis: Uncertain. Much improved on new meds. Weekly monitoring by case manager, S. Thompson.*

"Sad, isn't it?" Mimi Sloane said. "They all are. When you work around here, you go home at night wondering what it is that keeps you from becoming one of them. Maybe just a few genes or one neural kink. It's scary."

Danny closed the file and handed it to her.

"What are you going to do?"

"I need to go see him."

Sloane suggested they get together for lunch sometime. Danny said sure and hurried out, ditching the labcoat in a restroom.

Back in his car, he spread the Ocala map across the sizzling dashboard and searched for Rural Route 3. He couldn't find it. How could it not be on the map? Maybe it had another name.

He couldn't chance going back inside for directions. Lucky to get out the first time. Sooner or later he was going to run into someone who read the Jacksonville newspaper and had a memory for faces. His leg couldn't take another round trip anyway.

But driving around blindly wasn't a plan either. The gas-sucking Dart was back down to a quarter-tank and his net worth now stood at five dollars and change. He scanned the parking lot for someone he could get directions from. Across the way, a mother tugged the arm of a child stooping to pick a treasure off the pavement. Too far to shout. He'd only scare them.

The doors to the mental health center slid open and his friend with the aluminum foil hat stalked out, glancing around suspiciously, lips in constant motion. No help.

But there was someone behind him.

Danny jumped forward in the bucket seat, hitting his head on the car roof. It was the blonde woman he saw walking past Mimi Sloane's office.

She paused to slide on a pair of sunglasses from her purse. Danny studied her. Even with the shades, he was sure it was the same woman. And she still looked like Enya McKenzie.

She turned in the other direction and began walking.

"Hey!" he yelled out the window.

The car door stuck, as usual. He hammered it with his shoulder and spilled onto the asphalt, clambered up and began moving in her direction, willing one foot in front of the other.

"Hello. Excuse me. Could I talk to you?"

The woman turned and raised her sunglasses. They were twenty yards apart.

Danny froze. Either the fever had consumed him or he was standing in an Ocala parking lot staring at the same face he saw on the dock at the reunion.

Showing no recognition, the woman turned and resumed walking.

Damaged leg dragging behind, Danny huffed and puffed to within fifteen yards.

"Please. I have to talk to you. I think I know you."

The woman stopped again, but this time her expression changed, first to bewilderment and then to either shock or fear.

She pivoted and began to run, pumps clicking like tap hammers on the cement until she yanked them off and doubled her speed. It was no contest. Danny couldn't keep up.

"Stop! Please."

She veered off the sidewalk onto the asphalt. He watched helplessly as she weaved through cars until stopping at a white Honda Civic.

He reversed direction and faltered back to the Dart. The door was still open, keys in the ignition. The 360 V-8 could easily overtake the Civic.

Tires screeched as he climbed into the creaky front seat. The Civic peeled out the exit just as he cranked the ignition.

The starter groaned. Once, twice, then quit.

He hammered the steering wheel. President James Garfield wobbled on the dashboard, staring at him severely.

"You were supposed to bring me luck."

# 39

SARI PULLED a splinter from her hand and restacked the books on the cooler, leaving out *1984* because it was smaller than the rest. The tower was an inch shorter, but more stable. She made one other adjustment, tearing pages from the Danielle Steele paperbacks and stuffing them under the cooler to make it more level on the uneven concrete. Her earlier attempt to stand the cooler on one end and use the books to prop up the slanted side failed because the books wouldn't stay in place.

Light filtered through the *X* she cut in the carpet with the nail, illuminating the shadowed basement like a skylight. When she first saw it, she almost cried. A piece of furniture on top would have ended everything.

So close to freedom, but it still seemed like a mile. The boards were just out of grasp. The last fall was her fourth try. She dusted off her newest bruises and accepted that stretching wasn't going to cut it. She had to go airborne. Not far. Only a couple of inches. But whether it was an inch or a foot, it required the same difficult mechanical feat: rising vertically from a teetering stack of books on a wobbly ice chest on a crooked floor.

She visualized it in slow motion, like she was taught as a kid on the balance beam during three years of torturous gymnastics lessons, before her mother conceded her daughter was a klutz.

All about balance. Toes tight. Hips square. Slow, measured breaths. Knees bent. Straight up, like an arrow.

She rubbed her neck, took some deep breaths and climbed back on the cooler.

# 40

"THAT OUGHTA DO IT."

Danny watched impatiently as the elderly man named Harold wrenched jumper cable claws onto the posts of the Dart's battery for better contact.

He'd been jumping cars since he was a kid and it was all he could do to not push Harold out of the way to hurry things up. But he stayed patient, believing fate gave him a break when Harold pulled up next to the Dart with its raised hood and asked if he was having car trouble.

Two doctors ignored him when he asked for a jump, walking past like he was invisible. He was about to risk waving down the security guard when Harold came along. The jumper cables were in the Dart's wired-shut trunk. Not the first time the heap needed defibrillation.

Harold lifted his jaunty cap and wiped sweat with a polyester sleeve. Grease from the filthy engine stained his powder blue slacks.

"Crank the ignition, but wait 'til I get my engine revved."

The starter whirred and the Dart billowed clouds of white smoke as the flooded carburetor cleared.

Harold unhooked the jumper cables.

"Need a new battery, maybe an alternator," he said. "On the other hand, depending what they tell you it's gonna cost, you might want to look into getting new transportation. No sense throwing good money after bad."

Danny eased off the gas. The motor held steady. He got out and shook Harold's hand, slipping him a five-dollar bill. All he had left was loose change. The *Lottery Lunatic* was broke.

"You don't need to do that."

"It's a tip, for helping me."

"It didn't cost me anything."

"You got grease on your pants."

"Hell, my wife can get that out."

"Please, keep it. Harold, by any chance are you from around here?"

Harold laughed. "You could say that. Born and raised, not many who can make that claim."

"Have you ever heard of Rural Route 3?"

"Heard of it? I delivered milk and eggs on it for years when I was a young man."

Maybe fate really did bring Harold to him.

"Can you tell me the fastest way to get there?"

# 41

MAGNIFICENT SUNLIGHT streamed through the window. Ornate rusting burglar bars behind the dirty panes dissected the light with a halo effect, like a stained-glass window. Dust bunnies floated across the beams like angels. The brightness hurt her underground eyes, but the warmth nourished her skin.

In a small wood-paneled bedroom, Sari lay on gold shag carpet rubbing her scalp. The room was empty except for an unplugged alarm clock.

She had grabbed the boards on her third jump. After that, everything followed the steps she'd rehearsed in her head a thousand times: jackknife her feet through the opening and clamp her knees on the other side, rest, wrestle her hips up and through and rest again. At that point, her body was split like a woman sawed in half for a magician's trick.

The last step was the hardest. She knew it would be. Her shoulder got stuck trying to wrench it through the opening. Caught with her back twisted forty-five degrees, tendons burning, grip slipping, she imagined just letting go and dropping head-first to the dank floor. A quick end to everything.

But she squeezed her lungs empty, jerked with all her might and tore free, the jagged wood clawing bloody streaks down her arm. On top, she almost got pulled back down when she tried to roll away, tearing out a clot of hair that was tangled in the boards.

Still massaging her head, she stood and looked out the window. Nothing but green fields and patchy woods of pine and oak trees.

She ticked through the checklist. Step one: make sure the monster wasn't home. Step two: call 911.

Moving down a hall darkened by more wood paneling, she passed a bedroom and bath. A living room with peeling floral wallpaper opened off the hall. Movement.

Flattening against the wall, she saw dancing shadows on the ceiling, but heard no sound. She inched around the corner. It was a television, an old-style cabinet model tuned to a game show.

No car out front. He was gone. She found a phone in the kitchen, on the wall, a faded yellow rectangle with a rotary dial. *Click, click, click.*

Dead.

Disappointment, but not surprise. She knew the house sounds well and hadn't heard a phone ring since arriving.

The next step was to get help from a neighbor, but the view out the kitchen was the same as from the bedroom at the other end of the house. No houses or people. Only more fields and trees. She checked the front and back. Same thing.

A disappointment *and* a surprise. From the lack of outdoor sounds through the open basement windows, she knew they weren't in a densely populated place, but she expected to see signs of human life. She was in the middle of nowhere.

That left getting out and running. But how far was she from civilization? Her reserves were depleted. She couldn't make it far without more fuel. She'd take some food … and needed her shoes.

She found them in Kempler's bedroom closet, lined up neatly next to his, so big they made hers look like kids' shoes. Her rolled-up socks were on top. She sat on a race car bedspread and pulled the socks gingerly over her raw toes.

On the nightstand was an open Seminole High yearbook. She recognized the *Sweetheart Couple of the Year* picture of her and Danny, except Danny's throat had been slashed with red ink above an inscription: *I auta cry, I auta laugh, I auta write my autograph.*

Tightening the laces made her feel stronger. She started for the kitchen, but thought about the gun. An equalizer. She searched the nightstand. It was filled with porn magazines. Ugly stuff. Women in bondage and worse. She slammed the cabinet shut.

The key variable was how long the monster would be gone. It could be ten minutes or four days. Stick with the plan. Looking for the gun wasn't part of it. He probably kept it with him anyway.

She went to the kitchen. Stuck to the refrigerator with a Key West magnet was a receipt for three XXXL polo shirts: *Jaxon Kempler, Rural Route 3, Box 12, Ocala, FL.* So that's where she was. And Kempler was his real name, like he said in the death letter.

The refrigerator contained only a carton of milk and squeeze bottle of pancake syrup. The milk expired a month ago, but she grabbed the syrup. The cupboards were empty too, except for a cabinet above the sink crammed with boxes of pancake mix. She grabbed one. If she got stuck in the woods the syrup and mix would at least be edible.

She set the supplies on a red Formica dining table and foraged for a bag. When she found one, she picked up the pancake and syrup … and dropped them on the floor.

On the table, Danny's picture looked up from a newspaper under a headline: *LOTTO WINNER CHARGED IN GRISLY DRUG SLAYING*. A *Sun-Sentinel*, June 12. Danny really had been arrested. The monster had to be behind it.

Beneath it were more newspapers with more articles about Danny, from all around the state. At the bottom of the pile she came to a handwritten letter, a photocopy of the original. The margins were filled with block printing in red ink. She recognized that writing from the game pieces and death letter. Kempler's.

But something about the scribbled cursive in the letter also looked familiar.

*Dear Enya,*

*My name is Danny Teakwell. You probably already know it, but in case you don't. I'm the one who drove you home that night at Sugar Lake.*

The letter was dated December 19, 1974. She never knew Danny wrote to Enya. But why would she? The letter was sent four months after she broke up with him.

*I'm writing this letter because it's almost Christmas and I'm crying and I don't know what else to do. I'm not a very good writer. I know what I think, but it's hard to put it on paper. If you read this I hope you can hear what I'm trying to say even though I probably won't say it very good.*

*My friends and I did a horrible thing. We got you drunk and took advantage of you. It's hard for me to admit that to myself because I never thought I was that kind of a person. But I guess I am. It's a sad truth to live with.*

*What happened that night was our fault, not yours. That's the most important thing I want you to know.*

*I'm not writing to ask forgiveness. I don't forgive myself. I don't expect it from you. I had a girlfriend before everything happened. Her name is Sari Hunter. Maybe you know her from school. If someone hurt Sari like we hurt you, I'd want to kill them.*

*If it helps at all, I am paying for what I did and will for the rest of my life. I lost my friends. It turned out maybe they weren't such good friends anyway. But I also lost Sari. She meant more to me than anything.*

A tear rolled down Sari's cheek and splattered on the paper.

*I didn't plan what happened. While you were in the lake with Troy, John Mangrum told me a lie about Sari betraying me. That was my first mistake, listening to Mangrum. I wouldn't have believed him except Sari had sort of not told me the truth about where she was that night.*

Sari looked up. The sun made the faded red-gingham curtains glow. A 1982 Far Side calendar hung on a hook next to the sink. Twenty years and it finally made some sense.

*I loved Sari ever since we met. We grew up together before we went to Seminole High. That night in that moment, I thought I hated her. I hated all girls. I felt lost and scared.*

*When I swam across the lake and saw you on the sand something snapped in me. Mangrum told me some other lies, about you, that made it seem not as bad when it was happening. They wouldn't be excuses even if they were true.*

*I always loved Sugar Lake. It was a place to go and feel like you were far away even though you weren't. Troy Stoddelmeyer and I swam in it since we were kids. Until that night, my memories of Sugar Lake were hot summer days full of sunshine reflecting off clear water.*

*Not anymore. On our way home that night, the song Black Water by the Doobie Brothers was playing on the radio. It stuck in my mind and that's my memory of the lake now. Black water, a dark place to haunt nightmares.*

367

*This letter is my confession. You can use it that way if you need to. You can show it to your parents or take it to the police. I won't deny anything.*

*That night when you were getting out of the car I said I was sorry. It sounded stupid then and still does, but I really am. I heard a rumor you dropped out of school. I hope it's not true.*

*I've never been sure if there's a God, but I have been praying for you.*

*Danny Teakwell*

Jaxon Kempler had underlined the last sentence and printed in the margin, *There IS a GOD and hes coming to kick the holey shit out of you.*

Sari dropped the letter. *Mangrum.* That wicked liar. And Jaxon Kempler, a psychopath trying to destroy what was left. But why? And how did he get a copy of a letter Danny wrote to Enya twenty years ago?

She jammed the supplies in the bag. She'd go out the back door into the woods and work her way along the road to avoid running into Kempler if he came home. But when she wrenched the doorknob, the door didn't budge.

What the …? Three shiny gold deadbolt locks, just like the ones on the basement door, the ones she had stared at for nine days. The locks were double-keyed and there were no keys in them.

She ran to the front door. Same thing. Three deadbolts with no keys. Searching frantically, she found only one more door. It smelled like gasoline. The door to the garage he dragged her in from nine days earlier. Three more locks. No keys.

"It's okay. It's okay," she said, steadying herself and heading back to the kitchen. "You can go out a window."

But just as the reassurance left her lips, the image of the cathedral sunshine behind the burglar bars in the bedroom stopped her cold. Her eyes darted to the living room.

*No!* She sprinted to the kitchen. *Nooo! Not possible.*

Each window was fortified by the same rusting floral-pattern bars.

She dashed through the house, but it was a repeat in every room: iron bars behind dirty glass.

The bathroom was the last room and her last chance. The small window was opaque. She slid it open. Bars.

*A cage in a cage.* In nine days of planning, it never occurred to her she could still be trapped if she got out of the basement. How could she have not thought of that?

She slumped to her knees in the bathtub. *She hadn't thought of it!*

Resting her head against the tiles, she felt completely hopeless for the first time since he took her. So tired.

She snapped out of it and sat up straight. There *must* be a way out. *Think.* The bars are old. The basement wood was rotted. The window frames might be too. She'd find something to pry the bars loose. He must have some tools around. All she needed was time.

She was stepping out of the bathtub when she heard it, barely a buzz at first, but the sound amplified quickly. It was a car, traveling at high speed on the road out front. The motor roared louder and louder until it suddenly died.

The car turned in the driveway.

# 42

**THE VEHICLE RUMBLED** up the driveway. She couldn't make out the driver from the bathroom window. She ran to the living room as the car skidded to a stop, but still couldn't see through the sun glare on the dirty windshield. Holding her breath, she waited and watched.

The car door opened and the monster got out.

Sari ducked behind the curtain. Now what? Instinct said to fight. Logic said no because she'd lose again.

No way was she going back into the basement. Even if the death threat was another intimidation trick, she wasn't sure she could make it out a second time. Besides, he might spot the slashed carpet before she had a chance to try again.

The car door slammed.

She didn't see any choice except hiding in the back bedroom where she started.

A carving knife with a wood handle hung on a peg above the stove. She hesitated. He was so damned meticulous. If he noticed it missing, he'd come after her right away.

Footsteps on the porch.

Then that's the way it would be. She slid the knife off the peg and bolted down the hall as the top lock unlatched. Halfway, she remembered the pancake mix and syrup on the kitchen floor and raced to retrieve them as the second bolt turned.

Passing the bathroom, she saw the window was still open and went to shut it. She made it to the back bedroom just as the third lock clicked.

The monster came in singing. Not the Carpenters. A new song. Jim Croce with changed lyrics. "Big, bald, Albert Thumpet, that wild accountant and his crazy trumpet, deader than old King Kong, sent to where he don't belong."

She heard the door close, followed by what sounded like more latching. Was he already relocking the locks? She couldn't tell for sure above the singing.

He sounded awfully cheerful for someone about to commit murder. He had dumped the Croce song and was belting out *Knock Three Times* by Tony Orlando, punctuating the chorus with loud rapping on wood.

A clatter in the hallway. She peeked and saw a shiny new shovel propped against the wall, yellow proof of purchase tape still on the handle. *When I get back I'll dig a nice hole for you in the backyard.* So the letter wasn't just a threat.

Kempler came into view, crossing the kitchen wearing a purple polo shirt and bandage on his neck where she bit him. He switched songs again. *You've Lost That Lovin' Feeling* by the Righteous Brothers.

She looked around for something else to defend herself with. Nothing but the dusty alarm clock and some coat hangers in the closet. The cord from the clock could work as a garrotte—if she was ten times stronger. He'd flip her over his shoulder in a second. She set about fashioning a set of spiked knuckles from the wire hangers.

He was still singing. Good. It told her where he was.

She broke off pieces of wire and twisted them around her

knuckles. When she finished, she made a fist. Ten metal points stuck out at various angles. They looked pretty lethal. If the knife failed, she'd try for a clean shot at his eyes with the spikes.

Jaxon Kempler was getting in the groove with *Thank You Falettin Me Be Mice Elf* by Sly and the Family Stone when a loud knocking resounded through the house. At first Sari thought he had segued mid-chorus back to the Tony Orlando hit, but the singing died instantly.

*Rap, rap, rap.*

Someone was banging on the front door.

Silence.

*Rap, rap, rap.*

"Just a minute," Kempler said tentatively.

Heavy steps crossed the living room and Sari faced another dilemma. Should she run out and scream for help? The knocking was incessant. Who could it be? The only visitor in nine days was the woman he called Enya. He drugged her for that visit. Whoever was knocking, and they were doing it insistently, must be unexpected.

Jangling keys. Damn him. He really did relock the locks.

"You!" Kempler's voice.

"Let me in."

A woman.

"What ... what are you doing here?"

The door slammed. "What have you done, Jaxon?"

"I didn't do anything," he protested like a scolded child.

"I just saw Danny Teakwell at the mental health center."

Danny! Sari clamped a hand to her mouth.

"Teakwell? That's impossible."

"It's more than possible. He tried to stop me in the parking lot. What in the world have you done?"

"I—I ..." He murmured something Sari couldn't make out and retreated to the kitchen.

"Don't walk away, Jaxon. Look at me."

Whoever the woman was, she had some kind of power over him.

"Sit down," she said.

Chairs scraped on the kitchen tiles. They were at the red table.

"I only did what you wanted me to do, Enya."

"I told you, don't call me that."

The same woman as yesterday. A far out idea took shape. Enya somehow alive and behind everything? Using crazy Jaxon Kempler to get revenge?

Still no response from Kempler. What was happening?

"Wait a minute. What's that?" Kempler, a sudden edge to his words. "Hey, that's not supposed to—"

"Where did you get this letter?" the woman said.

Oh no. The letter from Danny. She left it on the table.

"I found it."

"Found it?"

"At your house. But it's not supposed to be out like that. I need to go check something."

Sari braced for a fight.

# 43

**DANNY CRUISED** past a bank clock. Almost two. Grady would be waiting for his call at the dock. He pulled into a gas station alongside a payphone and stretched out the window. Rolling in his last coins, he dialed the number. The boat was Grady's second home. He treated the phone like he owned it. He picked up on the first ring.

"Danny?"

"It's me."

"Are you okay?"

"I'm, uh, surviving."

"Where are you?"

"Calling from a payphone in …" Would Rodriguez know about the phone at the dock? "North Florida. I probably shouldn't say where. Better for your own protection. I only have a second, but promised I'd check in."

"You know they're looking for you everywhere."

"Fink filled me in and I saw the Jacksonville newspaper. Now they think I killed Troy and … took Sari."

"You always had a big way of doing things, son."

"Ha, I guess that's one way to look at it. I wanted to let you know I'm alive and hopefully on the right track to finding the real killer and … maybe …"

"Sari. I know. I can't wait to meet this young lady. Anything we can do to help from down here?"

"I need you to call someone. Myron Tamms. He's an old man who lived in Enya's house."

"Enya? Who's that?"

Danny had lost track of who knew what. "She's a girl from high school who may be the key to everything. Tamms said he came across something having to do with my case. Called it a *tragic mystery*, but I can't reach him."

"Okay, Myron Tamms. T-A-M-S?"

"Two *m*s. He's in the phone book."

"What do you want me to say to him?"

"Anything you can to make him trust you and explain the mystery. This guy's no kook. Hell, it's probably too late, but just in case."

"Too late? What do you mean by that? Are you telling me everything?"

"No."

A pause. "Alright. I'll call him. Tamms, with two *m*s."

"There's one other thing."

"What's that?"

"I love you, Grady."

The time ran out and the phone went dead.

A car raced up from behind, but it was just someone waiting to use the phone. He caught a glimpse of himself in the mirror and looked away. Wiping his sweaty hand on his pants, he jammed the Dart into gear and accelerated across the I-75 interchange, just like Harold told him to do. If the Samaritan was right, Rural Route 3 intersected his path in a couple of miles.

# 44

**KEMPLER GOT UP.** "There's some very strange things going on in this world."

Sari tightened her grip on the knife and curled the wire spikes.

"Sit back down, Jaxon. We need to get to the bottom of this right now. You broke into my house and took this letter?"

"I didn't *break* in, Enya. The window was unlocked. I'm just trying to help. You should be grateful instead of complaining." His voice was changing, monster returning, eclipsing the scolded boy.

"I'm not Enya. You know that. I'm Sabrina. I never should have told you about Enya. I made a serious mistake. You had no right to go into my house." Still calm, but less confident.

Sabrina? Who's Sabrina? Sari couldn't stand it. She slipped out of the bedroom and edged down the hall, ducking into Kempler's bedroom, just ten feet from the kitchen. When she poked her head out, all she could see was the monster's wide back stretching his purple polo shirt.

"You say you're Sabrina. I've been thinking about that. You're familiar, I assume, with multiple personalities? It's a rare disorder."

"I know what it is, Jaxon."

"Well, I know a lot more than you because a young medical man, Dr. Lardmore, once diagnosed me as having them. Of course, Lardass was wrong. Little quack. Mention other people live in your head and he automatically assumes you got multiple personalities. I told him it was only my mother, but you know medical men, they never listen. I tried to sue him for malpractice, but no lawyer would take my case, probably because they heard about the three lawyers in Daytona. But you know all that. Do you like hot chocolate?"

"No. We need to talk."

"I'm not asking if you want any," he said harshly. "I'm asking if you like it. Because if you didn't but woke up with a cup beside your bed, it would be a strong indicator you have multiple personalities. That's what happened in the famous case of Gina Rinaldi, well-documented in medical books."

"Jaxon, when's the last time you took your clozapine?"

"*Clozapine.* Sounds like acne medicine. *Quit popping that white crap all over the mirror. Use Clozapine.* I took some yesterday. I ran out for a while."

"Let's do this. We'll get in my car and go see Dr. Remington."

"Your car has a crummy radio and not enough leg room. Besides, Remington doesn't appreciate me. "

"Okay. We can go see Dr. Lazlo."

"Lazlo! Even worse. He's the one who should be on clozapine. Better yet, frontal lobotomy. I'd do it myself if they'd let me."

"Then I'll go alone. You can stay here. I'll be back in a little while."

"I can't let you go now. You know that."

Sari had a bad feeling about the way things were unraveling in the kitchen. Whoever the woman was, she no longer sounded like a coconspirator. She sounded frightened.

"I'm leaving. Do you understand?"

Sari waited for an explosion.

"Please don't go," Kempler whined. "Don't you want to know about Teakwell?"

# 45

**THE STATE TROOPER** had been behind him since he crossed I-75. Danny moved to the right lane. The trooper did the same.

Act normal. Just out for a drive in your rusted-out car with the door and trunk wired shut and duct tape for a window, vehicle of choice for serial killers everywhere. He slowed down and the trooper did the same. A white Jeep passed the trooper followed by a Mustang convertible. Drivers with clear consciences.

One way to tell for sure. The turn signals didn't work so he stuck his arm out and turned the corner past a motel. The Jeep came into view and kept going. The Mustang did the same.

The trooper turned after him and switched on flashing blue lights.

# 46

**FROZEN,** Sari listened as Jaxon Kempler summarized a killing spree that included stabbing an accountant named Albert Thumpet in North Dakota to assume his identity, mutilating John Mangrum and framing Danny for it and shooting Troy Stoddelmeyer on a dock in Jacksonville.

The story sounded like more crazy talk, except now she knew better. The newspapers confirmed at least the part about Mangrum. The visitor he called Enya stayed silent.

Kempler suddenly leaped out of his chair and spiraled. Sari dipped back and raised her weapons, but he stopped at the edge of the kitchen.

"I have everything documented if you don't believe me. You can check those papers on the table, but here's the latest. Read this headline."

The hyena laugh. Still no response from the woman who called herself Sabrina.

"The cops think Teakwell killed Stoddelmeyer too. I didn't even plan that, but you know the old saying. *The Lord helps y'all who helps y'all's selves.* Teakwell keeps trying to fuck everything up. I probably should've killed him on the dock with Stoddelmeyer, but I couldn't bring myself to do it because … well, you know."

"Jaxon, please let me go get help. You're not well."

"Help? I've got news for you, Enya, a thousand jigawatts to the cortex is not my idea of help."

"Why do you keep calling me Enya? You know my sister died a long time ago."

*Sisters!* So that was the connection. She never knew Enya had a sister.

"I believed you about that until I dug up Enya's grave and lost a good shovel in the process. Guess what was in it?"

"You dug up my sister's grave?"

"Correction. *Your* grave. At least, that's what I might be thinking. This is getting confusing, even for me. Whoever it was, her coffin was emptier than a breadbasket. I did it for you, *Sabrenya*, and my mother, of course. Two rapist scums down, a third on the way out. They hurt us, we hurt them. I wanted to keep Stoddelmeyer around longer because his cash came in handy, but progress can't be stopped."

"Enya wouldn't have wanted that. Don't you see?" she cried, composure breaking. "She was a kind person. A forgiving person."

"No one forgives rapists. Not me. Not Enya. I can't speak for you, whoever you are. Enya probably would want me to kill Teakwell too, but for me of all people to make some kid an orphan would not be normal."

Sari tried to assemble the pieces. The last part didn't make any sense, unless … add in the reference in the death letter to a child. She did the math. Sugar Lake, a night at the beginning of the school year. Enya drops out of school at Christmas. Commits suicide in June … ten months later. Enya pregnant from the night at Sugar Lake? And Kempler thinks Danny's the father?

"How is Ryan, anyway?"

"How do you know about Ryan?"

"Entering without breaking can teach you a lot of things."

Chair grating. "That's it. Listen good. I'm walking out of here and getting in my car. Don't try to stop me."

Sari heard a click.

"I won't, but my gun might. I lost my Luger in a river up in Jacksonville, thanks to Teakwell," he spat. "This one's not as accurate, but plenty good enough for stopping people from walking out and getting in their car. I dropped by Gunzo-Funzo to buy a replacement for the Luger, but they said I can't buy one because I'm a convicted mental patient. Do you believe that? Something called the fucking Brady Bill. Discrimination. We can't ignore it anymore."

"I'm your friend, Jaxon. You know I am. You don't want to hurt me."

"Of course not, but people don't kill people, guns do … and bookends in the shape of a clown and knives to the spine and surgical drilling and …"

# 47

**THE TROOPER RUSHED** up close on Danny, siren blaring. He guided the Dart onto a freshly mowed shoulder of scorched weeds, leaving the motor running.

A woman in a close-fitting brown uniform accentuating a wide butt climbed out of the car. Gold curls flared under a Mountie hat. Danny could see the dilapidated Dart reflected in her mirrored sunglasses as she approached the window.

He looked up and smiled.

"May I see your driver's license, sir?"

He had it, in his wallet, still waterlogged from last night's swim in the St. John's River, but if she didn't already know who he was, he'd just be surrendering by turning over his identification.

"What did I do? I was driving the speed limit. I signaled my turn."

"Emission control violation. This vehicle of yours leaves a trail of smoke halfway to Tampa. License, please."

Danny Teakwell, the nerd who picks cigarette butts off the beach, nailed for a crime against the environment.

"I think I left it at home."

"Where is home, sir? Are you an Ocala resident?"

"No, actually I'm from down south. Hollywood."

"You drove the entire state without your driver's license? That wasn't very good planning. I'm going to have to ask you to step out of the car."

He had nothing to lose. "Wait, you know what? I might have my license after all. What happened was I took it out of my wallet yesterday in St. Augustine when I rented a jet-ski because they wanted to hold it as a deposit, but now I'm thinking I put it back. I have my wallet right here." Brilliant, brainiac.

Trooper Tanzer, Badge No. 509, took a step back and slid her hand to the butt of her revolver as he reached for his back pocket.

He extracted the swollen slab of leather, opened it and handed it to her. "I accidentally took the wallet jet-skiing with me. Kinda wet."

She'd have probable cause to arrest him for felony stupidity if he kept talking.

"Please remove the license from the wallet."

The license hadn't been taken out since he bought the wallet three years ago and was melded to the plastic insert. He ended up tearing the flap out like it was made to be detachable and handing it to her.

"Registration?"

"Huh?"

"I need your vehicle registration."

"Oh boy, now that I know I don't have. Somebody stole it out of my glove compartment. Broke the window to do it." He motioned to the rear duct-taped window. "I would have given it to them if I knew they were gonna break the window."

Smiling, all relaxed and friendly.

"Sir, I need you to step out and move to the rear of the vehicle."

"No problem," he said, and punched the gas pedal to the floor.

# 48

"THERE'S ONE WAY to tell if you're Enya or not," Kempler said. "If Enya is already dead and you're her, putting a bullet in your head shouldn't have any effect. On the other hand, if you're who you say you are, the bullet will prove it. Let's do this nicely. Put your head on the table, Sabrenya."

The words rang cold and ominous. Sari looked at the knife and coat hanger spikes. They didn't look as threatening as before.

"Jaxon, I can help you, but you have to let me get you back to the hospital."

"Don't think so. Have you seen the kind of people they let live in that place? Believe me, this is going to hurt me more than it hurts you. Well, not really. Actually, I don't feel that much about it one way or the other. I guess Lazlo was right about something. I really do love you, but there's a fine line between love and death, as they say. I thought you were different, wearing the *Chain of Pain* and all. I'm not saying this to hurt your feelings, but you're not."

He'd flipped. Sari couldn't just stand there and let it happen. She inched out of the bedroom to the kitchen. Around the door frame she saw Kempler with his back to her. He held a large silver pistol pressed against the fine blonde hair of a woman … *who looked like Enya McKenzie.*

Her cheek was pressed on the table, blue eyes wet. "You don't want to kill me, Jaxon."

She saw Sari and her eyes widened. Sari put a finger to her lips. Three steps to reach him. A lump stuck in her throat and she found it hard to breathe.

"You keep saying that," Kempler said, "but I might *really* want to kill you. Sometimes a clean break is the best way to end a relationship. I read it in a book by a famous psychologist. He even has a TV show."

He launched into a rant about conflicts in relationships, lost in madness.

Sari raised the knife. Plunge it in his back. It's the only way. She took the first step into the kitchen.

"And don't try to play on my guilt. That's not going to work anymore."

Sari took the second step, holding the knife above her head.

"I'm blameless, a victim like everyone else. Just like Enya. Just like my mother and the rest of the *Chain* gang."

Sari took the last step, tightened her muscles and brought the knife down. But it stopped midway as Jaxon Kempler spun around and clamped her arm in an iron grip.

He put the gun barrel to her forehead, forcing her head back.

"Hello, Scrary! Did I ever mention I also have above-average hearing and an excellent memory for where I hang knives and hide secret letters? Thank you for remembering to set the table. I'll take that knife. *Now.*"

To the woman at the table: "Lift your head a trillionth of an inch and I'll repaint my kitchen with her."

Back to Sari, blue eyes glistening. "Let go of the knife," he said. "Hand it to me nicely."

When he loosened his grip, she yanked her arm away and

jumped back, squaring her body and holding the knife out like a sword.

"*Hah!* Nifty move."

*Go for the soft spot. Below the sternum.*

"But another very under-average idea. I filed this trigger down to a hairlip. It could go off just by me thinking about it. Even if you know how to knife fight, which I doubt, it will take at least one second for the tip of your knife—*my* knife—to reach my belly. Meanwhile, in that same second my high-velocity .45 caliber bullet will travel thirteen hundred feet, except, obviously, your skull will slow it down a little. Gimme the knife."

"Please. Give it to him," the blonde woman at the table whispered. "He'll hurt you."

Sari reluctantly lowered the knife. Kempler stepped in and wrenched it away.

"Women," he said. "Now that you're here, I'd like you to meet my case manager, Sabrina Thompson, who might also be her sister, Enya McKenzie. Sabrenya, this is my friend and prisoner, Scary Sari."

He turned back with a goofy smile. Sari's arm was already in motion. The coat hanger spikes struck him flush on the bridge of the nose. Blood squirted like a garden sprinkler. *But she missed the eyes.*

He grabbed her shirt and yanked her forward. "Godammit, Scrary, you can't just keep going around chomping into people's necks and ripping open their faces. It's rude." He leveled the gun at her chest.

The woman ran from the table. "Jaxon, no! Please."

"Fine," he sighed, then raised the gun and smashed it into Sari's face.

She crumpled. The woman who looked like Enya moved toward her in slow motion. The last thing she saw before blacking out was the clear blue sky beyond the barred windows.

# 49

DANNY TOOK the first turn before Trooper Tanzer made it back to her car, swerving onto a wide tree-lined street past a sign announcing he had entered Cripple Creek. He roared down short streets with inflated names past overbuilt houses with driveways filled with SUVs and minivans.

Left, right, left again. The siren was in full volume somewhere behind him. One plus: the faster he went the hotter the engine burned, reducing the exhaust trail.

He took a sharp corner, just missing a brick mailbox built like a fortress, and slammed on the brakes. The Willow Blossom Trail, exactly two houses long, ended with a stop sign and fence beyond it.

Which way? Instinct said left so he turned right—into a cul-de-sac.

He glided to a halt in the middle of an asphalt circle with a basketball hoop at the end. The siren grew louder. In his rearview mirror was another cul-de-sac.

Nowhere to go. So this was it.

On one side of the cul-de-sac sat a charming split-level ranch house with a white picket fence. A sprawling oak with a rope swing shaded the front yard. A golden retriever dozed beneath a birdhouse. Norman Rockwell couldn't have painted a prettier picture.

Except Rockwell would have painted it with the garage door closed. The gleaming Mercedes was out of place. On the other hand, the empty garage bay next to it looked pretty good to Danny.

He swung the wheel and idled up the driveway, turned off the key and coasted into the garage. To avoid the cacophony associated with battering open the driver's side door, he climbed out the passenger side and crawled on hands and knees toward the door leading into the house, scanning the wall for a doorbell button like the one Grady had in his garage.

There it was.

The siren closed in. Danny reached up and slapped the button. Nothing happened. Did it buzz inside? Maybe he could top off a perfect day and a soccer mom would come out and smoke him with her pink handgun. He stabbed the button again. The ceiling motor kicked in and the garage door rolled down on a grinding steel chain.

*Too damn slowly.* Ducked behind the Mercedes, he saw the trooper's blue lights in the windows of the house across the street just before the door sealed.

"Jesus, sweet Jesus," he exhaled.

"Are you the TV man?"

He opened his eyes to a chubby kid parked in the seat of a yellow plastic car, wearing a Superman costume and sucking on a banana.

Trooper Tanzer's radio crackled in the cul-de-sac.

"Well, now, I guess I am."

"Good, 'cause it's broke and I wanna watch *The Plastic Fantastic Rats*. My mom and me have been waiting for you. I'm Max. Five and a half."

"Nice to meet you. I'm Danny."

"How old?"

"Thirty-seven."

"Just thirty-seven?"

"And three-quarters."

Max nodded approvingly. "Come on," he said. "I'll show you where it is."

"Wait, wait. Hold on." He wanted to keep the kid talking in the garage. "What kind of set is it?"

"It's a Sony."

"What size?"

"Big."

"What's wrong with it?"

"It's broke. Come on," he said, wiping banana on his cape. "Hey, don't you have any tools?"

"I was just about to get them." Danny limped to the back of the Dart and took his time unwiring the trunk.

"What happened to your leg?"

"I got bit by a dog."

"Uh-oh. I better put Igor away. He chomped the mailman last week."

Of course he did. Danny gathered a screwdriver and rusty pliers.

"That's it?"

"All I need."

Max sniffed and stumbled into the house over untied shoe-laces. Danny followed him, entering a bright white kitchen with black appliances.

"*Mo-om*. The TV man's here."

A woman's voice came from upstairs, "I'm feeding the baby. I'll be down in a few minutes."

"Take your time," Danny hollered back.

"She's feeding my little sister, Nina. I call her Ninoid because

395

she looks like a space alien." Marching into the living room, "Here's the TV. Can you fix it in time for *The Plastic Fantastic Rats*?"

"We'll see."

# 50

**SABRINA LEANED** cross-legged against the basement wall, hands bound from behind with plastic ties.

The woman Kempler called Scary Sari sat slumped next to her, gaunt and pinched, also cuffed from behind. Blood clotted the left side of her face. Scrapes and bruises discolored her arms and legs.

She looked at the dirty mattress. A stubby toothbrush and tube of toothpaste were carefully arranged in the center. What had he done to her?

"Are you alright?" Sabrina asked softly.

Sari's lashes flickered. "Um, I'm not sure … what does my face look like?"

"Well … facial cuts bleed a lot. Sometimes they look worse than they are."

"That bad, huh?" She tried to laugh.

"It doesn't look very nice. Are you dizzy?"

"A little. My head hurts."

"What about your vision? Is it blurred?"

"Not sure. Hard to open my eye."

"My name's Sabrina Thompson. How did you get—"

"I'm Sari. Sari ... Hunter," she murmured.

The name took Sabrina's breath away. "Did you say Sari Hunter?"

"Mm-hm. You look like your sister."

"You knew Enya?"

"Sort of. I knew Danny. Danny ... Teakwell. Were you twins?"

"No, I'm two years older. We looked a lot alike. People always got us confused. How did you get here?"

"He brought me. Nine days ago ... I think that's right. I was part of his revenge plan. For your sister."

"How did you get out?"

She pointed with her chin.

"You made that hole?" she asked, incredulous.

"With a nail. I escaped. Almost. Then I got stuck and ..."

"Risked your life for a stranger. I don't know what to say. I'm so sorry. This is my fault." Sabrina hung her head. "It's all my fault."

"He said you were his case manager?"

"That's what they call it. I'm a social worker. I come out once a week to check on him, try to make sure he's taking his medication, drive him to the psychiatrist once a month. They call it monitoring, but it's not nearly enough, not for someone like Jaxon."

"You were so calm in the kitchen, even when he had the gun pointed at you."

"I wasn't feeling calm. That's just the best way to handle Jaxon. Usually. It didn't work this time."

"Did you really see Danny?" Sari said, lifting her head suddenly, startling Sabrina.

"I'm glad to see you moving."

"So you saw him?"

"I did. At the mental health center where I work."

"He's alright?"

"He seemed to be," she lied. Danny Teakwell did not look well.

"What was he doing there?"

"I'm not sure. I ran away from him. He caught me off guard. I knew right away his being there had something to do with Jaxon. I came straight here to find out what was going on."

"How did you know it had to do with the monster? That's what I call him, the monster."

"It's a long story."

"I'm not going anywhere."

"You need to rest."

"No, I don't. I've been trying to put together a puzzle with no pieces since he brought me here. I need to understand."

Sabrina got it. "Okay. I moved to Ocala to take the job at the mental health center last year, right after I got my degree. Didn't start college until I was thirty-two. I was what they call a nontraditional student. After a few months they assigned Jaxon to me. I wasn't ready for someone like him. He's been manipulating the system most of his life. He's unusual. Serious schizophrenic, but smart."

"Above average," Sari said.

"That's him. His intelligence helps him disguise his symptoms and he knows all the right answers when you ask about meds or how he's coping. I screwed up. I let him suck me in with his story."

"What happened?"

"His mother was raped and murdered when he was a child. Schizophrenia is genetic and usually doesn't show up until later, but the trauma triggered something. His behavior started getting more and more bizarre."

"Sad," Sari said, but any possibility of feeling sympathy for the monster was long gone.

"Back in the eighties he killed three men he thought were the ones who murdered his mother. The court found him not guilty by reason of insanity and committed him. He'd only been out a short time before I started working with him. In one of our counseling sessions, I made a big mistake. I told him something personal. About Enya."

"About the rape?"

"You know about that?"

"From Danny."

"They weren't the same situation, obviously, but Jaxon's story still resonated with me. Losing my sister was just so hard. When I told him what happened to Enya, he fixated on it right away. He's delusional. Thinks he has some kind of tangible bond with anyone who had a family member taken from them, especially if it involved rape."

"The *Chain of Pain*. I heard him talking about it in the kitchen."

"Exactly. He thinks I'm wearing it all the time. I never mentioned Enya again, but it was already too late. He wouldn't let go of it. Things got worse a couple months ago when I was taking him to see Dr. Remington and stopped by my house to pick up some files. I told him to stay in the car, but he followed me in. He saw a picture of me and Enya, saw how much we looked alike."

"You really do. I still remember her."

She tightened her lips. "Some mornings it's still hard to look in the mirror. Anyway, after he saw the picture he transferred his obsession about Enya onto me, kept saying he was going to avenge her death. I didn't take it seriously. I should have, but I didn't. He threatens people every day. If I had a dollar for every time he threatened Dr. Lazlo, I'd be a millionaire."

"He threatened me a lot too."

"And Enya died so long ago, what could he possibly do to avenge anything? Then I saw Danny Teakwell at the mental health center. I never told Jaxon any names, but the pieces snapped together. There just couldn't be any other explanation for why Danny Teakwell would be in Ocala chasing me across a parking lot."

"The letter Danny wrote to Enya," Sari said. "I read it before the monster came back. He knew about Danny from the letter. The rest of them too. All the names were in there."

"I know. Including yours," she said guiltily. "That's why I was so shocked when you told me who you are. All of this is just so … unbelievable. It can't all be true."

Sari wondered if she was thinking about Kempler's claim that he dug up Enya's grave. "I heard him call you Enya," she said.

"He started that not long after he saw the picture. That's when I knew he was going over the edge. I've been trying to get him recommitted for evaluation, but it's always the same old story—no beds available."

"I thought you were Enya. I never knew Enya had a sister."

"Not many people did. I spent my happy high school years in Georgia at the Isaac Institute for Religious Studies, a fancy name for a prison run by religious fanatics. My father sent me there. They kept me against my will until my eighteenth birthday."

Sari started to drift away, caught herself and jerked back to life. "What did you do … to deserve that?"

"I really think we should talk later, when you're feeling better. I wish I could do something to help you. These damned handcuffs." She wrestled against them, but the more she pulled the deeper they cut into her wrists.

"Keep going," Sari said. "There might not be a later."

The words hung heavy in the musty air.

"I ran away when I was twelve. Our father was abusive, not that he thought so. He insisted it was proper upbringing. Spare the rod, spoil the child, that was his life. We had rules for everything. No exceptions and strong penalties. He based them all in the bible. I hated God growing up. I didn't want to go to heaven because I thought God would be up there whipping all the children with a belt."

Noises from above.

"I wonder what he's doing," Sabrina said.

"Probably discussing our fate with his mother."

"Are you making fun of my mother?" Kempler shouted. He had the carpet above Sari's escape opening peeled back and was peering down snarling.

"So this is how you got out, Scrary. If you were going to be alive longer, I'd sue you for property damage. This was my mother's bedroom!"

The carpet slapped closed and he stomped away.

"Keep going," Sari said.

And Sabrina thought *she* was stubborn.

"Our older brother had already taken off, faked his age and enlisted in the army. I wanted Enya to go with me, but she wouldn't do it. She was always the good, obedient child, not that it saved her from many beatings."

A box of pancake mix fell through the hole in the carpet, landing on the floor with a thud.

"Ignore him," Sari said. "He's just trying to get our attention. What happened when you ran away?"

Sabrina nodded. "You understand him. I put on a lot of makeup and managed to buy a bus ticket. Had this fantasy I'd endear myself to some nice family and then send for Enya. Crazy, but what do you expect from a twelve-year-old? I made it to Key West before the police caught me. My father was as mad about the makeup as me running away. Called me a whore. I didn't even know what it meant."

"Where was your mother?"

"She died when we were little. I hardly remember her. Our father never remarried. It was like Enya and I became the women in his life. Not a healthy situation at all. After I ran away he shipped me off to the Isaac Institute so I could study the bible and rectify my soul. I did that until I turned eighteen and they had to let me go."

"Awful."

"It wasn't fun. Fifty girls stacked like cordwood in bunkbeds. Up at five for chores, classes all day, homework at night until bedtime. No television, no radio. Violate the rules? Off to solitary confinement you go. When I cried to our father about it, he said that's what I got for running away. It was that simple for him. The worse part was being taken away from Enya."

"Didn't you get to see her?"

"Just twice a year. They drove up in the summers when Enya got out of school and I'd go stay with them at Christmas."

"I'm surprised he didn't give you a second chance."

She nodded woodenly. "He missed the parts in the bible about forgiveness, but part of it was my fault. I ran away a second time during one of the Christmas breaks. After Enya killed herself, I didn't set foot out of the Isaac Institute until the day after my eighteenth birthday."

"What happened to your father?"

"I'm not sure. He stayed in Hollywood for a few years after Enya died, then moved out west somewhere. I haven't heard from him since. Don't want to. He may be dead by now."

"I'm sorry about what happened to Enya. I always have been. Danny was too. If you ever knew Danny, you wouldn't believe he could do something like that. I knew him most of my life and still could never figure it out. ... The letter helped some."

Sari fought to still the spinning in her head, struggling to assemble the next sentence. "What did Enya think ... about Danny?"

"She forgave him. She even forgave the other two because that's the way Enya was. And of course, she blamed herself for what happened. No surprise there. That's what we're taught to do."

Sari nodded. Brian Caberly.

"Danny's letter meant something to her. That's why I kept it all these years. Enya brought it to me the last time I saw her, only a week before she killed herself. She didn't want our father to find it. She also wrote a letter back to Danny. I still have that one too. She asked me to send it if I thought it was the right thing to do. I never did. I didn't want to give him the peace of knowing Enya forgave him."

"Do you hate Danny?"

"The truth? I hated all of them." She leaned on Sari to blow the gnats from her cut.

"Thanks."

"Do you think he was telling the truth about digging up my sister's grave?"

"He couldn't have. He said it was empty."

"Yeah."

"How did Enya—" Sari stopped.

"Drowned. In the Keys, with my father, which made everything even sadder, if that's possible, because our father hardly ever took us on vacation. They were in Marathon in a motel near the US 1 bridge. One night Enya said she was going for a walk and never came back. Her body washed up on the shore the next morning. They think she jumped off the bridge."

"Poor Enya. I'm so sorry. … Can I ask two more questions?" Sari said in a fading voice, life support systems switching to residual power.

"As many as you want."

"How did you know it was Danny at the mental health hospital … and who is Ryan?"

\* \* \*

He stopped mopping the blood from his face to marvel at the paper towel. *Wow.* Talk about absorbancy. No wonder *Consumer Guide* rated it number one.

"I have to admit it, Scrary," Kempler said to the bathroom mirror. "You are above average at hand-to-hand combat for a girl, especially one I practically starved to death."

He peeled two spooky cartoon bandages and stuck them in a cross on the bridge of his nose. They looked kinda cool. The ghost with the most.

On his way back to the kitchen he grabbed the shovel from the hallway. This was all getting to be too much trouble. The only good news was now he could go ahead and dig *three* graves.

Teakwell had pushed him farther than any normal person could take. The kid would just have to be an orphan.

A thermometer shaped like a duck nailed outside the kitchen window said it was ninety-six degrees. If he waited until dark he wouldn't have to sweat as much. But the entire case was starting to remind him of one of those movies where the crooks have a hundred chances to kill the good guys, but dick around until the good guys end up kicking their asses.

Scrary was getting like that. She had to go.

As for Sabrenya, well, that really was too bad. He'd just have to find another obsession.

Food would work for now. He was famished and would *kill* for a pizza. After he tied up the loose ends in the basement, he'd pick up a *Carnivore Extreme 5000* from Mama Debi's. In the meantime, he could stand to burn some calories.

What a great fitness infomercial grave-digging would be. *THE AB-DIGGINATOR.* Four easy payments of six bucks. That's all a decent shovel cost. *No assembly. Easy and fun. A Whole New You in THREE weeks, GUARANTEED.*

He unlocked the three locks on the back door and went outside.

# 51

**"WHAT DID HE SAY?"** Fink asked, sitting in his office curling and uncurling a paper clip around his finger.

"Said he thinks he's on the real killer's trail," Grady said. "Thinks the guy might have Sari too. Couldn't say where he was other than North Florida."

Chugging coffee, his third cup in an hour, Fink fixated on the hole in Lady Justice's forehead and wondered if he could make that good of a shot on purpose. It was two-fifteen. Almost time to meet Hauptmann at Alligator Paradise and take care of business.

He just wished he could shake the panicky feeling. Of course he would run out of benzos on the most fucked-up day of his life. The doctor who wrote his prescriptions chose this week to traipse off to Oregon for a nude meditation retreat. Fink spent the last two hours trying to find another pill mill with no luck.

"Did he sound okay?"

"No," Grady said crankily.

Nobody was in a good mood.

"Well, just think positively and I'll call you later."

"Yeah, yeah. Positively."

Fink dropped the receiver and buried his palms in his eye sockets. The stress was getting to be too much. Danny on the run, chasing a vicious killer, maybe even dead already, and here he was with a briefcase full of cash hijacked from his bank account using the power of attorney. He pictured his cross-examination: "Mr. Finkel, isn't it true that at the time of your client's demise, you were sitting in your office counting the money you just stole from his bank account?"

But there was no turning back now. He picked up the nine-millimeter and peeled off the sticky note. Below a yellow smiley face announcing *Today's Happy Reminders*, it said: *There's already a bullet in the chamber!!!*

He drained the coffee and headed for the elevator. The floor was empty. The lawyer married to the receptionist had left for his nephew's bar mitzvah rehearsal. The one she was just having sex with was in Costa Rica at a joint continuing legal education/bikini fitness program. The receptionist was gone too. A note taped to her Ouija board said she went home to feed her monkeys.

An accident on I-95 made him thirty minutes late pulling into Alligator Paradise. That would put Hauptmann in a worse mood than usual. He liked it. Taking control.

Alligator Paradise was more crowded than he expected. Nothing like funnel cakes, amusement park rides and a shitload of hungry reptiles to bring out the *touristas*. He circled the giant alligator sculpture in front and parked near the exit in case he needed to make a quick one.

*Don't screw up.* He double-checked everything. The money taped to the paperback books hadn't shifted. The recorder still worked. He locked back the hammer on the pistol, flipped on the safety and inserted the gun in his waistband. *Cocked and locked.* He wasn't crazy about having a cocked, loaded gun pointed at his junk, but Skaggs said it was the best way to save time if you needed to shoot someone in a hurry with a single-action pistol.

Climbing out into the searing heat, he buttoned his jacket to hide the protruding handgun, careful to keep the button microphone clear.

Twenty bucks for a ticket. Who are they kidding? He pocketed the stub in case he could claim it as a business deduction and made the five-minute trek past gift shops and a flamingo pen to the main pavilion.

No sign of Hauptmann. Just when he thought he'd catch him off-guard.

Brightly colored parrots with clipped wings flitted in the mangrove trees. Beady eyes watched from the lake. Fink stopped counting at ten gators. The sign said they ate an hour ago, but they looked hungry. On his left, roller coaster riders screamed each time the whooshing machine dipped thirty feet away.

"Hello Benjamin."

Right behind him. How'd he do that? And no fucking way: he was carrying a new soft leather briefcase like the one Fink wanted to buy.

"Hello Hauptmann," he spat, rattled, but determined not to surrender the edge this time.

"Nice lube job," Hauptmann laughed, waving at the styling gel. "Are you aware it's oozing down your neck?"

How'd you like your brains oozing down your neck? The words sounded good in his head.

"Never mind about that. You're late."

"Do you have the money?"

Oh, shit. The recorder. "Excuse me, Hauptmann. Gotta adjust the old apparatus." He turned and jammed his hand in his pants to switch on the recorder.

"I got it," he said, rotating back to face Hauptmann.

"The full hundred thousand?"

"I said I got it." He held up the briefcase. "It's right here."

Hauptmann smiled for the first time since they met two years ago. Fink saw his reflection in his gold tooth. No Coach Riley, but he looked alright.

"Good boy. I had bet myself you'd follow your usual pattern in life and fail. Thought I was going to have to break the bad news to your high-priced client. What would Teakwell say if he knew our big secret?"

Damn, he didn't want that part on tape. He changed the subject. "Nice briefcase. Bet you got it in South Beach."

"We're wasting time. Give me the money."

"Not yet. I need some guarantees."

"Please tell me you're not stalling because you didn't bring the money. That would prove to be a grave error, and that's your grave I'm referring to."

"Ooh, clever. I'm real scared." In truth, he was terror-stricken, which gave him a powerful urge to urinate. "You gonna shoot me right here with all these people around?"

"Maybe."

He had to be careful about pushing too far, but needed to get Hauptmann talking. He angled his chest to make sure the button mic stayed pointed at him.

Hauptmann brushed his jacket back, revealing a palm-sized chrome pistol in a belly holster.

"*Phfff.* You call that a gun? Looks like a cigarette lighter. Nice ladies' weapon though." The bulging semiautomatic in his own waistband steeled his confidence. It also pressed hard against his bladder. The three cups of coffee were screaming to be released.

The roller coaster swooped past, an ear-splitting combination of grinding steel and shrieking passengers that panicked the parrots and drowned out Hauptmann's next words.

"What?" Fink yelled.

"I asked if you were feeling okay."

"I feel just fine."

"You seem cockier than your usual cowardly self."

Just keep talking, asshole.

"Before we continue this negotiation, I need my own guarantee—that you have the money."

"Okay, I'll show it to you. But not out here. Behind that tree."

He pointed to a wide tangled cypress growing out of the platform next to the alligator pond.

Hidden behind the tree, he rested the briefcase on the railing and cracked it open. The alligators watched from below.

Hauptmann took a peek and nodded. Fink locked the case back up.

"So what kind of guarantees do you need? I suppose you want a promise I won't reveal your secret, especially to your fancy client."

Lately, Fink had been regretting his career choice.

"Oh hell, maybe Teakwell wouldn't even care," Hauptmann said. "He seems pretty laidback, the whole zen-surfer thing and all. Maybe he'd agree with you that a license to practice law is an unnecessary formality to defend someone's life in a murder prosecution. And, after all, what could three years of law school possibly teach a person that he can't pick up on his own?"

Fink did apply to law school once, but the only one that accepted him was unaccredited and in California. Of course, he never attended college either, so that was bound to be a sticking point.

Then one day at a yard sale with his Aunt Sylvia he stumbled on a set of used review books for the Florida Bar Examination. He bought them for ten bucks and began his legal education.

He studied hard. It wasn't like he took the unauthorized practice of law casually. Next he bought a set of Florida case reporters and statutes from the estate of a dead judge. He made up a Florida Bar ID number, rented some office space and was in business. In the back of his mind, he knew he'd get caught some day. He just wished it hadn't been by a blackmailer.

"Poor Teakwell. Entrusting his life to a complete fraud."

He felt bad enough about Danny without Hauptmann rubbing it in. It wasn't like he wanted to represent Danny. He talked him into it.

"Okay, Benjamin, you have my promise. You give me the hundred thousand dollars and I promise to keep your secret and not bother you ever again."

"Not so fast, Hauptmann. Or should I say Bugler? Why are you afraid to use your real name?"

He needed to move things along. Preoccupied with his lustful search for more alprazolam, he forgot to check how long the tape lasted.

"Zab Bugler. The fuck kinda name is that anyway?"

Bruno Hauptmann, née Zab Bugler, looked caught between surprise and murderous rage.

"Benjamin, I made it quite clear at the beginning to never use my real name. I'm curious as to the source of your newfound reckless courage. Perhaps you think I can't hurt you out here. Look around."

Fink looked.

"Look at the people. Are they watching us or are they absorbed in their own lives? Is that cypress tree providing plenty of cover? Pay attention to the sound of the roller coaster next time it comes by. Do you think those people who are not watching us and cannot see us would notice a pop from a small-caliber pistol? Hand over the money you stole from your client or I will have to consider shooting you and calmly walking away with your briefcase."

Another mistake, suggesting they go behind the tree. No matter. He was going to win this time.

"Look at you. *Bi-ig* man. Just a slimy slumlord."

That's how they met. Bugler came to him needing a lawyer to evict poor people behind on their rent from his crappy apartments. Fink just did the paperwork. He wasn't responsible for his clients' morals. The *Model Rules of Professional Conduct* said so. When they got in a fee dispute, Bugler tried to file a grievance against him with the Florida Bar, who said there was no record of a lawyer with that ID number. Bugler said he probably got the number wrong and would get back with them, but started extorting money instead.

"You talk real classy with your fancy education," Fink continued, leaning closer to make sure the recorder picked up every word. "But when it comes down to it, you're nothing but a pathetic, low-life blackmailer named Zab Bugler who lives in a condominium on Biscayne Boulevard, unit number four-three-nine, that's *four-three-niner*, phone number three-zero-five—" He found Bugler's property data with his new computer.

Bugler pulled the gun out, jerked back the slide and pointed it at his stomach. Fink jumped.

"Unbutton your shirt."

"Whoa. I'm willing to steal my client's money for you, but we're not going to get intimate."

"Are you wearing a wire? Never mind, I can see it where your disgusting hairy belly is pulling your shirt apart, you jackass. Hand over the recorder."

"No can do, Bugler. It's my only protection."

Until a few seconds ago he also had the nine-millimeter with fourteen rounds of ammunition for protection, but when he jumped the pistol dropped from his waistband to the bottom of his boxers, cold steel tearing at his testicles. He had to pee *so bad*.

Bugler palmed his gun and lowered it.

"This creates quite a predicament. Do you know what MAD is, Benjamin?"

"Mothers Against Drunk Driving? What do they have to do with this? You want me to give the money to charity?"

"Don't be an idiot, which I know is hard for you. I'm talking about Mutual Assured Destruction, the deterrence policy that kept the United States and Soviet Union from annihilating each other during the Cold War."

"No time for history lessons, Bugler."

"Neither side used their nuclear weapons in a first strike because each knew the other would have enough weapons left to destroy them. Mutual Assured Destruction. That's what you think you have going here, isn't it?"

"Something like that." He wasn't quite following.

"You believe that because of what you recorded you can destroy me. And, therefore, you think that I—acting out of rational self-interest—will elect not to destroy you."

"That's right." Fink hadn't reasoned it through quite that far, but that was the basic idea. "You tell my secret, I tell yours and we both go down."

"Not a bad plan. But even assuming you didn't screw up operating the recorder—a generous assumption—it has one major flaw."

"What's that?"

"There's no way you're leaving this place with that recorder." He raised the gun again.

The one friggin' time in his life Fink needed a gun he actually had one. What were the odds? The nine-millimeter would kick the crapola out of Hauptmann's wimpy pop-gun in a fair fight, but it was trapped in his drawers, the tip of the barrel poking his anus. If the safety failed, law students would be studying his products liability case for a hundred years.

"Fine, you want the money? You can have it." Fink held out

the briefcase. "Recorder too. Why should I care? It's not even my money."

"Very good. Nice that reasonable people can resolve their differences without bloodshed. Alternative dispute resolution. Isn't that what you lawyers call it?"

"That's a good one, Bugler. Here's another good one." Fink crouched ninja-style. "Make a move and I toss the briefcase and all the money in the water."

They glanced simultaneously at the pond below, crowded with alligators gathering for the next feeding.

"I see. You think I'll chase the money into the water and get eaten by the alligators, sort of a James Bond kind of ending, eh?"

Damn, he hadn't thought of that either. Good idea though. What difference did it make who thought of it first? Bugler was making fun of him, but Fink saw alarm in his eyes.

"That's right. I think you're such a greedy bastard that you'd rather risk getting eaten by gators than watch a sweet hundred grand sink into the muck."

Fink felt smug for a full half second, before Bugler made a quick step and grabbed the briefcase while jamming the gun into his stomach. He backed Fink against the tree out of view and shoved his gun hand down his trousers, probing for the recorder.

Now Fink had two guns, one outsized hand and a tape recorder in his pants, all squeezing his bloated abdomen.

It started as a drip.

*No!* He hadn't wet his pants since Jenny Stetweiler beat him up in the second grade. He fought to hold it back, but the drip became a trickle which surged into a sluice.

"What the hell? You're pissing on me?"

Bugler jerked the hand out, snatching the recorder, but leaving his gun behind. He stared in bewilderment at his dripping hand.

"You pissed on me. You fucking pissed on me! That's it. You are de—"

Fink didn't wait for him to finish. He yanked the briefcase free, wound up and let loose.

"Have fun swimming with the gators," he said triumphantly. "It's almost feeding time."

Except there was no splash. He was too wound up and the bag flew over his shoulder, missing the pond by a wide margin and landing near the roller coaster.

Bugler took off after it.

Fink started after him, but could barely move with the two handguns wedged between his soaking thighs. It was too late anyway. Bugler had already crossed the pavilion and entered the roller coaster area, beyond the orange mesh fence and sign that said *Warning: No Entry.*

He watched with disgust and self-loathing as Bugler snatched up the briefcase. Now he'd lost the recorder *and* Danny's money. He couldn't do anything right. Just once in his life he wished he could win at something.

Bugler waved at him mockingly just as the roller coaster rose up the hump. As it crested the peak, the riders squealed, arms flailing, feet wriggling.

Fink related to the look of sheer terror he saw on the face of a beefy passenger dressed incongruously in a matching tropical shirt and shorts with a cowboy hat and square-toed boots.

The parrots launched into their nineteenth nervous breakdown of the past twenty minutes.

It happened so fast that at first Fink thought he was imagining it, living out a fantasy. The roller coaster started to drop. The large rider with the cowboy boots looked even more petrified. Bugler was still waving and laughing. Then the rider's left boot slammed into Bugler's skull, cleanly decapitating him.

The cars roared by and disappeared over a ramp. No one

noticed Bugler crumpled in the grass.

Fink held his crotch and waddled to the scene like he was running tires on an obstacle course.

Except for his missing head, Bugler looked the same, still gripping the briefcase and recorder, both of which Fink pried loose.

Bugler's skull landed ten feet away. The half that remained intact looked like it was still smirking at him. Part of him, mostly the part in benzodiazepine withdrawal, wanted to run over and kick it like a football.

"So you thought you could beat me, didn't you, Bugler? Well, so did I."

He chunked back to the pavilion wiping icebergs of styling gel from his forehead.

The first cries of discovery arrived just as he returned to the cypress tree and leaned against the pond railing, gasping for breath.

Tourists raced to the scene oohing and ahhing. Some took snapshots. A goo-gooing tot pointed at the body with her pacifier.

The roller coaster finally screeched to a halt and Fink watched as security guards carried off a rider, who turned out to be an oilman from Texas, wearing a cowboy boot that hung at a ninety-degree angle from his ankle.

Fink pondered the professional possibilities. A defective design case against the roller coaster manufacturer by the Texan seemed winnable. Who still made roller coasters with people's feet hanging out? And a wrongful death claim by Bugler's survivors wouldn't be out of the question. His negligence in ignoring the warning sign to retrieve a bag of extorted money would complicate things, but Fink thought he could at least get a settlement.

*C'est la vie.* He knew that gig was over. Relieved to have

Danny's money back and Bugler out of his life, he dropped the recorder in the lake.

He deep-sixed the guns as well. Or tried to. A gator rose up and swallowed Bugler's pistol before it hit the water.

The swank leather case rested at his feet. He nudged it toward the water, but stopped. He could swear it was the same bag he saw in the window at the shop in South Beach. Maybe he was meant to have it. Bugler wasn't going to need it.

Behind the tree he transferred the cash from his shabby vinyl case, remembering to remove his business card from the plastic display pocket. He tore the cover from one of the paperbacks and scribbled on the blank side, *Free Books from the Literacy Counsel*. Something about it didn't look right.

He left the open briefcase and sign on a picnic table and swaggered toward the exit, wet pants matted against his thighs. Police and EMTs passed him running the other way.

# 52

SABRINA WATCHED helplessly as Sari's condition continued to deteriorate. Her injured eye had swelled shut. Her body heaved sporadically. She'd been quiet for several minutes. When Sabrina got a concussion in a car accident, the nurses kept her awake.

"Sari?"

No response.

She nudged her with her shoulder. "Sari, you okay?"

"Mm."

"Do you still want to talk?"

"You were going to answer my questions. About how you recognized Danny at the mental health center ... and who is ... what's his name?"

The abrupt reply startled Sabrina. She almost laughed in relief.

"I'm so happy you're still with me. His name is Ryan. Your questions go together. This is private and I'm not sure you're going to want to know it."

"I want to."

"I knew what Danny looked like because last weekend I went

to Hollywood to see him. Seminole High School was holding a reunion for the class of 1975. You might have known that."

Her chin moved slightly. "I was planning to go ... before he took me. You talked to Danny?"

"No, I just saw him for a few moments, through a window."

"What did he look like?"

Sabrina traced her face curiously. She still loved him. After all these years. A sworn affidavit wouldn't be more convincing than the look on her face. She suddenly found herself hoping a man she had despised all her life was okay.

"He's nice looking," she said. "Lean and tan, looks like he gets a lot of exercise."

Sari smiled. "Surfing. How did you know it was him?"

"I had his picture from a Seminole yearbook. He was sitting at a table inside the bar with a group of people. I was outside on the dock. He was easy to recognize. He doesn't look much different from his high school picture, just older."

"I don't understand. Why did you go to the reunion just to look at him through a window?"

"Well ..." She stopped. "That gets to your second question."

The basement door sprung open at the top of the stairs, splintering the frame.

"It's just me!"

Jaxon Kempler pounded down the stairs, pistol in one hand, bucket of cleaning supplies in the other. Purple and white bandages formed a cross on his nose. His shirt and pants were covered in dirt.

"Bad news, girls. I started working on your graves, but like all construction projects, this one has been delayed due to weather. It's too fucking hot. We assure you we are working to resolve the problem. Meanwhile, I hope you two have had a chance to get to know each other. You have a lot in common. You're both going to get shot in the head at close range with a hollow-point bullet."

"Jaxon, quit talking like that!"

"How am I supposed to talk? In French? *Ooh-la-la.*"

"*Focus!* Right here, right now. Think about what you're doing. Think about the consequences of your actions. I still believe in you. I still believe you don't really want to hurt us."

"Not in here. It's going to be a bitch to clean up. That's why I brought these cleaning supplies." He set the bucket down. "But I can't take a chance bringing you outside with little Houdini over there."

"She needs a doctor, Jaxon. Take off the handcuffs and let me take her to get help. You can stop now before it goes too far."

"Liar. It's way past too far. Don't you think I know that? I've already killed an accountant, drug dealer and a stockbroker this week and it's only Wednesday. Add to that kidnapping, assault with a deadly weapon and theft of property for taking your letter and I know where I'm going if I get caught. Wake up, Scrary!" he shouted.

"Can't you see she's suffering? Listen to your heart."

"Lazlo says I got no heart."

"Forget Lazlo. Just look at her. Let yourself feel compassion."

He stroked his chin.

"You're right. She's been a good prisoner, except for biting my neck and trying to poke my eyes out." The veins in his neck suddenly bulged. "And ruining my damn ceiling. That really pisses me off!"

He lowered his voice. "But because you still might be Enya— for you—I'll put her down quickly."

He grabbed Sari's hair and tilted her head back. "She won't feel a thing."

"Open up," he said, and slipped the gun barrel in her mouth.

Sari jerked her head and spit the gun out. "Fuck you."

"*Sari said fu-ck. Sari said fu-ck.* For that I'm going to wash your mouth out with soap. After I put the bullet down it, of course. No point cleaning twice. Inefficiency is one of the top three reasons most businesses fail."

He wrenched Sari's head.

"Quit fighting. You're going to ruin those nice teeth. I didn't give you that toothbrush and toothpaste for nothing." He reinserted the gun.

"Jaxon," Sabrina pleaded. "Think about your mother. She wouldn't want you to hurt Sari."

"That's where you're wrong. She's the one who just told me to get this thing over with. *Whoever liveth and believeth in me will have life everlasting.* Guess again."

*Bzzzzzzzz. Bzzzzzzzz.*

The doorbell upstairs.

Kempler spewed exasperation and loosened his grip.

*Bzzzzzzzzzzzzzzzzzzzzzzzz. Bzzzzzzzzzzzzzzzzzzzzzzzz.*

"Have you ever had one of those days where nothing goes right?" he said and turned for the stairs. "I'll be back. If either of you make a sound, the dirty blood of the dirty person wearing out my nice clean doorbell will be on your hands—not mine."

Upstairs, he crossed into the living room and unlocked the three deadbolts, humming *Who Can It Be Now?* Men at Work. You know it.

Was it possible he was so above average that he called in a pizza to Mama Debi's without a phone? That would really be something.

He opened the door, gun in hand, but there was nobody there. No crater-faced teenager holding a box. No junk car with a Mama Debi's Pizza light on top. Just his own fine wheels and Sabrenya's subcompact with the crummy radio and not enough legroom.

Maybe no one really rang the doorbell. His brain did buzz sometimes. He'd ask the girls if they heard it.

He started to close the door when he noticed a small figurine standing on the porch. It was a bushy-bearded guy with a receding hairline and a beer gut, wearing a suit. He looked pissed off.

"Dr. Lazlo? On my porch?"

*Oh-man. O-men.* A bad one. Couldn't be anything but. Why would the shrink send his tiny, plastic self to pop in unannounced unless it was bad news? But maybe it wasn't Lazlo. He didn't have a beard the last time he saw him. It could be a disguise.

The figurine stood on a square of white paper with writing on it. He bent down to read it.

It said "Look up."

He did.

Something was out of place. It was his new shovel, the one he left in the backyard, traveling toward his face at a high velocity.

\* \* \*

Furious crashing in the house above brought Sari back. Glass breaking, wood splintering. Sabrina was on her feet, unsteadily climbing the stairs, hands strapped behind her, shouting for help.

Then a loud pop and everything went silent. An audible period to an inciteful sentence.

A gun.

Danny hated guns.

Silence. Sari rocked onto her knees, pressed her back into the wall and inched to her feet. She tottered, but held steady.

Still no sound.

The locks unlatched and the doorknob turned.

# 53

JAXON KEMPLER crossed the threshold, unrecognizable but for his immense size and purple polo shirt. His face, neck, even his curly hair, were drenched in red—like Sissy Spacek at the end of the movie *Carrie* when they dropped the bucket of pig's blood on her.

His luminous blue lenses darted behind the red mask like the eyes behind a portrait in an old haunted house movie. Sounds gurgled from his throat.

Singing. It sounded like Three Dog Night.

He wiped his eyes. "Mama was right. This ain't no way to have fun."

Sabrina backtracked down the stairs. She made it to the bottom and sidestepped to Sari. No one spoke.

Kempler glared at Sari and then Sabrina, an inscrutable conjunction of rage, confusion and no expression at all.

The gun hammer locking into firing position broke the silence. He pointed the weapon at Sabrina.

"No!" Sari yelled. "Why would you hurt her? Forget listening to your heart. You don't have one. Use your stupid above-average brain! All she did was try to help you."

"Help me? By impersonating her sister? That's illegal. But you did remind me of something. I realize I owe you an apology. Have you ever had someone cut in front of you while you're waiting in line?"

Sari exhaled in disgust. Reasoning with him was pointless.

"Probably," he said. "And if you're like me, you want to kill them. *First come, first served* is a basic rule of Life. I almost forgot you've been waiting more than a week. You get to go first."

He swung the gun to Sari, pointing it straight at her broken heart.

"Go to hell."

"You're a strange girl, Scary Sari. You should be on your knees begging. Any last words?"

She straightened her shoulders. "Do it."

"Okey-dokey."

Sari didn't close her eyes. She saw Kempler's shoulder extend and arm tighten. His other hand swooped across and grabbed the pistol grip to steady his aim. She watched his index finger constrict on the trigger. A hairy mole twitched above his knuckle. Then she saw a figure hurl through the doorway, striking Kempler's back and knocking him forward into the stair railing.

The two-by-fours snapped. Kempler went over the edge. His skull hit the concrete with a loud crack. He lay motionless, sprawled awkwardly on the grimy floor, one arm stretched above his head like he was reaching for the gun, which landed a foot away.

"Danny?" Sari said, but there was no movement at the top of the stairs.

Sabrina started back up them.

Sari pushed off from the wall with her bound hands and weaved toward Kempler. She reached the gun and, in shuffling steps, moved it across the floor until she got it under the furnace.

Just as she did, something touched her calf. She would have jumped if she had the strength, but all she could do was rotate slowly in small steps.

It was Kempler, on his knees, teeth bared behind a devil's red face. She fell back against the furnace, barely escaping his thick bloody fingers reaching for her ankle.

The power came from a reservoir of pain and sorrow, resentment and regret, love and hate. She drew her leg back. The crossed bandages on his nose gave a perfect target.

Her knee hit with a crunch, hard enough to send him back to the floor. He lay still except for blue orbs blinking like turn signals.

Sari stood staring at him, lightheaded and wheezing to catch her breath. She placed a foot on his back to steady herself, then collapsed on top of him.

*  *  *

Danny was vaguely aware of something running in his eyes … liquid heat. He remembered hitting the floor after pushing Kempler, but now it felt like he was floating … in a sea of bubbles.

He didn't feel pain, which he didn't understand. The bullet hit him somewhere in the chest, knocking him down just as he was about to swing the shovel one more time. Maybe in the shoulder, but right now it didn't feel like he had a shoulder. Or a leg or ribs or anything.

Disembodied, drifting upwards. Peaceful, not a bad feeling.

Warbling in the distance. Angels with trumpets.

*Can't leave yet. Gotta help Sari.*

Not trumpets. Sirens. Finally tracked him down, found the Dart he left in the middle of the road. Good.

What did Myron Tamms want? Nice old guy. Got a girlfriend. Never called back. No, Danny was supposed to call him.

Warm energy stroking his forehead, whispering to him, taking him away.

He opened his eyes. He lucked out. He was with the angels. Enya McKenzie looked down on him, and she was smiling.

# 54

**HARSH FLORESCENT LIGHT** blinded him. He tried to move, but couldn't. IV needles stuck from each arm. A hose extruded from his heavily wrapped chest, snaking to a clear plastic box that bubbled like a bong. His leg throbbed like hell under a thin blue sheet. Detective Emilio Rodriguez sat as his bedside.

"How the hell are you, Teakwell?" he chirped brightly. "Welcome back."

"Sari Hunter," Danny said.

"She's okay. Banged up, but she's gonna be okay."

Danny closed his eyes, suspended on a cloud. *Sari okay ...* but Troy said the same thing on the dock. "Are you sure?" He hoped it wasn't a dream.

"Sure as we're sitting here, which might not seem too sure to you at the moment with all the dope they keep pumping into you. But you're a druggie, you probably like that."

"Explain to me, Detective, why of all the people, you're the one sitting here when I open my eyes. Isn't that some kind of constitutional violation? Cruel and unusual punishment?"

"I'm the only one allowed in. You're on a secure floor."

"I feel much safer."

"It's not to protect you, it's so you can't escape."

Danny coughed and doubled over, gripping the bed rails. "Good precaution."

Laughing, "I gotta give you credit, Teakwell. You're pretty tough for a skinny surfer boy. Or dude. Isn't that what you call each other? *Dudes*?"

"Where are we? You said welcome back."

"I meant to the land of the living. You've been out for a while. Docs have already done two surgeries on your leg. One to cut it open and one to sew it back shut. You're still in Ocala, in ICU."

"Out of your jurisdiction."

"This is a social call."

"Uh-huh."

He shrugged. "Apparently, I made a mistake. I'm a big person. I can admit it. Looks like you might actually be home free. The big guy's not talking, but the girls cleared you. Unbelievable story if it checks out. You can't really blame me."

Danny wasn't sure which girls he was talking about. "He's alive?"

"You wanna talk about a tough sonofabitch. You broke his arm, shattered his clavicle, fractured his skull in three places and he's already sitting up asking for pancakes."

"Guarded, I hope."

"Guarded, medicated and in restraints. Tomorrow, he'll be departing for Florida State Hospital pending trial for murder, kidnapping and a long list of other charges. He'll never see the light of day. I owe you that much."

"That's probably what they told the families of the three lawyers he killed."

"I read about that in his records. Not sure why they let him go the first time. I suspect some shrinks are in deep shit over there. But the laws are a lot tougher now and with three new

430

murders and everything else, he's never coming out."

"You said the girls. Sari?"

"Quite a lady. Not sure what she sees in you."

Danny tried to sit up. "Did he hurt her?"

"Easy, easy. I just told you she's okay. Relax and enjoy your narcotics. You'll hear it all soon enough. Suffice it to say she's another tough cookie. Kempler has a chunk missing from his neck and some nice needlepoint work on his nose, courtesy of your ex-girlfriend. Everyone back at the cop shop wants her autograph."

He picked a piece of lint from a tie decorated with pomegranates.

"According to the other one, the last thing that happened before the cops got there was your friend sending Kempler to the floor with a kick in the face."

"The other one? Enya? Is her name Enya McKenzie?"

"No, name's Sabrina. Sabrina Thompson, a social worker. We still got a lot to sort out. I'll level with you. That's why I'm here. Face it. It's gonna be a while before our relationship is purely social, you inviting me over to your beach house for luaus and shit. I got a million questions. Thought I'd seen everything, but this one makes it all look like cupcakes. Docs say I can't do it now, but as soon as possible."

Danny didn't hear the last part. He drifted back to sleep.

That was seven days ago, before Fink arranged for him and Sari to be transported south to Mercy Hospital in Hollywood, just a few blocks from Sand Dollar Lane where they grew up. From the ninth floor he could see their houses. In his old driveway, a kid with dark hair was dribbling a basketball. He hit a nice bankshot off a fancy glass backboard on wheels, a major improvement from the piece of plywood Danny and his dad nailed above the garage so many years ago. Next door at Sari's, an old woman roamed the front yard with a small dog on a leash.

He rinsed the plastic razor in the pan of warm water and adjusted a handheld mirror. Nurse Radison, the charge nurse, brought him the shaving supplies.

James Garfield stood next to the pan of water, all eight inches of him. The twentieth president brought him luck after all. One of the cops grabbed the plastic model from Thumpet's porch and gave it to Rodriguez.

Scraping away the stubble was slow going.

"So how are we doing?"

He jerked his head. "Oww!"

It was Radison, possessed of a preturnatural ability to sneak up on patients, standing in the doorway.

She shook her head disapprovingly. "Be careful! You've already wasted enough blood." The intercom called and she disappeared.

Danny hardly recognized himself in the mirror. More pale than he ever remembered. Freaky looking, especially with the slash of stitches down his forehead where Kempler cleaved him with a piece of glass during their fight.

The antibiotics dripping in his veins were working on the infection from the bullet hole in his leg. *Osteomyelitis*, the doctors called it. The bullet chipped his fibula. To fix the bone, they took part of it out.

"What did you put back in?" Danny asked.

"Nothing," the orthopedic surgeon said. "You don't really need a fibula."

Easy for him to say. Like everything else, the swelling had a technical medical name: *acute compartment syndrome*. To relieve the pressure, they sliced his calf from top to bottom and left it open for two days before sewing it back up.

"Can I still surf?"

"Impossible to say."

He had learned that was the answer to every medical question.

"Compartment syndrome can cause muscle or nerve damage, sometimes both. A lot will depend on physical therapy. Are you the kind of person who can commit to something and follow it through?"

Danny could almost hear Grady's laugh.

"For this, I hope I am."

The bullet in his shoulder nipped the subclavian artery, which Nurse Radison made him appreciate was a big deal during one of their touching bedside chats. Patting his hand with a fist, she said with moist eyes, "Lucky for you the cops were two steps behind or you would have bled out like a slaughtered pig."

The immediate loss of blood pressure made him pass out.

The chest doc was puzzled. "Let me make sure I have this right. After you were shot, you said you passed out."

"Yes. Almost immediately."

"I get that. That's what should have happened. But you also said you got up again, walked down a hall and pushed someone down some stairs."

"That's what they tell me. I don't have a clear memory of it."

"But how? It's not medically explainable. You should have been down for the count."

"I'm not sure. Because I had to, I guess."

The bullet also tore the apex of his lung, the reason he was hooked to the bong. The chest tube sucked out bloody air, trapping it in the bubbling chambers of water.

Kempler's shovel broke three ribs back in the graveyard. The doctor said they'd heal in due course without treatment, but would hurt like hell in the meantime.

"Really?" Danny said, but the physician missed the joke.

Good news came two days ago in the form of an official pronouncement delivered by Radison that his condition had been upgraded from *critical* to *serious, but stable.*

"What does that mean, you know, technically speaking?" Danny asked.

"It means quit your worrying, you'll be fine."

They graduated him to solid food. Lunch was rubber chicken, creamed corn and cold macaroni and cheese. Assuming no complications from food poisoning or other causes, Danny could be out in a week.

In the meantime, his story had boosted the get-well sector of the local economy. Flowers, balloons, cards—most of them from strangers—arrived daily. Janet Traynor, the *Hard Bite* reporter, sent an ostentatious orchid arrangement shaped like a surfboard with a note pleading for a live hospital room interview.

Hilariously, his public image had transformed overnight from lunatic killer to American hero. The phone rang nonstop, everyone from cable news to *People* magazine. He declined all interviews and asked the hospital operator to screen out media calls, but after Janet Traynor sneaked through by claiming to be Danny's pot dealer, they disconnected his room phone.

All in all, the hospital stay had been a much-needed vacation, just lying around like a fat cat while Nurse Radison fussed at and over him. No getting shot. No falling into graves. No new criminal charges. *And Sari was safe.*

He hadn't seen her. The guards were gone, but he was roombound per doctor's orders and, more relevantly, by all the medical accessories hooked into him. Same with Sari, they said. Everyone was mum about her condition. Radison cited patient privacy, but he also got the feeling she was trying to protect him from something. Rodriguez let slip that she'd been kept in Kempler's basement for more than a week without enough food.

Danny told Fink to get on the case. He showed up with the news yesterday.

"Are you sure you wanna know? You're not going to like it."

"Tell me."

"You're gonna want to kill the sonofabitch."

"Spill it."

"I'm telling you, you're going to want to kill him."

"I heard you the first time."

"Okay. First, I try to bribe one of the nurses for information, but she turns down the cash. Then I mention I'm your best friend and she tells me for free. Go figure human nature."

He adjusted his tie. "Remember, I'm only the messenger."

"Go on."

"Okay. The worst thing is Sari had a bad concussion and a gash on her head. The nurse said he, um, hit her with the butt of a gun."

Danny seethed.

"I know, I know. But she's going to be fine. No permanent damage."

"What else?"

"Well, you already know he starved … er, did not feed her well, but she's pretty much recovered from that. She's eating fine and has been getting IV nutrition from the start."

"Is that it?"

"She apparently has some other scrapes and bruises. But they're not serious and she's healing."

"Did he …"

"*No.* Sari told Rodriguez a definite *no* on that and they examined her to make sure. Apparently, he did drug her one time."

"I want to kill him, Fink."

"I told you," he said, throwing up his hands. "But if you do, you'll have to find another lawyer. I can't represent you."

"Here we go again. Back to where we started. Let me guess, defending vigilantes isn't one of your specialty areas."

"It's not that." His face drooped. "There's something I gotta tell you. How much time is left for visiting hours?"

They were both shaken when he left. It's not every day the person defending you of murder works into the conversation that he never bothered to go to law school. Danny couldn't really hold it against him. He did a helluva job, law license or not. The story about Bugler and the incident at Alligator Paradise topped the cake. Fink assured him the money from his bank account had been redeposited.

A talking head twitched soundlessly through the local news on a television suspended from the ceiling on brackets. There he was on the screen again. Same old mugshot. He changed channels.

The resting sun washed the room in peaches and cream. He looked at his old house again. The kid shooting baskets was gone.

How far to Sugar Lake from here? Maybe ten miles, if it was still there. How far to Enya McKenzie's pink house on Myrtle Street? Couple of miles at most.

He remembered when those places didn't exist. You're a kid shooting baskets in your driveway and nobody ever tells you about all the traps in life. All the bad choices, the wrong turns. All the chances to screw up.

Nurse Radison leaned her immense bosom across the threshold.

"*Go-od* news," she sang. "I just got permission from the hospital administration to personally pull the plug on you if you ever again let anyone bring alcohol into this room!"

He apologized for the third time and she moved on. She was referring to the two empty beer cans the cleaning crew found in his trash that morning.

Frank Calhoun, his old cellmate, smuggled them in. Danny declined to partake. Reducing alcohol consumption was one entry on his agenda for a new and improved life. Frank drank both.

He and Brenda were back together, their reunion a perfect picture of relationship compromise. Brenda offered to find another home for the Rottweiler, but Frank insisted that *Leonard4Ever*—as he renamed the new canine—stay, and even invited the dog to sleep with them. Brenda was so touched that she tried to drop the charges, but PETA objected on behalf of the deceased dachshund. Frank pled guilty to a misdemeanor in return for two hundred hours community service cleaning kennels at the Humane Society.

Grady was at the hospital every day. Danny had to kick him out in the afternoons to go open the Tradewinds.

"Think about those pirates moping around outside," Danny said. "Pitiful faces pressed against the glass. They won't know what to do with themselves."

"They're already moping because I told 'em they can't visit until you're discharged."

"Cheer them up with this news. I'm throwing a party at the Tradewinds just as soon as I get up and moving again. We'll make it a huge blowout. A celebration."

"There's a lot to celebrate." Grady said, patting Danny's arm.

"It's not for me. It's to celebrate my friends, especially you. Thank you, Grady. I'll never be able to repay your love and loyalty."

"What, you wanna arm wrestle for it? You celebrate what you want and I'll celebrate what I want. It's a free country. Let's just have the damn party."

Rodriguez popped in regularly for interrogation. Each time he left satisfied, he returned with something new. Today it was:

"One thing I haven't figured out is how you got away from the trooper chasing you after your traffic stop for polluting Ocala. I talked to her and she said"—reading from a spiral notebook—"*he just disappeared.*"

That reminded Danny to send restitution to the family with the dismantled Sony television in the middle of their living room. Poor little Max was probably bouncing off the walls from *Plastic Fantastic Rats* deprivation.

The local news switched to a live report at the courthouse. Fink?

He stood at the top of the courthouse steps behind a lectern with an American flag pinned hastily to the front. He was gesticulating wildly into a cluster of microphones that obscured the lower part of his face. His normally bouffant hair was slicked back and he'd ditched his glasses. He looked a little like Coach Pat Riley, who left the New York Knicks while Danny was still unconscious and was coming to Miami to coach the Heat. He turned up the sound.

"As I've maintained from the very beginning, Danny Teakwell is an innocent man."

Hear, hear.

"The State of Florida now agrees. I'm happy to report that just minutes ago State Attorney Arlo Pickering stipulated before Judge Kovacich to a dismissal of all charges. My client's bond has been relinquished. He is officially a free man. God bless America."

And to think Danny knew him way back before he was a fake lawyer.

"And so I say to you good citizens of my adopted state, speak up for justice, strike at oppression wherever it rears its ugly head, fight for what you believe in. Never give up, no matter what the odds."

"Mr. Finkel," shouted one of the media horde. "What cause do you plan to take on next?"

"Count me out. I'm quitting this nasty business. As of this moment, my law practice is officially closed."

The proclamation silenced even veteran news reporters. Poor Fink. The blackmailer was dead, but he decided the unauthorized practice of law had become too risky. What would he do now?

He was telling all of South Florida that very moment. "Next week, I start my new career. I'll be joining the *Hard Bite* news team, co-hosting a cutting-edge legal affairs show with Janet Traynor."

"What's it called?"

*"Justice or Just Crap?"*

The show, he explained, would feature local legal pundits analyzing miscarriages in the judicial system, beginning with Danny's case.

"Are the rumors true that your relationship with Janet Traynor is more than simply professional?"

"Please, please. My private life is off limits. Let's just say my new colleague has an amazing chest and leave it at that."

Perhaps irked by Fink's publicity for its major competitor, the station cut from the news conference back to the studio for a sports report. The Houston Rockets were still celebrating their sweep of the Orlando Magic in the NBA Finals.

Danny clicked off the television and picked up the letter again, the one Enya wrote twenty years ago that never got sent:

*Feb. 2, 1975*

*Dear Danny,*

*Thank you for your letter. I've thought about it a lot. I do forgive you. You helped me that night after everything happened. My sister said that doesn't matter, but it did to me.*

*The rumor about me dropping out of school is true. I had to. I'm pregnant. I hid it as long as I could, but my father found out and made me quit school. My father is making me have the baby and put it up for adoption.*

439

*After that, I'll be moving to Georgia to the same school as
my sister. That's at least one good thing. I'll get to be with
my sister again. Life has been hard without her. For now, I'm
at home, not doing much, reading a lot and cooking and
cleaning.*

*Don't dwell on me. One of the books I've been reading is
called Man's Search for Meaning by a man named Viktor
Frankl. He was in a Nazi concentration camp during the
war. From everything he saw he learned to believe there is
a meaning to all suffering. That no matter what gets taken
from us, we still have the freedom of our own attitude, to
choose our way under any set of circumstances.*

*I'm trying to look at things that way. You should too. Go on
with your life. Use your freedom to choose your own way. I'm
going to be okay.*

*My father will be home from work soon and I'm supposed to
have dinner on the table so I'll go.*

*Enya McKenzie*

The tears came once more. Enya consumed so much of his
psychic space for so long, but he had been clueless the whole
time about who she really was. A hopeful, forgiving person. A
strong person. Not someone who would take her own life.

Sabrina brought him the letter two nights ago. Danny
couldn't help but gawk when she walked in.

"I'm Sabrina," she said quickly.

"They told me. I thought you were Enya."

"I know. You're not the only one."

She dragged a chair to the bed and sat down. "There's no
preparing you for what I'm about to say, but after everything
that's happened, I decided I owe it to you."

She removed a piece of paper from her purse. Danny noticed
red marks on her wrists.

"First, read this," she said, handing him Enya's letter. "Fair
warning. It's going to be a shock."

440

He read it.

"You have a son. Enya was his mother. His name is Ryan. Ryan Marshall. He's twenty years old and lives in Oregon."

Danny didn't say anything.

She explained that Ryan was adopted at birth by a couple in Portland, a geologist and a high school English teacher. He attends a local college studying fine arts, but spends most of his time trying to get a recording deal for his alternative rock band, *Suzy Loves Jill.*

"He looks just like you. Even the long blond hair like in your yearbook picture. I had to be sure. That's why I came to the reunion."

"You were on the dock."

"Yes."

The resemblance to her sister was so strong it was hard to maintain eye contact.

"When Enya put Ryan up for adoption she filled out a form for the Florida birth parent registry. It lets adopted children get information about their birth parents when they reach legal age. After Enya's death I was able to add my name to the registry. Several months ago Ryan contacted me."

Nurse Radison stuck her head in. Danny waved her away.

"We started corresponding. I flew out to meet him, taking what I had about Enya to show him. There isn't much. A few pictures, a scrapbook, some artwork ... that's it."

She wiped her face with a tissue she had been shredding in her hands. "I never planned on telling you any of this. Do you understand?"

"I think so."

"A lot changed for me that day in Kempler's house. What he did to you and Sari, to everyone, it was my fault. If I hadn't told him about Enya, none of it would have happened."

"It was Kempler's fault, maybe mine, but not yours. You shouldn't think that way."

"See, that's another thing. That day, from listening to Sari, from watching her face—that face! I don't think I've ever seen a more expressive face."

Danny actually laughed. "It's true."

"When she talked about you, I realized you couldn't be the person I had conjured up and spent my life ..."

"Hating? It's okay. I've hated myself for twenty years for what happened."

"Then Sari saved my life in the kitchen and you saved us both in the basement. I knew I had to let go of those feelings, especially after seeing Enya's letter again. I hadn't looked at it in years. Rereading it, everything hit me. I've been betraying her memory for all these years—who she was and what she wanted. So have you."

"I've been trying to honor her memory. I swear."

"How? By punishing yourself?" She studied his face. "I want to make a deal."

"With me?"

"I won't spend my life blaming myself for what Kempler did if you'll stop blaming yourself for my sister's death."

She stuck out her hand. Danny shook it.

"Ryan's asked a lot of questions about his biological father. I played dumb. Now I'd like to tell him about you. I mean, if it's okay. It's your decision—and a big one—so you should think about it. I think it could help him."

"If you think it's a good idea, of course. I'd do anything I could to help."

"I also never told him his mother committed suicide. I said she died in an accident. I guess it's time to be honest about that too," she said. Her shoulders sagged.

It was a day for painful revelations all around. Danny weighed his words carefully.

"I have something to tell you too," he said. "I don't know if it will make things better or worse. It's about Enya and … how she died."

That's when he revealed the news he learned from Myron Tamms, the *tragic mystery* that eluded him. Tamms turned up at the hospital in a state of great agitation only an hour after Danny arrived from Ocala.

"It was that cousin of yours who started it all," Tamms said.

"Cousin?"

"You know, the one who owns the air conditioning business."

"Oh, that cousin. I apologize, Mr. Tamms. He's not really my cousin."

"I figured."

"But what does Roy Chambers have to do with my case?"

"Did he mention to you that they had to move the AC unit closer to the house? He said that whoever installed it was most likely a bit dull. I believe his precise words were *friggin' moron*. They had to dig it up and move the whole shebang, concrete base and all."

Danny remembered Chambers' phone message. "He did say something about that."

"There's your mystery," Tamms said.

When Tamms went out to level the ground and lay some sod, he hit something hard with the rake. Smooth and gray, he thought it was a shell, so he dug around it with a hand trowel.

"It wasn't a shell. Oh, no, no. It was a skull. A human skull, fractured in several places. I saw more bones, but stopped right there. I wanted to talk to you before calling the police. I've been following your case."

He rubbed smudges from his Buddy Holly glasses with a hospital tissue and pulled a wad of papers from his back pocket.

"I went to the library and researched human anatomy. I'm no expert, but the size of the skull and bones seem to strongly indicate a young person. All I could think about was the girl's bedroom."

"Frozen in time," Danny said.

Danny sent him to Rodriguez. Excavating Tamms' backyard unearthed the skeleton of a female in her teens according to a preliminary report. Blunt head trauma was the likely cause of death, judging from the skull fissures. Danny told Rodriguez about the empty coffin at the Westbrook Cemetery. Rodriguez found no record of anyone drowning in Marathon Key in June 1975. He opened a homicide file on Enya McKenzie.

As Danny told the story, Sabrina pulled closer. She spoke before he finished.

"My father," she said. "He killed my sister."

She cupped her hands and blew into them. "The signs were there. I refused to see them. My brother was suspicious right away. At the funeral he asked point blank if I considered the possibility that our father killed her. I yelled at him, rejected it completely, but that was only because I had the same thought."

"It would be hard for anyone to accept their father could do something like that."

"I saw Enya a week before she died, a month after she gave birth. She and my father came up to visit. That's when she gave me the letters, yours and hers. She was upbeat, positive, just like in her letter. That was my sweet sister, the eternal optimist. She was actually excited about coming to the Isaac Institute because we'd be together. It was only a week later the principal called me out of bible study to tell me she committed suicide."

She squeezed her hands together. "My father."

"It's not official. Everything is very preliminary."

"That's what happened. I know it now. That's the sickest part. If you knew my father, it all fits. In his warped religious kingdom, having sex out of wedlock was a sin worse than murder. And to get pregnant by it? Forget it. When he found out, he whipped Enya. Beat his defenseless pregnant daughter. Can you believe it?"

Danny didn't want to believe it. If Rodriguez didn't find McKenzie, he might go after him himself.

"What about the drowning story?" he said.

"He made it up. He must have. Which means the whole funeral and empty casket were just a ruse to cover his tracks."

"Seems like it would have been easier to make up a story that she ran away."

"That wouldn't have worked. I tried hard, twice, to get Enya to run away with me, but she wouldn't do it. He knew that and knew I knew it. I would never have stopped searching for her. Never."

Nurse Radison was at the door again, pointing vigorously at her watch. Something in Danny's face must have spoken to her because she moved along.

"I visited that grave so many times," she said, shaking her head. "Laid flowers every time ... on an empty hole in the ground. Our father was crazy, but not stupid. The grave and funeral service gave credence to everything. I remember asking him at the funeral if I could look at her one last time. He said no because fish bites had disfigured her. I begged him to let me just kiss her head and say good-bye. He told me I was sick."

Nurse Radison finally burst in and announced that visiting hours were long over. Danny started to protest.

"It's okay. It's time for me to go," Sabrina said. "I'm tired and have to drive back to Ocala in the morning. We'll talk more. Remember our deal."

Danny put the letter down and turned away from the afternoon sun, burrowing his head in the pillows. The hall was unusually quiet. No food trays clattering, no orders from Radison resounding. The only sound was the tranquil bubbling of the water box attached to the catheter in his chest.

He closed his eyes. Sabrina's words kept returning. The best thing he could do to honor Enya would be to abide by her letter. *Use your freedom to choose your own path.* He wasted half a lifetime wallowing in guilt, believing that to do anything else would betray his debt to Enya. But he had it backwards. *Go on with your life.*

Pitter-patter footsteps pulled him back to the outside world. They started at the end of the hall near the nurses' station. The steps grew quicker and noisier. A heavier, slower set of feet plodded behind.

"Well look who's here," said a young girl's voice.

Danny opened his eyes to see Jessica Jewell, oval face smiling, dressed sportily in polka-dot shorts, rubber baseball cleats and a Slagger-Jewell Funeral Home teeshirt and cap. Her father, Jarrod Jewell, Jr., stepped into view behind her, wearing a matching cap and teeshirt and carrying a cardboard box.

"I'm sorry to disturb you," he said. "She insisted."

"Come on in. It's great to see you, Jessica."

"I *told* you, Dad." Jessica ran and hopped on Danny's bed.

"Be careful!" Jewell admonished, shifting the box uneasily.

"It's okay," Danny said. "Just don't pull out any of these tubes."

"Hmm." She pressed a finger to her lips. "If that tube coming out of your boob was a little higher, you could be getting aspirated."

"Jessica!" Poor Jewell, hemmed in on all sides by his family of renegade morticians. "Embalming is not a nice subject to discuss with someone who's … not feeling well."

Danny laughed. "Hopefully I won't need any aspirating for a long time. But when I do, I'll be sure I come to you."

"No joke?"

"No joke."

"You hear that, Dad. I got my first customer, and he's not even dead." Bouncing on the bed, "Show him what we brought.

We got you a present, Danny. You'll never guess what it is in a million years."

"A present? You didn't have to do that."

"I bought it with my own money. You're going to love it. It's just what you need. Gimme that box."

She sprung off the bed and plucked the corrugated container from her father's hands, setting it carefully on Danny's lap. He heard scratching inside.

"I tried to talk her out of it," Jewell apologized. "I told her it's against hospital rules. She came back with *You let Grandpa sleep in a casket.* What could I say?"

Danny unfolded the flaps and peeked inside. A chubby hamster with bulging eyes and a white patch on his back sniffed warily.

"Isn't he the cutest? He's a little scared right now. You need to pet him to get him to relax. Do you just love him?"

"Of course I do. Who wouldn't love a cute little guy like this?"

"Now you won't be alone anymore. What are you going to name him? It's a him."

"Let's see, what do you think would be a good name?"

"How about *Jarrod Jewell, Senior,* after my grandpa?"

Jewell groaned.

"I'm not sure about that one," Danny said. "That would be quite a mouthful every time I had to call him."

She tugged her bottom lip. "I didn't think about that. How about Wilhelm? He invented embalming fluid."

"Maybe something a little lighter."

"I know! Patches. He's got that cute little patch on his back."

"I like that. Hello, Patches." The hamster replied with a pellet.

"He likes it too. I think he smiled."

They were on their way to baseball practice. Jewell coached the *Slagger-Jewell Sluggers.* Jessica played right field and sang the national anthem before every practice.

"I don't know why they don't let me sing it before real games," she said. "Dad, why not?"

"I also have something for you," Jewell said, handing him an envelope. "It's a car title made out to you. It came in the mail. I have no idea why we got it. "

The title to the Dart. He gave the funeral home address to the kid at the gas station when he bought the car, never thinking he'd actually send it. Danny thanked him and apologized for lying about his name. Jewell said he understood.

When they left, Danny tucked Patches under the bed just in time before Radison popped in. The hamster stayed quiet, temporarily forestalling summary eviction, but his hours were numbered. He'd get Grady to smuggle him out.

He tried to feed Patches the leftover creamed corn, but the hamster wasn't stupid. He was leaning over the bed coaxing the animal to at least try the tapioca pudding when he sensed someone in the room. Busted.

"I'm surprised you're still here. Didn't you know that surf's up?"

Danny lurched, ripping an IV tube from the syringe taped to his arm.

Sari sat in a wheelchair dressed in a white hospital gown, brown eyes glistening. A butterfly bandage crossed the corner of her eye. She was too thin. Her fingers were wrapped in gauze and her arms bore signs of fading bruises. She was the most beautiful sight he had ever seen.

"I haven't been able to find a board big enough to carry all this crap."

She laughed and wheeled to the edge of the bed, reached out and grabbed his hand. He squeezed and all he could think or feel was *Sari*. Just that. No words, just energy.

Finally whispering, "I'm so sorry for getting you into this mess."

"You saved me. Sabrina too." She smiled. "My guardian angel."

And for a moment Danny was twelve years old again, standing in Sari's backyard under the shade of the big mango tree, watching her open the silver package with the gold ribbon. The music box with the ceramic angel inside, the one he gave her the day he moved away, just before she gave him the poem cut from construction paper.

"*The Heart of the Heart,*" he said.

Sari leaned and wrapped her arms around him. They drew closer until they got tangled in the web of tubes and wires and started laughing, then crying.

# EPILOGUE

**A PICTURE PERFECT** Saturday afternoon on the boardwalk and the beach was buzzing. Danny shifted his weight on the cane, watching the workers tear down the flaking plywood sign for *Chattie's Swimsuits and Beach Apparel*. Inside, a man in white overalls feathered joint compound over sheetrock. An electrician wired heavy duty outlets for the planers.

Everything was official. Fink hooked him up with a real lawyer. Next month Danny would be making custom surfboards in his own shop. The thought of working for an honest living again made him almost unbearably happy. The new sign was on the way. *Nine Lives Surf Shop*. Grady's idea.

Three weeks since they let him out of the hospital. The pain in his ribs subsided a little more each day. The cut on his forehead had mostly healed. His chest still ached when he took deep breaths, but that was normal. A week ago, they took the stitches out of his leg and gave him the green light to start physical therapy. He threw himself into it and was already making progress. The PT said his knotty leg muscles were an asset. Go tell the critics, surfing is good for something after all. If he kept it up, there was no reason he couldn't surf again.

That morning he traded his crutches for a cane and used it to make the trip down the boardwalk, brushing aside Grady's remonstrations. As usual, the geezer was right again. His calf ached like hell, chest too.

Rehabbing the leg and planning the surf shop consumed most of his time. He went to church last Sunday, keeping the promise he made in the graveyard. It wasn't so bad. The preacher was a convicted felon who talked about redemption. He planned to go back.

At night he hung with the crew at the Tradewinds. Over the anguished cries of everyone except Grady, he drank water. The urge to consume alcohol shrunk as the fog of depression lifted. It felt good to wake up with a clear head. Tonight was the big party. He'd celebrate then.

*Biberty Leach-Fest*, as Fink billed it on the invitations. It was supposed to be *Liberty Beach-Fest*, but typos occurred, despite Fink swearing he was off the pills. Danny vetoed his first two choices, *Bugler's Ball* and *OOO*, the latter of which Fink claimed stood for the three circles of life, while also having a pleasing Doo-wop sound, but later admitted was an acronym for *Orgy, Orgy, Orgy*.

The party had taken on a life of its own with more than two hundred guests. What the hell. Sari was coming.

He hadn't seen her since that first afternoon in the hospital. Her parents picked her up and drove her across the state to Bradenton where they retired.

They talked on the phone a few times, keeping it light, neither ready to relive the events. Just like in the old days, her mom could pick up a phone and talk for an hour before passing it along, but now Danny enjoyed it. With Sari groaning *Mo-om* in the background, June played matchmaker, inviting Danny to come stay with them.

He was so excited he hardly slept the night before, even after an emotionally draining trip to Oregon. Hiding in the corner of a dark college club, he enjoyed a night of music from *Suzy Loves Jill*. He liked their edgy originals.

Ryan played rhythm guitar and keyboards. There was no mistaking the resemblance. Such a surreal feeling. Like most college bands, *Suzy Loves Jill* had lousy equipment. Danny visited a Portland lawyer and arranged to become an anonymous benefactor, setting up an account to pay for gear and studio time. It was all he could think to do. Ryan already had a real father. Sabrina was working on a plan for them to meet.

Studying the surf shop, Danny wondered if it was too late to change the plans and make the entire front out of glass. A Latina in a bikini whizzed by on roller blades. "Way to go, Danny!"

At least the media onslaught had died down, as journalists found other newsworthy causes. Locally, it was a twelve-year-old bank robber in Miramar whose little sister drove the getaway car. *Justice or Just Crap?* devoted its entire premier episode to the important case, highlighted by Fink's emotional interview with the robber's fifth-grade teacher. She was in the middle of extolling the defendant's penmanship when she broke down under intense cross-examination and dramatically confessed the boy had a reputation for eating too many snacks and grabbing the ankles of opposing players at soccer games.

He took a last look at the surf shop and began the trek home. The aroma of grilling burgers and hot dogs wafted from the Sea Dog near the paddleball courts. Behind him a tourist caused a traffic jam feeding popcorn to a network of highstrung seagulls. An old woman with skin like rawhide sat in the shade of a coconut palm weaving a hat from green fronds.

Danny walked for ten minutes before stopping. He hobbled to the edge of the boardwalk and rested on the cane. Detective Rodriguez called that morning. They located Aaron McKenzie in a graveyard in Scottsdale, Arizona. He died three years ago from colon cancer. Rodriguez thanked him for the party invitation and asked if he should bring anything.

He gazed out at the pale green sphere. The afternoon storm clouds were moving in, blanketing the water with dark shadows. A pelican skimming a foot off the water dipped to snatch a fish. Shallow waves collapsed on the shore, liquid concave mirrors reflecting the sun from behind his shoulder. The sheen folded into foam, again and again. Reliable. Reassuring.

Danny thought about Sugar Lake. The past and the present. He grieved for Troy and even Mangrum. He thought about Jaxon Kempler and Aaron McKenzie, about the dark side. In everyone. He thought about Enya and felt the familiar undertow pulling at him, but didn't succumb.

He made a deal with Sabrina. He shook her hand.